A COLDER WAR

ALSO BY CHARLES CUMMING

Typhoon

The Trinity Six

The Thomas Kell Novels

A Foreign Country

A Colder War

The Alec Milius Novels

A Spy by Nature

The Spanish Game

A COLDER WAR

CHARLES CUMMING

St. Martin's Griffin
New York

This is a work of fiction. All of the characters, organizations, and events portrayed in this novel are either products of the author's imagination or are used fictitiously.

www.stmartins.com

Grateful acknowledgment is made for permission to reprint from the following: Epigraph on page vii from *The Double-Cross System* by Sir John Masterman. Published by Vintage. Reprinted with permission from The Random House Group Limited. Excerpt from "Postscript" from *Opened Ground: Selected Poems 1966–1996* by Seamus Heaney. Copyright © 1998 by Seamus Heaney. Reprinted with permission from Farrar, Straus and Giroux, LLC.

The Library of Congress has cataloged the hardcover edition as follows:

Cumming, Charles, 1971–
A colder war / Charles Cumming.
p. cm.
ISBN 978-1-250-02061-1 (hardcover)
ISBN 978-1-250-02060-4 (e-book)
1. International relations—Fiction. 2. Spy stories. 3. Suspense fiction. I. Title.
PR6103.U484C65 2014
823'.92—dc23

2014010053

ISBN 978-1-250-02554-8 (trade paperback)

St. Martin's Griffin books may be purchased for educational, business, or promotional use. For information on bulk purchases, please contact the Macmillan Corporate and Premium Sales Department at 1-800-221-7945, extension 5442, or write to specialmarkets@macmillan.com.

First published in Great Britain by HarperCollins Publishers

First St. Martin's Griffin Edition: June 2015

10 9 8 7 6 5 4 3 2 1

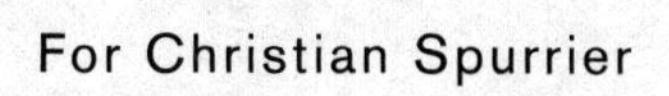
For Christian Spurrier

Certain persons have a natural predilection to live in that curious world of espionage and deceit, and attach themselves with equal facility to one side or the other, so long as their craving for adventure of a rather macabre type is satisfied.

—JOHN MASTERMAN, *THE DOUBLE-CROSS SYSTEM*

. . . You are neither here nor there,
A hurry through which known and strange things pass
As big soft buffetings come at the car sideways
And catch the heart off guard and blow it open.

—SEAMUS HEANEY, "POSTSCRIPT"

TURKEY

1

The American stepped away from the open window, passed Wallinger the binoculars, and said: "I'm going for cigarettes."

"Take your time," Wallinger replied.

It was just before six o'clock on a quiet, dusty evening in March, no more than an hour until nightfall. Wallinger trained the binoculars on the mountains and brought the abandoned palace at Ishak Pasa into focus. Squeezing the glasses together with a tiny adjustment of his hands, he found the mountain road and traced it west to the outskirts of Dogubayazit. The road was deserted. The last of the tourist taxis had returned to town. There were no tanks patrolling the plain, no *dolmus* bearing passengers back from the mountains.

Wallinger heard the door clunk shut behind him and looked back into the room. Landau had left his sunglasses on the farthest of the three beds. Wallinger crossed to the chest of drawers and checked the screen on his BlackBerry. Still no word from Istanbul; still no word from London. Where the hell was HITCHCOCK? The Mercedes was supposed to have crossed into Turkey no later than two o'clock; the three of them should have been in Van by now. Wallinger went back to the window and squinted over the telegraph poles, the pylons, and the crumbling apartment blocks of Dogubayazit. High above the mountains, an airplane was moving west to east in a cloudless sky, a silent white star skimming toward Iran.

Wallinger checked his watch. Five minutes past six. Landau had pushed the wooden table and the chair in front of the window; the last of his cigarettes was snuffed out in a scarred Efes Pilsen ashtray now bulging with yellowed filters. Wallinger tipped the contents out of the window and hoped that Landau would bring back some food. He was hungry and tired of waiting.

The BlackBerry rumbled on top of the chest of drawers; Wallinger's only means of contact with the outside world. He read the message.

VERTIGO IS ON AT 1750. GET THREE TICKETS.

It was the news he had been waiting for. HITCHCOCK and the courier had made it through the border at Gurbulak, on the Turkish side, at ten to six. If everything went according to plan, within half an hour Wallinger would have sight of the vehicle on the mountain road. From the chest of drawers he pulled out the British passport, sent by diplomatic bag to Ankara a week earlier. It would get HITCHCOCK through the military checkpoints on the road to Van; it would get him onto a plane to Ankara.

Wallinger sat on the middle of the three beds. The mattress was so soft it felt as though the frame was giving way beneath him. He had to steady himself by sitting farther back on the bed and was taken suddenly by a memory of Cecilia, his mind carried forward to the prospect of a few precious days in her company. He planned to fly the Cessna to Greece on Wednesday, to attend the Directorate meeting in Athens, then over to Chios in time to meet Cecilia for supper on Thursday evening.

The tickle of a key in the door. Landau came back into the room with two packets of Prestige filters and a plate of *pide*.

"Got us something to eat," he said. "Anything new?"

The *pide* was giving off a tart smell of warm curdled cheese. Wallinger took the chipped white plate and rested it on the bed.

"They made it through Gurbulak just before six."

"No trouble?" It didn't sound as though Landau cared much about the answer. Wallinger took a bite of the soft, warm dough. "Love this stuff," the American said, doing the same. "Kinda like a boat of pizza, you know?"

"Yes," said Wallinger.

He didn't like Landau. He didn't trust the operation. He no longer trusted the Cousins. He wondered if Amelia had been at the other end of the text, worrying about Shakhouri. The perils of a joint operation. Wallinger was a purist and, when it came to interagency cooperation, wished that they could all just keep themselves to themselves.

"How long do you think we'll have to wait?" Landau said. He was chewing noisily.

"As long as it takes."

The American sniffed, broke the seal on one of the packets of cigarettes. There was a beat of silence between them.

"You think they'll stick to the plan or come down on the one hundred?"

"Who knows?"

Wallinger stood at the window again, sighted the mountain through the binoculars. Nothing. Just a tank crawling across the plain: making a statement to the PKK, making a statement to Iran. Wallinger had the Mercedes license plate committed to memory. Shakhouri had a wife, a daughter, a mother sitting in an SIS-funded flat in Cricklewood. They had been waiting for days. They would want to know that their man was safe. As soon as Wallinger saw the vehicle, he would message London with the news.

"It's like clicking refresh over and over."

Wallinger turned and frowned. He hadn't understood Landau's

meaning. The American saw his confusion and grinned through his thick brown beard. "You know, all this waiting around. Like on a computer. When you're waiting for news, for updates. You click refresh on the browser?"

"Ah, right." Of all people, at that moment Paul Wallinger thought of Tom Kell's cherished maxim: "Spying is waiting."

He turned back to the window.

Perhaps HITCHCOCK was already in Dogubayazit. The D100 was thick with trucks and cars at all times of the day and night. Maybe they'd ignored the plan to use the mountain road and come on that. There was still a dusting of snow on the peaks; there had been a landslide only two weeks earlier. American satellites had shown that the pass through Besler was clear, but Wallinger had come to doubt everything they told him. He had even come to doubt the messages from London. How could Amelia know, with any certainty, who was in the car? How could she trust that HITCHCOCK had even made it out of Tehran? The exfil was being run by the Cousins.

"Smoke?" Landau said.

"No, thanks."

"Your people say anything else?"

"Nothing."

The American reached into his pocket and pulled out a cell phone. He appeared to read a message, but kept the contents to himself. Dishonor among spies. HITCHCOCK was an SIS Joe, but the courier, the exfil, the plan to pick Shakhouri up in Dogubayazit and fly him out of Van, that was all Langley. Wallinger would happily have run the risk of putting him on a plane from Imam Khomeini to Paris and lived with the consequences. He heard the snap of the American's lighter and caught a backdraft of tobacco smoke, then turned to the mountains once again.

The tank had now parked at the side of the mountain road, shuffling from side to side, doing the Tiananmen twist. The gun turret swiveled northeast so that the barrel was pointing in the direction of Mount Ararat.

Right on cue, Landau said: "Maybe they found Noah's Ark up there," but Wallinger wasn't in the mood for jokes.

Clicking refresh on a browser.

Then, at last, he saw it. A tiny bottle-green dot, barely visible against the parched brown landscape, moving toward the tank. The vehicle was so small it was hard to follow through the lens of the binoculars. Wallinger blinked, cleared his vision, looked again.

"They're here."

Landau came to the window. "Where?"

Wallinger passed him the binoculars. "You see the tank?"

"Yup."

"Follow the road up. . . ."

". . . Okay. Yeah. I see them."

Landau put down the binoculars and reached for the video camera. He flipped off the lens cap and began filming the Mercedes through the window. Within a minute, the vehicle was close enough to be picked out with the naked eye. Wallinger could see the car speeding along the plain, heading toward the tank. There was half a kilometer between them. Three hundred meters. Two.

Wallinger saw that the tank barrel was still pointing away from the road, up toward Ararat. What happened next could not be explained. As the Mercedes drove past the tank, there appeared to be an explosion in the rear of the vehicle that lifted up the back axle and propelled the car forward in a skid with no sound. The Mercedes quickly became wreathed in black smoke and then rolled violently from the road as flames burst from the engine. There was a second explosion, then a larger ball of flame. Landau swore very quietly. Wallinger stared in disbelief.

"What the hell happened?" the American said, lowering the camera.

Wallinger turned from the window.

"You tell me," he replied.

2

Ebru Eldem could not remember the last time she had taken the day off. "A journalist," her father had once told her, "is always working." And he was right. Life was a permanent story. Ebru was always sniffing out an angle, always felt that she was on the brink of missing out on a byline. When she spoke to the cobbler who repaired the heels of her shoes in Arnavutkoy, he was a story about dying small businesses in Istanbul. When she chatted to the good-looking stallholder from Konya who sold fruit in her local market, he was an article about agriculture and economic migration within Greater Anatolia. Every number in her phone book—and Ebru reckoned she had better contacts than any other journalist of her age and experience in Istanbul—was a story waiting to open up. All she needed was the energy and the tenacity to unearth it.

For once, however, Ebru had set aside her restlessness and ambition and, in a pained effort to relax, if only for a single day, turned off her cell phone and set her work to one side. That was quite a sacrifice! From eight o'clock in the morning—the lie-in, too, was a luxury—to nine o'clock at night, Ebru avoided all e-mails and Facebook messages and lived the life of a single woman of twenty-nine with no ties to work and no responsibilities other than to her own relaxation and happiness. Granted, she had spent most of the morning doing laundry and cleaning up the chaos of her apartment, but thereafter she had enjoyed a delicious lunch with her friend Banu at a restaurant in Besiktas, shopped for a new dress on Istiklal, bought and read ninety pages of the new Elif Shafak novel in her favorite coffeehouse in Cihangir, then met Ryan for martinis at Bar Bleu.

In the five months that they had known one another, their relationship had grown from a casual, no-strings-attached affair to something more serious. When they had first met, their get-togethers had taken place almost exclusively in the bedroom of Ryan's apartment in Tarabya, a place where—Ebru was sure—he took other girls, but none with whom he had such a connection, none with whom he would be so open and raw. She could sense it not so much by the words that he whispered into her ear as they made love as by the way that he touched her and looked into her eyes. Then, as they had grown to know one another, they had spoken a great deal about their respective families, about Turkish politics, the war in Syria, the deadlock in Congress—all manner of subjects. Ebru had been surprised by Ryan's sensitivity to political issues, his knowledge of current affairs. He had introduced her to his friends. They had talked about traveling together and even meeting one another's parents.

Ebru knew that she was not beautiful—well, certainly not as beautiful as some of the girls looking for husbands and sugar daddies in Bar Bleu—but she had brains and passion, and men had always responded to those qualities in her. When she thought about Ryan, she thought about his *difference* from all the others. She wanted the heat of physical contact, of course—a man who knew how to be with her and how to please her—but she also craved his mind and his energy, the way he treated her with such affection and respect.

Today was a typical day in their relationship. They drank too many cocktails at Bar Bleu, went for dinner at Meyra, talked about books, the recklessness of Hamas and Netanyahu. Then they stumbled back to Ryan's apartment at midnight, fucking as soon as they had closed the door. The first time was in the lounge, the second time in his bedroom with the kilims bunched up on the floor and the shade still not fixed on the standing lamp beside the armchair. Ebru had lain there afterward in his arms, thinking that she would never want for another man. Finally she had found someone who understood her and made her feel entirely herself.

The smell of Ryan's breath and the sweat of his body were still all over Ebru as she slipped out of the building just after two o'clock, Ryan snoring obliviously. She took a taxi to Arnavutkoy, showered as soon as she was home, and climbed into bed, intending to return to work just under four hours later.

Burak Turan of the Turkish National Police reckoned you could divide people into two categories: those who didn't mind getting up early in the morning and those who did. As a rule for life it had served him well. The people who were worth spending time with didn't go to sleep straight after *Muhtesem Yuzyil* and jump out of bed with a smile on their face at half past six in the morning. You had to watch people like that. They were control freaks, workaholics, religious nuts. Turan considered himself to be a member of the opposite category of person: the type who liked to extract the best out of life; who was creative and generous and good in a crowd. After finishing work, for example, he liked to wind down with a tea and a chat at a club on Mantiklal. His mother, typically, would cook him dinner, then he'd head out to a bar and get to bed by midnight or one, sometimes later. Otherwise, when did people find the time to enjoy themselves? When did they meet girls? If you were always concentrating on work, if you were always paranoid about getting enough sleep, what was left to you? Burak knew that he wasn't the most hard-working officer in the barracks, happy to kill time while other, better-connected guys got promoted ahead of him. But what did he care about that? As long as he could keep the salary and the job, visit Cansu on weekends, and watch Galatasaray games at the Turk Telekom every second Saturday, he reckoned he had life pretty well licked.

But there were drawbacks. Of course there were. As he got older, he didn't like taking so many orders, especially from guys who were younger than he was. That happened more and more. A generation coming up behind him, pushing him out of the way. There were too many people in Istanbul; the city was so fucking crowded. And then there were the dawn raids, more and more of them in the last two years—a Kurdish problem, usually, but sometimes something different. Like this morning. A journalist, a woman who had written about Ergenekon or the PKK—Burak wasn't clear which—and word had come down to arrest her. The guys were talking about it in the van as they waited outside her apartment building. *Cumhuriyet* writer. Eldem. Lieutenant Metin, who looked like he hadn't been to bed in three days, mumbled something about "links to terrorism" as he strapped on his vest. Burak couldn't believe what some people were prepared to swallow. Didn't he know how the system worked? Ten to one Eldem had riled somebody in the AKP, and an Erdogan flunkie had spotted a chance to send out a message. That was how government people always operated. You had to keep an eye on them. They were all early risers.

Burak and Metin were part of a three-man team ordered to take Eldem into custody at five o'clock in the morning. They knew what was wanted. Make a racket, wake the neighbors, scare the blood out of her, drag the detainee down to the van. A few weeks ago, on the last raid they did, Metin had picked up a framed photograph in some poor bastard's living room and dropped it on the floor, probably because he wanted to be like the cops on American TV. But why did they have to do it in the middle of the night? Burak could never work that out. Why not just pick her up on the way to work, pay a visit to *Cumhuriyet*? Instead, he'd had to set his fucking alarm for half past three in the morning, show himself at the precinct at four, then sit around in the van for an hour with that weight in his head, the numb fatigue of no sleep, his muscles and his brain feeling soft and slow. Burak got tetchy when he was like that. Anybody did anything to rile him, said something he didn't like, if there was a delay in the raid or any kind of problem—he'd snap them off at the knees. Food didn't help, tea neither. It wasn't a blood sugar thing. He just resented having to haul his arse out of bed when the rest of Istanbul was still fast asleep.

"Time?" said Adnan. He was sitting in the driver's seat, too lazy even to look at a clock.

"Five," said Burak, because he wanted to get on with it.

"Ten to," said Metin. Burak shot him a look.

"Fuck it," said Adnan. "Let's go."

The first Ebru knew of the raid was a noise very close to her face, which she later realized was the sound of the bedroom door being kicked in. She sat up in bed—she was naked—and screamed, because she thought a gang of men were going to rape her. She had been dreaming of her father, of her two young nephews, but now three men were in her cramped bedroom, throwing clothes at her, shouting at her to get dressed, calling her a "fucking terrorist."

She knew what it was. She had dreaded this moment. They all did. They all censored their words, chose their stories carefully, because a line out of place, an inference here, a suggestion there, was enough to land you in prison. Modern Turkey. Democratic Turkey. Still a police state. Always had been. Always would be.

One of them was dragging her now, saying she was being too slow. To Ebru's shame, she began to cry. What had she done wrong? What had she written? It occurred to her, as she covered herself, pulled on some knickers, buttoned up her jeans, that Ryan would help. Ryan had money and influence and would do what he could to save her.

"Leave it," one of them barked. She had tried to grab her phone. She saw the surname on the cop's lapel badge: TURAN.

"I want a lawyer," she screamed.

Burak shook his head. "No lawyer is going to help you," he said. "Now put on a fucking shirt."

LONDON, THREE WEEKS LATER

3

Thomas Kell had only been standing at the bar for a few seconds when the landlady turned to him, winked, and said: "The usual, Tom?"

The usual. It was a bad sign. He was spending four nights out of seven at the Ladbroke Arms, four nights out of seven drinking pints of Adnams Ghost Ship with only the *Times* quick crossword and a packet of Winston Lights for company. Perhaps there was no alternative for disgraced spooks. Cold shouldered by the Secret Intelligence Service eighteen months earlier, Kell had been in a state of suspended animation ever since. He wasn't out, but he wasn't in. His part in saving the life of Amelia Levene's son, François Malot, was known only to a select band of high priests at Vauxhall Cross. To the rest of the staff at MI6, Thomas Kell was still "Witness X," the officer who had been present at the aggressive CIA interrogation of a British national in Kabul and who had failed to prevent the suspect's subsequent rendition to a black prison in Cairo, and on to the gulag of Guantanamo.

"Thanks, Kathy," he said, and planted a five-pound note on the bar. A well-financed German was standing beside him, flicking through the pages of the *FT Weekend* and picking at a bowl of wasabi peas. Kell collected his change, walked outside, and sat at a picnic table under the fierce heat of a standing gas fire. It was dusk on a damp Easter Sunday, the pub—like the rest of Notting Hill—almost empty. Kell had the terrace to himself. Most of the local residents appeared to be out of town, doubtless at Gloucestershire second homes or skiing lodges in the Swiss Alps. Even the well-tended police station across the street looked half asleep. Kell took out the packet of Winstons and rummaged around for his lighter; a gold Dunhill, engraved with the initials P.M.—a private memento from Levene, who had risen to MI6 chief the previous September.

"Every time you light a cigarette, you can think of me," she had said with a low laugh, pressing the lighter into the palm of his hand. A classic Amelia tactic: seemingly intimate and heartfelt, but ultimately deniable as anything other than a platonic gift between friends.

In truth, Kell had never been much of a smoker, but recently cigarettes had afforded a useful punctuation to his unchanging days. In his twenty-year career as a spy, he had often carried a packet as a prop: a light could start a conversation; a cigarette would put an agent at ease. Now they were part of the furniture of his solitary life. He felt less fit as a consequence and spent a lot more money. Most mornings he would wake and cough like a dying man, immediately reaching for another nicotine kick start to the day. But he found that he could not function without them.

Kell was living in what a former colleague had described as the "no-man's-land" of early middle-age, in the wake of a job which had imploded and a marriage which had failed. At Christmas, his wife, Claire, had finally filed for divorce and begun a new relationship with her lover, Richard Quinn, a twice-married hedge fund Peter Pan with a £14 million townhouse in Primrose Hill and three teenage sons at St. Paul's. Not that Kell regretted the split, nor resented Claire the upgrade in lifestyle; for the most part he was relieved to be free of a relationship that had brought neither of them much in the way of happiness. He hoped that Dick the Wonder Schlong—as Quinn was affectionately known—would bring Claire the fulfillment she craved. Being married to a spy, she had once told him, was like being married to half a person. In her view, Kell had been physically and emotionally separate from her for years.

A sip of the Ghost. It was Kell's second pint of the evening and tasted soapier than the first. He flicked the half-smoked cigarette out into the street and took out his iPhone. The green messages icon was empty; the mail envelope identically blank. He had finished the *Times* crossword half an hour earlier and had left the novel he was reading—Julian Barnes's *The Sense of an Ending*—on the kitchen table in his flat. There seemed little to do but drink the pint and look out at the listless street. Occasionally a car would roll down the road or a local resident drag past with a dog, but London was otherwise uncharacteristically silent; it was like listening to the city through the muffle of headphones. The eerie quiet only added to Kell's sense of restlessness. He was not a man prone to self-pity, but nor did he want to spend too many more nights drinking alone on the terrace of an upmarket gastropub in west London, waiting to see if Amelia Levene would give him his job back. The public enquiry into Witness X was dragging its heels; Kell had been waiting almost two years to see if he would be cleared of all charges or laid out as a sacrificial lamb. With the exception of the three-week operation to rescue Amelia's son, François, the previous summer, and a one-month contract working due diligence for a corporate espionage firm in Mayfair, that was too long out of the game. He wanted to get back to work. He wanted to *spy* again.

Then—a miracle. The iPhone lit up. "Amelia L3" appeared on the screen. It was like a sign from the God in whom Kell still occasionally believed. He picked up before the first ring was through.

"Speak of the devil."

"Tom?"

He could tell immediately that something was wrong. Amelia's customarily authoritative voice was shaky and uncertain. She had called him from her private number, not a landline or an encrypted Service phone. It had to be personal. Kell thought at first that something must have happened to François, or that Amelia's husband, Giles, had been killed in an accident.

"It's Paul."

That winded him. Kell knew that she could only be talking about Paul Wallinger.

"What's happened? Is he all right?"

"He's been killed."

4

Kell hailed a cab on Holland Park Avenue and was outside Amelia's house in Chelsea within twenty minutes. He was about to ring the bell when he felt the loss of Wallinger like something pulling apart inside him and had to take a moment to compose himself. They had joined SIS in the same intake. They had risen through the ranks together, fast-track brothers winning the pick of overseas postings across the post–Cold War constellation. Wallinger, an Arabist, nine years older, had served in Cairo, Riyadh, Tehran, and Damascus before Amelia had handed him the top job in Turkey. In what he had often thought of as a parallel, shadow career, Kell, the younger brother, had worked in Nairobi, Baghdad, Jerusalem, and Kabul, tracking Wallinger's rise as the years rolled by. Staring down the length of Markham Street, he remembered the thirty-four-year-old wunderkind he had first encountered on the IONEC training course in the autumn of 1990, Wallinger's scores, his intellect, his ambition just that much sharper than his own.

But Kell wasn't here because of work. He hadn't rushed to Amelia's side in order to offer dry advice on the political and strategic fallout from Wallinger's untimely death. He was here as her friend. Thomas

Kell was one of very few people within SIS who knew the truth about the relationship between Amelia Levene and Paul Wallinger. The pair had been lovers for many years, a stop-start, on-off affair which had begun in London in the late 1990s and continued, with both parties married, right up until Amelia's selection as chief.

He rang the bell, swiped a wave at the security camera, heard the lock buzzing open. There was no guard in the atrium, no protection officer on duty. Amelia had probably persuaded him to take the night off. As "C," she was entitled to a grace and favor Service apartment, but the house belonged to her husband. Kell did not expect to find Giles Levene at home. For some time the couple had been estranged, Giles spending most of his time at Amelia's house in the Chalke Valley, or tracing the ever-lengthening branches of his family tree as far afield as Cape Town, New England, the Ukraine.

"You stink of cigarettes," she said as she opened the door into the hall, offering up a taut, pale cheek for Kell to kiss. She was wearing jeans and a loose cashmere sweater, socks but no shoes. Her eyes looked clear and bright, though he suspected that she had been crying; her skin had the sheen of recent tears.

"Giles home?"

Amelia caught Kell's eyes quickly, skipping on the question, as though wondering whether or not to answer it truthfully.

"We've decided to try for separation."

"Oh, Christ, I'm so sorry."

The news acted on him in conflicting ways. He was sorry that Amelia was about to experience the singular agony of divorce, but glad that she would finally be free of Giles, a man so boring he was dubbed "The Coma" in the corridors of Vauxhall Cross. They had married each other largely for convenience—Amelia had wanted a steadfast, backseat man with plenty of money who would not block her path to the top; Giles had wanted Amelia as his prize, for her access to the great and the good of London society. Like Claire and Kell, they had never been able to have children. Kell suspected that the sudden appearance of Amelia's son, François, eighteen months earlier, had been the relationship's last straw.

"It's a great shame, yes," she said. "But the best thing for both of us. Drink?"

This was how she moved things on. *We're not going to dwell on this, Tom. My marriage is my private business.* Kell stole a glance at her left hand as she led him into the sitting room. Her wedding ring was still in place, doubtless to silence the rumor mill in Whitehall.

"Whiskey, please," he said.

Amelia had reached the cabinet and turned around, an empty glass in hand. She gave a nod and a half smile, like somebody recognizing the melody of a favorite song. Kell heard the clunk and rattle of a single ice cube spinning into the glass, then the throaty glug of malt. She knew how he liked it: three fingers, then just a splash of water to open it up.

"And how are you?" she asked, handing him the drink. She meant Claire, she meant his own divorce. They were both in the same club now.

"Oh, same old, same old," he said. He felt like a man at the end of a date who had been invited in for coffee and was struggling for conversation. "Claire's with Dick the Wonder Schlong. I'm house-sitting a place in Holland Park."

"Holland Park?" she said, with an escalating tone of surprise. It was as though Kell had moved up a couple of rungs on the social ladder. A part of him was dismayed that she did not already know where he was living. "And you think—"

He interrupted her. The news about Wallinger was hanging in the space between them. He did not want to ignore it much longer.

"Look, I'm sorry about Paul."

"Don't be. You were kind to rush over."

He knew that she would have spent the previous hours picking over every moment she had shared with Wallinger. What do lovers eventually remember about each other? Their eyes? Their touch? A favorite poem or song? Amelia had almost word-perfect recall for conversations, a photographic memory for faces, images, contexts. Their affair would now be a palace of memories through which she could stroll and recollect. The relationship had been about much more than the thrill of adultery; Kell knew that. At one point, in a moment of rare candor, Amelia had told Kell that she was in love with Paul and was thinking of leaving Giles. He had warned her off, not out of jealousy, but because he knew of Wallinger's reputation as a womanizer and feared that the relationship, if it became public knowledge, would skewer Amelia's career, as well as her happiness. He wondered now if she regretted taking his advice.

"He was in Greece," she began. "Chios. An island there. I don't really know why. Josephine wasn't with him."

Josephine was Wallinger's wife. When she wasn't visiting her husband in Ankara, or staying on the family farm in Cumbria, she lived less than a mile away, in a small flat off Gloucester Road.

"Holiday?" Kell asked.

"I suppose." Amelia had a whiskey of her own and drank from it. "He hired a plane. You know how he loved to fly. Attended a Directorate meeting at the Station in Athens, stopped off on Chios on the way home. He was taking the Cessna back to Ankara. There must have been something wrong with the aircraft. Mechanical fault. They found debris about a hundred miles northeast of Izmir."

"No body?"

Kell saw Amelia flinch and winced at his own insensitivity. That body was her body. Not just the body of a colleague; the body of a lover.

"Something was found," she replied, and he felt sick at the image.

"I'm so sorry."

She came toward him and they embraced, glasses held awkwardly to one side, like the start of a dance with no rhythm. Kell wondered if she was going to cry, but as she pulled away he saw that she was entirely composed.

"The funeral is on Wednesday," she said. "Cumbria. I wondered if you would come with me?"

5

The agent known to SVR officer Alexander Minasian by the cryptonym "KODAK" had near-perfect conversational recall and a photographic memory once described by an admiring colleague as "pixel sharp." As winter turned to spring in Istanbul, his signals to Minasian were becoming more frequent. KODAK recalled their conversation at the Grosvenor House hotel in London almost three years earlier:

Every day, between nine o'clock and nine thirty in the morning, and between seven o'clock and seven thirty in the evening, we will have a person in the teahouse. Somebody who knows your face, somebody who knows the signal. This is easy for us to arrange. I will arrange it. When you find yourself working in Ankara, the routine will be the same.

KODAK would typically leave his apartment between seven and eight o'clock in the morning, undertake no discernible countersurveillance, drive his car or—more usually—take a taxi to Istiklal Caddesi, walk down the narrow passage opposite the Russian consulate, enter the teahouse, and sit down. Alternatively, he would leave work at the usual time, take a train into the city, browse in some of the bookshops and clothing stores on Istiklal, then stop for a glass of tea at the appointed time.

Whenever you have documents for me, you only need to go to the teahouse at these times and to present yourself to us. You will not need to know who is watching for you. You will not need to look around for faces. Just wear the signal that we have agreed, take a cup of tea or take a coffee, and we will see you. You can sit inside the café or you can sit outside the café. It does not matter. There will always be somebody there!

Of course KODAK did not wish to establish a pattern. Whenever he was in the area around Taksim, day or night, he would try to go to the teahouse, ostensibly to practice his Turkish with the pretty, young waitress, to play backgammon, or simply to read a book. He frequented other teahouses in the area, other restaurants and bars, often purposefully wearing near-identical clothing.

If it suits you, bring a friend. Bring somebody who does not know the significance of the occasion! If you see somebody leaving while you are there, do not follow them. Of course not. This would be dangerous. You will not know who I have sent to look for you. You will not know who might be watching them, just as you will not know who might be watching you. This is why we do not leave a trace. No more chalk marks on walls. No more stickers. I have always preferred the static system, something that cannot be noticed, except by the eye which has been trained to see it. The movement of a vase of flowers in a room. The appearance of a bicycle on a balcony. Even the color of a pair of socks! All these things can be used to communicate a signal.

KODAK liked Minasian. He admired his courage, his instincts, his professionalism. Together they had been able to do significant work; together they might bring about extraordinary change. But he felt that the Russian, from time to time, could be somewhat melodramatic.

If you feel that your position has been compromised, do not show yourself at the teahouse or at the Ankara location. Instead, obtain or borrow a cell phone and text the word BESIKTAS to my number. If this is not possible, for whatever reason—you cannot obtain a signal, you cannot obtain a phone—go to a phone box or other landline and speak this word when there is an answer. If we contact you using this word, it is our belief that your work for us has been discovered and that you should leave Turkey.

It seemed highly improbable to KODAK that he would ever be suspected of treachery, far less caught in the act of handing secrets to the SVR. He was too clever, too cautious, his tracks too well covered. Nevertheless, he remembered the meeting points, and the crash instructions, and committed the numbers associated with them to memory.

There are three potential meeting points in the event of exposure. Remember them. If you say BESIKTAS ONE, a contact will meet you in the courtyard of the Blue Mosque at the time agreed. He will make himself known to you and you will follow him. If you consider Turkey to be unsafe, make your way across the border to Bulgaria with the message BESIKTAS TWO. Do not, under any circumstances, attempt to board an airplane. A contact will make himself known to you at the time agreed, in the bar of the Grand Hotel in Sofia. In exceptional circumstances, if you feel that it is necessary to cross into former Soviet territory, where you will be safer and more easily escorted to Moscow, there are boats from Istanbul. You will always be welcome in Odessa. The code for this crash meeting is BESIKTAS THREE.

6

It had dawned on Thomas Kell that the number of funerals he was attending in a calendar year had begun to outstrip the number of weddings. As he traveled north with Amelia in a packed first-class carriage from Euston, he felt as though the change had occurred almost overnight: one moment he had been a young man in a morning suit throwing confetti over rapturous couples every third weekend in summer; the next he had somehow morphed into a veteran fortysomething spook, flying in from Kabul to bury a friend or relative dead from alcohol or cancer. Looking around the train gave Kell the same feeling: he was older than almost everyone in the carriage. What had happened to the intervening years? Even the ticket inspector appeared to have been born after the fall of the Berlin Wall.

"You look tired," Amelia said, looking up from an op-ed in *The Independent*. She had taken to wearing half-moon reading glasses and almost looked her age.

"Gee, thanks," Kell replied.

She was seated opposite him at a table sticky with half-eaten croissants and discarded coffee cups. Beside her, oblivious to Amelia's rank and distinction, a clear-skinned student with an upgraded ticket to Lancaster was playing solitaire on a Samsung tablet. Both had their backs to the direction of travel as the fields and rivers of England whistled by. Kell was jammed in at a window seat, trying to avoid touching thighs with an overweight businesswoman who kept falling asleep in a Trollope novel. He had packed a bag because he was planning to stay in the north for several days. Why hammer back to London when he could go walking in Cumbria and eat two-star Michelin food at L'Enclume? There was nothing and nobody waiting for him back home in Holland Park. Just the Ladbroke Arms and another pint of Ghost Ship.

Kell was wearing a charcoal business suit, a white shirt, and a black tie; Amelia was dressed in a dark blue suit and black overcoat. Their funereal garb drew occasional sympathetic stares as they walked across Preston station. Amelia had booked a cab on SIS and, by half past twelve, they were wandering around Cartmel like a married couple, Kell checking into his hotel, Amelia calling the office more than once to ensure that everything back in London was running smoothly.

They were eating chicken pie in a pub in the center of the village when Kell spotted George Truscott at the bar, ordering a half pint of lager. As assistant to the chief, Truscott had been lined up to succeed Simon Haynes as "C" before Amelia had stolen his prize. It had been Truscott, a corporatized desk jockey of suffocating ambition, who had authorized Kell's presence at the interrogation of Yassin Gharani; and it had been Truscott, more than any other colleague, who had gladly thrown Kell to the wolves when the Service needed a fall guy for the sins of extraordinary rendition. Roughly three minutes after taking over as chief, Amelia had dispatched Truscott to Bonn, dangling the top job in Germany as a carrot. Neither of them had seen him since.

"Amelia!"

Truscott had turned from the bar and was carrying his half pint across the pub, like a student learning how to drink during Fresher's Week. Kell wondered if he should bother disguising his contempt for the man who had ruined his career, but stage-managed a smile, largely out of respect for the somber occasion. Amelia, to whom false expressions of loyalty and affection came as naturally as blinking, stood up and warmly shook Truscott's hand. A passerby, glancing at their table, would have concluded that both were delighted to see him.

"I didn't know you were coming, George. Did you fly in from Bonn?"

"Berlin, actually," Truscott replied, hinting archly at work of incalculable importance to the secret state. "And how are *you*, Tom?"

Kell could see the wheels of Truscott's ruthless, back-covering mind turning behind the question; that cunning and inexhaustibly competitive personality with which he had wrestled so long in the final months of his career. Truscott's thoughts might as well have appeared as bubbles above his narrow, bone-white scalp. *Why is Kell with Levene? Has she brought him in from the cold? Has Witness X been forgiven?* Kell glimpsed the tremor of panic in Truscott's wretched and empty soul, his profound fear that Amelia was about to make Kell "H/Ankara," leaving Truscott with the backwater of Bonn, a Cold War EU hang-up barely relevant in the age of Asia Reset and the Arab Spring.

"Oh, look, there's Simon."

Amelia had spotted Haynes coming out of the gents'. Her predecessor produced a beaming smile that instantly evaporated when he saw Kell and Truscott in such close proximity. Amelia allowed him to kiss both her cheeks, then watched as the male spooks became stiffly reacquainted. Kell barely took in the various platitudes and clichés with which Haynes greeted him. Yes, it was a great tragedy about Paul. No, Kell hadn't yet found a permanent job in the private sector. Indeed it was frustrating that the public enquiry had stalled yet again. Before long, Haynes had shuffled off in the direction of Cartmel Priory, Truscott trotting along beside him as though he still believed that Haynes could influence his career.

"Simon wanted to give the eulogy for Paul," Amelia said, checking her reflection in a nearby mirror as she put on her coat. They had polished off their chicken pies, split the bill. "He didn't seem to think it would be a problem. I had to put a stop to it."

Having collected his knighthood from Prince Charles the previous autumn, Haynes had appeared at The Sunday Times Oxford Literary Festival, spoken at an Intelligence Squared debate at the Royal Geographical Society, and enthusiastically listed his favorite records on *Desert Island Discs*. As such, he was the first outgoing chief of the Service to be seen to be actively benefiting, both commercially and in terms of his own public profile, from his former career. For Haynes to have given the eulogy at Wallinger's funeral would have exposed the deceased as a spy to the many friends and neighbors who had gathered in Cartmel under the impression that he had been simply a career diplomat, or even a gentleman farmer.

"A bad habit we've acquired from the Security Service," Amelia continued. She was wearing a gold necklace and briefly touched the chain. "It'll be memoirs next. Whatever happened to *discretion*? Why couldn't Simon just have joined BP like the rest of them?"

Kell grinned but wondered if Amelia was giving him a tacit warning. *Don't go public with Witness X*. Surely she knew him well enough to realize that he would never betray the Service, far less breach her trust?

"You ready for this?" he asked, as they turned toward the door. Kell had been drinking a glass of Rioja and drained the last of it as he threw a few pound coins onto the table as a tip. Amelia found his eyes and, for an instant, looked vulnerable to what lay ahead. As they walked outside into the crystal afternoon sunshine, she briefly squeezed his hand and said: "Wish me luck."

"You'll be fine," he told her. "The last thing you've ever needed is luck."

He was right, of course. Shortly after three o'clock, as the congregation rose as one to acknowledge the arrival of Josephine Wallinger, Amelia assumed the dignified bearing of a leader and chief, her body language betraying no hint that the man three hundred people had come to mourn had ever been anything more to her than a highly regarded colleague. Kell, for his part, felt oddly detached from the service. He sang the hymns, he listened to the lessons, he nodded through the vicar's eulogy, which paid appropriately oblique tribute to a "self-effacing man" who had been "a loyal servant to his country." Yet Kell was distracted. Afterward, making his way to the graveside, he heard an unseen mourner utter the single word "Hammarskjöld" and knew that the conspiracy theories were gathering pace. Dag Hammarskjöld was the Swedish secretary of the United Nations who had been killed in a plane crash in 1961, en route to securing a peace deal that might have prevented civil war in the Congo. Hammarskjöld's DC6 had crashed in a forest in former Rhodesia. Some claimed that the plane had been shot down by mercenaries; others that SIS itself, in collusion with the CIA and South African intelligence, had sabotaged the flight. Since hearing the news on Sunday, Kell had been nagged by an unsettling sense that there had been foul play involved in Wallinger's death. He could not say precisely why he felt this way—other than that he had always known Paul to be a meticulous pilot, thorough to the point of paranoia with preflight checks—yet the whispered talk of Hammarskjöld seemed to cement the suspicion in his mind. Looking around at the faceless spooks, ghosts of bygone ops from a dozen different Services, Kell felt that somebody, somewhere in the cramped churchyard, knew why Paul Wallinger's plane had plunged from the sky.

The mourners shuffled forward, perhaps as many as two hundred men and women, forming a loose rectangle, ten deep, on all four sides of the grave. Kell saw CIA officers, representatives from Canadian intelligence, three members of the Mossad, as well as colleagues from Egypt, Jordan, and Turkey. As the vicar intoned the consecration, Kell wondered, in the layers of secrecy that formed around a spy like scabs, what sin Wallinger had committed, what treachery he had uncovered, to bring about his own death? Had he pushed too hard on Syria or Iran?

Trip-wired an SVR operation in Istanbul? And why Greece, why Chios? Perhaps the official assumption was correct: mechanical failure was to blame. Yet Kell could not shake the feeling that his friend had been assassinated; it was not even beyond the realm of possibility that the plane had been shot down. As Wallinger's coffin was lowered into the ground, he glanced to the right and saw Amelia wiping away tears. Even Simon Haynes looked cleaned out by grief.

Kell closed his eyes. He found himself, for the first time in months, mouthing a silent prayer. Then he turned from the grave and walked back toward the church, wondering if mourners at an SIS funeral, twenty years hence, would whisper the name "Wallinger" in country churchyards as a shorthand for murder and cover-up.

Less than an hour later, the crowds of mourners had found their way to the Wallinger farm, where a barn near the main house had been prepared for a wake. Trestle tables were laid out with cakes and cheese sandwiches cut into white, crustless triangles. Wine and whiskey were on standby while two old ladies from the village served tea and Nescafé to the great and the good of the transatlantic intelligence community. Kell was greeted with a mixture of rapture and pity by former colleagues, most of whom were too canny and self-serving to offer their wholehearted support on the fiasco of Witness X. Others had heard word of his divorce on the Service grapevine and placed consoling hands on Kell's shoulder, as if he had suffered a bereavement or been diagnosed with an inoperable illness. He didn't blame them. What else were people supposed to say in such circumstances?

The flowers that had lain on Wallinger's coffin had been set out at one end of the barn. Kell was standing outside, smoking a cigarette, when he saw Wallinger's children—his son, Andrew, and his daughter, Rachel—bending over the floral tributes, reading the cards, and sharing a selection of the written messages with each other. Andrew was the younger of the two, now twenty-eight, reportedly earning a living in Moscow as a banker. Kell had not seen Rachel for more than fifteen years, and had been struck by her dignity and grace as she supported her mother at the graveside. Andrew had wept desperately for the father he had lost as Josephine stared into the black grave, frozen in what Kell assumed was a medicated grief. Yet Rachel had maintained an eerie stillness, as if in possession of a secret that guaranteed her peace of mind.

He was grinding out the cigarette, half listening to a local farmer telling a long-winded anecdote about wind farms, when he saw Rachel bend down and pick up a card attached to a small bunch of flowers on the far side of the barn. She was alone, several meters from Andrew, but Kell had a clear view of her face. He saw Rachel's dark eyes harden as she read the card, then a flush of anger scald her cheeks.

What she did next astonished him. Leaning down, and with a brisk flick of her wrist, she skidded the flowers low and hard toward the edge of the barn, where they hit the whitewashed wall with a soundless thud. Rachel then placed the card in her coat pocket and returned to Andrew's side. No words were exchanged. It was as though she did not want to involve her brother in what she had just seen. Moments later Rachel turned and walked back toward the trestle tables, where she was intercepted by a middle-aged woman wearing a black hat. As far as Kell could tell, nobody else had witnessed what had happened.

The barn had become hot and, after a few minutes, Rachel removed her coat, folding it over the back of a chair. She was continually in conversation with guests who wished to convey their condolences. At one point she burst into laughter and the men in the room, as one, seemed to turn and look at her. Rachel had an in-house reputation for beauty and brains; Kell recalled a couple of male colleagues constructing Christmas-party innuendos about her. Yet she was not as he had imagined she would be; there was something about the dignity of her behavior, the decisiveness with which she had dispatched the flowers, a sense in which she was fully in control of her emotions and of the environment in which she had found herself, that intrigued Kell.

In time, she had made her way to the far side of the barn. She was at least fifty feet from the coat. Kell, carrying a plate of sandwiches and cake toward the chair, took off his own coat and folded it alongside Rachel's. At the same time, he reached into her outside pocket and removed the card.

He glanced across the barn. Rachel had not seen him. She was still deep in conversation, her back to the chair. Kell walked quickly outside, crossed the drive, and went into the Wallingers' house. Several people were milling about in the hall, guests looking for bathrooms, staff ferrying food and drink from the kitchen to the barn. Kell avoided them and walked upstairs.

The bathroom door was locked. He needed to find a room where he would not be disturbed. Glimpsing posters of Pearl Jam and Kevin Pietersen in a room farther along the corridor, Kell found himself in Andrew's bedroom. There were framed photographs from his time at Eton above a wooden desk, as well as various caps and sporting mementos. Kell closed the door behind him and navigated past various items of clothing that were strewn on the floor. He took the card from his jacket pocket and opened it up.

The inscription was in an eastern European language that Kell assumed to be Hungarian. The note had been handwritten on a small white card with a blue flower printed in the top right-hand corner.

Szerelmem. Szívem darabokban, mert nem tudok Veled lenni soha már. Olyan fájó a csend amióta elmentél, hogy még hallom a lélegzeted, amikor álmodban néztelek.

Had Rachel been able to understand it? Kell put the card on the bed and took out his iPhone. He photographed the message, left the bedroom, and returned to the barn.

With Rachel nowhere to be seen, Kell removed his overcoat from the chair and, by simple sleight of hand, replaced the card in her coat pocket.

It had been in his possession for no more than five minutes. When he turned around, he saw that she was coming back into the barn and walking toward her mother. Kell went outside for a cigarette.

Amelia was standing on her own in front of the house, like someone at the end of a party waiting for a cab.

"What have you been up to?" she asked.

At first, Kell thought that she had spotted him lifting the card. Then he realized, from Amelia's expression, that the question was merely a general enquiry about his life.

"You mean recently? In London?"

"Yes, recently."

"You want an honest answer to that?"

"Of course."

"Fuck all."

Amelia did not react to the bluntness of the response. Ordinarily she would have smiled or conjured a look of mock disapproval. But her mood was serious, as though she had finally arrived at a solution to a problem that had been troubling her for some time.

"So you're not busy for the next few weeks?"

Kell felt a jolt of optimism, his luck about to change. *Just ask the question,* he thought. *Just get me back in the game.* He looked out across a valley sketched with dry-stone walls and distant sheep, thinking of the long afternoons he had spent brushing up his Arabic at SOAS, the solo holidays in Lisbon and Beirut, the course he had taken at City Lit in twentieth-century Irish poetry. Filling up the time.

"I've got a job for you," she said. "Should have mentioned it earlier but it didn't seem right before the funeral." Kell heard the gravel-crunch of someone approaching them across the drive. He hoped the offer would come before they were cut off midconversation. He didn't want Amelia changing her mind.

"What kind of job?"

"Would you go out to Chios for me? To Turkey? Find out what Paul was up to before he died?"

"You don't *know* what he was up to?"

Amelia shrugged. "Not all of it. On a personal level. One never does." Kell looked down at the damp ground and conceded the point with a shrug. He had dedicated most of his working life to the task of puncturing privacy, yet what did a person ultimately know about the thoughts and motives of the people who were closest to them? "Paul had no operational reason to be in Chios," Amelia continued. "Josephine thinks he was there on business, Station didn't know he was going."

Kell assumed that Amelia suspected what was obvious, given Wallinger's reputation and track record: that he had been on the island with a girl and that he had been careful to cover his tracks.

"I'll tell Ankara you're coming. Red carpet, access all areas. Istanbul ditto. If it's coming from me, they'll open up all the relevant files."

It was like getting a clean bill of health after a medical scare. Kell had been waiting for such a moment for months.

"I could do that," he said.

"You're on full pay, yes? We put you on that after France?" The question was plainly rhetorical. "You'll have a driver, whatever else you need. I'll make arrangements for you to have a cover identity while you're there, should you need it."

"*Will* I need it?"

It was as if Amelia was holding back a vital piece of information. Kell wondered what he was signing up for.

"Not necessarily," she said, though her next remark only confirmed his suspicion that there was something else in play. "Just tread carefully around the Yanks."

"What does that mean?"

"You'll see. Tricky out there at the moment."

He was struck by the intensity with which Amelia was speaking.

"What are you not telling me?" he asked.

"Just find out what happened," she replied quickly, and took his wrist in a gloved hand, squeezing hard at the bone as though to stem the flow of blood from a wound. Amelia's steady eyes held Kell's, then flicked back in the direction of the wake, at the mourners in black filing out of the barn. "Why was Paul on Chios?" she said, and there was agony in the question, a powerful woman's despair that she had been unable to protect a man whom perhaps she still loved. "Why did he die?"

For a moment Kell thought that her composure was going to crack. He took Amelia's arm and squeezed back, the reassurance of a friend. But her strength returned, as quickly as the sudden gust of wind that blew across the farm, and whatever Kell was about to say was cut short.

"It's simple," she said, with the trace of a resigned smile. "Just find out why the hell we're all *here*."

7

Kell had packed his bags, cleared out of his room, and canceled his reservation at L'Enclume within the hour. By seven o'clock he was back in Preston station, changing platforms for an evening train to Euston. Amelia had driven to London with Simon Haynes, having called Athens and Ankara with instructions for Kell's trip. He bought a tuna sandwich and a packet of crisps on the station concourse, washed them down with two cans of Stella Artois purchased from a catering trolley on the train, and finished *The Sense of an Ending*. No colleague, no friend from SIS had elected to join him on the journey home. There were spies from five continents scattered throughout the train, buried in books or wives or laptops, but none of them would run the risk of publicly consorting with Witness X.

Kell was home by eleven. He knew why Amelia had chosen him for such an important assignment. After all, there were dozens of capable officers pacing the corridors of Vauxhall Cross, all of whom would have jumped at the chance to get to the bottom of the Wallinger mystery. Yet Kell was one of only two or three trusted lieutenants who knew of Amelia's long affair with Paul. It was rumored throughout the Service that "C" had never been faithful to Giles; that she had perhaps been involved in a relationship with an American businessman. But, for most, her links to Wallinger would have been solely professional. Any thorough investigation into his private life would inevitably turn up hard evidence of their relationship. Amelia could not afford to have talk of an affair on the record; she was relying on Kell to be discreet with whatever he found.

Before going to bed he repacked his bags, dug out his Kell passport, and e-mailed the photograph of the Hungarian inscription to an old contact in the National Security Authority, Tamas Metka, who had retired to run a bar in Szolnok. By seven the next morning Kell was in a cab to Gatwick and back in the dreary routine of twenty-first-century flying: the long, agitated queues; the liquids farcically bagged; the shoes and belts pointlessly removed.

Five hours later he was touching down in Athens, cradle of civilization, epicenter of global debt. Kell's contact was waiting for him in a café inside the departures hall, a first-posting SIS officer instructed by Amelia to provide a cover identity for Chios. The young man—who introduced himself as "Adam"—had evidently been working on the legend throughout the night: his eyes were stiff with sleeplessness and he had a rash, red as an allergy, beneath the stubble on his lower jaw. There was a mug of black coffee on the table in front of him, an open sandwich of indeterminate contents, and a padded envelope with the single letter *H* scribbled on the front. He was wearing a Greenpeace sweatshirt and a black Nike baseball cap so that Kell could more easily identify him.

"Good flight?"

"Fine, thanks," Kell replied, shaking his hand and sitting down. They exchanged pleasantries for a few minutes before Kell took possession of the envelope. He had already passed through Greek customs, so there was now less danger of being caught with dual identities.

"It's a commercial cover. You're an insurance investigator with Scottish Widows writing up a preliminary report on the Wallinger crash.

Chris Hardwick." Adam's voice was quiet, methodical, well rehearsed. "I've got you a room at the Golden Sands hotel in Karfas, about ten minutes south of Chios Town. The Chandris was full."

"The Chandris?"

"It's where everybody stays if they come to the island on business. Best hotel in town."

"You think Wallinger may have stayed there under a pseudonym?"

"It's possible, sir."

Kell hadn't been called "sir" by a colleague in over a year. He had lost sight of his own status, allowed himself to forget the considerable achievements of his long career. Adam was probably no older than twenty-six or twenty-seven. Meeting an officer of Kell's pedigree was most likely a significant moment to him. He would have wanted to make a good impression, particularly given Kell's links to "C."

"I've arranged for you to pick up a car at the airport. It's booked for three days. The Europcar desk is just outside the terminal. There's a couple of credit cards in Hardwick's name, the usual PIN number, a passport of course, driver's license, some business cards. I'm afraid the only photograph we had of you on file looks a bit out of date, sir."

Kell didn't take offense. He knew the picture. Taken in a windowless room at Vauxhall Cross on September 9, 2001. His hair cut shorter, his temples less grayed, his life about to change. Every spy on the planet had aged at least twenty years since then.

"I'm sure it'll be fine," he said.

Adam looked up at the ceiling and blinked hard, as though trying to remember the last in a sequence of points from a mental checklist.

"The air traffic control officer who was on duty the afternoon of Mr. Wallinger's flight can meet you tonight at your hotel."

"Time?"

"I said seven."

"That's good. I want to move quickly on this. Thank you."

Kell watched as Adam absorbed his gratitude with a wordless nod. *I remember being you,* Kell thought. *I remember what it was like at the beginning.* With a pang of nostalgia, he pictured Adam's life in Athens: the vast Foreign Office apartment, the nightclub memberships, the beautiful local girls in thrall to the glamour and expense accounts of the diplomatic life. A young man with a whole career ahead of him, in one of the great cities of the world. Kell put the envelope in his carry-on bag and stood up from the table. Adam accompanied him as far as a nearby duty-free shop, where they parted company. Kell bought a bottle of Macallan and a carton of Winston Lights for Chios and was soon airborne again above the shimmering Mediterranean, checking through the e-mails and texts that had collected on his iPhone before takeoff.

Metka had already sent through a translation of the message seen by Rachel.

My dear Tom,

It is always good to hear from you and I am of course happy to help.

So what happened to you? You took up poetry? Writing Magyar love sonnets? Maybe Claire finally had the sense to leave you and you fell in love with a girl from Budapest?

Here is what the poem says—please excuse me if my translation is not as "pretty" as your original:

My darling. I cannot be with you today, of all days, and so my heart is broken. Silence has never been this desperate. You are asleep, but I can still hear you breathing.

It is really very moving. Very sad. I wonder who wrote it? I would like to meet them.

Of course if you are ever here, Tom, we must meet. I hope you are satisfied in your life. You are always welcome in Szolnok. These days I very rarely come to London.

With kind regards,
Tamas

Kell powered down the phone and looked out of the window at the wisps of motionless cloud. What Rachel had reacted to so strongly was obvious enough: a message from one of Wallinger's grieving lovers. But had Rachel understood the Hungarian or recognized the woman's handwriting? He could not know.

The plane landed at a small, functional, single-runway airport on the eastern shore of Chios. Kell identified the air traffic control tower, saw a bearded engineer on the tarmac tending to a punctured Land Cruiser, and took photographs of a helicopter and a corporate jet parked on either side of an Olympic Air Q400. Wallinger would have taken off only a few hundred meters away, then banked east toward Izmir. The Cessna had entered Turkish airspace in less than five minutes, crashing into the mountains southwest of Kütahya perhaps an hour later.

The island's taxi drivers were on strike so Kell was glad of the rental car, which he drove a few miles south to Karfas along a quiet road lined with citrus groves and crumbling, walled estates. The Golden Sands was a tourist hotel located in the center of a kilometer-long beach with views across the Chios Strait to Turkey. Kell unpacked, took a shower, then dressed in a fresh set of clothes. As he waited in the bar for his meeting, nursing a bottle of Efes lager and an overwhelming desire to smoke indoors, he reflected on how quickly his personal circumstances had changed. Less than twenty-four hours earlier, he had been eating a tuna sandwich on a crowded train from Preston. Now he was alone on a Greek island, masquerading as an insurance investigator, in the bar of an off-peak tourist hotel. *You're back in the game,* he told himself. *This is what you wanted.* But the buzz had gone. He remembered the feeling of landing in Nice almost two years earlier, instructed by the high priests at Vauxhall Cross to find Amelia at any cost. On that occasion, the rhythms and tricks of his trade had come back to him like muscle memory. This time, however, all that Kell felt was a sense of dread that he would uncover the truth about his friend's death. No pilot error. No engine failure. Just conspiracy and cover-up. Just murder.

Mr. Andonis Makris of the Hellenic Civil Aviation Authority was a thickset islander of about fifty who spoke impeccable, if overelaborate English and smelled strongly of eau de cologne. Kell presented him with Chris Hardwick's business card, agreed that Chios was indeed very beautiful, particularly at this time of year, and thanked Makris for agreeing to meet him on such short notice.

"Your assistant in the Edinburgh office told me that time was a factor," Makris reassured him. He was wearing a dark blue pin-striped suit and a white shirt without a tie. Self-assured to the point of arrogance, he gave the impression of a man who had, some years earlier, achieved personal satisfaction in almost every area of his life. "I am keen to assist you after such a tragedy. Many people on the island were shocked by the news of Mr. Wallinger's death. I am sure his family and colleagues are as keen as we are to find out what happened as soon as is possible in human terms."

It was obvious from his demeanor that Makris bore no sense of personal responsibility for the crash. Kell assumed that he would want to take the opportunity to shift the blame for the British diplomat's demise onto the shoulders of Turkish air traffic control as quickly as possible.

"Did you meet Mr. Wallinger personally?"

Makris was taking a sip of white wine and was halted by the question. He swallowed in his own good time and dabbed his mouth carefully with a paper napkin before responding.

"No." The voice was even in tone, a trace of American in the accent.

"The flight plan had been filed before I arrived on my shift. I spoke to the pilot—to Mr. Paul Wallinger—on the radio as he checked his instruments, taxied to the runway, and prepared for takeoff."

"He sounded normal?"

"What does 'normal' mean, please?"

"Was he agitated? Drunk? Did he sound tense?"

Makris reacted as though Kell had impugned his integrity.

"Drunk? Of course not. If I sense that a pilot is any of these things, I will prevent him from flying. Of course."

"Of course." Kell had never had much time for thin-skinned bureaucrats and couldn't be bothered to summon an apology for whatever offense his remark might have caused. "You can understand why I have to ask. In order to complete a full report on the accident, Scottish Widows needs to know everything . . ."

As though he had already grown tired of listening, Makris leaned down, picked up a slim briefcase and set it on the table. Kell was still speaking as two thick thumbs operated the sliding locks. The catches popped, the lid sprang open, and Makris's face was momentarily obscured from view.

"I have the flight plan here, Mr. Hardwick. I made a copy for you."

"That was very thoughtful."

Makris lowered the lid, passing Kell a one-page document covered in hieroglyphs of impenetrable Greek. There were boxes where Wallinger had scrawled his personal details, though no address on the island appeared to have been provided.

"The flight plan was to take the Cessna over Aignoussa, then east into Turkey. It is customary for Cesme or Izmir to take immediate responsibility for aircraft entering Turkish airspace."

"This is what happened?"

Makris nodded gravely. "This is what happened. The pilot told us he was leaving our circuit and then changed radio frequency. At this point, Mr. Wallinger was no longer our responsibility."

"Do you know where he was staying on Chios?"

Makris directed his eyes toward the flight plan. "Does it not say?"

Kell turned the sheet of paper around and held it up for inspection. "Hard to tell," he said.

Makris pursed his lips, as if to imply that Chris Hardwick had caused secondary offense by his failure to read and understand modern Greek. He took back the flight plan, studied it carefully, and was obliged to admit that no address had been given.

"There seems to be only Mr. Wallinger's residence in Ankara," he conceded. Clearly, this was a minor breach in aeronautical protocol. Kell suspected that, first thing in the morning, Makris would hunt down a junior colleague at the airport and take significant pleasure in reprimanding him for the oversight. "But there is a telephone number," he said, as though to compensate for the clerical error.

"A telephone number on Chios?"

Makris did not need to look back at the code. "Yes."

According to a preliminary report sent to Amelia the day before the funeral, Wallinger had used his own logbook and JAR license to hire the Cessna in Turkey and his own passport to enter Ankara, but had then left no trace of his movements once he arrived on Chios. His cell phone had been switched off for long periods during his stay and there was no activity on any Wallinger credit card, nor on his four registered SIS legends. He had effectively spent a week on Chios as a ghost. Kell assumed that Wallinger had been with a woman, and was trying to conceal his whereabouts from both Josephine and Amelia. Yet the lengths he had gone to suggested that it was equally plausible he had been making contact with an agent.

"Do you recognize the number?"

"Do I *recognize* it?" Makris's reply was effortlessly condescending. "No."

"And have you heard anything about what Mr. Wallinger was doing on Chios? Why he was visiting the island? Any rumors around town, newspaper reports?"

Kell accepted that his questions were what is known in the trade as a "trawl," but it was nevertheless important to ask them. It did not surprise him in the least when Makris suggested with a light cough that Mr. Hardwick was exceeding his brief.

"Paul Wallinger was just a tourist, no?" he said, raising his eyebrows. It was clear that he had no desire to improvise an answer. "I certainly have not spoken to anybody, or read anything, which suggests other interests. Why do you ask?"

Kell produced a bland smile. "Oh, just background for the report. We need to ascertain whether there was any chance that Mr. Wallinger deliberately took his own life."

Makris tried to appear appropriately dignified as he considered the grave matter of Paul Wallinger's possible suicide. It had doubtless occurred to him that such a verdict would absolve Chios Airport entirely of any responsibility in the crash, thus ending, at a stroke, the possibility of a lawsuit against the engineer who had checked the Cessna.

"Let me ask around," he replied. "To be perfectly honest with you, I have not yet even discussed the crash with my colleagues in Turkey."

"What about your engineers?"

"What about them, please?"

"Have you ascertained who was on duty the afternoon of the flight?"

"Of course." Makris had prepared for this, the most sensitive section of the interview, and dealt with it as Kell had expected he would. "Air traffic control is not accountable for maintenance and engineering. That is a separate department, a separate union. I assume that you will be holding other meetings with other employees in order to obtain a more full picture of the tragedy?"

"I will." Kell experienced another craving for a cigarette. "Do you happen to have the name of the engineer to hand?"

Makris appeared to weigh up the good sense of denying the man from Scottish Widows this simple request. At some cost to his equilibrium—his neck did an agitated roll and there was another delicate cough of irritation—he wrote down the name on the back of the flight plan.

"Iannis Christidis?" Kell studied Makris's spidery handwriting. With this and the phone number he had more than enough leads to plot Wallinger's movements in the days leading up to his death.

"That is correct," Makris replied. And to Kell's surprise he immediately stood up and drained the last of his wine. "Now will there be anything else, Mr. Hardwick? My wife is expecting me for dinner."

As soon as Makris had left the hotel, Kell went back to his room and dialed the number using the hotel landline. He was connected to a recorded answering service, but the message was in Greek. Heading back downstairs he dialed the number again, asked the receptionist to listen to the message and to give a rough translation of what was being said. To his frustration he was told that the voice was a default, computer-generated message with no person or corporation named. Kell, by now hungry and thinking about dinner, returned to his room to ring Adam.

"The engineer who worked on Wallinger's plane was called Iannis Christidis. Can you see if there's anything recorded against?"

"Sure."

It sounded as though Adam had woken up from a siesta. Kell heard the bump and scratch of a man looking around for a pen, the noise of a dog barking in the background.

"With a name like Christidis you'll probably get the Greek phone book, but see if he has a profile on the island."

"Will do."

"How are your reverse telephone directories for Chios?"

"I'm sure we can work something out."

Kell read out the number from the flight plan, checked that Adam had taken it down correctly, then mentally switched off. Having watched the headlines on CNN, he went for a grilled sea bass and a Greek salad at a restaurant halfway along the beach. From his table on a moonlit terrace he could see the distant lights of the Turkish coast, blinking like a runway.

At ten o'clock, smoking a cigarette at the edge of a high tide, he felt the pulse of a message coming through on his phone. Adam had sent a text.

STILL WORKING ON IC. NUMBER IS FOR A LETTING AGENCY. VILLAS ANGELIS. 119 KATANIKA, ON THE PORT. PROPRIETOR LISTED AS NICOLAS DELFAS.

8

Alexander Minasian, the SVR *rezident* in Kiev, the Directorate C officer whose recruitment of KODAK would surely make him a legend in the halls of Yasenevo, was a ghost on visits to Turkey. Sometimes he would come by airplane. Sometimes he would cross by car or truck from Bulgaria. On one occasion, he had taken a train across the frontier at Edirne. Always under alias, always using a different passport. Three times on the KODAK operation, Minasian had taken a ship from Odessa—his favored method of reaching Turkey—later meeting the asset in a room at the Ciragan Kempinski Hotel. They had drunk chilled red Sancerre and talked of the political and moral benefits of KODAK's work. Showing good instincts from the very beginning, the asset had always refused to meet undeclared SVR officers on Turkish soil, as well as cutouts and NOCs. KODAK would deal only with Minasian, whom he knew simply as "Carl."

Their arrangement was straightforward. Whenever there was product to be shared, KODAK would present himself at one of two cafés in Ankara or Istanbul and produce the agreed signal. This would be seen by a member of the embassy staff and a telegram would be immediately sent to Kiev. For reasons that Minasian had always accepted and understood, KODAK did not believe in handing over every piece of information or intelligence that crossed his desk. The product he chose to share was always "cherry-picked" (KODAK's phrase, one that Minasian had been obliged to look up) and usually of the highest quality.

"I'm not interested in giving you streams of reporting about investment goals, energy budgets, crystal ball stuff. That's what's going to get me caught. What I choose to give you, when I choose to give you it, will be hard, actionable intelligence, usually with very high clearance."

There were two dead letter boxes in Istanbul. One in the men's bathroom of a tourist restaurant in Sultanahmet owned by a former KGB officer, long since retired and now married to a Turkish woman who had borne him two sons. A dry cistern in the second of two recently modernized cubicles, detached from all plumbing, was ideal for the purposes of leaving memory sticks, hard drives, and documents—whatever KODAK wished to pass on.

The second site was located among the ruins of an old house—said once to have belonged to Leon Trotsky—on the northern shore of Buyukada, an island in the Sea of Marmara. This was KODAK's preferred location, because the asset was friendly with a journalist on Buyukada who lived adjacent to the site, so that any journeys made to the island could pass as social visits. KODAK had recently expressed his distaste for the cistern—though of course it had been thoroughly cleaned and disinfected during the bathroom renovations—complaining to Minasian that he felt "like Michael Corleone going to shoot somebody" whenever he lifted the lid to make a drop. Minasian had promised to find a third site, although KODAK seemed increasingly fond of the box on Buyukada, concealed as it was among the ruins and protected from rains and vermin.

It was toward this box that Minasian was headed, though his journey, as always, was to be a six-hour masterpiece of countersurveillance, involving two changes of clothing, five different taxis, two ferries (one north to Istinye, the other south to Bostanci), as well as three miles on foot in Besiktas and Beyoglu. Only when Minasian was certain that he had picked up no surveillance did he board the private vessel at Marinturk Marina and make the short crossing to Buyukada.

While on the island he still exercised caution. It was possible that MIT or the Americans could have advanced surveillance on Buyukada and pick Minasian up on foot (no vehicles were allowed on the island, only bicycles and horse-drawn carts). For this reason he effected his second change of appearance in a restaurant near the ferry terminal, leaving by a rear exit. Having completed a circuit of the island by cart, Minasian instructed the driver to take him within three hundred meters of the Trotsky house, completing the last section of his journey on foot.

He was carrying a leather shoulder bag, in which he had placed his changes of clothing, as well as a pair of swimming trunks and a towel. During the warmer months, Minasian would often take a swim before collecting the product. Anything to add to a sense of blameless leisure. Today, however, he was keen to return to Kadikoy on the ferry so that he could dine with a male friend in Bebek. For this reason, he went directly to the location, discerned that he was alone, and removed the contents left for him the previous day.

The paper was folded and protected from the elements by a transparent plastic folder that had been bound with a rubber band. This was usual. Minasian opened it and immediately photographed the contents. To his surprise, he saw that there was only one piece of information.

LVa/UKSIS Tehran (nuclear) Massoud Moghaddam.
Cryptonym: EINSTEIN

9

The offices of Villas Angelis were located above a small, family-run restaurant on the harbor in Chios Town. Kell reached the first floor by an external staircase at the side of the building, knocking on a part-frosted glass door through which he could see a small, strip-lit office occupied by a woman in her late thirties. The woman looked up, turned an inquisitive squint into a welcoming smile, then crossed the room and invited Kell to enter with a flourish of bosom and bonhomie.

"Hello sir, hello, hello," she said, on the correct assumption that Kell was a visitor to the island and spoke no Greek. She was wearing a floral print summer dress and blue espadrilles that were squashed by her swollen feet. "Come and sit down. How can we help you?"

Kell shook the woman's hand and settled into a small wooden chair facing her desk. Her name was Marianna and she was no taller than the water cooler beside which she was standing. The screensaver on her computer showed a photograph of an elderly Greek couple, whom Kell took to be her parents. There were no photographs on the desk of a husband or boyfriend, only a framed formal portrait of a small child in shorts—her nephew?—flanked on either side by his parents. Marianna was not wearing a wedding ring.

"My name is Chris Hardwick," Kell said, handing over his card. "I'm an insurance investigator with Scottish Widows."

Marianna's English was good, but not good enough to untangle what Mr. Hardwick had told her. She asked Kell to repeat what he had said, while studying the card closely for further clues.

"I'm investigating the death of a British diplomat. Paul Wallinger. Does that name mean anything to you?"

Marianna looked very much as though she wanted the name to mean something to her. Her eyes softened, so that she was looking at Kell with something like yearning, and her head tilted to one side in an effort to accommodate the question. In the end, however, she was obliged to admit defeat, responding in an apologetic tone that suggested frustration with her own ignorance.

"No, I'm sorry that it does not. Who was this man? I am sorry that I cannot help you."

"It's quite all right," Kell replied, smiling as warmly as he could. To the left, a poster of the Acropolis was peeling off the wall. Beside it, three digital clocks in pale gray cases displayed the time in Athens, Paris, and New York. Kell heard the sound of footsteps on the external staircase and turned to see a man of similar age and build to Andonis Makris pushing through the door of the office. He had thick eyebrows and a heavy black mustache, with two different shades of dye battling for prominence in his hair. Seeing Kell in the chair, the man grumbled something in Greek and moved toward the farthest window in the room, throwing open a set of shutters so that the office was suddenly flooded with morning sunlight and the noise of gunning mopeds. It was clear to Kell that the man was Marianna's boss and that his words had been some sort of reprimand to her for a sin as yet undetected.

"Nico, this is Mr. Hardwick." Marianna offered Kell a conciliatory smile, which he interpreted as an apology in advance for her boss's erratic temperament. She then began tapping something into her computer as Nicolas Delfas crossed the room and invited Kell to move to a seat beside his own desk. The body language was page-one machismo: *I'm in charge now. Men should deal with men.*

"You're looking to rent a place?" he asked, offering up a dry, bulky handshake.

"No. I'm actually an insurance investigator." Delfas had braced his arms across his desk and was busily searching for something among a pile of papers. "I was just asking your colleague if your office had had any dealings with a British diplomat named Paul Wallinger?"

The word "diplomat" was barely out of Kell's mouth before Delfas looked up and began shaking his head.

"Who?"

"Wallinger. Paul Wallinger."

"No. I don't want to talk about this. I don't know him. I did not know him."

Delfas met Kell's eye, but his gaze quickly slid back to the desk.

"You don't want to talk about him or you don't know who he was?"

The Greek began moving objects on the top of a battered black filing cabinet, an exertion that caused him to breathe more heavily and to shake his head in frustration. After a few moments he looked at Kell again, as though surprised to see that he was still in the office.

"Sorry?" he said.

"I was asking if you had met Mr. Wallinger."

Delfas pursed his lips, the bristles of his thick mustache momentarily obscuring the base of his nose.

"I have told you, I do not know about this man. I don't have any questions to answer. What else can I help you with?"

"Wallinger's flight plan listed your office as a contact number on Chios. I wondered if he had rented a property from Villas Angelis?"

Kell glanced at Marianna. She was still absorbed in her computer, though it was clear that she was listening to every word of the conversation:

her ears and cheeks had flushed to scarlet and she looked tense and stiff. Delfas barked something at her, then uttered a word—"*gamoto*"—which Kell assumed to be a close Greek cousin of "fuck."

"Look, Mr., uh . . ."

"Hardwick."

"Yes. I do not know what it is you are talking about. We are very busy here. I cannot help you with your enquiries."

"You didn't hear about the accident?" Kell was amused by the idea that Delfas and Marianna were "busy." The office had all the bustle and energy of a deserted waiting room in a branch-line railway station. "He took off from Chios Airport last week," he said. "His Cessna crashed in western Turkey."

At last Marianna turned her head and looked at the two men. It was obvious that she had remembered Wallinger's name, or was at least familiar with the circumstances of the accident. Delfas, seeming to sense this, stood up and tried to usher Kell toward the door.

"I do not know about this," he said, adding what sounded like a further brusque denial in his native tongue. Pulling at the door, he held it open with his eyes fixed on the ground. Kell had no choice but to stand and leave. Long exposure to liars—good and bad—had taught him not to strike in the first instance. If the perpetrator was being willfully stubborn and obstructive it was better to let them stew.

"Fine," he said, "fine," and turned to Marianna, nodding a warm farewell. As he left, Kell quickly scanned the room for evidence of CCTV and burglar alarms, making a rapid assessment of the locks on the door. Given that Delfas was plainly hiding something, it might be necessary to arrange a break-in and to take a closer look at the company's computer system. Kell informed him that Edinburgh would be in "written contact regarding Mr. Wallinger's relationship with Villas Angelis" and said that he was grateful for the opportunity to have spoken to him. Delfas muttered: "Yes, thank you" in English, then slammed the door behind him.

The office opening hours and telephone number were engraved in a sheet of hard white plastic at the base of the external stairs. Kell was studying the notice and thinking about arranging for a Tech-Ops team to fly out to Chios when a far simpler idea occurred to him. The muscle memory of a cynical old spook. He knew exactly what he had to do. There was no need to organize a break-in. There was Marianna.

10

Recruiting an agent is an act of seduction," an instructor at Fort Monckton had told a class of eager SIS pups in the autumn of 1994. "The trick with agents of the opposite gender is to seduce them without, well, *seducing* them."

Kell remembered the ripple of knowing laughter that had followed that remark, a room full of high-functioning trainee spooks all wondering what would happen if they one day found themselves in a situation where they were sexually attracted to an agent. It happened, of course. To gain the trust of a stranger, to convince a person to believe in you, to compel them to act, sometimes against their own better instincts—was that not the first step to the bedroom? Good agents were often bright, ambitious, emotionally needy: to run them required a mixture of flattery, kindness, and empathy. It was the spy's job to listen, to be in control, to remain strong, often in the face of impossibly difficult circumstances. The men employed by SIS were often physically attractive, the women also. Several times in his career, Kell had been in situations where, had he wanted to, it would have been easy to take a female agent to bed. They came to rely on you, to trust and admire their handler completely. Right or wrong, the mystique of spying was an aphrodisiac. For much the same reason, the atmosphere within the four walls of Thames House and Vauxhall Cross had often been likened to a bordello, particularly where younger employees were concerned. Secrecy bred intimacy. Officers could only discuss their work with other officers. Often they would do so at night, over a drink or two in the MI5 bar, or a local pub in Vauxhall. Inevitably, one thing led to another, both at home and abroad. It was the way of the business. It was also one of the reasons the divorce rate in SIS was as high as in Beverly Hills.

The trick with agents of the opposite gender is to seduce them without, well, seducing *them.* Kell sat on the harbor wall at quarter to three, the instructor's words running through his mind as he kept an eye on the first-floor windows of Villas Angelis. At exactly one minute past three, Marianna and Delfas emerged to begin their hour-long lunch break. Delfas went into the restaurant downstairs, to be greeted by several nodding patrons who were seated at tables beneath a burgundy awning. Marianna began to walk south along the harbor road. Kell followed her at a discreet distance and watched as she went into a restaurant adjacent to the ferry terminal. From his position on the street he had clear sight of her table. There was a second door at the side of the restaurant through which he could enter without being seen. He would sit down, order some food, then contrive a reason to walk past.

He took five hundred euros out of an ATM, entered the restaurant, nodded at a waitress, and sat down. Within a minute, Kell had a menu open in front of him; within two, he had ordered sausages, fried potatoes, and salad, as well as a half-liter bottle of sparkling water. Marianna was on the opposite side of the room, beyond the bar, one of perhaps fifteen or twenty other customers spread out around the restaurant. Kell could not see her table, but had glimpsed the top of her head when he walked in.

As soon as the waitress had brought the water, Kell stood up and headed toward the bar. He turned right, ostensibly looking for the toilets, but made a point of staring at Marianna's table. Sensing movement in her peripheral vision, she looked up and instantly recognized Kell. She smiled warmly and set aside the book she was reading.

"Oh, hello." Kell managed to convey a look of complete surprise as he came to a halt beside her. He was pleased to note that Marianna was blushing.

"Mr. Harding!"

"Hardwick. Call me Chris. Marianna, yes?"

She looked embarrassed not to have remembered his name. "What are you doing here?"

Kell turned and nodded back in the general direction of his table. "Same as you, I suppose. Just having some lunch."

"Have you eaten?"

Marianna looked at the chair opposite her own, as though mustering the courage to invite Kell to join her.

"I've just ordered," he replied, adding a warm smile. "What have you got there? Some soup? Looks delicious."

Marianna looked down at what appeared to be a bowl of clear chicken soup. She lifted up the spoon. For a moment, Kell wondered if she was going to offer him a taste.

"Yes, soup. I am very sorry about Nico."

Kell played dumb with the name. "Nico?"

"My boss . . ."

"Oh. Him. Yes, that was frustrating."

She appeared to have run out of things to say. Kell looked ahead toward the door of the bathroom.

"Sorry," she said, taking the cue. "I didn't mean to stop you."

"No, no," Kell replied. "It's really nice to see you. I enjoyed meeting you this morning." Marianna appeared not to know how to react to the compliment. Her hand moved toward her face and the tips of her fingers brushed her eyebrows. Kell hooked the ensuing silence with an appropriate amount of bait. "I was just frustrated. It would have been useful to find out why Mr. Wallinger had your number."

Marianna looked as though she was in possession of the answer to Mr. Hardwick's simple question.

"Yes," she replied, her hand reaching for the spine of the book, as though to reassure herself about something. The flush had gone from her cheeks and she looked eager to continue the conversation. "Nico can be difficult in the mornings."

Kell nodded, allowing another brief silence to envelop them. Marianna shot a nervous glance toward the bar.

"Where are my manners?" she said. "You are a guest in Chios. Would you like to eat at my table? I can't leave you on your own."

"Are you sure?" Kell felt the small but unmistakable buzz of a successfully executed plan.

"Of course!" Marianna's natural bustle and bonhomie was suddenly in full flood. She looked buoyant. "I can tell the waitress to bring your food to my table. That is, if you'd like me to?"

"I would like that very much."

After that, it was easy. Kell hadn't recruited an unconscious asset for over a year, but the tricks of the trade, the grammar of a successful pitch, were second nature to him. "If you're doing it properly," the same instructor at the Fort had told the same 1994 class, "a recruitment shouldn't feel cynical or manipulative. It should feel as though both parties want the same outcome. It should feel as though the prospective agent requires something from you, and that you can meet that requirement."

And so it was that Kell discovered the limits of Marianna Dimitriadis's loyalty to Nicolas Delfas.

From the outset, he avoided talking about Wallinger. Instead, Kell concentrated on finding out as much about Marianna as possible. By the time they were eating dessert—a rice pudding flavored with lemon—he knew where she had been born, how many brothers and sisters she had, where those siblings lived, the names of her best friends, how she had come to work at Villas Angelis, why she had remained on Chios (rather than pursue a career in Thessaloniki in public relations), as well as the identity of her last boyfriend, a German tourist who had lived with her for six months before returning to his wife in Munich. In her natural warmth and good cheer, Kell detected the loneliness of the maiden aunt, the romantic and social frustration of the lifelong spinster. He rarely shifted his gaze from Marianna's lively and melancholy eyes. He smiled when she did; he listened as carefully and as intelligently as she required. He was certain that, by the time it came to settle the bill, she would agree to the simple task that he was about to set her.

"I've got a problem," he said.

"You do?"

"If I can't find out why Paul Wallinger used the number of your office on his flight plan, my boss is going to go crazy. He'll have to send somebody else out to Chios, I'll get the blame, the whole thing will take weeks and cost a fortune."

"I see."

"Forgive me for saying this, Marianna, but I felt like Nico was hiding something from me. Was that the case?" His companion's eyes dropped to the table. Marianna began to shake her head, but Kell could see that she was smiling to herself. "I don't mean to pry," he added.

"You're not prying," she replied instantly. She looked up and gazed into his eyes, a look of yearning with which he had become familiar throughout the meal.

"What was it then?"

"Nico is not very . . ."—she searched for the correct adjective—"kind." It was not the word that Kell had been expecting, but he was glad of it. "He does not like to help people unless they can help him. He does not like to involve himself in anything . . . complex."

Kell nodded in appreciation of Marianna's stark analysis of character. The waitress passed their table and Kell took the opportunity to order an espresso.

"How would it be complex?" he asked. "Was he involved in business with Mr. Wallinger?"

A burst of laughter and a beaming smile told Kell that this was not the case. Marianna shook her head.

"Oh, no. There was nothing wrong in their relationship." She glanced out of the window. A ferry was easing into the harbor, passengers on the bow waving at the mainland. "He just decided not to help you." Marianna could see that Mr. Hardwick was affronted by Delfas's belligerence. "Do not take it personally," she said, and for a moment Kell thought that she was going to reach for his hand. "He is like this with everyone. I am not like that. Most Greek people are not like that."

"Of course."

The moment had arrived. Kell felt the bulge of five hundred euros in his wallet, money that he had been prepared to offer Marianna in exchange for her cooperation. He had laid a private bet with himself that he would not need it.

"Would you be prepared to help me?" he asked.

"In what way?" Marianna was blushing again.

"Can you tell me what Nico wasn't prepared to say? It would save me a lot of trouble."

If Marianna experienced a moment of ethical conflict over the matter, it passed in no more than a second. With a matter-of-fact sigh, her loyalty to her boss was shaken off like a passing fad.

"From my memory," she said, taking Kell into her immediate confidence, "Mr. Wallinger was staying in one of our villas. For a week."

"Then why didn't Nico tell me that?"

She shrugged. It seemed that they were both at the mercy of a stubborn and irascible man. "He came into the office to collect the keys."

Kell buried his surprise. The news of the sighting was like a vision of Wallinger coming back from the dead.

"You met him?"

"Yes. He was very nice, a quiet man, quite serious." Marianna hesitated, taking a risk with Mr. Hardwick's ego. "I thought he was very tall—and extremely handsome!"

Kell smiled. That sounded like Paul.

"So he was on his own?"

"Yes. Although I saw him later that day. With somebody else."

"Oh. Who was that?" Kell was about to say: "A woman?" when he checked himself. "Another tourist?"

"A man," Marianna replied matter-of-factly. Kell wondered if her memory was playing tricks on her. It was not the answer he had been expecting. "I walked past their table," she said. "One of the cafés near my office."

Kell found that he was turning Amelia's words over in his mind. *Tread carefully around the Yanks. Tricky out there at the moment.*

"This man. Was he American by any chance?"

Kell was concerned that he was asking too many questions. He was relying on the atmosphere of broad agreement which had grown up between the two of them, a relaxed complicity.

"I don't know," Marianna replied. "I never saw him again."

"Was he as handsome as Mr. Wallinger?"

Kell put a grin on the question, trawling for a description in a way that he hoped would not raise Marianna's suspicions.

"Oh, no!" she said, obliging him. "He was younger, but he had a beard, and I don't like beards. I think the villa was rented by a woman. In fact, I am sure of that, because I spoke with her on the telephone."

This was the name Kell needed. Find the woman and he could find the man. He was sure of it.

"I don't want to get you into trouble," he said, suggesting quite the opposite with his eyes.

"What do you mean?"

"All I would need is a copy of the rental agreement. If there's nothing sinister or illegal going on, it would really save me a lot of . . ."

Marianna did not even bother to hear him out. They were friends now—perhaps more than that. Mr. Hardwick had successfully earned her trust. She leaned forward and at last touched the top of his wrist. Kell heard the buzz of a moped as it tore along the port, the crack of seagulls circling above the restaurant.

"No problem," she said. "Where are you staying? How would be the best way of sending it? I could fax?"

Three hours later, lying on his bed, almost halfway through *My Name Is Red,* Kell heard a knock at the door of his hotel room. He opened it to find the same receptionist who had assisted him with the recorded message the previous evening. She was holding up a piece of paper.

"Fax."

Kell tipped her five euros and went back into the room. Marianna had sent through the rental agreement, as well as a short handwritten note scribbled at the top of the page: "Great to meet you! Hope to see you again!" The document was dual-language, so Kell was able to see that the villa in question had been rented, at a cost of €2,500, for the seven days prior to the crash. There was no sign of Wallinger's name on the document, only the signature and date of birth of a woman who had given a Hungarian passport and cell phone number for ID. Seeing her handwriting, Kell felt the mystery of Rachel's note opening in front of him like a blooming flower. Checking the camera roll on his iPhone, he saw that there was a clear match with the signature on the rental agreement.

He was on the phone to Tamas Metka within minutes.

"Tom!" he exclaimed. "Tell me. Why am I so popular all of a sudden?"

"I need a profile on somebody. Hungarian passport holder."

"Is he the poet?"

Kell laughed. "Not he. She. Our usual arrangement?"

"Sure. The name?"

"Sandor," Kell replied, reaching for a packet of cigarettes. "Cecilia Sandor."

11

The force of her grief had astonished Rachel Wallinger. She had spent the greater part of her adult life thinking that her father was a liar, a cheat, a man of no substance, an absence from the heart of his own family. Yet now that he was gone, she missed him as she had never missed anyone or anything before.

How was it possible to grieve for a man who had betrayed her mother, time and again? Why was she suffering for a father who had shown her so little in the way of attention and love? Rachel had not respected Paul Wallinger, she had not even particularly liked him. When asked by friends to describe their relationship, she had always given a version of the same response—"He's a diplomat. We grew up all around the world. I hardly ever saw him." Yet the truth was more complex and one she kept to herself. That her father was a spy. That he had used his family as cover for his clandestine activities. That his secret life on behalf of the state had afforded him an opportunity to enjoy a secret life of the heart as well.

At fifteen, while the Wallinger family was living in Egypt, Rachel had come home early from school to find her father kissing another woman in the kitchen of their house in Cairo. She had walked into the garden, looked up at the house, and seen them together. She had recognized the woman as a member of staff from the embassy. In that moment, her entire understanding of family life had been obliterated. Her father was transformed from a man of strength and dignity, a man she trusted and whom she adored with all her heart, into a stranger who would betray her mother and whose affection for his daughter was apparently meaningless and inchoate.

What had made the discovery even worse was her father's realization that he had been spotted. The woman had left the house immediately. Paul had then come out into the garden and had tried to convince the teenage Rachel that he had merely been comforting a distraught colleague. *Please do not mention this to your mother. You do not know what you have seen.* In her state of shock, Rachel had agreed to the cover-up, but her complicity in the lie changed the nature of their relationship for good. She was not rewarded for keeping the secret; in fact, she was punished. Her father became distant. He withdrew his love. It was as though, as the years went by, he perceived Rachel as a threat. There were times when she felt that *she* was the one who had betrayed *him*.

What Rachel witnessed that day also affected the way she formed and conducted her own relationships in later life. As she grew older, she became aware of trusting no one, of playing games with prospective lovers, of testing men for evidence of duplicity and cunning. Intensely private and concealed, Rachel was habitually drawn to men whom she could not have or could not control. At the same time, particularly in her early twenties, she was often dismissive of those who showed her genuine kindness and affection.

In the months after the incident in Cairo, Rachel had made it her business to pry into her father's personal affairs, developing an obsessive fascination with his behavior. She had cross-checked dates in his diaries; investigated "friends" to whom he had introduced her at seemingly benign family gatherings; eavesdropped on telephone calls whenever she found herself passing her father's office at home or standing outside her parents' bedroom.

Then, years later, a reminder of the day that had changed everything.

Only weeks before her father's death, Rachel had discovered a letter that he had written to yet another mistress. Sent to the family flat in Gloucester Road. Rachel had recognized the stationery, the handwriting, but not the name of the person to whom the letter had been originally addressed in Croatia: Cecilia Sandor. The envelope was marked "Address Unknown" and there was a demand for excess postage. Rachel had intercepted it before her mother had looked through the morning post.

She could still recite parts of the letter from memory:

I cannot stop thinking about you, Cecilia. I want your body, your mouth, the taste of you, the smell of your perfume, your conversation, your laughter—I want all of it, constantly.

I cannot wait to see you, my darling.

I love you

P x

More than fifteen years after Cairo, Rachel had felt the same wrenching shock that she had experienced as a teenager looking up at the kitchen window. At thirty-one, she was no moralist. Rachel was under no illusions about marital infidelity. But the letter only served to remind her that nothing had changed. That her father would always put his own life, his own passions, his other women, in front of his love for his wife and daughter.

So why, then, was she grieving him so intensely? Driving back to London the day after the funeral, Rachel had been suddenly so overwhelmed by loss that she had pulled her car over onto the hard shoulder of the motorway and sobbed uncontrollably. It was like being under a spell, a thing she could neither break nor control. As soon as the wave of grief had passed, however, she had felt restored and able to carry on driving, thinking up ways to cheer up her mother, even if it was just by spending time with her so that she was not left on her own.

This ability to organize her behavior, to compartmentalize her feelings, was a characteristic that Rachel had observed in her father. He had been a tough and opinionated man, perceived by many as arrogant. From time to time, Rachel herself had been accused of being distant and cold, usually by boyfriends who had been drawn to her self-confidence and energy, but eventually repelled by her refusal to conform to their expectations of her.

When she considered the many traits that she had inherited from her father, particularly now that he was gone, it felt to Rachel as though he was living inside her and that she would never shed his influence. Nor, now, did she want to. Her feelings about him in the aftermath of his death had become altogether more complex. She was angry with Paul for keeping her at such an emotional distance, but remembered the rare moments when he had held her, or taken her to dinner in London, or watched her graduation at Oxford, with great yearning. Rachel wished that he had not betrayed his family, but she also regretted never having confronted him about his behavior. Her father had probably gone to his grave knowing that his daughter resented him. The guilt Rachel felt about that was at times overwhelming.

They were so similar. That was the conclusion she had drawn. At odds all her adult life, because they were alike in so many ways. Was that why they had come for her? Was that why she had been approached?

Spying in the DNA. Spying as a talent passed down through the generations.

12

With the tide in his favor, Kell could have swum to Turkey in a couple of hours. It was less than ten kilometers from Karfas to Cesme; a ferry from Chios Town would have got him there in forty-five minutes. Instead, sticking to the itinerary arranged by London, he flew back to Athens and took a bumpy afternoon plane to Ankara, landing a little after five o'clock and losing his bag for an hour in the late afternoon chaos of an overstaffed Turkish airport.

Douglas Tremayne, Wallinger's number two in Ankara and the acting head of station, was waiting for him in the arrivals area. Kell couldn't work out whether his presence at the airport was an indication of the seriousness with which he was taking the Wallinger investigation, or evidence of the fact that Tremayne was bored and starved of company. He was wearing a pressed linen suit, an expensive-looking shirt, and enough aftershave to water the eyes of anyone within a twenty-foot radius. His hair had been carefully combed and the brown brogues he was wearing polished to a brilliant shine.

"I thought we were meeting for dinner?" Kell asked, shouldering his bag as they headed toward the car park. Tremayne was an unmarried former army officer with a fill-in-the-blanks personality whom Kell had briefly worked alongside in the late 1990s when both men had been stationed in London. Along with several other colleagues, Kell had formed the opinion that Tremayne had not yet found the courage to admit to himself, far less to others, that he was gay. Personable to an almost suffocating degree, he was best enjoyed in small doses. The prospect of spending the next several hours in his company, not to mention two full days and nights at the British embassy combing through the Wallinger files, filled Kell with a sense of despondency bordering on dread.

"Well, I had some time on my hands, I know what the taxi drivers are like round here, thought I'd surprise you so we could make a start on things in the car."

Given that Tremayne was declared to the Turkish authorities, there was a chance that anything they discussed in the vehicle would be recorded and relayed back to MIT, the Turkish intelligence service.

"When did you last have this thing swept?" Kell asked, swinging his luggage into the trunk. There was a dent in the left back panel of the car, an unhealed scar from a collision in Ankaran traffic.

"Don't worry, Tom. Don't worry." Tremayne opened the passenger door for him, like a chauffeur anticipating a tip. "Picked it up yesterday afternoon." He patted the roof for good measure. "Clean as a whistle."

"But you're followed?"

Tremayne waited until he had sat in the driver's seat and switched on the engine before replying.

"By the Iranians. By the Russians. By the Turks. Isn't that part of my job description? To suck up surveillance so that the likes of you can go about your business?"

If such a status bothered him, Tremayne did not betray his distress. He was the quieter breed of spook, grown somewhat lazy, certainly happy to serve time in the shadow of more dynamic colleagues. Wallinger had been the star in Turkey, Amelia's point man for the restructuring of SIS operations in the Middle East, heading up a team of hungry young officers eager to recruit and run operations against the myriad targets presented to them in Ankara and beyond. Tremayne would not have considered himself in the running for head of station.

Within minutes Tremayne's Volvo was crawling along a standard-issue Turkish highway, Kell reviving a sense he dimly recalled of Ankara as a soulless city, deposited on the Steppe, buildings of no recognizable age or tradition strewn across an erratic landscape. He had visited the city on two previous occasions, solely for meetings with MIT, and could recall nothing of the trips save for a January blizzard that had given the British embassy the look of an Alpine ski lodge.

"So we've been battening down the hatches, trying to come to terms with the whole thing." Kell's mind had wandered; he wasn't sure how long Tremayne had been monologuing about Wallinger. "I wasn't able to go to the funeral, as you know. Had to mind the fort. How was it?"

Kell cracked a window and lit a cigarette, his fourth since landing.

"Difficult. Very moving. A lot of old faces there. A lot of unanswered questions."

"Do you think he might have crashed the plane deliberately?"

Tremayne had the decency to make a momentary, glancing eye contact as he pitched the question, but the timing of it still irked Kell.

"You tell me. Did Paul strike you as the suicidal type?"

"Not at all." Tremayne's response was quick and forthright, though he added a caveat, like a quick adjustment to the steering wheel. "Truth be told, we didn't see a great deal of each other. We didn't fraternize. Paul spent the majority of his time in Istanbul."

"Any particular reason for that?"

Tremayne hesitated before responding. "It's an attack Station."

"I'm well aware of that, Doug. That's why I said 'particular reason'."

Kell was trawling again, for anything: Wallinger's assets—conscious or unconscious—his contacts, his women. The files and telegrams he would pore over in the next forty-eight hours would give an official version of Wallinger's interests and behavior, but there was no downside to the raw intel of gossip and rumor.

"Well, for one thing, he loved the city. Knew it like the back of his hand, enjoyed it as Istanbul deserves to be enjoyed. Things are always more formal here. Ankara is a government town, a policy town. As you will be aware, most of the important discussions on Iran, on Syria and the Brotherhood, are taking place in Istanbul. Paul kept a lovely house in Yenikoy. He was surrounded by his books, his paintings. That's where Josephine would visit him. She loathed Ankara. The children did, too."

"Rachel came here?"

Tremayne nodded. "Only once, I think."

Kell took out his iPhone and checked the screen for activity. There was a single text, which turned out to be a welcome message from his mobile phone provider, and three e-mails, two of which were spam. It was a bad, addictive habit he had developed after spending too many solitary days and nights in London without sufficient intellectual stimulation: a craving for news, for the tiny narcotic fix of contact from the outside world. Most days he hoped for a friendly message from Claire, if only to reassure himself that she had not entirely vanished from his life.

"Is that the new one?" Tremayne asked.

"I've no idea." Kell put the iPhone back in his pocket. "Tell me what Paul was working on when he died. Amelia said you'd be able to bring me up to speed."

A change of gear and Tremayne crawled toward a red light.

"I suppose you've heard about the Armenian fiasco?"

It was a reminder to Kell that he had been out of the loop for too long. Whatever operation Tremayne was referring to had not even been mentioned by Amelia in Cartmel.

"Assume that I'm starting at zero, Doug. The decision to send me here was only taken two days ago."

The traffic light began to flash. Tremayne moved off in bunched suburban traffic, passing beneath a giant billboard of José Mourinho advertising what appeared to be contents insurance.

"I see," he said, plainly surprised by Kell's ignorance. "Well, best described as a bloody farce. Eight-month joint operation with the Cousins to bring a high-ranking Iranian military official across the border. Everything going like clockwork from Tehran, he gets as far as the frontier with his courier, Paul and his opposite number in the CIA about to pop the champagne and then—bang!"

"Bang?"

"Car bomb. Asset and courier both killed instantly. Paul apparently had the whites of his eyes, the Cousin bloody *filmed* him. It's all in a report you'll read tomorrow." Tremayne overtook a truck belching fumes into the Ankaran evening and changed into a lower gear. "Amelia didn't tell you?"

Kell shook his head. *No, Amelia didn't tell me.* And why was that? To save face, or because there was more to the story than a simple botched joint op?

"The bomb was planted by the Iranians?"

"We assume so. Remote controlled, almost certainly. For obvious reasons we weren't able to get a look at the wreckage. It's as though we were allowed to glimpse our prize, and then that prize was snatched from our grasp. A very deliberate snub, a power play. Tehran must have known about HITCHCOCK all along."

"HITCHCOCK was the cryptonym?"

"Real name Shakhouri."

Again, Kell wondered why Amelia had not told him about the bomb. Had the operation been spoken of at the funeral? Were there half a dozen conversations in the barn about HITCHCOCK to which he had not been privy? He felt the familiar, numb anger of his long exclusion from privileged information.

"What's the American line on what happened?"

Tremayne shrugged. He was of the view that the post-9/11 Cousins were a law unto themselves, best treated with deference, but kept at arm's length as much as possible. "You're meeting them on Monday," he said. There was a note change in Tremayne's voice, as if he was about to apologize for letting Kell down. "Tom, there's something I need to discuss with you."

"Go on."

"The CIA head of station here. I assume you've been told?"

"Been told what?"

Tremayne stretched the muscles in his neck, releasing another puff of aftershave into the car. "Tom, I've been made aware of your situation. I've known about it for some time." Tremayne was referring to Witness X. It sounded as though he wanted Kell's gratitude for remaining circumspect. "For what it's worth, I think you were strung up."

"For what it's worth, I think I was too."

"Hung out to dry to protect HMG. Made a scapegoat for the numberless failings of our superiors."

"And inferiors," Kell added, squeezing the cigarette out of the gap in the window. In that moment, passing a group of men standing idly beside the road, he knew exactly what Tremayne was about to tell him. He was back in the room with Yassin Gharani, back in Kabul in 2004, with a pumped-up CIA officer throwing punches in the face of a brainwashed *jihadi.*

"Jim Chater is in town."

Chater was the man whose reputation and good name Kell had protected at the expense of his own career. That naïveté, in itself, had been a principal component of his anger in the past two years, not least because he had never received adequate thanks for suppressing what he knew about the worst aspects of Chater's conduct. Gharani had been beaten senseless. Gharani had been waterboarded. For his uncommitted sins he had then been dispatched to a black site in Cairo and—when the Egyptians were done with him—to Cuba and the prolonged humiliations of Guantanamo. And Chater was now the man with whom Kell would have to discuss the death of Paul Wallinger.

Kell turned to Tremayne, wondering why "C" hadn't warned him. Amelia had placed her own needs—her desire for her affair with Paul never to become public knowledge—above the good sense of putting Kell into an environment in which he would clash with one of the men he held responsible for terminating his career. Perhaps she had seen a benefit in that. As Tremayne, in an effort to locate Kell's hotel, began taking directions from a Turkish sat-nav, Kell reflected that Chater was a rogue element, a running sore in the otherwise cordial relationship between the two services. However, Amelia had presented him with an opportunity, a chance for explanations, for closure. Something cold stirred inside Kell, a dormant ruthlessness. The chance to do business with Jim Chater in Turkey was also the chance to exact a measure of revenge.

13

Massoud Moghaddam, a lecturer in chemistry at Sharif University, a commercial director with responsibility for procurement at the Natanz uranium enrichment plant near Isfahan, and a CIA asset recruited by Jim Chater in 2009, known to Langley by the cryptonym EINSTEIN, woke as usual shortly before dawn.

His routine did not vary from morning to morning. He left his wife sleeping, showered and brushed his teeth, then prayed in the living room of his two-bedroom apartment in northern Tehran. By seven, his six-year-old son, Hooman, and eight-year-old daughter, Shirin, were both awake. Narges, his wife, had washed and was preparing breakfast in the kitchen. The children were now old enough to dress themselves, but young enough still to make an apocalyptic mess at the table whenever the family sat together for a meal. At breakfast time, Massoud and Narges usually ate *lavash* bread with feta cheese and honey; the children preferred their bread with chocolate spread or fig jam, most of which ended up in crumbs and splatters on the floor. While mummy and daddy drank tea, Hooman and Shirin gorged on orange juice and made jokes about their friends. By eight, it was time for the children to leave for school.

Their mother almost always walked them to the gates, leaving Massoud alone in the apartment.

Doctor Moghaddam wore the same outfit to work every day. Black leather shoes, black flannel trousers, a plain white shirt, and a dark gray jacket. In the winter he added a V-neck pullover. He wore a cotton vest under his shirt and rarely, if ever, removed the silver necklace given to him by his sister, Pegah, when she had moved to Frankfurt with her German husband in 1998. Most mornings, to avoid the rush hour traffic that blighted Tehran, Massoud would ride the subway to Sharif or Ostad Moin. On this particular day, however, he had an evening appointment in Pardis, and would need the car to drive back into the city after supper.

Massoud drove a white Peugeot 205 that he kept in the car park beneath his apartment building. He would joke to Narges that the only time he was ever able to accelerate beyond twenty miles an hour in Tehran was on the ramp leading out of the car park. Thereafter, like every other commuter heading south on Chamran and Fazlollah Nouri, he was stuck in a permanent, hour-long crawl of traffic. The Peugeot was not air-conditioned, so he was obliged to drive with all four windows down, allowing every molecule of air pollution and every decibel of noise to accompany him on his journey.

On certain mornings, Massoud would listen to the news on the radio and to intermittent traffic reports, but he had recently concluded that each of these was as pointless as the next; there were now so many subway construction sites in Tehran, and the city so overwhelmed by traffic, that the only solution was to drive as assertively as possible along the shortest geographical route. Come off any of the main arteries, however, and he ran the risk of being redirected by traffic police, or stopping altogether behind a broken-down truck. Today, with smog shrouding the Alborz mountains, Massoud eased his irritation by plugging an MP3 player into the stereo and clicking to *The Well-Tempered Klavier.* Though certain notes and phrases were hard to detect against the noise of the highway, he knew the music intimately and always found that Bach helped to ease the stress of a hot summer morning in near-permanent four-lane gridlock.

After almost an hour, he was at last able to loop down from Fazlollah Nouri onto Yadegar-e-Emam. Massoud was now within a few hundred meters of the university car park, although there were still two sets of traffic lights to negotiate. It was fiercely hot, and his shirt was soaked with sweat. As he came to a halt, a pedestrian walked past the driver's window, the smoke from his mint cigarette drifting into the car, a smell that reminded Massoud of his father. Up ahead, he could see yet another traffic cop directing yet another group of jousting cars. All around him, the ceaseless, Bach-drowning cacophony of horns and bikes and engines.

Massoud glanced in his opposite sideview mirror, preparing to push into the outer lane so that he could later make the turn onto Homayunshahr. A motorbike was snaking through a gap in traffic, about two meters from the Peugeot. If Massoud pushed out, there was a chance he would knock the bike over. Looking again in the mirror, he saw that there was a helmeted passenger riding pillion behind the driver. Best to let them pass.

The motorbike did so, but drew up alongside the Peugeot. To Massoud's surprise, the driver applied the brakes and stopped. There was space in front of him in which to move, yet he had come to a halt. The driver bent forward and seemed to look at Massoud through a black visor that threw sunlight into the car. Massoud heard a muffled word spoken under the helmet—not Persian—but lost his concentration when the lights turned green and he was obliged to engage first gear and shunt toward the turning.

It was only when he sensed a weight magnetizing to the rear door, pulling down on the Peugeot's suspension like a flat tire, that Massoud realized what had happened and was seized by black panic. The bike was gone, swerving directly in front of the car, then angling back in a fast

U-turn into the river of traffic moving on the opposite side. In desperation, Massoud reached for his seat belt, the engine still running, and pulled the belt across his chest as he tried to open the door.

Witnesses to the explosion later reported that Dr. Massoud Moghaddam had one foot on the road when the blast shaped toward him, obliterating the front section of the Peugeot 205 but leaving the engine almost intact. Four passersby were injured, including a customer emerging from a nearby café. A nineteen-year-old man on a bicycle was also killed in the attack.

14

Kell spent the next two days, from half past eight in the morning to ten o'clock at night, in Wallinger's office on the top floor of the British embassy. SIS Station was reached through a series of security doors activated by a swipe card and a five-digit PIN. The last of the doors, leading from the Chancery section into the Station itself, was almost a meter thick, heavy as a motorcycle and watched over by a CCTV camera linked to Vauxhall Cross. Kell was required to open a combination lock and turn two handles simultaneously before pulling the door toward him on a slow hinge. He joked to one of the secretaries that it was the first exercise he had taken in almost a year. She did not laugh.

In accordance with Station protocols the world over, Wallinger's computer hard drive had been placed inside the strongbox prior to his departure for Greece. On the first morning, Kell asked one of the assistants to remove it and to reboot the computer while he made a brief mental inventory of the personal items in Wallinger's office. There were three photographs of Josephine on the walls. In one, she was standing in a damp English field with her arms around Andrew and Rachel. All three were wearing outdoor coats and smiling broadly beneath hoods and caps—a happy family portrait. On Wallinger's desk there was a further framed picture of Andrew wearing his Eton morning suit, but no photograph of Rachel from her own school days. The *Daily Telegraph* obituary of Wallinger's father, who had served in the SOE, was framed and hung on the far wall of the office beside another large picture of Andrew rowing in an eight at Cambridge. Again, there was no comparable photograph of Rachel, not even of her graduation day at Oxford. Kell knew very little about Wallinger's children, but suspected that Paul would have enjoyed a closer and perhaps less complicated relationship with his son, largely because of the broad streak of unemotional machismo in his character. There was very little else of a personal nature in the room, only an Omega watch in one of the desk drawers and a scuffed signet ring, which Kell could not recall ever having seen on Wallinger's hand. Finding the largest desk drawer locked, he had asked for it to be opened, but found only painkillers and vitamin pills in half-finished packets, as well as a handwritten love letter from Josephine, dated shortly after their wedding, which Kell stopped reading after the first line out of respect for her privacy.

The hard drive gave him access to the SIS telegrams that Wallinger had sent and received in the previous thirteen months, copies of which were also being read by one of Amelia's assistants in London. Wallinger's internal communications within the Station, and to the wider embassy staff, had not been automatically copied to Vauxhall Cross, but Kell found nothing in the intranet messages to the ambassador or first secretary which appeared out of the ordinary. Amelia had gone over the heads of SIS vetting to ensure that Kell was given immediate DV clearance to read anything in Turkey that might help him to piece together Wallinger's state of mind, as well as his movements, in the weeks leading up to his death. He was permitted to read four "eyes-only" telegrams on Iranian centrifuges that had been seen only by H/Istanbul, Amelia, the foreign secretary, and the prime minister. The classified internal report into the failed defection of Shakhouri Mirzai had been copied to Jim

Chater, who had added his own remarks in anticipation of a similar CIA report into the incident. Kell could find nothing in the manner in which the recruitment of Mirzai had been handled, nor in the planning and execution of the operation, that seemed problematic or misjudged. As Tremayne had suggested, the Iranians must have been alerted to the defection, likely because of an error in Mirzai's tradecraft. Only by talking to Chater face-to-face would Kell be able to get a fuller picture.

On his third afternoon in Ankara, Kell took a taxi to Wallinger's suburban villa in Incek, a property owned by the Foreign Office and occupied by successive heads of station for most of the previous two decades. Turning the key in the front door, Kell reflected that he had searched many homes, many hotel rooms, many offices in his career, but had only had cause to snoop on a friend once before—when searching for Amelia the previous year. It was one of the healthier house rules at SIS and MI5: staff were required to sign a document pledging not to investigate the behavior of friends or relatives on Service computers. Those caught doing so—running background checks on a new girlfriend, for example, or looking for personal information about a colleague—would quickly be shown the door.

The villa was starkly furnished in the modern Turkish style with very little of Wallinger's taste apparent in the decor. Kell suspected that his *yali* in Istanbul would be quite different in atmosphere: more cluttered, more scholarly. It appeared as though a cleaner had recently been to the property, because the kitchen surfaces were as polished as a showroom, the toilets blue with detergent, the beds made, the rugs straightened, not a speck of dust on any shelf or table. In the cupboards, Kell found only what he would have expected to find: clothes and shoes and boxes; in the bathroom, toiletries, towels, and a dressing gown. Beside Wallinger's bed there was a biography of Lyndon Johnson; beneath the television downstairs, box sets of all five seasons of *The Wire*. The villa, as soulless as a serviced apartment, revealed very little about the personality of the occupant. Even Wallinger's study had a feeling of impermanence: a single photograph of Josephine on the desk, another of Andrew and Rachel as children hanging on the wall. There were various magazines, Turkish and English, paperback thrillers on a shelf, a reproduction poster of the 1976 Winter Olympics in Innsbruck. Kell read through a few scribbled notes in a foolscap pad and found an out-of-date diary in the desk, but no hidden documents, no letters concealed behind pictures, no false passports or suicide note. Wallinger had kept a tennis racket and a set of golf clubs in a cupboard under the stairs. Feeling somewhat foolish, Kell checked for a hidden compartment in the handle of the racket and for a false bottom in the golf bag. He discovered nothing but some old tees and two hardened sticks of prehistoric chewing gum. It was the same story upstairs. Checking behind drawers, unscrewing lampshades, looking under cupboards—Wallinger had hidden nothing in the house. Kell moved from room to room, listening to the intermittent sounds of birdsong and passing cars in the suburban street outside, and concluded that there was nothing to find. Tremayne had been right—Wallinger's heart had been in Istanbul.

Kell was in a bathroom adjacent to the smaller of two spare bedrooms when he heard the front door opening and then slamming shut. The sound of a set of keys falling onto the surface of a glass table. Not an intruder; it had to be someone who had legitimate access to the villa. A cleaner? The landlord?

Kell left the bathroom and walked out onto the landing. He called out: *"Merhaba?"*

No reply. Kell began to walk downstairs, calling out a second time: "*Merhaba?* Hello?"

He could see down into the hall. A faint shadow moved across the polished floor. Whoever had come in was now in Wallinger's office. As he reached the midpoint of the stairs, Kell heard a reply in a singsong accent he recognized instantly.

"Hello? Somebody is there, please?"

A woman came out of the office. She was wearing blue leggings and a black leather jacket and her hair was grown out and tied at the back. Kell hadn't seen her since the operation to save François Malot, in which she had played such a crucial role. When she saw him, her face broke into a wide smile and she swore excitedly in Italian.

"Minchia!"

"Elsa," Kell said. "I wondered when I'd run into you."

15

They hugged each other in the hall, Elsa wrapping her arms around Kell's neck so tightly that he almost lost his balance. She smelled of a new perfume. The shape of her, the warmth in her greeting, reminded Kell that they had almost become lovers in the summer of the Malot operation, and that only his loyalty to Claire, allied to a sense of professional responsibility, had prevented that.

"It is so amazing to see you!" she said, raising herself up on tiptoes to kiss him. Kell felt like a favorite uncle. It was not a feeling he enjoyed, yet he remembered how easily Elsa had broken through the wall of his natural reticence, how close they had become in the short time they had spent together. "Amelia sent you?" she asked.

Kell was surprised that Elsa did not know that he was going to be in Ankara. "Yes. She didn't tell you?"

"No!"

Of course she didn't. How many other Service freelancers were working on the Wallinger case? How many other members of staff had Amelia dispatched to the four corners of the earth to find out why Paul had died?

"You're picking up his computers?"

Elsa was a Tech-Ops specialist, a freelance computer whiz who could decipher a software program, a circuit board, or a screen of code as others could translate pages of Mandarin, or sight-read a Shostakovich piano concerto. In France, a summer earlier, she had unearthed nuggets of intelligence in laptops and BlackBerries that had been critical to Kell's investigation: without her, the operation would certainly have failed.

"Sure," she said. "Just picked up the keys."

She glanced toward the glass table. Kell saw the keys resting against the base of a vase containing fake plastic flowers.

"I guess that's what you call good timing," he told her. "I was about to start downloading the hard drive."

Elsa's face screwed up in confusion, not merely at the obvious overlap in their responsibilities, but also because she knew that, to Kell, computer technology was a gobbledygook language of which he had only a rudimentary understanding.

"It's a good thing I am here, then," she said. It was only then that she let go of his hands, pivoting back in the direction of the office. "I can tell you which plug goes in the wall and which one goes in the back of the computer."

"Ha, ha."

Kell studied her face. He remembered the natural ebullience, a young woman entirely at ease in her own skin. Running into Elsa so suddenly had lifted his spirits out of the despondency that had plagued him for days. "When did you get here?" he asked.

She glanced outside. She had three earrings in her right lobe, a single stud in the left. "Yesterday?" It was as though she had forgotten.

"You're going into the Station at some point?"

Elsa nodded. "Sure. Tomorrow, I have an appointment. Amelia wants me to go through Mr. Wallinger's e-mails." She pronounced "Wallinger" in two separate parts—"Wall" and then a Scandinavian "Inga"—and Kell smiled. "Is that not correct, Tom Kell? Wallinger?"

"It's perfect. It's your way of saying it."

It was good to hear the music of her voice again, the mischief in it. "Okay. So I take a look at this man's computers, take the phones and maybe the drives back to Rome for analysis."

"The phones?" Kell followed her into the office and watched as Elsa powered up Wallinger's desktop.

"Sure. He had two cell phones in Ankara. One of the SIM cards from his personal phone was recovered from the airplane."

Kell did not disguise his astonishment. *"What?"*

"You did not know this?"

"I'm playing catch-up." Elsa squinted, either because she did not understand the expression, or because she was surprised that Kell appeared so far off his game. "Amelia only brought me in a few days ago."

During the operation in which they had first worked together, Kell had spoken to Elsa about his role in the interrogation of Yassin Gharani. She knew that he had been sidelined by SIS, but made it clear that she believed in Kell's innocence. For this, she occupied a special place in his affections, not least because her trust had been more than Claire had ever been able to afford him.

"You're going to Istanbul?" she asked.

"As soon as I'm done with the Americans. You?"

"I think so, yes. Maybe. There is Wallinger's house there? And, of course, a Station."

Kell nodded. "And where there is a Station, there are computers for Elsa Cassani."

The booting desktop played an accompaniment to Kell's remark, a rising scale of digitized notes issuing from two speakers on Wallinger's desk. Elsa tapped something into the keyboard. It was only then that Kell saw the ring on her finger.

"You got engaged?" he said, and experienced a sense of dismay that surprised him.

"Married!" she replied, and held up the ring as though she expected

Kell to be as pleased as she was. Why was he not glad for her? Had he become so cynical about marriage that the prospect of a woman as lively, as full of promise, as Elsa Cassani walking up the aisle filled him with dread? If so, these were cynical, almost nihilistic thoughts of which he was not proud. There was every chance that she would find great happiness. Plenty did. "Who's the lucky man?"

"He is German," she said. "A musician."

"Rock band?"

"No, classical." She was about to show Kell a photograph from her wallet when his phone began to ring.

It was Tamas Metka.

"Can you speak?" The Hungarian explained that he was calling from a phone box across the street from the bar in Szolnok. Kell gave him the number of the secure telephone in Wallinger's bedroom and walked upstairs. Two minutes later, Metka rang back.

"So," he said, a strain of irony in his voice. "Turns out you may have met this Miss Sandor."

"Really?"

"She used to be one of us."

Why wasn't Kell surprised? Wallinger was most likely having yet another affair with yet another female colleague.

"A spook?"

"A spook," Metka confirmed. "I took a look at the files. She worked several times alongside SIS, Five. She was with us until three years ago."

"'Us' meaning she's Hungarian?"

"Yes."

"Private sector now?"

"No." There was a smothering roar on the line, the sound of a truck or bus driving past the phone booth. Metka waited until it had passed. "Nowadays she owns a restaurant on Lopud."

"Lopud?"

"Croatia. One of the islands off Dubrovnik."

Kell was sitting on Wallinger's bed. He picked up the biography of LBJ, turned it over in his hand, skimmed the quotes on the back.

"Is she married?" he asked.

"Divorced."

"Kids?"

"None."

Metka emitted a gusty laugh. "Why do you want to know about her, anyway? You fallen in love with a beautiful Magyar poet, Tom?"

So Cecilia was beautiful, too. Of course she was.

"Not me. Somebody else." Kell had replied as though Wallinger was still alive, still involved with Sandor. "Why did she leave the NSA?"

A phone rang on the ground floor of the villa. Kell heard Elsa's voice as she answered—*"Pronto!"* Maybe it was her husband calling. Putting the book back on the bedside table, it fell open to a page that had been marked by what looked like a photograph. Kell picked it up.

"I'm not certain why," Metka replied. Kell, now only half listening, turned the photograph around. He was astonished to see that it was a picture of Amelia.

"Say that again," he said, buying time as he came to terms with what he was looking at.

"I said I don't know why she left us. What I saw of her file showed that it was in '09. Voluntary."

In the photograph, which had been taken perhaps ten or fifteen years earlier, in the full flush of Amelia's affair with Wallinger, she was sitting in a crowded restaurant. There was a glass of white wine in front of her, a blurred waiter in a white jacket passing to the left of her chair. She was tanned and wearing a strapless cream dress with a gold necklace that Kell had seen only once before: it was identical to the one Amelia had worn at Wallinger's funeral. She was perhaps forty in the picture and looked extraordinarily beautiful, but also profoundly content, as though she had at last attained a kind of inner peace. Kell could not remember ever having seen Amelia so at ease.

"She still had security clearance," Metka was saying. "There was nothing negative recorded against her."

Kell put the photograph back in the book and tried to think of something to say. "The restaurant?" he asked.

"What about it?"

"You got a name? An address on Lopud?"

He knew that he was going to have to find Cecilia Sandor, to talk to her. She was the key to everything now.

"Oh, sure," said Metka. "I've got the address."

16

The embassy of the United States of America was a low-roofed complex of buildings in the heart of the city, flat as the Pentagon and defended by black metal fencing ten feet high. The contrast with the British embassy, a lavish imperial throwback in an upmarket residential neighborhood overlooking downtown Ankara, could not have been starker. While the Brits employed a single uniformed Turk to run routine security checks on vehicles approaching the building, the Americans deployed a small platoon of buzz-cut, flak-jacketed Marine Corps, most of them hidden behind tungsten-strengthened security gates designed to withstand the impact of a two-ton bomb. You couldn't blame the Yanks for laying things on a bit thick; every wannabe *jihadi* from Grosvenor Square to Manila wanted to take a pop at Uncle Sam. Nevertheless, the atmosphere around the embassy was so tense that, as he pulled up in a rattling Ankaran taxi, Kell felt as though he were back in the Green Zone in Baghdad.

After fifteen minutes of checks, questions, and pat-downs, he was shown into a small office on the first floor with a view onto a garden in which somebody had erected a small wooden climbing frame. There were various certificates on the walls, two watercolors, a photograph of Barack

Obama, and a shelf of paperback books. This, Kell was told, was where Jim Chater would meet him. The choice of venue immediately raised Kell's suspicions. Any discussion between a cadre CIA officer and a colleague from SIS should, as a matter of course, take place inside the CIA's Station. Was Chater planning a blatant snub, or would they move to a secure speech room once he arrived?

The meeting was scheduled for ten o'clock. Twelve minutes had passed before there was a light knock on the door and a blond woman in her late twenties entered wearing a suit and a clip-on smile.

"Mr. Kell?"

Kell stood up and shook the woman's hand. She introduced herself as Kathryn Moses and explained that she was an FP-04 State Department official, which Kell dimly recalled as an entry-level ranking. More likely she was CIA, an errand girl for Chater.

"I'm afraid Jim's running late," she said. "He's asked me to step in. Can I get you a coffee, tea, or something?"

Kell didn't want to lose another five minutes of the hour-long meeting in beverage preparation. He said no.

"Any idea what time he'll be here?"

It was then that he realized Ms. Moses had been sent deliberately to stall him. Settling into a rolling chair behind the desk, she gave Kell a brief, appraising glance, adjusted the sleeves of her jacket, then spoke to him as though he were a Liberal Democrat minister visiting Turkey on a two-day fact-finding tour.

"Jim has asked me to give you an overview of how we see things right now developing locally and in the Syrian-Iranian theater, particularly with reference to the regime in Damascus."

"Okay." It turned out to be a mistake to imply consent, because Moses now cleared her throat and didn't draw breath until the clock on the office wall had moved to within a few second-hand clicks of half past ten. There was background on the State Department decisions to move the Istanbul consulate out of town and to share an airbase with the Turks at Incirlik. Moses had views on the "contradictory" relationship with Prime Minister Tayyip Erdogan and was pleased that the "shaky period" in the run-up to the invasion of Iraq—a veiled reference to Turkey's refusal to cooperate with the Bush administration—was now a thing of the past. In the view of the Obama administration, she said, the Turkish leadership had come to the realization that membership of the EU was no longer a viable goal, nor was it particularly in the country's interests. Indeed, despite accepting seven billion euros in aid from the EU over a period of ten years, Mr. Erdogan wanted "to turn Turkey's face to the south and to the east," establishing himself as "a benign Islamic Calvinist"—not a phrase coined by Kathryn Moses—with Turkey as "a beacon for the rest of Muslim north Africa and the Middle East, a modern, functioning capitalist buffer state existing peaceably between east and west."

"If I could just ask why you think I need to hear this?"

But Moses was deaf to Kell's entreaties. Chater had put the screws on her and she would not risk incurring his wrath by allowing Thomas Kell to slip from her grasp. She had been told to keep him busy, and keep him busy was what she intended to do.

"Just a moment," she said, and actually raised her hand, as though Kell had been rude to interrupt. "If I could just finish, because Jim was keen that you have some sense of where we are on all this, before you guys get together. As you probably know, the prime minister has been highly critical of U.S. policy in the Middle East, hostile toward Israel, particularly in respect of the 2010 flotilla, but happy to allow NATO radar systems on the soil of the republic and certainly supportive, in a tacit sense, of the overthrow of Assad as an Iranian/Russian client state. In other words, Mr. Kell, we see the Turkish leadership at the present time as contradictory. Mr. Erdogan has reined in the military, stabilized the *lira,* overseen a boom in exports and foreign—particularly Gulf Arab—investment, but at the same time attempted to rewrite the constitution to amass greater power. The man in the street sees him as a sultan, and has no problem with the increasingly moralistic and authoritarian tone of the leadership. Those with an instinctive fealty to Ataturk, of course, view him as a demagogue." Kell had to admire her chutzpah: Chater had probably given her ten minutes' notice, but she was speaking with the fluency and confidence of a university lecturer. "So what do we have here?" At last she glanced at some notes on her desk. "An Islamist in sheep's clothing, rolling back the secular state and causing long-term damage to the region as a consequence, or the one guy in this part of the world that the West can actually do business with?"

Kell produced a smile to acknowledge that Moses had played a clever hand. "You tell me," he said. "You seem to have all the answers. I thought I was here to discuss the death of Paul Wallinger."

But Moses did not get a chance to answer Kell's question. As though he had been waiting in the wings of a theater for a cue, Jim Chater walked into the office. Summoning Kell to his feet with outstretched arms, he took him into a tight bear-hug embrace with all the warmth and authenticity of a Judas kiss.

"Tom. So great." The American broke off and stepped back to take a look at Kell, his mouth a wry grin, his gas-blue eyes fired up and doing their best impression of rapport. Chater looked just as Kell remembered him: short, physically fit, and egregiously self-satisfied. He was wearing two days of stubble, stonewashed denim jeans, and a pair of Nike sneakers. "Sorry to keep you waiting. Couldn't be helped. How's Kathryn been treating you? She give you her grand theory on how we're all at the center of the universe? Turkey the most important country east of New York, west of Beijing?"

"Something like that." Ordinarily, Kell might have conjured a chuckle here to make Chater feel top dog; in the old days, he had always worked on the assumption that it was best to flatter the Cousins. Now, though, as a free agent, he found that he wanted to retain some dignity; Kell no longer thought of himself as a company man. When he looked at Jim

Chater, he didn't see a chummy Yank, a trusted ally, a man with good points and bad. He saw a human being who had abandoned the better part of himself in a cell in Kabul. Kell remembered the stench and the violence and the vengeance of that place and felt the shame of his own complicity in it every day.

"So how long you in town for?" Chater asked.

Kell had tickets to leave for Istanbul on the night train, but the CIA didn't need to know that.

"A few days," he replied.

Kathryn was watching them with quiet, underling deference. Kell hoped that she would soon leave.

"Yeah? And you're havin' a good time?"

"I wouldn't exactly put it that way."

Even a man as impregnable to self-doubt as Jim Chater recognized that he had been gauche. It was time to pay his respects to Kell's friend and colleague.

"Of course. Of course not. Look, Tom. We were all of us here shocked by the news about Paul. Such a tragedy. Such a senseless waste. I sent a note on behalf of my staff to London. I don't know if you saw that?"

Kell said that he hadn't, a response that opened a convenient door for Chater.

"That's right, so where are you now? I heard you were out. I heard you were in. What's your status? How can we help you?"

Kathryn chose this moment to ease out of the room. ("I'm going to leave you gentlemen to it.") Kell shook her hand, said how nice it had been to meet her, and caught a beat of appreciation in the interaction between Moses and Chater. Just in the timing of his glance as she opened the door to leave; the body language of a job well done.

"Clever," he said, nodding after her. "Interesting."

"You bet," Chater replied, but Kathryn's absence had an immediate effect on Chater's mood. He looked suddenly as Kell remembered him from Kabul: cynical, calculating, indifferent. "So," he said, rubbing the palm of his hand across the razored grays of his scalp, "you never answered my question."

"I'm back. Amelia wants answers. She sent me."

"Right." There was both a measure of doubt and a hefty dose of condescension in the tone of Chater's response. "So what rank are we talking? You're coming in as H/Ankara? Nothing like new blood to excite us, Tom."

Kell knew the game that was being played. Did Thomas Kell have the clearance, the status, to deserve a full briefing on HITCHCOCK from James N. Chater III? Or was he just a glorified coroner, tying up the loose ends of Paul Wallinger's life?

"We're talking STRAP 3 clearance," Kell replied pointedly. "Same as it always was. Same as it will always be. Doug Tremayne isn't going to be running our Station, if that's the question you're trying to ask."

"I know what question I'm trying to ask." Chater's blue eyes were fixed on Kell's even as he twisted his rolling chair from side to side. "So you're still her friendly face? You trust 'C' after everything she's put you through?"

Kell recognized the interrogator's trick. "We both want answers," he replied, ducking under the provocation. "The past is a foreign country."

A sound came out of Chater's nose like a man having difficulty identifying the source of an unusual smell. He began to smile.

"So you're no longer Witness X? I heard Gharani was paid off by her majesty's government. Tom Kell isn't going to have his day in court?"

"Who are you asking for, Jim? Yourself or for the agency?"

Chater's arms went up suddenly, like an act of mock surrender, before clasping his hands behind his head. It looked as though he was about to tip back in the chair. He said nothing, but the smile held.

"On Paul's accident," Kell said. It was already ten forty-five. "On the crash. We think engine failure at this point. There was no black box, obviously. We're just trying to piece together Paul's final movements, tie up any loose ends."

"You got loose ends, Tom?"

It might have been the question of a concerned ally, but it was more likely an attempt to unsettle Kell by implying that SIS was disorganized. "We're fine," he replied.

"Paul was on vacation at the time?"

"Yup."

"On Chios?"

"That's right."

"He had a place there?"

"Not that I'm aware of."

Chater glanced out of the window. His eyes seemed to focus momentarily on the climbing frame.

"He have a girl out there?"

Kell sensed that Chater already knew the answer to his own question. "Again, not that I'm aware of."

"So what the fuck was he doing?"

"That's the loose end."

Kell thought that he could hear children playing outside, but when he looked into the garden, there were none. Chater was asking too many questions.

"I heard you got divorced."

"Where did you read that? *Foreign Affairs*?" Kell was annoyed, but certainly not surprised, by the intrusion. It was trademark Chater to go creeping around in a colleague's private life—asking questions, hearing things on grapevines—and then to bring up his findings in a meeting.

"Don't recall," Chater said, clearly lying. "Maybe *The National Enquirer*?" Suddenly he sat bolt upright in his chair and leaned forward at the desk, another shit-eating grin spreading out across his face. "So, we gotta get you a girl while you're in town."

"You pimping on the side, Jim?" Chater seemed stumped for a witty comeback. "Thanks, but I'll be fine."

It looked as though Chater had taken offense, or had at least lost interest in the subject. He looked down at the surface of the desk.

"So, engine trouble, huh?"

Another question about Chios. Kell was certain now that the Cousins had information of their own about Wallinger's accident. He took a risk, to gauge what reaction the name would generate. "I've got people talking to the engineer who worked on Paul's plane before takeoff," he said. "Iannis Christidis."

It was as though Chater had been fed a piece of bad news through an earpiece. He twitched, touching the side of his neck. The recovery was just as rapid—all of this within much less than a second—but the relaxed, carefree way in which he said: "Oh, yeah?" betrayed a profound disquiet.

"Yeah." Kell employed a straightforward bluff. "There was a small problem with the Cessna on the way in from Ankara. Paul had asked Christidis to check it out."

"Is that right?" Chater glanced at his watch. "Hey, we need to get this thing done. I got an eleven o'clock."

"I've been saying that since ten."

"Touché," Chater replied.

"Can we at least talk about Dogubayazit?"

Chater looked at Kell as though he had tried to offer him a bribe. "In *here*?"

"Where, then?" Kell took Chater's gaze back out of the window. "I'm not the one who decided to hold this meeting next to a playground."

"Kathryn's fault," he replied, stacking the blame on a colleague as easily as he had secured the wrists of Yassin Gharani. "She didn't know who you were. She didn't know why you were here." Chater's excuse bounced around the room in search of a good home. He held Kell's gaze. "Well, look, we don't have an option to move now," he said. "We'll have to do this another time."

"When?" Kell looked pointedly at his watch. "This afternoon? Tomorrow morning?"

He knew that within five minutes of the meeting ending, Chater would be upstairs in the CIA Station working a trace on Iannis Christidis.

"Not going to work," the American replied. "I'm flying to D.C. at midday tomorrow, full up until then."

"When do you get back?"

Chater seemed to find the answer at the top of the security wall surrounding the playground. He was craning his neck as he said: "About a week."

The Cousins knew something. Chater's obstinacy spoke volumes about the CIA's position on Wallinger.

"I'm going to trust that these walls don't have ears," he said. Outside the room, a man walked past in the corridor saying: "Sure, yeah, six." Chater was no longer looking out of the window. "We are expecting your report into HITCHCOCK. Any idea of a time frame on that?"

"Imminent."

"What does that mean? Tomorrow? The next day? Or does it have to fly with you to D.C. and back?"

That at least earned Kell a smile. "About a week, Tom, yeah. We still have some"—Chater enjoyed reviving the phrase—"loose ends."

They had reached the end of the road. Three minutes were left on the clock, but Jim Chater seemed to be glancing at the second hand every twenty seconds.

"Any chance I can speak to Tony Landau?" Kell asked.

Landau was the CIA officer who had accompanied Wallinger to the Iranian-Armenian border.

"Sure," Chater replied. "If you can get to Houston." Kell was about to respond when Chater sucked up the remaining time. "Look. You ask me, we don't even know for sure if HITCHCOCK was in the vehicle. Whole thing could have been a bluff. Did your agent even exist?"

It was an astonishing accusation, not least because it implied that SIS had been fooled into running an Iranian agent provocateur. Why was Chater going down this route?

"Nobody can confirm the sighting, Tom. Nobody knows who was in the car."

"Come off it," Kell replied. "You guys shot a fucking *video*."

"Which showed nothing. Passenger had a beard like a mulberry bush. No way of telling it was Shakhouri Mirzai."

"What are you trying to tell me? That your sources in Iran have seen Mirzai walking the streets? That Iranian intelligence set the whole thing up, sacrificing two employees in the process?"

"Who's to say they were employees?" Chater shot Kell a look that he could only interpret as contempt for Wallinger's botched role in the operation. "Could have been anybody. Could have been two patsies on a life sentence, making an extra buck for their families." Chater stood up from the desk, rubbing what looked like a bite on his left arm. "Look, it'll all be in my report." It was clear that the discussion was over. "I'll see you in a week, Tom. You take it easy."

Kell had been obliged to hand in his cell phone when he entered the embassy. It was given back to him by a shaven-headed Marine, but was now operationally useless: Chater's team, though unlikely to do so, had nevertheless been given more than an hour in which to strip the phone and fit it with state-of-the-art surveillance software. So Kell walked to a café three blocks from the embassy, wrote down the numbers for Marianna and Adam, took the SIM out, then binned the phone and called Marianna from a phone box across the street, using a card purchased at a nearby *bakkal*.

"Marianna, it's Chris Hardwick calling."

"Chris!"

Her voice was sprightly and excitable. Kell guessed that she was alone in the office; if Delfas had been looking over her shoulder, she would have sounded more circumspect. They exchanged pleasantries for a few minutes—Kell catching up on all of Marianna's family news—before eventually broaching the subject of the Sandor villa.

"Do you remember mentioning that you saw Paul Wallinger talking to someone at one of the restaurants near your office?"

If Marianna was surprised by the line of questioning, the speed and enthusiasm of her answer did not suggest it.

"Of course, yes. The man with a beard."

"That's right. What restaurant were they in? The one below your office?"

Marianna had already told him that this was not the case, but Kell needed a starting point from which to discover the true location.

"No, no," she said, predictably enough. "I think it was Marikas. In fact, I'm sure it was Marikas."

"How do you spell that?" In the cramped, noisy phone booth, Kell scrawled down the name. After that it was just a question of winding things down. "I've got a feeling I went there for a coffee one morning."

"Yes," said Marianna. "You probably did."

Kell cleared his throat. He asked three more questions about Marianna's family, correctly remembering the names of her mother and father, then intimated that he was being called into a meeting. "Hopefully my report will be ready by the end of the week," he said.

"You must have worked so hard, Chris." Marianna sounded slightly crestfallen that the conversation—indeed, the relationship—was drawing to an inevitable end. "I so wish we could meet again," she said.

Kell was aware of the cruel absurdity of his lies. In the old days, he had sometimes drawn satisfaction from simple manipulations of this kind; but no longer. An easy facility for deceit, an ability to make a lonely woman feel cherished was hardly a talent of which a man of forty-four could be proud.

"Me too," he said, and hated himself.

"So when will you come back to see me?" Marianna asked.

Kell could picture her in the solitude of the office, her face slightly flushed, seagulls clacking outside. *Recruiting an agent is an act of seduction.*

"I don't suppose for a long time," he replied, trying not to sound cold and distant. "Unless I get out to Greece for a holiday."

"Well, it would be wonderful to see you again," she said. "Please let's stay in touch."

"Yes. Let's."

Kell hung up, extracted the card, and lit a much-needed cigarette. He began walking in the direction of his hotel. At the edge of a well-tended municipal park he spotted another public phone box, queued for two minutes behind a tracksuited Syrian, then dialed the number in Athens.

Adam Haydock was at his desk.

"I've got some jobs for you."

"Go ahead, sir."

Across the street, two bored cops were checking driver's licenses at random from passing cars and mopeds. Turkey: still a light-touch police state.

"It'll mean going to Chios with a Tech-Ops team. It'll mean getting clearance from London."

"From Amelia?" Adam asked.

"From 'C,'" Kell replied.

17

Kell woke before dawn on the Istanbul sleeper with a coronary headache and a raging thirst directly linked to the bottle of Macallan he had polished off the night before with two young Turkish businessmen who were en route to Bulgaria for a three-day conference on "white goods." Two ibuprofen and half a liter of water later, Kell was gazing out of the scratched window of his four-man sleeper compartment drinking a cup of sweetened black Nescafé and listening to the snores of the mustachioed widower occupying the bunk below his own.

The train shunted into Haydarpasa station just after six o'clock. Kell zipped up his bag, bade farewell to his traveling companions, and took a ferry across the Bosporus to Karakoy. Ordinarily he might have felt the traditional romantic excitement of the Western traveler arriving by sea in one of the great cities of the world, but he was in a frustrated mood, hungover and tired, and Istanbul felt like just another staging post on his quest to solve the riddle of Paul Wallinger's death. He might just as well have been arriving in Brussels or Freetown or Prague. There would be endless meetings at the consulate. There would be long telephone calls to London. He would have to spend many hours searching Wallinger's *yali* in Yenikoy. An indoor life. At no point—if past experience was anything to go by—would he have the chance to relax and to enjoy the city, to visit the Topkapi, for example, or to take a boat trip to the Black Sea. He remembered visiting Istanbul as a twenty-year-old university student, Claire at his side on their first summer together as boyfriend and girlfriend. They had stayed for five days in a cheap backpacker's hostel in Sultanahmet, surviving on *raki* and chickpea stews. A few months later, on the eve of his twenty-first birthday, Kell had received the tap on the shoulder from SIS. It was like remembering a bygone era. His twenty-year-old self was now a stranger to him; Claire had walked the streets of Istanbul with a different man.

He texted Claire then walked through sporadic crowds toward the Galata Bridge. It was a warm, blustery morning. Ferries were bumping the quay, eight lanes of traffic stalled in both directions in the rush-hour crush of Kennedy Avenue. Men were selling steamed mussels and blackened husks of corn from makeshift barbecues erected beside the newspaper kiosks and ticket booths on the promenade. Kell bought a copy of the *International Herald Tribune* and walked along the lower, pedestrianized section of Galata Bridge, aiming for a restaurant that he knew fifty meters along the walkway. Above him, clumps of men were fishing from the eastern side of the bridge; thin plastic lines dropped down in front of the restaurant, near-invisible against the bright clouds and silver waters of the Bosporus. A young, unshaven waiter showed Kell to a table adjacent to a group of German tourists who were drinking glasses of tea and staring at a fold-up map of Turkey. As he sat down, Kell immediately pointed at a photograph of some fried eggs on a five-language, laminated menu. The waiter smiled, said: "Chips?" and Kell nodded, eager to see off his hangover.

It was only then, settling into his chair and looking out across the water at the boats on the swollen sea, at the far Asian shore, that the city at last began to open up for him, the magic and the romance of Constantinople. Kell was himself again. To the southeast, he could see birds twisting on warm swells above the minarets of Hagia Sophia; to the north, the huddled wharfs and buildings of Galata, splashed by sun. He drank a double espresso, smoked a Winston Light, and read the headline stories on the *Tribune* as a sudden wind cracked the pages of his newspaper. A tourist poster of Cappadocia was tacked to the wall of the restaurant. Kell mopped up the yolks of his fried eggs with hunks of soft white bread, ordered a second cup of coffee, then paid his bill.

Half an hour later he was walking into the dimly lit lobby of the Grand Hotel de Londres, an old-world Istanbul institution a stone's throw from the British consulate. The small, red-carpeted lobby was empty save for a cleaning lady dusting a framed oil painting on the stairs. Above her, an ancient glass chandelier rattled in the draft of the street door as it closed behind Kell. A tap on the reception desk bell summoned a voluminous man from an office hidden behind a small brown door. Kell signed the register in his own name, handed over his battered passport, and took his bags upstairs in a cramped lift to a bedroom with views over Beyoglu and, in the distance, a slim, shimmering strip of the Golden Horn.

Around eleven o'clock, having showered and shaved and swallowed two more painkillers, he wandered downstairs. He wasn't due at the consulate until after lunch and wanted to finish *My Name Is Red* in the hotel bar. He took the stairs, passing the same cleaning lady, who had now made her way to the second floor, where she was reverently wiping the glass on a framed picture of Ataturk.

Kell heard their conversation long before he saw their faces. A singsong English, decorated by laughter, and the elegant, well-spoken tones of his old friend and colleague, suddenly not in London anymore, but staying in the very same hotel.

Amelia Levene and Elsa Cassani were seated opposite each other on an ornate sofa in the resident's lounge looking, for all the world, like a mother and daughter who had just returned from a sightseeing trip to Sultanahmet. Kell instantly sensed the rapport between them; it had been evident in the timbre of Amelia's voice, a particular softness that she employed only with trusted friends and confidantes. Elsa was plainly in awe of her, yet her manner was not nervous or overly respectful; she seemed relaxed, even slightly mischievous in Amelia's company. There were two glasses of tea in front of them, on small white saucers, and a packet of Turkish chocolate biscuits, doubtless bought at a nearby shop.

"We must stop meeting like this," Kell said as he walked toward them. Amelia looked up and smiled at the joke. Elsa turned to see who had spoken and seemed to suppress a desire to yell *"Minchia!"* again at the sight of him.

"I was wondering when you'd get here," Amelia said, glancing pointedly at her watch. "Elsa told me you were on the sleeper?"

"And I thought you were in London," he replied, and could not work out if he was pleased to see her or irritated that Amelia had yet again kept him out of the loop. They kissed one another and a waiter appeared, asking Kell if he would like a drink. He ordered a tea and sat beside Elsa, wondering how long it would take for somebody to tell him what the hell was going on.

18

An hour later, Kell had his answer. At Amelia's suggestion they left Elsa to work at the hotel and went for a walk through the streets of the city, arm in arm at certain points, at others split by surges of oncoming pedestrians on Istiklal Caddesi. Amelia was wearing a floral-print headscarf and a tweed jacket with patches on the elbows; Kell thought that she looked like a lady-in-waiting attending to the queen at Sandringham, but wasn't in the mood to tease her. More casually dressed in jeans and a sweater, he smoked as he walked, pressing Amelia for answers.

"You didn't tell me about the SIM they recovered from the wreckage."

"There's a lot I haven't been able to tell you, Tom."

Amelia's reaction was typically inscrutable. An elegantly dressed Turk with a gleaming bald patch and polished brown brogues was sitting on a plastic stool in front of a shop window in which balls of wool of different colors were displayed in small wooden boxes. He was playing a lute and singing a mournful song. Beside him, a boy in a Besiktas football shirt was eating a pretzel.

"How was Ankara?" Amelia asked, watching them.

Kell could only assume that she had good reason to be so evasive. On

Ankara, he hardly knew where to begin: Chater's conduct at the embassy had been both a calculated snub to Kell's uncertain status and an apparent attempt to avoid helping SIS with their enquiries into Wallinger's death. He didn't want to start by telling Amelia about that. As far as she was concerned, anything Kell said about Chater would have to be filtered through his own animus against the man who had poleaxed his career. He *wanted* Chater to be hiding something; Amelia knew that as well as he did.

So he talked about the long hours at SIS Station and was struck by how often Amelia interrupted him to ask supplementary questions, to cross-check a fact, to be certain that Kell had accurately recalled the details of the many files and telegrams he had read in Wallinger's office. The conversation took them north toward Taksim Square, where they doubled back along Istiklal, stopping briefly to browse in an English-language bookshop where Amelia bought *Team of Rivals,* "because everyone I know is reading it." When, finally, she had stopped asking questions about HITCHCOCK, Kell returned to the SIM.

"Who went through the wreckage? Who found the phone?"

"The Turkish authorities. I had somebody there acting as a liaison for the family. He managed to get hold of the phone and bring it back to London."

"And?"

They stopped walking. Amelia adjusted her scarf and turned one hundred and eighty degrees, looking north along the broad street. They were no more than twenty feet from the entrance to the Russian consulate. Ordinarily Kell would have pointed this out, as an amusing curiosity, but did not want to interrupt Amelia's train of thought.

"There are some numbers that we're still trying to trace."

"What does that mean?"

"It means that it's too early to say."

Of course. Even with a colleague as trusted as Thomas Kell, Amelia would not disclose anything more than was absolutely required by the demands of the conversation. Kell concealed his anger at being treated like a second-rate gumshoe. "Too early to say" meant that Elsa—or one of her ilk—had dragged something off the SIM which would be useful in the context of a secondary piece of intelligence; without that, there was no point in getting anybody's hopes up. Amelia would tell him only what he needed to know. As he looked up at the first-floor windows of the consulate, wondering if somebody inside was having Moscow kittens at the sight of "C" loitering in the road, Kell felt something of the same frustration he had experienced in his meeting with Chater. To be obstructed in his work was one thing; to be finessed, even patronized by his friend, quite another.

"You might find that one of the numbers was to a former Hungarian intelligence officer named Cecilia Sandor."

It was a cruel strike, but something in Kell had wanted to wound Amelia.

"Who?"

He put his arm across Amelia's back and tried to steer her away down the street. She seemed to flinch at the contact, knowing that Kell was about to break bad news.

"Paul was on the island with her."

"On Chios?"

"Yes."

He allowed Amelia to process what he had told her. It took only a couple of seconds, but in that time Amelia seemed to separate herself from the thick crowds on Istiklal, from the laughter of passing couples, the chatter and music of the street.

"They were seeing each other?"

"Looks that way. She left flowers and a handwritten note at the funeral. She rented a villa on the island. They stayed there for about a week."

Amelia began to walk more briskly, as if to surge away from what Kell was telling her. "How do you know Sandor was NSA?"

"You ever come across Tamas Metka?" Amelia shook her head. "Old contact of mine from Budapest. Met him when he was in London about ten years ago. I had him run the name. Sandor is midthirties. Quit Hungarian intelligence in 2009 to run a restaurant in Croatia. Before that, according to Metka she did plenty of operational stuff with us, with the grass skirts, too." "Grass skirts" was an old in-house euphemism for MI5. "It might be worth cross-checking her name with Paul's operations. That's probably how they met."

"Probably," Amelia muttered.

He wanted to tell her about the photograph, to lift her spirits, to say that Paul had kept a picture of her beside his bed until the day he died. But what would be the point? Soon enough Amelia would find a way of suppressing her feelings. He knew how effectively, even cynically, she could disentangle her head from her heart. It was how she had lived for thirty years with the knowledge that she had given up her only child for adoption at birth: by compartmentalizing her feelings, by rationalizing the pain. Yet the thought occurred to him: if Wallinger had kept a ten-year-old photograph of Amelia in a book beside his bed, what had Amelia retained as her own private keepsake?

"I understand that you've asked Adam Haydock to trace the engineer who worked on Paul's plane?"

"That's right."

"And to look at some CCTV on Chios? Is that correct?"

Kell explained that Wallinger had been observed talking to a bearded man in a restaurant on the harbor. He wanted to float a theory that the individual in question had been Jim Chater, but didn't want to give Amelia the opportunity to tell him that he was being absurd.

"Who saw him?"

"The woman who rented the villa to Sandor. Marianna Dimitriadis."

"Was he American?"

"No idea," Kell replied. "She didn't get an accent."

They had arrived at the southern end of Istiklal. A small red tram was moving slowly along the boulevard, two young boys hanging off the back running board. Kell dropped the cigarette he had been smoking and suddenly felt hot. He took off his sweater.

"At first it looked as though Paul had covered his tracks because he didn't want Josephine to know that he was having an affair." Amelia produced a quiet, knowing snort. "But did he have other reasons to be there? Operational reasons?"

"I've told you that. He had no business . . ."

"My question was rhetorical. What if he was meeting a contact off the books?" Kell pointed out that Wallinger had shelved his passport, his credit cards, and his cell phones after landing on Chios. That was an awful lot of cover for a dirty weekend.

"Perhaps he didn't want *me* to know he was there."

Kell admired Amelia's candor, not least because she had saved him from making an identical observation.

"Oh, come off it," he replied. "How long is it since you two were an item?"

"We were never 'an item,' Tom."

That shut him up. Kell watched a stray cat scampering under the wheels of a parked van, tracking its progress downhill along a side street cloaked in scaffolding. There was a strong smell of frying fish; he imagined that the cat was trying to locate the source of it.

"Hungry?" Amelia asked. She, too, had reacted to the warmer weather, removing her jacket and looping it over her arm. There was a large, brightly lit restaurant across the street, manned by white-aproned chefs tending to metal containers of food displayed in high windows. The place looked cheap and popular; most of the tables were already occupied.

"How about that place?" Kell suggested, as a jackhammer drill started up in the distance.

"Perfect," said Amelia, and they went inside.

19

Amelia's choice of seat was telling. Rather than pick a vacant table in the window, with a view out onto Istiklal, she jammed herself into a noisy corner of the restaurant alongside a geriatric Turk sporting an antediluvian hearing aid. Even if he spoke or understood English, it was unlikely that the man would be able to hear what Kell and Amelia were saying; less likely still that he would then go running to MIT with a verbatim account of their conversation.

Kell ordered lamb shanks and mashed potatoes; Amelia a lamb stew with a side order of pureed eggplant that had the look and texture of baby food. Within a couple of mouthfuls they had both pronounced the food to be "disgusting," but ate as they talked, sipping from glasses of sparkling water.

"You haven't talked about your meeting with Jim Chater," she said.

"I thought I'd wait for a full moon. Why didn't you tell me he was out here?" Amelia produced another trademark look of inscrutability, adjusting the sleeves of her blouse. Kell felt a rising irritation once again. "I'm assuming there's method in all this madness," he said.

"Come again?" Her tone of voice suggested that Kell was being unnecessarily provocative.

"Why didn't you mention it? Why haven't you asked me about him until now?"

"You sent a report last night, didn't you?"

"Which you've seen?"

Kell was surprised to discover that Amelia had not read his account of the meeting with Moses and Chater, which he had telegrammed to London shortly after he had finished talking to Adam Haydock in Athens.

"I wanted to hear it from the horse's mouth," she said, as though she were paying Kell a compliment.

"Well here's the horse," he replied, biting off a mouthful of bread.

To avoid creating an impression of bias, Kell reproduced the characteristics of the meeting as blandly and as factually as he could: the Moses monologue; Chater's obvious time-wasting; the American's brusque reaction to Kell's questions about HITCHCOCK. When it came to Iannis Christidis, Kell told Amelia only that he felt Chater was already familiar with the name.

"Iannis Christidis," she repeated. "The one you've asked Adam to track down?" Her interest was piqued. "You really think Jim recognized the name?"

Kell had to proceed carefully. To suggest as much to Amelia, with the clear inference that the CIA had been involved in Wallinger's crash, would be a grave accusation.

"Who knows?" he said, fudging it. "I thought I saw something. I might have been projecting."

"Projecting what?"

Kell shot her a look. It had been many months since they had last spoken about what had happened in Kabul.

"Look. You know there are decisions I made which I regret . . ."

"Okay, okay," Amelia said quickly, as though Kell had embarrassed her. Angered as much by this as by his own persistent need to explain his actions, he lapsed into silence. "Oh, for Christ's sake, Tom. Don't be like that. I just don't want us to get sidetracked. I want to know about Chater's state of mind."

"Why?" Kell replied quickly.

"Because I have doubts about him too."

It was an extraordinarily loaded remark, and one that Kell seized on.

"What do you mean?"

Amelia pushed her plate to one side; it was immediately scooped up by a passing waiter. She dabbed her mouth with a paper napkin and glanced toward the window.

"You haven't asked me the obvious question," she said, following the progress of a child who was walking past the restaurant.

"Obvious question? About what? Your doubts? Where are we on this?"

Her head snapped back toward him. "What am I doing here?" There was a rare surge of melodrama in her tone of voice, perhaps even a measure of panic. Kell recalled that he had asked that exact question in the resident's lounge of the Hotel de Londres. Amelia, as was typical of her present mood, had declined to answer.

"Okay, then. Why are you in Istanbul? Something breaking in Syria?"

She turned back toward the window. They had both been keeping an intermittent watch on any new customers who came into the restaurant: looking for repeating faces; checking the obvious observation points across the street. But this wasn't tradecraft. Something was plainly bothering Amelia. She seemed to be weighing up the good sense of what she was about to say.

"We lost another Joe."

"What?"

"In Tehran. On Monday. Assassinated."

Kell had seen the news reports. He had assumed, like everybody else, that the Mossad had carried out the assassination.

"The guy in the car. The scientist? He was an *asset*?"

"One of Paul's, yes. Cryptonym EINSTEIN."

"Jesus." To recruit a scientist on the inside of the Iranian centrifuge program was a major coup both for Wallinger and for SIS; to lose him to a black op was a body blow. "Who took him out?"

Amelia shrugged with her eyes. Either she knew, and couldn't say, or, more likely, had no idea who had carried out the attack and wasn't prepared to trade in theories.

"The point is that we lost HITCHCOCK three weeks ago, Paul in a plane crash, EINSTEIN on Monday. That's more assets than we've dropped in AF/PAK in seven years." Kell, still eating, bit down on a brittle chip of lamb shank and had to pick a tiny piece of bone out of his mouth. Amelia, with the tact of a croupier, looked away. "When you went through Paul's telegrams, through the files," she said, "did anything jump out?"

"Meaning?"

"Meaning did anything strike you as odd? Anything at all about the things he was saying and doing?"

"Everything I looked at seemed above board," he replied. "Commonplace, even. Doug Tremayne was looking at the agent handling, farming out Paul's assets to new officers. There was no point in giving that to me because I'm not going to be around long enough to play an operational role."

The old man at the next-door table was eating fruit salad and made a slurping sound, as though disappointed by Kell's answer. Amelia appeared to be about to speak when she stopped herself.

"Jesus, spit it out," he said.

"What if I was to offer you H/Ankara?"

The job was everything he had hoped for—his reputation cleared; a sense of purpose and direction restored to his life. Yet Kell did not experience the elation he might have expected. He was arrogant enough to believe that he deserved such a position, but Amelia's offer seemed to contain a warning. Why would "C" take the considerable risk of appointing Kell H/Ankara if she did not expect to extract a quid pro quo?

"That's enormously flattering," he said, and put a cautious hand on Amelia's arm. He was thanking her, but not yet saying yes, not yet saying no.

"Do you think you'd be interested?" Amelia's head was tipped forward, as though she were looking at him over half-moon spectacles. "Could you see yourself based out here? Three years? Four?"

"I don't see why not."

"Good," she replied. Then, as if there was no more to be said on the subject, she returned to what appeared to be troubling her.

"Did you come across a reference to Ebru Eldem?"

The old Turkish man rose from his seat, leaving behind the half-eaten bowl of fruit salad. Kell followed him with his eyes, but his mind was back in Wallinger's office, sifting through files and telegrams, trying to summon the name from among a hundred others.

"Journalist?" he asked, more in hope than expectation, but Amelia nodded, encouraging him to expand. "Arrested a few months ago," he said, dredging up the Eldem story. "Usual Turkish setup. Hack writes something critical of Erdogan, gets banged up as a terrorist for her troubles."

"That's the one."

"What about her?"

"She was an American asset."

"Okay." It was a lunch of surprises. "Recruited by your old friend, Jim Chater. Chater complained to Paul when she was arrested."

"Paul told you this?"

"Last time he was in London, yes. Said she was the third journalist on the Cousin's books to have been jailed in the region."

"Were they all Turks?"

"Yes."

"Eldem is a political reporter?"

If Amelia was impressed that Kell had remembered such a seemingly insignificant biographical detail, she did not show it. "Yes. For *Cumhuriyet*."

"But that's par for the course round here," he said. "There are eight hundred journalists in prison in Turkey. That's more than there are in *China*."

"Is that right?" Amelia absorbed the statistic. After a moment's pause, she added: "Well, we've also lost academics. We've also lost students. We have a NOC in Ankara who reported direct to Paul; he's lost a senior source in the EU. Fired about six months after we took him on."

Like the vague physical discomfort that presages an illness, Kell had a sense that Amelia was about to tell him something profoundly troubling. Would it be the quid pro quo, or would it be something about Paul? Uncomfortable at the prospect of continuing their conversation in their current position—a mother and child were about to settle into the vacated seat beside them—Amelia suddenly stood up, put on her jacket, and led Kell out of the restaurant. They were some distance away, walking down a deserted cobbled street east of the Galata Tower, when she finally returned to the subject.

"What I'm about to tell you, I want to tell you as a friend." She looked at Kell and, with no more than a glance, asked for his absolute discretion.

"Of course." He put his hand on her back. This time Amelia did not flinch. "I think Simon Haynes dropped the ball in the last weeks of his tenure."

"Go on."

"I think certain things escaped his attention. During the transition, I was still so affected by what had happened in France"—she was referring to the kidnap and rescue of her son—"that I didn't pay close enough attention to something that now seems very obvious." Amelia turned down a narrow, deserted street that had been soaked by a burst pipe; water was gurgling out of a ruined building, pouring down one side of the road. "Over a four-year period, a number of joint operations with the Cousins have been undermined. HITCHCOCK and EINSTEIN the worst, no question, but others going back three years. In London, in the U.S., in Turkey, Syria, Lebanon, Israel."

"What do you mean 'undermined'?"

"I mean that the numbers are out. I mean that too many things have gone wrong. I've looked at the history, at the statistics, and we're losing too many assets, too much strategic advantage, too much product."

"You think there's a leak?"

It was the question every spy hoped he would never have to ask. A mole was the secret state's profoundest fear, the paranoid nightmare of its guarded and cautious inhabitants. Philby. Blake. Ames. Hanssen. The names kept coming, generation after generation, traitor breeding traitor, an entire bureaucratic class feeding on itself, on paranoia and double-think. Amelia, acknowledging Kell's question with a glance, asked for—of all things—a cigarette, which he lit for her as they walked.

"I don't know its nature," she said. "But I don't think it's technical."

Was that better or worse? Human betrayal was morally more repugnant but, typically, less damaging than a compromised communications link. If, say, the Iranians or the Israelis, the Russians or the Chinese, had a line into SIS's telegram system, the Service was finished, because it was the end of secrets. If, on the other hand, there was a mole, he or she was identifiable; by definition, their days were numbered.

"I've had to be bloody careful." Amelia held the cigarette in the tips of her fingers and inhaled on it like a sixth-form prefect. "I've had everything checked and double-checked. Every mainframe, telegram, e-mail, you name it. Passwords changed, keypads, Augean stables job."

"I didn't know," Kell said, and shrugged out a momentary cramp in his right shoulder. "And still the leaks keep coming?"

"And still the leaks keep coming." Amelia tossed the cigarette into an oil-streaked puddle of water. She had taken no more than two puffs. "There are names," she said. "The same people copied on the same intelligence, attending the same meetings, seeing the same CX."

"Us or them?"

"Both," she said.

"How many?"

"Too many. Dozens on our side of the Atlantic, dozens on theirs. I could be investigating this thing until my ninetieth birthday. I could make Angleton look level-headed." They rounded another corner. Two men were playing backgammon at a small table in front of a shoe shop. One of them looked up and smiled at Amelia, apparently appreciating the presence of an elegant, well-dressed woman in his gray neighborhood. Ever the politician, she smiled back. "Too many suspects," she said, in a flat voice. "I have little idea who sees what we see once it crosses the pond. The mole could be State Department, could be Langley. Christ, it could be the White House." Kell listened to the fading rattle of the backgammon dice. "But," Amelia said.

"But," Kell repeated. A boat moaned on the Bosporus.

"There are specific people I want to look at. Four, to be precise. One is Douglas Tremayne."

Kell felt an instinctive sense that Amelia had the wrong man: Tremayne didn't fit the profile of a traitor, but he knew that such thoughts were the spycatcher's Achilles' heel. Everyone was a suspect. Everyone has his reasons. *"Doug?"* he said.

"I'm afraid so." Amelia again removed her jacket and looped it over her arm. "The other, on our side, is Mary Begg."

"Never heard of her."

"Works on the Middle East Directorate at the Cross. Came to us from Five just after you left. She's seen most things. Been involved. It could be her."

"And the others are Yanks?" Kell asked, wondering with an accumulating envy if Begg had been his like-for-like replacement.

Amelia nodded. "I've got a team in Texas. In Houston. Taking a very close look at Tony Landau. His fingerprints were all over HITCHCOCK, all over EINSTEIN. He had access to most of the files relating to the corrupted assets."

"*Most* of the files," said Kell pointedly.

Amelia appeared to appreciate the fact that Kell had noticed the caveat. “He didn’t know about Eldem. The circulation on her was very low.”

Kell knew what Amelia was going to tell him. Chater had known about Eldem, had possibly betrayed her to the Turks. Kell was going to be asked to soak Chater’s laptops and phones, to follow him into bathrooms, to sleep under his bed. He was going to be presented with an opportunity to avenge Kabul.

“That’s why you’re here,” she said, right on cue. “The Cousins have a young officer here. Ryan Kleckner.”

“Kleckner,” Kell replied, caught off guard. He had never heard the name.

“He’s had the same access. Attended the same meetings. We’ll be looking at Begg; I have someone on Tremayne. I want you to take on Kleckner. I’ll give you everything you need to make an assessment of his behavior, to include or exclude him as a suspect.”

Kell nodded.

“A month before he flew to Chios, a week before Dogubayazit, Paul came to London. I confided in him as I am confiding in you.”

“Paul knew about the mole?” Kell asked.

“Yes.”

“And the Americans? Did you raise your concerns with them?”

“Christ, no.” Amelia shook off the idea like a sudden chill. “Go to the Cousins with an accusation like that? It would shut everything down. Every joint op. Every shared bite of intelligence. Every ounce of carefully nurtured trust since Blake and Philby.”

“So Paul was the only one who knew?”

“Wait.” Amelia held up a hand to interrupt him. They had come to the bottom of the hill, the crowded Galata Bridge now visible to the southwest, heavy traffic funneling in both directions along Kemeralti Caddesi. “I’ve got to be completely honest with you. I cannot say, hand on heart, that Paul is above suspicion.” Kell saw the conflict in her, knew the consequences if Wallinger proved to be the mole. “But we have to stop this thing. We have to find out where the leaks are coming from. I've had to shut almost everything down. All the joint ops, limit the circulation on too many reports. The Cousins don't understand it and they're getting restless. Everything we're doing in Turkey, in Syria, with the Iranians, the Israelis, it's all being affected. I can't *move* until this thing is resolved." Amelia was chopping the air with her hand. "You've got to try to get answers quickly, Tom," she said, curling the hand into a fist. "If we can't get anything on Kleckner, I'll have to go to the Americans. Soon. And if the mole turns out to be one of ours . . ."

"Curtains," said Kell.

They stood in silence for a moment.

"What did Paul say about the leaks?" Kell asked.

Amelia seemed surprised by the question. "He agreed to look into it," she said. "He said he didn't trust Kleckner, didn't like Begg. Something not right about her. We agreed never to discuss my theory using any of the usual channels. No telegrams, no telephones, nothing."

"Sure." Kell waited for Amelia to continue. When she remained silent, gazing at the cluttered horizon beyond the minarets encircling the Golden Horn, he prompted her by saying: "And?"

She turned toward him. To Kell's surprise, her eyes were stung with tears.

"And I never saw him again."

20

There was nobody on the beach.

Iannis Christidis sat alone on the damp, low-tide sand, listening to the near-silent rhythm of the folding waves, his brain numb with alcohol. It was perhaps two or three o'clock in the morning; he had long since lost track of time. Reaching into the breast pocket of his shirt, he pulled out a crumpled packet of Assos and clumsily tapped three cigarettes onto the hard sand. He let two of them roll away on the wind and pressed the third to his lips. Then he reached into the pocket of his trousers for a lighter.

A last smoke for a condemned man. He could not even taste the tobacco. The first inhalation of smoke tilted his head back so that he was looking up at the black sky, tracing stars in the blinking double vision of his drunkenness, then a gasp as he rocked forward and groaned and fell to one side.

Christidis picked himself up. He pressed his fist into the sand and sat up straight. He looked out at the water again, at the black night, the silhouette of a fishing boat moored fifty meters from the beach. This was his island. This had been his life. This was the decision he had made and the mistake was too great now, the shame and the guilt. Everything to live with, nothing to live for.

He was sure now that he was going to do it. He put the cigarette in his mouth and began to scrape at the ground in front of him with both hands, like a dog burying a bone. He was pulling back the wet clods and piling them up at his feet so that his shins and the tops of his knees were soon covered in thick sand.

As a child he had played on this beach.

He choked on the cigarette, the smoke doubling back on the wind and stinging his eyes. He spat it out on the ground, spittle running down his chin so that he had to wipe it away with his sleeve. He reached around and felt his wet trousers, taking out the wallet and tossing it into the hole he had made. Taking off his watch and his wedding ring and throwing those in, too. He started to put the sand back, to cover up the hole, the waves suddenly louder, as if the tide was rushing in to carry him away. A ship must have passed in the strait a few minutes before. Iannis was able to realize that. Maybe he wasn't as drunk as he thought he was.

He packed the last of the sand over his personal belongings, stood up, and stamped down with his feet. He wasn't even sure why he was burying things on the beach. So that they could identify him. So that they would know that he was gone. Otherwise someone might walk past in the next few hours and steal the wallet, the ring, the watch. Christidis began to take off his trousers and underpants, his shirt, threw the packet of cigarettes on the sand. Balancing on one leg, he took off first one sock, then the other. He wondered why he was still wearing them. Why hadn't he taken off his socks? His whole head was suddenly black with the noise of the sea and the night and the fear of what he was about to do.

Christidis stumbled forward. He hoped that somebody was watching him and that they would stop him from moving forward. But nobody came. He walked into the water and felt the sand suddenly subside beneath him, a steep cliff dropping away beneath his feet. He was up to his chest, the sea in his mouth, spluttering and gasping for air. But he began to swim, heading away from the shore. Moving.

All of the alcohol and the dread were suddenly out of him. He was swimming past a boat, heading out into the open water. He almost reached out and touched the stern, but knew that if he did, he would never let go. He went past the boat, turned and looked back at the rocking silhouette. The beach was grades of blacks and browns and Christidis was out of breath. He thought of his clothes on the flat wet sand and the wallet buried in the shallow hole beside them. All of that his past now. His life.

He was treading water, looking back at Chios, the salt in the water crackling in his ear. *Don't be a coward,* he told himself. *Don't go back to what you are living through.* He had tried to face the wall of his shame. He had thought that time would make everything all right. But he had been wrong.

He turned and continued swimming. Moving east in the direction of the Turkish coast, taking himself farther and farther away from Chios. Getting tired now. Starting to worry. Getting cold. He knew that was a good thing. He knew that it meant the sea would eventually take him.

21

Kell was sure that it wasn't Tremayne. He knew next to nothing about Landau or Begg. He wanted to suggest to Amelia that Chater would most probably have had equivalent or superior access to the same CIA intel as Ryan Kleckner and was therefore just as much of a suspect in the molehunt. Almost in the same thought, he wondered if Amelia had instructed a third party to look into Chater's affairs. That was surely possible. Since Wallinger's death, Amelia's behavior had been more than secretive: she had been deliberately opaque, even obstructive. She knew that Kell could not be relied upon to give Chater a fair hearing; she would have asked a trusted comrade to put the watch on the American. But who?

He stopped himself. Kell was in the center of the Galata Bridge, directly above the restaurant where, a few hours earlier, he had eaten breakfast. The same fishermen were probably dropping the same lines over the same southern section of the bridge. And Kell realized that, less than half an hour after listening to Amelia's theory, he was already lost in Angleton's wilderness of mirrors, the place where your friend is your enemy, the place where your enemy is your friend.

"Tom?"

Amelia had stopped and turned around a few meters ahead of him. A taxi passed within inches of her extended elbow as she rested her hands on her hips.

"Sorry," Kell muttered. He moved to catch up. There was an overwhelming smell of landed fish on the bridge.

"I said that Josephine Wallinger is in Istanbul. At the house in Yenikoy. I was going to go and see her."

"Is that a good idea?"

"You think it's a *bad* idea?"

You tell me, Kell thought, and remembered that Amelia possessed that same cold center that he had glimpsed in so many of his colleagues, the chill in the jaded soul. He knew the emotional territory: the quiet, always conscious desire to go face-to-face with an adversary, to prove one's superiority, often while wearing a mask of kinship and warmth. Amelia had betrayed Josephine time and again. Was that not enough for her? Yet despite all of their shared passion, all of Amelia's learning and brilliance, her great beauty, her success, Paul had always returned to his wife. Did Amelia feel, finally, humiliated by that? She was as ceaselessly competitive in matters of the heart as she was in matters of the state. This was more than a question of survival. Amelia Levene embodied the nailed-down principle that a pedigree SIS officer should never come off second best.

"I said I'd drop round for a cup of tea at about four." She glanced at her watch. "It's already quarter to. Join me?"

"Sure."

She had flagged down a taxi within seconds. The driver made a jerking, unnecessary chicane through cluttered traffic, lurching north toward the Unkapani Bridge. Kell thought to strap himself in before remembering that no cab in the history of Turkish transportation had ever boasted a functioning rear seat belt. Amelia remained impassive throughout. She had told Kell that she wanted to ask Josephine if Paul had ever mentioned the mole; yet he wondered if he would be party to that conversation when it took place. More likely Amelia wanted him by her side to dilute the intensity of her encounter with Josephine. It was not a question of whether or not Josephine knew about the affair—a wife *always* knows—but simply the extent to which she would be prepared to forgive Amelia for her transgressions.

His cell phone sounded, a text pinging in. Kell took it out and looked at the screen. Claire had replied to his earlier message:

> SEEMS LIKE YESTERDAY. WE WERE SO HAPPY, TOM. WHAT HAPPENED? IT ALL SEEMS SUCH A WASTE. X

"You all right?" Amelia asked, seeing the change in his expression. He was familiar with the sudden, parabolic shifts in Claire's mood. When she was lonely or frightened about the future, she would try to draw close to him; when she was content and happy in her new life with Richard, she would treat Kell as a failed state. Nevertheless, in that moment he felt an extraordinary yearning for his wife, and for what he had lost. Though Kell knew that he wanted a different future, there were still times when he wished that he had been able to resolve his differences with Claire so that they could have lived peaceably together. She was right. It all seemed such a waste.

"I'm fine," he said. "Just Claire."

It was another half hour before they located the house, a modest *yali* on the shore of the Bosporus, built by a rich Ottoman trader in the late nineteenth century and then renovated by a faceless landlord who rented it to the Foreign and Commonwealth Office at extravagant cost. They rang the bell, waited for almost two minutes, then heard the fast, light step of someone clipping down a flight of stairs. Kell was certain it was not Josephine. The movements were young, quick, almost weightless.

At first he did not recognize the young woman who opened the door. Her hair was shorter and dyed blond. Her large brown eyes, the lashes dark with mascara, were luminous and kind. Her skin was lightly tanned, so that freckles had begun to appear around her nose and at the tops of her arms. She was wearing a dark blue summer dress; the straps of a cream bra were slightly loose across her shoulders. There was a bracelet around one of her ankles and the toenails of her neat bare feet were painted scarlet red. It was Rachel.

"Hello. I remember you. Amelia."

"Hello. That's right. We met in Cartmel."

The two women shook hands and Rachel turned to look at Kell. He had responded instantly to something in her expression and manner, and felt the chest-shifting surge of attraction. Looking at Rachel's photographs in the Ankara station, watching her at the funeral, he had felt nothing of this. Rachel was not his type. But there was a force and an honesty in the penetration of her gaze that winded him. Kell had not felt such a thing for months, years even, and it was extraordinary to experience it again. He looked toward Amelia, then back at Rachel, who was studying his face with the calm, almost amused self-assurance of a plastic surgeon wondering which bit to cut first.

"Tom," said Kell, extending his hand. Against his better judgment, he found that he held her gaze, stirring up the chemistry between them. Perhaps the whole thing was just a mirage. Perhaps Rachel was just fitting his face to the mourners at her father's funeral, wondering if she had spoken to him, trying to remember if he had offered his condolences. That might explain why she was looking at him so intently.

"Hello, Tom," she said. She had a radiant, guileless smile that lit up her face; it was as though she had already made up her mind to like him. "I'm Rachel. You've come to see Mum."

"Yes," said Amelia, before Kell did.

She led them into a hall cluttered with rugs and lamps and pictures. Full-bodied and graceful, a bombshell figure. Kell could smell her perfume as she walked ahead of them and felt as though Amelia was reading his every thought. In another room, he could hear Josephine talking on the telephone. He wanted to keep watching this beautiful woman, to decide if he had imagined what had just occurred or whether his sense of her was correct. Had there been a genuine connection between them or had he simply fallen victim to the trap of beauty? "Mum's talking to a friend," she said, turning to look at him. That gaze again. "She won't be long. Would you like some tea?"

The question took them into a kitchen awash in natural light. High windows, crisscrossed by narrow wooden frames, offered a panoramic view across the Bosporus to the Asian side. The waters were so close it was as though the room were floating on pontoons. Amelia said: "What a beautiful view," and Kell enjoyed the fact that Rachel made no effort to respond to the observation. Yes, it was a beautiful view. Everybody mentioned that. What else was there to say about it?

He stopped beside a sturdy wooden table on which various books and files had been piled up. Amelia took off her jacket and placed it over the back of a wicker rocking chair that looked as though it had been attacked, over a period of many years, by generations of giant moths.

"Sorry, I should have taken that," said Rachel, indicating the jacket, though she made no effort to hang it up. Instead, she opened a door out onto a white-painted veranda so that a rush of warm sea air funneled into the house. Then she crossed the room and placed a kettle on a lit ring of gas. All of this captivating to Kell, who was enjoying the sight of a beautiful woman weaving her spell.

"Pappa loved tea," she said, stretching toward a corner of the kitchen where boxes of Twinings and Williamson teas wrestled for space with glass jars of beans and pasta. That movement—which showed off the curve of her breasts and very slightly raised the hem of her dress so that Kell could see the smooth tanned edge of her thigh—struck him as premeditated, though it could just as easily have been a sign of Rachel's complete lack of self-consciousness. Nevertheless, he decided that she was being deliberately provocative and told himself to park whatever nascent feelings of lust he was experiencing.

"Have you been out here long?" Amelia asked.

"Two days," Rachel replied. She appeared to be enjoying the process of being hospitable in her father's house; protective of Josephine; a first line of defense against visiting mourners. Rachel turned again, rose onto tiptoes, opened a cupboard, and pulled down two china cups. Then she turned and caught Kell staring at her. He held her gaze, letting her know with a glance that he was aware of her beauty, of the game she was playing, and that he was enjoying it.

"Sugar?"

"Two, please," he said. Amelia, he knew, took it black. She made a comment about how nice it was to be served tea from a mug "in the English fashion," rather than from a "tiny little glass," as was the custom in Turkey. Again, Rachel did not respond to the observation. If she had something to say about something, she would say it; if she didn't, she would not. Kell guessed that she was the sort of person who could very easily sit through an awkward silence. He liked that about her.

"Did you know my father?" she asked, passing him his cup of tea. The mug had a reproduction of the Botticelli *Venus* on one side. A siren singing him onto the rocks.

"Yes," he replied. "I'm very sorry."

"What did you think of him?"

Kell felt Amelia's sliding glance as the question caught them both off guard. Rachel's tone of voice, allied to the directness of her gaze, demanded an honest answer. She would not want to deal in platitudes; he knew that much about her already.

"He was a good friend. It was the nature of our business that I saw too little of him. He was cultured. He was clever. Always such good company."

What might he have added? That he thought Paul Wallinger, for all his learning and brilliance, possessed that dangerous streak of selfishness—it was the fashion nowadays to call it narcissism, even sociopathy—that ultimately damaged anyone who came too close to him. Kell might have said that Rachel's father had taken women for his pleasure, for years and years, discarding them when he was done. That he had allowed Amelia to fall in love with him, thereby jeopardizing her career, but had lacked the will—or perhaps the courage—to break with Josephine and to marry her, despite the fact that they were so well suited. Had he admired Paul for sticking with Josephine, to guarantee the Foreign Office perks, the school fees, while roaming the world as a free man, for all intents and purposes a bachelor at liberty to behave as he pleased? Not particularly. None of it, in final analysis, was Kell's business. You never knew what private accommodations married couples made with each other.

"Your father was also very good at his job," he added, because Rachel looked like she wanted to hear more.

"I'll second that," Amelia replied, trying to make a smiling eye contact with Rachel, who seemed to be avoiding her gaze. Kell sensed that Amelia wanted to get out of the room and to find Josephine; Rachel was making her feel uneasy.

"So you're another spook?"

The question was directed at him with a look of nonchalance. Kell met it with a grin.

"I don't know." He looked across at Amelia, who was staring into her cup. "What am I these days?"

The chief of the Secret Intelligence Service was saved from conjuring a suitably witty response by the arrival of Josephine Wallinger, who had paused in the doorway of the kitchen, as though taking in the view for the first time. Kell was shocked by her appearance. She looked tired and browbeaten, as though everything Paul had ever done—his spying, his womanizing, even his death—had conspired to ruin her.

"Did you know that the Turkish word for 'Bosporus' is the same as the word for 'throat'?"

"I did not know that," Amelia replied, moving toward her with arms outstretched. The two women embraced. As Josephine said: "Thank you for coming. How lovely to see you," Kell looked at Rachel in an effort to discern whether or not she knew about her father's affair with Amelia. There was no observable change in her expression.

"You know Tom, of course?"

Amelia ushered Josephine toward Kell. She smelled of tears and face cream. He kissed her on both cheeks and said how good it was to see her. When she thanked him for coming to the funeral, Rachel interjected, saying: "Oh, were you there? I didn't notice you," and Kell tried to unpick the implication of the remark. Was it an insult, a way of flirting with him, or simply a throwaway line?

For some time they idled in chitchat: Kell, Josephine, and Amelia sitting on various armchairs and sofas dotted around the open-plan kitchen. Rachel moved from room to room, from floor to floor, but honored Kell with a glance whenever she returned to the kitchen. Having waited for the correct moment, Amelia invited Josephine to accompany her on a walk around Yenikoy. That gave Kell the chance to smoke a long-awaited cigarette on the veranda. It was no surprise when he heard the click of the door behind him and turned to see that Rachel was coming outside to join him.

Round two.

"Got a spare one of those?"

"Sure."

He dug out the packet of Winston Lights, slid out a single cigarette, and tilted it toward her. She took it and he offered her a light, cupping his hand around the flame to protect it from gusts of sea wind. The tips of her fingers touched the back of his hand as she inhaled on the flame and withdrew from him.

"I always think it looks as though it's coming to a boil."

It took Kell a moment to realize that Rachel was talking about the Bosporus. The observation was entirely apt. The churning waters ahead of them seemed to be bubbling in a fury of surging tides and winds.

"You go out on it much? Did your father take you?"

"Once," she said, and exhaled a funnel of smoke that bent in front of his face and rushed off, evaporating on the breeze. "We took a ferry out to Buyukada. Have you been there?"

"Never," Kell replied.

"One of the islands in the Sea of Marmara. Summer tourists, mostly, but Pappa had a friend who lived out there. An American journalist."

As soon as he heard the word "American," Kell thought of Chater, of Kleckner, of the mole. He wondered who the journalist was to whom Rachel was referring. Just as quickly, like the smoke turning sharply from her lips, she changed the subject.

"Why did you say that he was good at his job? How is a spy a good spy? What made Pappa better than anyone else?"

Kell would happily have spent the rest of the afternoon answering that question, because it was his area of particular expertise, a subject he had studied and thought about for the better part of his adult life. He began with a simple observation.

"Believe it or not, it's a question of honesty," he said. "If a person is clear about what they want to achieve, if they set about achieving that goal objectively and with precision, more often than not they will succeed."

Rachel looked confused. Not because she did not understand what Kell was trying to say, but because she did not necessarily accept it.

"Are you talking about life or are you talking about spying?"

"Both," Kell replied.

"It all sounds a bit self-help."

Kell laughed off the insult. "Thanks," he said, but her next remark caught him off guard.

"Are you saying my father wasn't a liar?"

He would have to proceed carefully. It was all very well sharing a flirtatious cigarette with an attractive woman on the shores of the Hellespont, but that woman was also the daughter of a man who had recently been killed. Kell was the gatekeeper of Paul Wallinger's reputation. Whatever he told Rachel about her father, she would remember for the rest of her life.

"We lie," he said. "I have lied in my career. It wasn't something your father was immune to, either. But let's face it, deceit isn't exactly unique to espionage." She frowned again, as if she thought that Kell was trying to wriggle off a hook. He looked up at the house, then out across the water. "Architects lie. Ship captains lie. I was trying to make a different point. That we achieve our best results by presenting ourselves honestly. That goes for all relationships, don't you think? And what I do, what your father did, was ultimately about making relationships."

Rachel drew deeply on the answer and smoked in silence. A ketch passed within a hundred meters of the *yali*. Kell followed its progress, enjoying the drum tautness of the full sails, the clean white churn of the wake.

"I loathe spies," she said.

Kell laughed at this, but Rachel was looking out across the water and would not meet his gaze.

"Explain," he said, trying to deny to himself that a woman he desired, whose good opinion he already coveted, had deliberately insulted him.

"I think it killed something off in Pappa," she said. "A part of him dried up inside. I began to think that he had a piece missing from his heart. Call it decency. Call it tenderness. Honesty, perhaps."

And Paul knew that, Kell thought, remembering the abundance of photographs of Andrew in Ankara, the comparative absence of pictures of Rachel. Wallinger knew that his bright, beautiful, perceptive daughter had seen through him. He knew that he had lost her respect.

"I'm sorry to hear you say that," he said. "I really am. I hope you won't always feel that way. I don't think it's true of Paul. He was capable of great kindness. He was a decent man." Kell tripped on the words as he said them, because he knew they were platitudes designed to comfort a woman who was long past any desire to be falsely reassured. He tried a different approach. "What we do—the people we are obliged to work with, the ends we are asked to justify—takes its toll. It becomes impossible to remain above the fray. Does that make sense? In other words, we are blackened by our association with politics, with the secret world." Even as he said this, Kell could feel a contrary argument rising inside him. There had been decency in Paul Wallinger only when it was in Paul Wallinger's interests to be decent; when it served him to be ruthless, he was ruthless. "What's the line from Nietzsche? He who fights with monsters should see to it that he himself does not become a monster—"

Rachel interrupted him, tossing her cigarette out to sea. "Right," she said impatiently, as though Kell was a freshman trying to impress her with cod philosophy. He felt embarrassed and opted for greater simplicity. "What I'm trying to tell you is that we are all the sum of our contradictions. We all make mistakes. They fuck you up, your mum and dad, but your mum and dad also do a pretty good job of fucking themselves up, too."

That made her grin. At last. It was lovely to see it again, the flattering radiance of Rachel Wallinger's smile. Kell tossed his cigarette into the water, but they remained on the veranda.

"So what mistakes have you made, Tom?" she said, and touched his arm, as though she imagined that she did not have his full attention. Had Kell possessed an ounce more self-confidence in that moment, a watertight assurance that it would not offend her, he would have reached for Rachel, looped his hand around her waist, pulled her toward him, and kissed her. But he could no more make a pass at Wallinger's daughter than he could imagine making a pass at Amelia Levene.

"Lots," he replied. "And all of them bound by the Official Secrets Act. You'll have to wait for my memoirs."

She smiled again and looked south at the vast suspension bridge linking European Istanbul to the Asian side. At night it was lit by a thousand blue lights, a sight Kell always enjoyed. He would have liked to take Rachel to one of the restaurants in Moda or Ortakoy, to order oysters and Chablis, to talk for hours. He hadn't felt that way about a woman in years.

"How well do you know Amelia?" she asked.

Kell heard a warning in the question, perhaps the implication that Rachel knew about the affair. He smothered his concern with a joke.

"Well enough that if she had spinach in her teeth, I would tell her."

Rachel did not laugh. She was still looking south, toward the bridge.

"Mum doesn't trust her."

"No?"

"She thinks she knows more about Dad's accident than she's letting on."

That was unexpected. Nothing to do with the affair. Everything to do with the crash. Kell did his best to reassure her.

"Please don't worry about that," he said. "All of us are trying to find out what happened. That's why I'm here. That's why they've gone off for a walk."

"You're talking to me like I'm too young to hear the grown-ups' secrets."

"You know that's not true. Nobody thinks that, Rachel. Least of all me."

"We've only just met. You don't know me."

He wanted to tell her that he had met her before; or, at least, that he had watched her and seen what she had done with the flowers at her father's funeral. The flare of anger in her eyes, flinging the bouquet into the wall, a gesture at once violently dismissive of Cecilia Sandor and instinctively defensive of her mother. Kell remembered how Rachel had gone to Andrew afterward, almost as if she was protecting him from the consequences of their father's deceit. She had removed the card before Andrew had had the chance to see it. Kell still did not know if Rachel had been able to understand the Hungarian text on the card or had simply recognized the handwriting.

A noise inside the house. Josephine and Amelia returning from their walk. Kell wished that he had been privy to their conversation; Amelia tiptoeing around Josephine's resentment of the woman who had almost stolen her husband. Rachel opened the door and went back into the room. Kell caught a knowing look on Amelia's face as she registered that the two of them had been outside together.

"I wish you wouldn't smoke, darling," Josephine said, smiling benignly at Kell as though he were a chauffeur who had been killing time waiting for his boss. "What time's your thing tonight?"

"What thing?" Amelia asked.

"I've been invited to a party," Rachel replied.

"Some colleague of Paul's," Josephine added blandly, still looking at Kell. "Perhaps you know him. American diplomat. Ryan Kleckner."

22

Kell reacted quickly, a rapid improvisation.

"That's odd. I had a meeting with someone who was going to the same party. Kleckner. He works at the consulate here, right?"

"Right," Rachel replied.

"I think somebody caught someone's eye," Josephine added, shooting Rachel an arch look. In that moment Kell realized that Kleckner had asked Rachel as his date.

"Mum, I met him for five minutes at the wake. He knew I was coming out to Istanbul. He just very sweetly invited me to his party."

"Is it a big thing? A dinner?" Kell's voice was steady but he was aware of trying to make himself feel less physically tense. If the party was an intimate dinner for a dozen of Kleckner's closest friends, he had no chance of crashing; if most of expat Istanbul was invited, he could tag along.

"Some bar. Bleu. Have you heard of it?"

Amelia obviously hadn't, but she said: "Yes" because she knew what Kell was trying to do. He wanted to get into Kleckner's circle, wanted to have a chance to go eye-to-eye with his target.

"I'm not sure I want to go on my own," she said. "I won't know anyone."

Josephine began to speak. "Then just stay here with . . ."

Amelia did not allow her to finish. "Take Tom," she said, throwing out the idea as casually as Kell had tossed his cigarette into the Bosporus. "He's always complaining that he's too old for nightclubs but too young to stay at home."

Rachel seemed to enjoy that line. "Are you always complaining about that?" she asked, with a knowing tilt of the head. Kell muttered: "I've never said that in my life," while all three women grinned at him. Rachel enjoyed the sight of his momentary discomfort and took up Amelia's suggestion. "Come with me, then," she said. "It'll be fun. You can be my chaperone."

Chaperone, Kell thought two hours later as he stared into the steamed-up mirror of his hotel bathroom, wiping away the condensation to reveal a face smothered in shaving foam, his hair wet from the shower. *Chaperone.* He opened the bathroom door and shaved as the steam slowly cleared. He thought of the line in *Moonraker* about Bond's reluctance to shave twice in the same day and a smile curled in the mirror. Thomas Kell was not a vain man, but he was vain enough to want to look good for Rachel Wallinger. Moving closer to the glass he spotted a single black hair protruding from his left earlobe, two more in his nostrils. He pulled them out, his eyes watering. There was a hair dryer in the wardrobe, but Kell drew the line at that, toweling himself dry and then dressing in jeans, desert boots, and a pale blue shirt that had been laundered by the hotel in Ankara.

He had arranged to meet Rachel at the base of the Galata Tower. She was there before he was, pivoting on wedge heels in a belted black dress, a pair of Ray-Bans with powder blue frames shielding her eyes from the fading evening sun. He kissed her on both cheeks and recognized her perfume, though he could not place it. Perhaps a colleague had worn it at SIS.

"Did you eat?" she asked.

Kell had ordered a sandwich from room service and wolfed it after the shower, but said: "No," because he hoped that Rachel was hungry. He wanted to sit with her for a while, to get to know her, just the two of them.

"Shall we get something quick?"

"Good idea."

They found a small contemporary place hidden in the warren of bars and restaurants north of the tower and sat at an angle to each other, eating *meze* and drinking a bottle of chilled Turkish red. Rachel did not ask any questions about the crash, nor did she seem interested in probing Kell for further information about her father's career. Instead, they talked about their respective lives in London, Rachel explaining that she was about to start a new job in publishing after working for several years as a teacher. Kell made no mention of his suspension from the Service, but sketched out the basic facts of his divorce and his current life in London.

"Do you get on well with your wife?" she asked.

"Broadly speaking."

"What does that mean?"

"It means that we're still friends, even though both of us feel betrayed by the other."

"Then you can't be friends."

"I disagree. It just takes time." Rachel produced a knowing smile. "What about you?" he asked. "Ever been married?"

Rachel arched her eyebrows, as though Kell was being old-fashioned. "Never," she said. "Don't imagine I ever will be."

"Why do you say that?"

"I'll tell you another time. Right now I'm happier grilling you." She looked quickly to one side of the table. "Do you miss your wife?"

Kell drew her eyes back to his. "I miss her company, of course. She's a fantastic person. We spent most of our adult lives together." He placed a packet of Karelia filters on the table, like an opening bid in a game of poker. "You could say that there are times when I miss the *structure* of what we had, the ease of two people who knew each other very well and were comfortable in each other's company. But I don't miss the other stuff."

"What stuff?"

Kell avoided talk of adultery and rows and opted instead for a subject that he hoped would draw Rachel away from the forensic dissection of his marriage.

"I wanted to have children. I *still* want to have children. We weren't able to do that."

She looked at him as though he had betrayed Claire. "Is that why you left her?"

"No," Kell replied instantly. "It was more complicated than that."

Rachel chose that moment to stand up and go to the bathroom, leaving Kell alone at the table, half listening to the conversations of his fellow diners. He had been on only two dates since Claire's departure for the more fertile slopes of Primrose Hill, on both of which he had gleaned an astonishing amount of personal information from his respective companions, never to see them again. It was one of the anomalies of life on the divorce circuit: everybody had a story to tell, everybody had baggage they were eager to unload. There was precious little privacy, but a refreshing lack of obfuscation. The time for concealment, for presenting a false self, seemed to pass as people crossed the Rubicon of forty. What you saw was, at long last, what you got.

It was the same talking to Rachel, whom Kell might have expected to be more circumspect. Sitting with her was like sitting with the promise of better times ahead. It was an odd thing to articulate to himself, but he felt something of his old strength returning, as though he was being shown the best of a world of which he had grown tired. Rachel was provocative and honest, she was beautiful to look at, she made him feel alive and enthused. It was an effort, in fact, to conceal from her the extent to which he was already bewitched.

Bar Bleu was a five-minute walk downhill along a street that smelled of sewage, where cats nipped in and out of rusted scaffolding pipes and a moped screamed in high gear, struggling with the slope. At one point, walking along cobbles ruptured by years of Istanbul traffic, Rachel stumbled under the weak streetlights and Kell reached quickly across to prevent her tripping. The moment passed in an instant, but it was like an old-fashioned test of chivalry that he had passed with ease.

"Quick reactions," she said, briefly touching the top of his hand as Kell released her arm. The tips of her fingers were soft and cold in the night. He felt the scratch of one of her rings against his wrist.

"The training kicked in," he joked. "My world is a jungle of threats."

Rachel laughed and they smoked a cigarette on the final stages of the walk, arriving at the entrance of Bar Bleu at the same time as a pimped four-by-four with tinted windows and an inevitably personalized license plate. The doors opened and two expensively maintained, stilettoed Turkish girls emerged from the back, followed by gelled boyfriends in designer shirts. A valet attendant slipped into the driver's seat and the traffic that had bunched up behind it on the narrow street was allowed to pass.

"Brave new world," Kell muttered.

A black-jacketed bouncer gave Kell the up-and-down and nodded him toward a clipboard-wielding hostess. Under the heading "Ryan K Birthday," Kell could see the words "Rachel Wallinger + 1." An overweight Indian man with a shaved head and a ten-thousand-dollar wristwatch was jammed in against a wall.

"Who were you meant to come with?" Kell shouted as they pushed through the crush of drinkers at the front of the bar. The temperature had gone up by ten degrees.

"You," she replied. "I texted Ryan to tell him I was bringing someone. He said he'd heard of you."

Kell had worked with countless CIA officers over a period of twenty years. Jim Chater was the ranking American spy in the region. The name Thomas Kell was probably as well known at Langley as it was at Vauxhall Cross. He concluded that there was no darker implication to Kleckner's remark.

"What does he look like?" he asked Rachel as a waitress angled past, carrying a tray of cocktails above her head. Kell leaned back in a rope-a-dope, allowing the tray to pass close to his head.

"Can't really remember," Rachel replied, shouting now because the music in the bar—Kell knew it was Beyoncé, but couldn't name the track—was apocalyptically loud.

"Rachel!"

And there he was. Ryan Kleckner. A worked-out, tanned, good-looking American with teeth that glowed slightly blue under the bright lights of the bar. Kleckner was wearing jeans and a crisp white shirt, unbuttoned sufficiently to reveal a loose nest of chest hair, and appeared to be the lodestone around which dozens of party girls and Eurotrash lotharios were orbiting in a frenzy of coke and tequila. Rachel was in his arms as Kleckner kissed both her cheeks. He locked on to Kleckner's eyes and smiled broadly as Rachel introduced them.

"Tom! Wow, hi, thanks for coming." He was nodding, smiling, enveloping Kell in goodwill. "Honored that you're here. Know a lot about you."

This almost an aside, a remark to exclude Rachel, as though Kleckner was paying private tribute, spy to spy. Rachel, meanwhile, was shuffling around in her handbag, saying: "I bought you something, a present" as another waiter twisted past with a tray of cocktails.

"What is it?" Kleckner asked, taking what looked like a paperback book that Rachel had wrapped in red paper. There was a birthday card stuck to the top of the package.

"Open it," she said, shouting over the music. Kell was hot. He wanted a drink. He craved another cigarette but it was a three-day voyage back to the entrance through the drinkers and partygoers standing four deep at the bar.

Kleckner opened the card first. From what Kell could ascertain, it was a Larson cartoon. The American took a moment to stare at it, then burst into laughter. Kell didn't ask to take a look. The paperback was a copy of *Hitch-22,* the memoirs of the late British journalist Christopher Hitchens. Kleckner appeared to swallow some measure of disappointment. A flicker of irritation passed across his face, like a software glitch, before he found the words to thank Rachel.

"This is the *God Delusion* guy, right?" Kleckner glanced again at the cover. Kell reckoned it was ten to one the American was a practicing believer. "Journalist who backed the U.S. on Saddam?"

"That's right!" Rachel was shouting. "But not *The God Delusion. God Is Not Great.* Sort of the same thing."

Kleckner did not respond. He looked as though he wanted to set the present to one side, as an error of judgment by the pretty British girl, and to continue enjoying his evening. Rachel appeared to sense this and, as a tall, redheaded woman tapped Kleckner on the shoulder, shared a look with Kell, relaxing her mouth into a mock frown.

"Clearly not a fan of the Hitch," she said.

"Clearly," Kell replied. "I'll get us a drink."

That turned out to be a promise that was hard to keep. For all of twenty minutes, Kell queued at the bar, jostled and squeezed on all sides by a dozen men trying to catch the eye of the bartenders, all of them soaked in sweat and aftershave. When, finally, he had paid for two caipirinhas and ferried them back, Kell found Rachel tucked in a corner sofa talking to Kleckner and a second, unidentified man who was wearing a Hawaiian shirt and a silver chain necklace. There was a large ice bucket on a table in front of them, two Laurent-Perriers and a bottle of designer vodka nestled among the glittering cubes.

"You should have had a glass of champagne," Kleckner shouted, placing a sturdy and welcoming hand on Kell's shoulder as he stooped to sit with them. The second man, bald and squat as Bob Hoskins, introduced himself as "Taylor, colleague of Ryan's." Kell filed the name away for his ten o'clock. Taylor said: "We were just talking about Erdogan."

The conversation allowed Kell the chance to take Kleckner's political temperature, though he never strayed far from established State Department lines. Erdogan, in Kleckner's view, "wants his head on coins, his face on banknotes. Guy wants streets named after him, to out-Ataturk Ataturk." This was not exactly news; indeed, it was a view shared by Kell and most of his former colleagues at SIS. Kell felt that Rachel made the most interesting contribution to the conversation.

"Don't you think the Ataturk cult is sort of fatal to Turkey?" she said, looking to Taylor first, her eyes level with his sweat-soaked shirt. "I think it stops them moving forward, thinking in fresh ways. He's held in such reverence, and on the one hand that's a wonderful thing, because he's a sort of a Mandela figure here, the spiritual leader of the nation. But it's maybe time to move on? They can't seem to move out from behind the shadow of this immense father figure. They're like children in that sense."

Taylor was closer in age to Kell and observably flattened by champagne and vodka. His washed-out eyes stared at Rachel's, trying, without evident success, to engage his brain sufficiently to respond to what she had said. Kleckner, who had been drinking at twice Taylor's rate, had no such problem.

"I know what you mean," he said, with a self-assurance that was almost patronizing. "Like a kind of North Korean brainwashing. They're comforted by him. They worship him. They walk into a post office and his picture is on the wall. Nobody wants to betray that legacy. Nobody wants to question it or criticize him and maybe then move up to the next gear."

"Except fuckin' Erdogan," Taylor muttered, slugging another mouthful of Laurent-Perrier. He twisted his neck in the direction of the toilets, as though weighing up the tactical and strategic consequences of making a break for the bathroom. There were heavy crowds between the sofa and the doors. He appeared to decide against it and swiveled back to make a beady eye contact with Kell. "What about you, Tom?"

"We're all defined and held back by national myths," Kell replied. Ordinarily he would have ducked the question, but the competitor in him wanted to outgun Kleckner. "The Russians have the Rodina. Everything flows from that concept. The Motherland, a near-masochistic willingness to subordinate to a strong leader."

"Yeah, talk about not being able to fucking move on," Taylor muttered. "Talk about sabotaging your own future."

Rachel smiled as Kell pressed ahead. "And the Americans have it, too. Land of the free. Home of the brave. The right to bear arms. Question those principles too strongly and you'll be run out of town as a socialist."

"You got a problem with those principles, Tom?" Rachel asked. Kell relished her archness, but noticed that Kleckner was looking at both of them very intently.

"Not at all. Why would I have a problem with freedom? Or bravery?" Taylor screwed his face up and shook his head, seeking solace in another mouthful of champagne. "I'm just trying to make the point that if a politician, in the American context, strays too far from the rights of the individual, if he or she appears to promote an idea of collective, rather than personal, responsibility, then they're going to get hammered in the newspapers and hammered at the polls."

For a moment, it felt as though Kleckner was going to respond, but the American kept his counsel. Perhaps it was all getting a bit serious for a twenty-ninth birthday party. Jay-Z had started singing "Empire State of Mind" and a tanned blonde in a micromini had appeared at Kleckner's side. Taylor finally made a move to the bathroom, allowing the girl to slip into his seat while keeping her hand firmly on Kleckner's thigh. She whispered something in his ear, shooting Rachel a quick look of search and threat. Kell couldn't tell if they were more than friends. More likely the blonde was just another Istanbul party girl who liked to drape herself around handsome American diplomats.

"Another drink?" he asked Rachel, who looked as though she was regretting coming to the party.

"Sure," she replied, with a soft glance.

Kell stood up and moved through the crowds to the bar. What to make of Kleckner? Kell remembered the line in Macbeth. *There's no art to find the mind's construction in the face.* Kleckner looked like a *believer.* If not a patriot, exactly, then certainly a young man possessed of a certain idealistic zeal. At that age, everybody wanted to make a difference. Would it matter to Ryan Kleckner *how* he made that difference, or would it simply be a question of influence for its own sake? Could such a person be selling Western secrets to Moscow, to Iran, to Beijing? Of course.

Kell looked back in the direction of the sofa. He saw Kleckner's gaze fastened onto Rachel's, attentive and solicitous, the micromini blonde edged out by their body language, looking every bit the unwelcome guest as she perched on Taylor's chair. Kell suddenly regretted sounding off about national myths. He regretted leaving to buy another round of drinks. He felt all of the separateness and the weight of his age in this place filled with youth and music and beauty. Too old for nightclubs, too young to stay at home.

A space opened up at the bar. Kell angled into it, lodging a territorial elbow on the counter, but felt the pulse of his phone vibrating in his back pocket. He reached for it and answered a blocked call.

"Tom? It's Adam Haydock."

Kell could barely hear. He shouted at Haydock to wait and abandoned his place at the bar, pushing through the crowds to the exit. "Can you hear me now?"

Kell wondered what was so important that it couldn't wait until morning. "Sure," he replied.

"I thought I should tell you." There was a conspiratorial edge to Adam's voice.

"Tell me what?"

"Iannis Christidis is dead."

23

Kell walked several meters away from the bar, down the quiet street.

"Dead how?"

"His body was spotted in the water by a local fisherman. They found his clothes, his wallet, on a beach near his home. Alcohol in his bloodstream off the charts."

"Drowned, then."

"Looks that way. Looks like suicide."

Kell's instinct told him that Christidis had been killed on the orders of Jim Chater. Chater knew that Kell had got to him. He knew that Christidis had secrets to spill. The engineer who had worked on Wallinger's plane—had most probably tampered with it—needed to be taken out of the equation.

"He leave a note?"

"Not that I'm aware of."

Kell could hear the indistinct thump of the Bar Bleu music receding into the distance. A taxi drove past him, braked, then accelerated away when Kell turned his back to the road.

"Where are you?"

"At the embassy. I have a couple of good sources on Chios. One of them heard about Christidis on the island grapevine. Called me about half an hour ago."

"You need to fly . . ."

Haydock was ahead of him. "Already booked. I'm leaving Athens in about six hours. I'll get over there, ask around, find out the whole story. Can I call you at lunchtime?"

"Do that, yes. Get as much information about his state of mind as possible. Ask around the other airport engineers. Get into his house, his phones, get a drink with his friends. You'll need money." Kell knew that he was preaching to the converted. Adam was SIS-trained to the eyeballs and would have done all of these things as a matter of course. But Kell was thorough and, in some sense that he could not precisely articulate or understand, keen to pass on tips and expertise to a junior officer, to a younger version of himself. "If there's a suicide note, the police will have it. Other people will want to see it. You need to get there first. Get to the note before they do."

"Yes, sir." Adam sounded slightly daunted. "Who else is going to want to see it? You mean journalists?"

"I'm not worried about journalists. You can pay them. I'm worried about Cousins. Tread carefully around the Yanks."

Kell was distracted by something in his peripheral vision, someone coming down the street. He looked up and saw Rachel walking toward him, smoking a cigarette. He gestured toward her—an apologetic smile with a raised hand—and wished Haydock luck with his trip.

"There's something else, Tom."

"What?"

Rachel was now beside him, lovely in the pale cream light of the street. He gestured again, this time at the phone, as though the person calling him was wasting his time.

"Fragments of CCTV came back from the restaurant."

"Fragments."

"The man sitting with Mr. Wallinger. He has a beard."

Kell looked at Rachel. He did not want to mention her father by name. He angled the phone closer to his mouth so that he would not be overheard.

"We knew that, didn't we?"

"We did. The images are very poor. Indistinct."

"Has London seen them? Worked the pixels or whatever it is those guys do?"

Again Kell wondered if the bearded man in the Chios footage, sitting at the outdoor table with Wallinger, would turn out to be Jim Chater. Rachel had taken out her own phone and was checking the screen for messages.

"There's not much. London can't get anything out of it," Adam said. "Only this."

"What?"

"The table seems to be set for three."

"They're sure about that?"

Rachel looked up from her phone. Listening to everything.

"Three sets of knives, forks, napkins. Three wineglasses. A jacket on the back of a chair, Wallinger and the beard in the other two."

"Could have been beard's jacket."

"It's pink," Adam replied briskly.

"Well, you never know. Nice weather. The Mediterranean. Certain men feel confident wearing pastels."

Kell bounced his eyebrows at Rachel. *Two more minutes.* She indicated that there was no rush. Smiling at him as she did so, her lips reddened by lipstick. Kell felt the hum of the wine at dinner, the caipirinha, the inch and a half of vodka he had shot before leaving the hotel. Rachel's calves, raised on the wedge heels, were tanned and sinuous, the belt of her black dress corset-tight around her waist. She was not slim or willowy like so many of the girls in the bar. She had curves, an hourglass in jet black.

"Anything else on the table?"

Adam seemed to appreciate his attention to detail.

"Yes. Glad you mentioned that. I might have forgotten."

A Porsche with diplomatic plates growled past, a bespoke-suited Mastroianni at the wheel, an impossibly beautiful girl beside him. *Italian embassy,* Kell thought, and saw Rachel tracking the car with her eyes.

"Forgotten what?" he asked.

"There's a digital camera on the table in front of the jacket. Between the knife and fork. Silver, pocket-size. Might belong to whoever was sitting there."

"But we have no idea who that was? There are no other angles on the CCTV? Security cameras on the dock? Another bar or shop, farther along the promenade?"

"I'm still looking."

Sandor. Was Cecilia the owner of the pink jacket? But why would Paul have dealt his mistress into a meeting with Chater? Kell knew that he had to go to Croatia to speak to her. To find out who else had been at the table with Wallinger. Let Amelia cope with the molehunt for now; she was the only one with the power to control what did and did not make its way to the Cousins.

"Good luck," he told Adam, then pocketed the phone and crossed the street to talk to Rachel.

24

Sorry," Kell told her. "Work."

"That's all right. I wondered where you'd gone. Went outside for a cigarette and saw you talking."

"I was meant to be buying you a drink."

Rachel scrunched up her nose, shook her head like a shiver. "I've probably had too much already." Kell took out a packet of cigarettes and offered her one. This time Rachel lit her own. No need to touch his cupped hands. "What do you make of Ryan?" she asked.

"Seems nice enough. Good-looking fucker."

The response produced a cheeky smile. "*Isn't* he? I think he might be quite clever, too. I hardly spoke to him at the funeral."

Kell found himself saying: "There's no art to find the mind's construction in the face."

Rachel joke-choked on her cigarette and stared at him. "What does *that* mean, Shakespeare?"

"I'm just saying. He might be clever. He might be good-looking. But he might also be a wanker."

"Isn't that true of anybody?"

"Of course." They began walking back up the street toward the bar. "Not my kind of place," he said, in an attempt to change the subject.

"Mine neither." Rachel inhaled on the cigarette, touching the back of her neck. "The first place to be blown up in the event of a revolution."

She was exactly right. Bar Bleu had been wall-to-wall with that new international class—overeducated, overprivileged—who are dedicated solely to the accumulation of wealth and status and to the satisfaction of vast, insatiable appetites. That had been one of the noticeable things about Kleckner. The people at the party—intellectually incurious, devoid of self-doubt, somehow making a virtue of distilled greed and social ambition—had happily wallowed in the Eurotrash nirvana of the bar. Girls, coke, champagne, designer labels. It was all there, all on show, all for the taking. Yet Kell had sensed in Kleckner a reluctance fully to embrace such a lifestyle. Had he found himself part of a fast diplomatic and entrepreneurial expat set, swinging from bar to bar, from nightclub to nightclub, and simply decided to enjoy it for what it was? Or was there an operational agenda, an advantage to be gained from doing so?

"I ought to say good-bye to Ryan."

Rachel had decided on behalf of both of them that they would not be going back to the party. Five minutes later she had emerged from the bar with a smile on her face and a promise that their night was not yet over.

"So," she said, looping her hand through Kell's arm and guiding him down the street. She was holding his body close to hers. "Where are you taking me?"

Kell could smell her perfume, his arm enclosing her waist, the suppleness of her.

"Where do you feel like going?" he asked.

"How about your hotel?"

25

They were in a taxi, knees touching, knees not touching, Kell's heart racing like a gambler waiting on the turn of a card. Rachel looked across at him and said: "So who was on the phone earlier?"

This was more than a little icebreaking small talk in the backseat of a midnight cab. He realized that she had been biding her time before asking the question.

"A colleague in Athens."

"Something about Pappa?"

"Perhaps."

"What does *that* mean?" The same rush of anger that had scalded her cheeks, the same sudden hardening of the eyes as she read the card at the wake, suddenly passed across Rachel's lovely face and changed its character completely. She was distant from him, brittle and cold.

"Sorry, instinct," Kell said, scrambling for an excuse. "We're not supposed to talk about operational . . ."

"Yeah, yeah, yeah," she replied, staring out of the window as the taxi stopped at a set of lights. They were no more than fifty meters from the walls of the British consulate. "Fucking spies."

She was drunk. Perhaps stress and alcohol and grief played out inside her as rage. Kell took Rachel's hand. She allowed him to press his fingers against hers, but she did not respond to his touch. He would have preferred it if she had flinched and retracted her hand.

"It was someone at the embassy in Athens who's looking into the crash that killed your father."

She turned toward him, her dark eyes beginning to forgive him, perhaps realizing that she had overreacted.

"What's the person's name?"

"Adam."

"Adam what?"

"Haydock."

The taxi was coming to a halt beside the Hotel de Londres. It had started to rain. Kell hoped that Amelia or Elsa weren't nursing brandies in the bar or he'd have a lot of explaining to do at his ten o'clock.

"Did you make that up?"

Kell passed a ten-*lira* note to the driver. "You'll never know," he said.

Rachel did not laugh.

"Jesus, Rachel. His name is Adam Haydock. Okay? I didn't make it up."

She walked three paces ahead of him, clipping up the steps of the hotel. A man was selling roses in the rain. He offered one to Kell, as though it would help him to make amends with the pretty girl, but Kell ignored him and walked inside. Rachel was already in the lobby. Whatever chemistry had built up between them, whatever promises their bodies had made to each other on the street outside the bar, had evaporated. And yet Rachel was still in his hotel.

Kell watched her walk into the lounge. To his relief, it was empty. No sign of Amelia, nor of Elsa. Just a parrot in a cage, a picture of Ataturk on the wall. The bar at the far end of the room was closed, the lights dimmed.

"Just like Studio 54 in here." Rachel's voice was deadpan as she turned to face him. Her anger had subsided, she still looked bruised by Kell's evasiveness, but she was letting him back in.

"Your father had a meeting on Chios before he died." Kell knew that he had to be frank with her. "We're trying to find out who he was talking to. The identity of the man."

"Man?" she said.

"Yes. Man. Why?"

Rachel puffed out her cheeks and turned away from him, touching the tassels of a velvet-upholstered cushion.

"You don't need to finesse me, Tom," she said. "I know who my father was. I know what he was like. You don't have to protect me from him."

How to reply to such a remark? A person can invite you to be forthright and honest, but they will often resent you for that honesty as soon as it shows its face. What Rachel knew about her father's behavior with other women, the manner in which he had conducted himself as a husband, would affect every relationship she would make in the future. Kell was in possession of extraordinarily sensitive information about Paul Wallinger's private life: his relationship with Amelia Levene, his affair with Cecilia Sandor. He should not and could not divulge that information to his daughter.

"I know I don't," he said. "None of us is perfect, Rachel. Your father was a complicated man, but he loved you very much. You and Andrew meant the world to him."

It was a platitude, and Rachel treated it as such, allowing Kell's words to evaporate in the gloom of the deserted lounge like a half-heard announcement on a PA system.

"You don't know that he loved me. How can you know that?" Kell thought of Wallinger's office in Ankara, the photographs only of Andrew, and said nothing. "He was with his mistress."

Though he was not surprised, Kell still felt unnerved. "Yes," he replied, because there was no point in denying that.

"Does everybody know? Everyone at MI6?"

"Would it matter if they did?"

"It would matter to Mum. She feels humiliated. She's so ashamed, you know?"

"And you want to protect her."

Rachel nodded. Her rage and fury were gone. She was composed and thoughtful, breathtakingly beautiful in the extinguished light of the room.

"Amelia knows that your father was staying with a woman. Adam Haydock knows about it. Very few other people. The investigation into his death is being handled by a small team. Amelia put me in charge of it."

Rachel's eyes narrowed slightly. "Why does there need to be an investigation?"

Kell risked her wrath a second time.

"Rachel, I don't want to have to say this to you. Believe me. I would much prefer to be allowed to tell you everything that's going on. But I would lose my job if I told you why we are investigating the crash. Does that make sense?"

"Yes, it makes sense," she said quietly, and perhaps there was a memory of the day, ten years earlier, when her father had finally sat Andrew and Rachel down and told them that Daddy wasn't really a diplomat. Daddy was an officer with the Secret Intelligence Service. A spy. Paul, perhaps with Josephine at his side, proudly holding her husband's hand, would have asked for his children's absolute discretion, pointing out the legal and security requirements for total secrecy. The privilege of privileged information. Rachel knew the rules.

"Thanks for understanding." Kell put his hand on her shoulder, an awkward, hapless rekindling of touch. Behind him, the parrot in the lounge was woken from a slumber and squawked loudly, saying something in Turkish that broke the silence. Rachel looked across at the cage, shrugged, and produced a brittle laugh.

"How do we get a drink?" she said, walking out into the lobby and looking around for a member of staff. Kell assumed that the duty manager was making his rounds of the hotel.

"I think they're closed for the night," he replied.

"A statement of the obvious, Thomas Kell." His physical desire for her was once again as intense as it had been on the street, the memory of her waist, the smell of her perfume.

"I've got a bottle of vodka in my room," he said. He didn't want to spend an hour in the lobby of the hotel dancing around the subject. He wanted Rachel in his bed. He wanted either to restore the charge between them or for Rachel to go home to the *yali*.

"Have you now?" she said, all of the glint and mischief returning to her face.

"I have. Only got one glass, though."

"Only one glass? That's a shame."

And with that, Rachel turned around, leaned over the bar, plucked a highball from below the counter, straightened up, and breezed past him, holding the glass aloft like a trophy.

"Now you have two."

There was a moment, as soon as they were in the room, when Rachel walked away from Kell, toward the window, as though building up her courage. He waited for her, for the right moment. When she turned to look at him, he moved toward her and took her face in his hands and kissed her for the first time. And soon they were tearing at each other, desire and pleasure flooding through Kell like an opiate. Every doubt and moment of loneliness and pain he had felt in the past months and years were leaving him. For so long, in the aftermath of his marriage, he had felt a kind of deadness at the center of himself, his emotional existence completely stalled, incapable of finding other women attractive, and increasingly convinced that whatever passion and carnality he had once possessed had been extinguished by his divorce, by the gradual realization that more than half of his life was now done and visible only in the rearview mirror of regret and bad choices. Kell had no children to show for himself, no legacy save for the fiasco of Witness X. That was to be his monument. And yet, in the space of a few hours, he had met a woman who had somehow swept away his fury and his impotence as decisively as she had flung aside the flowers at the funeral, igniting something within Kell which felt like *life* again.

"I thought you only invited me up here because you wanted a drink?" she said, curling into the nook of his neck and shoulder an hour later. Kell was breathing in the smell of her skin, wanting her again.

"Very rude of me," he said.

"Something about vodka."

The bottle and the glass were where he had left them before leaving to meet her, the chaperone taking a shot for his nerves. Kell reached for the bottle and, with an extended, unsteady hand, poured six inches into the glass.

"Sorry. Slightly overdid it," he said, encouraging Rachel to sit up and take a drink.

"Jesus! Who do you think I am? Amy Winehouse?"

He looked at her arms and her breasts, at the very slight swell of her belly, nothing perfect or airbrushed about her body, just the raw femininity of her, smells of sex and perfume and alcohol mingling in the night. For a time they sat up in silence, sharing the vodka, touching thighs and stomachs and hands, until Rachel eventually rose from the bed and walked into the bathroom, absolutely devoid of self-consciousness or vanity in every movement of her body. Of all things, Kell wanted to check the messages on his phone and was about to scramble around on the floor looking for his trousers when he told himself to relax, to get back into bed and to forget about Iannis Christidis and Ryan Kleckner for five minutes and just to enjoy himself. How many times did a man get to do this in his life? Candor and tenderness and the soul connection of an exquisite woman? He heard the toilet flushing next door, the whine of Rachel running a rusty tap, the mundane and commonplace sounds made by couples in the moments following intense intimacy. He had forgotten all about them.

The bathroom door swung open. Rachel came out wearing a towel. She smiled at Kell and picked up their clothes from the floor, throwing them together in a cluttered pile on the ottoman beneath the window.

"So you were at the funeral?" she said. "Funny I didn't notice you."

"Insulting, even," Kell replied. "I noticed *you*."

"You did? Well I suppose of course you did . . ." They were both aware of the sadness at the edge of what had begun as a playful exchange.

"I saw you reading a note on a bunch of flowers. I saw you throw the flowers at the wall."

Rachel had been in the process of removing the towel and climbing back into bed. She tightened it around her and stared at Kell, as though he had glimpsed something far more private than the naked body momentarily exposed to him.

"You *saw* that?"

He nodded. He reached for her and unhooked the towel, making space in which she could lie down beside him. Then, without thinking, Kell lied.

"What was that about? Why did you throw the flowers away?"

Rachel turned over onto her stomach, pulling a loose white sheet over her back. He helped her, freeing the sheet as it caught on her foot. He could see the marks on her skin where he had scratched and bitten her. Rachel was staring down at the mattress, and for a long time said nothing. Eventually she moved off the bed and walked across the room toward the pile of clothes. From beneath her crumpled black dress she retrieved her handbag. She popped the catch on the bag, reached inside, and removed a crumpled blue envelope, which she passed to him. The envelope had been stamped in France and was addressed to Cecilia Sandor. The handwriting belonged to Paul Wallinger.

"What is this?" Kell asked.

But he already knew.

26

ead it," said Rachel.

Hotel Le Grand Coeur et Spa
Chemin du Grand Coeur
73550 Meribel
Savoie
France

December 28th

My darling Cecilia,

As promised, a letter to you on the Grand Coeur stationery, because I know how you love a nice hotel—and hate and distrust e-mail!

I'm sitting in the bar of the hotel, pretending to work, but only thinking about you and how much I miss you and wishing it was you that was here, just the two of us, skiing and talking and making love and walking in these glorious mountains.

Kell felt an odd surge of sympathy for Wallinger, the adulterer who fancied himself in love and whose shabby secret had been exposed. At the same time, he was horrified that Rachel had come into possession of the letter. He could not imagine what effect the contents would have had on her.

I wonder where you are now, at this moment? What you're doing? Are you finding enough to do with the restaurant closed? Cecilia, I want to tell you that there is not five minutes that go by when I am not thinking of you. I was skiing with Andrew this afternoon and you were in my head and in my heart all the time, I felt filled up by your love and by the love that I feel for you. All my married life—all my adult life, in fact—I feel that I have been searching for you, for a woman with whom I feel absolutely free to be who I am, to say what I want to say, to act without reprimand or guilt or falsity of any kind. At forty-six years old! It's ridiculous.

The words "adult" and "who I am" were underlined twice, as though Wallinger had finally abandoned any pretense at gravitas and was writing in the mode of an adolescent.

Sometimes I feel like I've wasted so much of my life in lies and in living in a way that was profoundly unhealthy, not just for me, but for my family and even for friends that I have let down and betrayed with this double life of the heart and the mind that I have been living for too long now. I want it all to stop. I just want to be with you and to draw a line under everything, to stop working in this bloody job and to commit myself to you and to our love. I have met the woman I want to spend the rest of my life with. I want us to build something together.

Rachel was standing at the window, the towel again wrapped around her body, looking out onto the city through a tiny gap in the shutters. Kell did not know what to make of the letter. If Paul had been deeply in love with Cecilia, why had he kept a photograph of Amelia in a book beside his bed? Had he been giving serious consideration to quitting, or was that the philanderer's way of keeping a mistress keen and tenter-hooked? And who were the "friends" he was referring to? Amelia, certainly. But who else had Paul trampled on? Had there been other adulteries with Service wives?

Cecilia, I am craving you. I cannot stop thinking about you. I think about the summer, how you left the keys for me outside your house. I let myself in and you were waiting for me. I don't think I had ever seen you looking so beautiful as you did that day. Your skin was tanned, your mouth waiting for me. I wanted to take my time with you. I was so desperate for you because we'd been talking all week and I was craving you. I remember what you tasted like—suntan lotion and saltwater and the sweetness of you. I remember you coming, the ecstasy of it, and I was glad that I had given you that, because every second I was with you was a paradise.

Kell put the letter down. He had read enough. It felt as though this was now all that he would remember of Paul. He would no longer be a spy or a friend or a father; he would just be the man who had lost himself to a mistress in an oblivion of infatuated sex. To Kell's relief, Rachel turned around and made a joke.

"I've seen her photograph. She looks like a fucking Na'vi."

"What's a Na'vi?" Kell asked. He wanted to match her arch mood.

"You know. *Avatar.* Six-foot-six blue gimp from another planet. She's so fucking tall she looks like a kind of plant. Fake tits, too."

Kell folded the letter and placed it on the table beside the bed.

"You know I can remember the afternoon when he wrote that," she said. "He told me he had a report to write. He couldn't go into Meribel with me. I was looking forward to spending time with him, because he'd been skiing with Mum and Andrew in the morning." Kell doubted this. He felt that Rachel was lying to herself in order to pile further blame onto her father. "But, no, work had to come first. The whole week I really thought he and Mum were finally happy. She did too. They'd had problems in the past, you know?" Kell nodded. "I remember them kissing and holding hands as they walked down the street. Something as simple as that. Something old-fashioned between a husband and wife." Rachel shook her head and smiled. "But of course my father was the sort of person who could act like the family man with his wife and his son and his daughter, then write that shit in the afternoon to a Hungarian whore half his fucking age."

"Rachel . . ."

"It's okay. I'm not angry. I sound angrier than I am. Believe me, I've had enough time to get to know who my father was. It's just upsetting that that week now means nothing, because he was thinking about fucking the Na'avi all the time. Composing this shit in his head. Getting it all down in the bar while he was pretending to write a report on spies. I found lots more letters. Maybe ten of them. That's the only one from him though. You notice the neat, controlled handwriting—no mistakes, no crossings out? Typical controlling Pappa. The other letters are all from the Na'avi. She can hardly spell, ignorant cow."

"So the card at your father's funeral. The flowers. They were from her? She was sending him a private message, one that your mother wouldn't be able to understand, but you recognized her handwriting?"

"Yes."

For some time they said nothing. Kell eventually went to the bathroom. When he came back into the room, Rachel was still standing by the window.

"Come back to bed," he said.

She did so, wordlessly, and curled into him again. He knew that there would be no more talk. Kell set an alarm for eight, and closed his eyes, his hand stroking Rachel's back as she drifted off to sleep. He was listening to her breathe when she whispered: "You are lovely."

He kissed her forehead.

"You are too," he replied, wondering how long it had been since he had said those words, how long it had been since he had heard them.

27

It was always the same afterward. Walking back down the same quiet street, catching the eyes of strangers. How quickly his exhilaration changed to shame. The men in the teahouses, the women scrubbing flagstones on a front porch—all of them watching him. All of them seeming to know exactly what he had done.

Douglas Tremayne boarded the tram. It was crowded. He felt himself hemmed in against other bodies, other men. He had washed afterward and his skin felt soft and feminine. He was aware that he smelled of soap, his hair still damp where it met the collar of his shirt. People staring at him. Strangers. Turks. The Englishman in his brown brogues and burgundy corduroy trousers. A tweed jacket in Istanbul. Tremayne liked to dress smartly but he always felt that the passengers on the tram were judging him.

He replayed the night's events in his mind. The same old patterns. The exchanges were beginning to blend into one another. Sometimes he would forget where he had been, what had occurred, even in which city it had happened. He knew places all over Turkey.

There was always that sense beforehand of losing control, of his better self rendered powerless. It was just a thing that he was obliged to do, and until he did it, there could be no calm and equanimity in his system. He would know no peace of mind. Tremayne thought of it as an addiction and treated it as such, though he had never told a soul, never sought help, never succumbed to a confession.

Where did these impules come from? Why had he turned out this way? Why did he always make the same rotten decisions?

The tram stopped. In the distance, a minaret. More passengers crowding him up. More strangers. The stink of morning sweat and the smell of his own perfumed skin. A mingling. Tremayne touched the back of his neck, felt the dampness of his hair, wondered if this time he had finally been caught. Watched. Photographed. Filmed.

Perhaps it was what he wanted. A release from this secret life. A release from all the guilt. The guilt and the shame.

28

Kell slept for no more than an hour. At dawn, he became aware of Rachel creeping out of bed and gathering up her clothes from the ottoman. His eyes closed, his head turned toward the window, he heard her going into the bathroom, emerging a few minutes later wearing the hourglass black dress and the wedge heels of the previous evening. She approached the bed and leaned over to kiss him.

"Walk of shame," she whispered. "Go back to sleep."

"You should stay."

"No. Got to go home."

They kissed again, and he held her close to him, but the heat between them had gone. She stood up, smoothed down the dress, waved at him with rippling fingers, and walked out of the room.

Kell immediately sat up. Istanbul was muffled by the shuttered windows, by curtains that closed out the dawn light, but he could still hear the city awakening, traffic and the lone cry of the muezzin. Rachel would easily find a taxi outside the Londres and, within half an hour, be back at home, creeping upstairs in the *yali,* past the sleeping Josephine, to snooze for the rest of the morning. He only hoped that she would not encounter Amelia downstairs, back from a dawn run or en route to an early breakfast. Walk of shame indeed.

He opened the curtains and the shutters, went to the bathroom and took a shower, then ordered breakfast to his room. Just after six thirty, too soon for the coffee and eggs to have been prepared, there was a knock at the door. Rachel? Had she forgotten something?

Wearing just a towel around his waist, Kell opened the door.

"Thomas! I am a married woman now. Cover yourself!"

It was Elsa, grinning.

"Thanks for the warning," he said. "What are you doing up so early?"

"This," she said, thrusting a file in his direction. "I have been working on it since I saw you. It is a long night. Amelia ask me to make some background on Cecilia Sandor. This is what I find out. It is all so very sad, Tom. How I hate wasted love."

29

The file was a bible of grief. E-mails from Cecilia to her closest friend in Budapest, mourning the loss of Paul. Telephone calls to a doctor in Dubrovnik, whom Elsa had identified as a psychiatrist specializing in "addiction and bereavement." Cecilia had visited Internet sites about death and heartbreak and signed into an English-language chat forum in which she had discussed her feelings of loss with total strangers around the world. She had joined a yoga class on Lopud, was having massages every forty-eight hours, therapy three times a week. She had bought self-help books from Amazon, spent £2,700 on a two-week trip to the Maldives. She had read widely on plane crashes—specifically the many newspaper reports and web articles relating to Wallinger's accident—and closed her restaurant for ten days as soon as she had heard about his death. To Kell's astonishment, he saw that Sandor had also made an anonymous donation of a thousand pounds to the SIS Widows' Fund.

Further checks of her e-mail had shown that Wallinger's mistress had flown by easyJet from Dubrovnik to Gatwick the day before the funeral and had reserved a seat on the same train that Kell and Amelia had taken from Euston. Kell realized that they had been seated no more than a carriage apart. Cecilia had been booked onto a return London train in midafternoon, a flight back to Dubrovnik the following day. She had most probably bought the flowers in Preston, driven direct to the farmhouse, left the bouquet and card in the barn, then returned to the station. One of the e-mails sent to her friend in Budapest—badly translated by Internet software—showed that Cecilia had not attended the funeral service itself.

Kell read the file over breakfast. At nine o'clock he rang Elsa in her room, congratulated her on a job well done, and asked if there had been any specific references, in any of the research, to Jim Chater or Ryan Kleckner.

"No," she said, her voice falling away. Perhaps she felt as though she had let Kell down. "I do not think so, Tom. I can check this."

"Don't worry," Kell told her. She had been up all night and sounded weary. "Get some rest. You deserve it."

The British consulate was a glorious, humbling remnant of Empire, a three-story nineteenth-century neoclassical palace in the heart of Beyoglu, no more than a hundred meters from Kell's hotel. An attack by suicide bombers a decade earlier had resulted in the death of the British consul-general and more than twenty others. Kell could remember exactly where he was—eating lunch with Claire on a glorious November afternoon in London—when he had heard about the attack on the BBC.

"All because of bloody Bush," Claire had said, pointing at images of the president, who had been in town for talks at 10 Downing Street. Kell had ducked the argument, as he always did with Claire when it came to cause and effect on terror. "If Blair had just kept us out of Iraq," she said, "none of this stuff would be *happening.*"

Amelia beat him to the meeting by an hour. Kell walked into the Station just before ten to be informed by "C" that she had been "up since six" and was "keen to get down to business."

"You look knackered," she said as she spun the locks, clockwise, counterclockwise, on the secure speech room. An alarm sounded as Kell lifted the lever and pulled on the deadweight of the door. The combination of the physical effort involved in this and the screech of the alarm served only to intensify his hangover. He felt as though he had left the better part of his brain comatose on a pillow in the Hotel Londres.

"Nice and warm in here," Amelia quipped, reacting to the intense cold of the air-conditioning. It was a feature of secure speech rooms around the world: it was not unknown for officers to attend meetings wearing scarves and overcoats.

Amelia sat at one end of a conference table set with chairs for eight; Kell took a seat halfway down, having sealed the doors behind him. He was carrying a double espresso from an automated coffee machine on the ground floor, his third of the morning.

"How was the party?" Amelia asked as she lifted several files and printouts from a black leather briefcase, piling them on the table in front of her.

"Fun," Kell replied. "Eurotrash bar below Galata. Expats and rich Turks. Fun."

"And Rachel?"

"What about her?"

"Was she fun too?"

Up since six. Kell felt the forensic, all-seeing penetration of the Levene gaze. Had Amelia spotted Rachel leaving the hotel? It was pointless lying to her; she knew that he was attracted to Rachel. Kell felt like a passenger at an airport passing through a state-of-the-art X-ray machine; every bone and muscle of his guilt glowing like a bomb.

"She's great," he said. "An old soul. Clever. Funny. The chaperone had a good time."

Amelia nodded, seeming to accept this. "Is she interested in ABACUS?"

Kell frowned. "*ABACUS?*"

"I didn't tell you?" Amelia shuffled around in the files, a sudden visual reminder of the plate-spinning chaos into which the new job had thrust her. "Cryptonym for Kleckner."

"Right," Kell said, watching her as his head throbbed.

"So?"

Kell would enjoy answering the question. Rachel certainly hadn't been interested enough in Ryan Kleckner to stay at his party for more than an hour. She had then come back to Kell's hotel room and released herself to him with a passion and a finesse that had astonished him. All of this suggested that, at least for the time being, Rachel Wallinger was more interested in Thomas Kell.

"Hard to say," he replied, distracted by a specific visual memory of Rachel's spine as she moved beneath him, the way the pale bedroom light had cast shadows in the dips and hollows of her back. He downed the last dregs of the espresso. "She flirted with him a little bit. Kleckner certainly looked fond of her."

"Fond?" Amelia was frowning. "Do the Cousins *do* fond? ABACUS doesn't strike me as the type."

"What do we know about him?" Kell hoped to draw Amelia away from Rachel with the question. Retrieving a narrow file from the pile of papers, she duly obliged, giving him full spectrum background on Kleckner's career (seven years in the CIA, three of them in Madrid, two of them in Turkey); his education (high school in Missouri—valedictorian—followed by SFS at Georgetown); his family history (parents divorced when Kleckner was seven, the father never to be seen again). There was—as Kell had suspected—a decent helping of religious fervor in the Kleckner lineage (the adored mother was an energetic Catholic schoolteacher who ran her own prayer group), allied to good, old-fashioned American patriotism (Kleckner had an older brother who had served two tours in Iraq, a younger sister who had returned to her day job as an ER doctor in Belleville having volunteered for a six-month secondment to Bagram in 2008). At twenty-two, Kleckner had been a star on the Georgetown rowing squad, paying his way through college by working nights as a hospital porter. After a short stint as an unpaid intern for a Republican congressman in St. Louis, he had applied for a position with the Central Intelligence Agency.

"Self-starter. Overachiever," said Kell. "Possible loner?"

"Nothing wrong with that," Amelia replied, rapping her fingers on Kleckner's résumé. "I would have thought Langley was pleased to have him."

"Would you give him a job?" Kell was suddenly nauseous with hunger, the eggs and white bread of the Londres breakfast now just acid in his gut. Amelia produced an official State Department photograph of Kleckner and flashed Kell one of the smiles she reserved for boys.

"He is *awfully* handsome," she said, spinning the picture along the table toward Kell. He stared at the photograph. Kleckner looked as effortlessly seductive as a matinee idol. "IQ in the high hundreds," she said. "Eyes like Gregory Peck. *Pecs* like Gregory Peck, most probably. Of *course* I'd give him a job."

"Sexist," Kell replied. Through the small window in the door of the secure speech room he spotted a bowl of bananas and felt like a dying man who has glimpsed a source of fresh water in the Nefud desert. "So we soak him?" he asked, knowing that it would be a long time before he could get outside to eat something. Too many alarms. Too many locks. Too much conversation.

"Oh, we soak him," Amelia replied. "By this time next week we'll know more about young Mr. Kleckner than he knows about himself."

She wasn't exaggerating. For the next half hour Amelia Levene was at her very best: thorough, imaginative, ruthless. She wasn't just "C," the Whitehall Dame-in-waiting. Her passion seemed to have returned, her love of the game. If she was worried that her legacy would be another Philby or Blake, a traitor to destroy the transatlantic relationship, she did not show it. Kell glimpsed some of the restless energy and enthusiasm that had marked Amelia out in her late thirties and forties. She was as focused and as forensic as he had seen her in many years. This was the woman Paul Wallinger had fallen in love with. The best SIS officer—male or female—of her generation.

It transpired that many of her ideas for the blanket coverage of Ryan Kleckner were already in place. A ten-man team, seconded from the Security Service, had put foot surveillance on ABACUS on half a dozen occasions. They were currently on standby in Istanbul, ready to go full-time as soon as Kell gave the word. Amelia had instructed Elsa to cut out the Wi-Fi at Kleckner's residence, thereby allowing a local asset Turk Telekom engineer to fit microphones in the kitchen, bathroom, bedroom, and living room of his apartment. The roof of Kleckner's car—a Honda Accord—had been "painted" in the small hours of Friday morning by a team from the Station while it was parked on the street. The vehicle was now visible to satellites should Kleckner decide to go AWOL, although, as Kell pointed out, those satellites were mostly American-controlled, and therefore functionally useless (Amelia conceded the point with a grunt of disdain). Cameras were also being planted in any café, hotel, or restaurant where ABACUS had shown a "pattern." It was known that he frequented a gym four blocks from his home and liked to visit a small teahouse off Istiklal whenever he found himself in Beyoglu. ("There's a waitress there," Amelia said. "He likes her.") Both locations would have near-total visual coverage. At least once a month, Kleckner could be found attending Mass at the Church of St. Antony of Padua, the largest Catholic cathedral in Turkey. Catherine West, wife of a declared SIS officer whom Amelia had known for many years, had been given instructions to attend the same Mass and to report on Kleckner's behavior and appearance, providing a description of anyone who came into contact with him. Information could very easily be passed between members of the congregation, most obviously by anyone sitting next to Kleckner in a pew. When Kell asked about them, Amelia confirmed that similar operations were already under way against Douglas Tremayne and Mary Begg. Tony Landau was also being watched in the United States.

"And then there's Iannis Christidis," she said.

"He's not going to be much use to us."

"I'm aware of that." Amelia looked down the table and frowned. "What are your thoughts?"

It sounded like a test. Kell summoned as much intellectual energy as his jaded state would allow.

"I think we should wait for Adam to report," he replied, discovering some of his old talent for circumspection. "He's only just arrived on Chios. Let's give him a chance to talk to the police, to the airport people, to Christidis's friends and family."

"You think that will change your mind about things?"

Amelia was still staring down at the papers in front of her. He knew that she would brook no half truths or evasions.

"Change my mind about what?"

She knew him so well. Kell sensed what was coming.

"I think you believe the Americans got to him." Amelia stood up, ostensibly to stretch her legs in the cramped, chill confines of the room, but also perhaps to make a physical point to Kell by standing over him. "That Jim Chater was the bearded man on Chios, that Paul made the mistake of telling him your theory about the mole, and that Chater had him killed as a result."

Hearing the theory spoken aloud made it sound, for the first time, slightly absurd. But Amelia was entirely correct. She had articulated precisely what Kell believed had happened.

"I think that's the most likely scenario, yes," he conceded. "Given the way Chater reacted in Ankara."

Amelia walked around the table and tapped the lever on the sealed door. Through the glass Kell saw Douglas Tremayne walking into the Station. In town from Ankara, looking like an army officer on a day off at the races: polished brogues, a tweed jacket, even burgundy trousers.

"I would merely advise you to keep your mind open."

There was no tone of condescension in Amelia's voice as she sat down, not even a warning. Just a friend's wise counsel. Play the pieces on the board, not the opponent.

"I hear what you're saying," Kell replied.

"Good." Amelia picked up a file. Kell recognized the cover. It was the Sandor report. She began to tap it on the table, as though beating out the rhythm to a song. "It's just that I don't entirely buy this."

"Elsa's report?"

"No. I think that's first rate. As far as it goes." She opened a random page of the report and ran her finger along the text. "I just don't buy the trail of breadcrumbs. It's too perfect." Amelia began to detail Cecilia's behavior as a list of bullet points. "The book from Amazon. The yoga. The massages. If you were going to create a legend for a girl who had lost the love of her life, would you do it any differently than this?"

Kell felt the room invert. If what Amelia was suggesting was true, Wallinger had been played. "I guess not," he replied, without conceding her point. It seemed too far-fetched. "What are you suggesting? That it's a fiction?"

"I'm just suggesting that you need to keep your mind open. That we need to look into it. Cecilia Sandor may very well have been a former Hungarian intelligence officer who opened a restaurant in Lopud and just happened to fall in love with Paul Wallinger. She may very well be so heartbroken that she's taking herself off to therapy three times a week and pouring out her heart on chat forums. But she might equally have been an SVR honey trap tasked with recruiting H/Ankara."

For several seconds Kell was rendered speechless, his sleep-deprived mind trying to work through the myriad implications of what Amelia was suggesting.

"You still think Paul might have been the mole?"

Amelia merely shrugged, as though Kell had asked after nothing more significant than the state of the weather.

"I would be very surprised, of course," she replied quietly.

"So Sandor found a line into his telegrams, his e-mails? Decrypted his laptop, duplicated his phone? Surely he wouldn't have been that stupid?"

"Pretty girls do funny things to middle-aged men, even the *non*stupid ones," Amelia replied curtly. Kell could not tell if this was a generalized statement of despair at male behavior, or a specific warning to steer clear of Rachel. "All I'm asking is that we consider all possibilities. We are still no closer to identifying the source of the leaks. Meanwhile, the Office is still running on half power, unable to do meaningful business with the Americans or to make significant progress on dozens of operations in the region. You know that."

"Of course I know that."

Kell took a moment to reflect as Amelia produced a bottle of mineral water from her briefcase and drank from it. Would it ease her suffering to know that Paul had fallen for a false god, for a love that did not exist? Would Amelia have preferred it that way? Or was she simply looking to avenge Sandor for stealing the heart of the man she had loved? The hunt for the mole and the hunt for the truth about Wallinger's death seemed to be bound together in her heart.

"You should go to Lopud," she said, as if to confirm this. "Take a look at her."

"You're happy for me to leave Kleckner to the team for a few days?"

"More than happy. We've got him well covered."

"Then of course. I'll go to Lopud."

"It's a holiday island," Amelia told him, as though Kell was unaware of this. "An hour from Dubrovnik by ferry. One big hotel at the end of town, a necklace of restaurants around the bay. You could fly in for seventy-two hours, play the businessman on a weekend break. Pop in for dinner at Sandor's restaurant. Bump into her if she goes for a swim. Let's see if Cecilia is who she says she is. Let's run the rule over the poor, grieving girlfriend."

30

Traveling on a French-Canadian passport under the name "Eric Cauques," Sebastien Gachon took a scheduled flight to Zagreb in the early hours of April 11. In the Croatian capital, he hired an Audi A4, fixed his iPod into the music dock, and listened to an audiobook recording of the novel *Dead Souls* as he drove—within the speed limit at all times—southeast along the motorway to the coastal city of Zadar.

As arranged, a second vehicle was waiting for Gachon in the car park of his hotel. In the recess beneath the spare wheel, he found the knife and a weapon with sufficient ammunition. That night, he ate well in an Italian restaurant, went to a bar to find a girl, paid her six hundred euros to spend the night in his room, but asked her to leave at three o'clock in the morning after she had satisfied him and he was ready to sleep. Gachon arranged for a taxi to come to the hotel to collect the girl. They exchanged telephone numbers, though he gave her a cell phone which would cease to function within forty-eight hours. Her working name was "Elena." She told him that she was from a small town to the west of Chisinau in Moldova.

The following morning, Gachon drove along the coast road toward

Dubrovnik. Due to an accident near Split, there was heavy traffic and he was two hours behind schedule by the time he arrived at his hotel. Using a public phone box in the old town, he obtained final confirmation of the target's position from his controller and received the go-ahead for the operation. To Gachon's frustration, he was instructed to wait in Dubrovnik for an extra twenty-four hours and to take the ferry to Lopud no earlier than Saturday morning. The other elements of the plan were to be observed as arranged. The water taxi would still be waiting to take him off the island at the jetty of the Lafodia Hotel at 2330 hours.

No explanation was given for the delay.

31

Kell didn't bother traveling to Lopud under alias. If Cecilia Sandor was a Russian asset, a freelancer in the pay of the Iranians, the Chinese, or the Mossad, any false identity he attempted to use on the island would be ripped apart in a matter of minutes. As soon as Sandor became suspicious of Kell, she would trace him to his hotel, have his legend run through a database, and conclude that he was hostile. Pretending to a Greek real estate agent that he was an insurance investigator from Edinburgh was one thing; posing as Chris Hardwick to a former Hungarian intelligence officer with possible links to the SVR quite another.

For the same reason, he didn't suggest taking Elsa along for cover, even if Amelia could have spared her. Yes, a couple always drew less attention than a single man, in almost any environment, but Kell wanted to leave his options open. Having a "girlfriend" in tow might limit his access to Sandor. If she was as innocent as she appeared, Kell could introduce himself at the restaurant as a friend and colleague of Paul's and try to ascertain what had happened on Chios in the days leading up to the crash. He was also—if he was honest with himself—keen to avoid being trapped in quasi-romantic cover with Elsa. Kell was troubled by his desire to get back to Istanbul, and to Rachel, as soon as the operation would allow.

London had booked him into the Lafodia, the large hotel that Amelia had described at the southwestern edge of Lopud Town. There were two separate groups attending conferences at the hotel, as well as a number of holidaying families; Kell was grateful for the natural cover of crowds as he wandered back and forth from the beach or strolled along the pedestrianized path that curled around the bay in a half-mile crescent.

Sandor's restaurant—Centonove—was located some distance from the hotel, inside a small converted house a few meters from the shoreline. There were half a dozen tables positioned on a terrace overlooking the bay, several more inside the restaurant itself. No vehicles were permitted on the island, so the necklace of bars and restaurants along the bay were undisturbed by passing traffic.

On his first full day on Lopud, a Saturday, Kell passed Centonove perhaps seven or eight times without setting eyes on Sandor. GCHQ were tracking her phone and laptop but had failed to inform him that Cecilia was spending most of the day in Dubrovnik "visiting a friend for lunch and then meeting a decorator in the afternoon." When it transpired that Sandor was scheduled to work the Sunday evening shift at the restaurant, Kell booked a table for eight o'clock and spent the rest of the day at the Lafodia, reading a novel, swimming in the sea, and e-mailing Rachel. He was not permitted to tell her that he was on Lopud, nor would he have wanted to, for obvious personal reasons. Nevertheless, it was a source of agitation to Kell that he was obliged to lie to her, to give the impression that he was "in Germany on business." It was like a reminder of the many years he had spent with Claire, unable to tell her where he was going, who he was meeting, the nature of the covert business he was conducting on behalf of the secret state. Furthermore, he sensed that Rachel *knew* he was deceiving her and that any relationship that might develop between the two of them would be compromised as a result.

Kell woke late on Sunday morning with the idea of walking to a ruined fort above the bay and carrying out basic distance surveillance on Sandor's apartment, which was located directly above Centonove. Rachel had sent an e-mail overnight, complaining that she had been to "an amazingly boring party filled with amazingly boring people" at a nightclub on the Bosporus.

> Things are very quiet and dull here without you, Mr Kell. When are you coming back from Berlin? xxx

The route to the fort began in the back streets of Lopud town and quickly wove uphill along a rocky path that meandered through a forest of pine and cypress. From the bay, Kell had spotted what appeared to be an abandoned shepherd's hut halfway up the hill. Leaving the path and picking his way through thick undergrowth, he located the hut and—having ensured that he was concealed from view—trained a set of binoculars across the water at Centonove. There was no sign of Sandor, only the bald middle-aged waiter whom Kell had passed on three occasions, as well as a smattering of tourists eating lunch on the terrace. Cheltenham had triangulated Sandor's cell phone to the building, so Kell assumed that she was upstairs in her apartment. The shutters were closed and the veranda outside her kitchen, on the southern side of the building, deserted.

He swept the binoculars along the bay, left into town, right toward the Lafodia. It was almost midday and the heat was intensifying. Kell could see children splashing in the shallows, tourists in rented kayaks embarking on trips around the island, the ferry from Dubrovnik slowing on approach to the terminal. The normal buzz and drift of island life. He would like to bring Rachel here. Just a few nights together, a chance to sleep late, to catch some sun, eat good food. Instead Kell knew that it would be at least two months, perhaps three, before he was done with Kleckner and free to leave Istanbul, and only then for a short break before returning to Ankara. In that time, who knew what would happen to Rachel? Chances are she would soon head back to London and he would never see her again.

He waited another five minutes in the shade of the hut. Still no sign of Cecilia. Standing up and shouldering the binoculars, Kell returned to the path, removing his shirt and continuing uphill toward the fort. Within ten minutes he had emerged from the forest to find himself among the ruins at the summit of an arid, rocky outcrop. He rested against a wall and tried to recover his breath, sipping from a bottle of water and wiping the sweat from his face. Behind him, to the southeast, Dubrovnik glittered in the midday sun. To the north, Kell could make out the tiny hulls of motorboats and yachts crisscrossing the strait. He checked his phone for messages, but there was nothing from Elsa, nothing from Rachel, nothing from London. He took several pictures of the ruins, then began the descent, passing two elderly British tourists as he tracked back through the forest. Halfway down, he again dropped off the path, clambered through the undergrowth, and returned to the cover of the shepherd's hut.

This time, Kell sat with his back to a shattered wooden door. The sun was at its zenith and he was aware of the danger of light reflecting off the surface of the binoculars as, once again, he trained them on Centonove. The door began to itch against the small of his back and he put his shirt on, smacking at his neck to kill an insect that had settled on his wet skin. He picked up the binoculars and traced along the bay, focusing on the cluster of tables outside the restaurant.

And there she was. Cecilia Sandor. Emerging from the ground-floor entrance and making her way across the path to the terrace. The binoculars were powerful enough for Kell to make out the precise features of her face. He was surprised by what he saw. She was not a naturally beautiful woman; indeed, it looked as though Cecilia had used fillers extensively beneath her eyes and on her mouth. Her upper lip had the absurd and unmistakable swell of collagen, her vast breasts out of all proportion to an otherwise reedy frame. Seeing how tall she was, Kell thought instantly of Rachel's nickname—the Na'vi—and grinned as a bead of sweat dripped down his back. Behind him, perhaps fifty meters away, he heard a group of three or four people walking past on the path. One of them was whistling a chunk of Tchaikovsky—either *Swan Lake* or *The Nutcracker,* Kell never knew the difference—and the melody lodged in his mind as he continued to watch the terrace.

Cecilia emerged from the restaurant carrying a bottle of water. She placed the bottle in front of an elderly couple, then spoke to a man of about thirty-five who was wearing sunglasses and a red polo shirt. The man was seated alone at the table farthest from the entrance. He had finished eating; there was an espresso cup on the table in front of him, and he was smoking a cigarette. Cecilia picked up what appeared to be a small metal tray on which the man had placed some euros to pay for his meal and held the tray in her hand as they spoke to each other. Then the man placed his hand on the small of Cecilia's back, rested it there, and caressed her. Cecilia did not react until, as much as ten seconds later, the man moved his hand down toward her buttocks, at which point she eased him away and stepped back from the table.

What had Kell just seen? It was impossible to know whether Cecilia had moved his hand away out of irritation, or simply because she did not want other customers at the restaurant to see what was happening.

Kell knew immediately what he had to do. Standing up, he left the binoculars beside the hut and moved as fast as he could back toward the path. He was wearing shorts and sneakers, and the plants and trees picked at his skin as he struggled through the undergrowth. It was essential that he try to identify the man before he left the restaurant. Kell began to jog along the path, his phone jumping in his back pocket as he descended toward the town. He was soon completely drenched in sweat and taking deep gulps of air as he ran, cursing his addiction to cigarettes. The phone began to ring but he ignored it. Within three minutes he had reached the end of the forest path and could turn toward the bay through the narrow back alleys of the town. His pace was slowing, but he urged himself on, formulating a plan as he ran and knowing that he could rest and catch his breath as soon as he was within a stone's throw of the restaurant.

Reaching the harbor, Kell found himself among thick crowds wandering around the shops and cafés close to the pier. He assumed these were mostly passengers from the midday ferry that he had observed approaching the island half an hour earlier. The sight of a sweating, panting Englishman with a roasted face drew stares as he turned north and began to jog toward Centonove. Within a minute, the terrace of the restaurant was in sight. Within another ten seconds, Kell could see that the man in the red shirt had left. He swore under his breath and stopped running, his lungs stinging, gasping for air, his head, neck, arms, and legs broiled by the afternoon sun.

Kell looked up. To his relief, he could see the man coming toward him on the path. There was an elderly lady in front of him, dressed in black widow's weeds, as well as a middle-aged British couple whom Kell recognized from the Lafodia.

This was his only chance. Kell was going to take a crazy risk, of the sort that he might have tried on the IONEC twenty years earlier, to prove an aptitude for courage and quick thinking. It was operationally near-suicidal, yet he had no choice.

The British couple were within ten meters of where Kell was standing. Hoping that they would pass without seeing him, he turned his back to stare at a rack of postcards outside a small shop. If they stopped and tried to talk to him, to offer help to a struggling tourist, the plan would be unworkable. Kell was still desperately short of breath and continued to gasp for air as he picked up one of the postcards. To his relief, the British couple walked past without stopping.

He immediately put the postcard back, turned around, and moved into the center of the path, effectively blocking it. With sweat pouring down his face, Kell made direct, pleading eye contact with the man in the red shirt as he walked toward him. The man frowned and slowed his pace, recognizing that Kell was trying to communicate with him. Putting his weight unsteadily on his left foot, but adding no further exaggeration to his already disheveled appearance, Kell raised his hand and took the gamble.

"Do you speak English?"

"Sure." It sounded like a Balkan accent. The man was perhaps closer to forty than thirty-five, but good-looking and fit. He was wearing a chunky metal watch on a tanned wrist, pressed linen trousers, and a pair of expensive-looking deck shoes. The red polo shirt had a Lacoste crocodile on the chest.

"Could I ask a big favor?"

"Favor?"

"Do you have a phone I could borrow?"

The words were no sooner out of Kell's mouth than he remembered that he had forgotten to switch off the sound on his own iPhone. If it rang in his back pocket, he was finished.

"You need make a call?" The man looked genuinely alarmed at the sight of the medically unstable British jogger standing before him.

"Just to my hotel," Kell replied. He nodded toward the white hulk of the Lafodia, a quarter of a mile along the bay. He could not risk putting his hand into his back pocket and feeling for the mute switch on the phone. He would just have to pray that it didn't ring. "My wife. I came out without my . . ."

To Kell's amazement, Lacoste quickly extracted a Samsung from his hip pocket, swept his thumb over the screen, and handed him the unlocked phone. "You have the number?"

Kell nodded and muttered heartfelt thanks, then began tapping out the number of his private U.K. cell phone, which he had left in the safe in his room. It began to ring. He heard the automated message responding on voice mail.

"*Welcome to the O2 messaging service. The person you are calling is unable to take your call . . .*"

Kell knew that he would have to improvise a nonexistent dialogue with his "wife" and hope that it sounded credible.

"Hi. It's me." An appropriate pause. "I know. Yes. Don't worry. I'm fine." Another delay. Lacoste was staring at him, his expression entirely blank. "I'm just borrowing a phone off a very kind passerby. I think I've torn a muscle in my leg." Another pause. It occurred to Kell that he would later be able to hear his own improvised performance, recorded for posterity. "No, I'm fine. But could you ask the hotel to send down one of their buggies? I don't want to have to limp back."

Kell took the weight off his injured leg and winced to accentuate a burst of imaginary pain. Lacoste could not have been less interested in the nuances of Kell's performance: he was looking out across the bay and seemed to be perfectly happy waiting for the call to end.

"Or maybe sprained it," Kell said, hearing a sustained tone as the messaging service cut him off. "I'm not sure." He counted out two more seconds, long enough for his imaginary wife to question the seriousness of his injury and perhaps the good sense of asking the hotel to rush to his assistance. Then Kell said: "Yeah, maybe you're right" as Lacoste turned to face him once again. Kell tried to study the features of his face as closely as possible, to commit them to memory. "Look, I'd better get off the line," he said. "I'm using someone's phone and he needs to get away."

Kell had assumed that Lacoste could speak English and had been listening to every word of the phantom conversation. To his surprise, however, Cecilia's mystery man merely frowned and bounced his eyebrows, suggesting that he did not fully comprehend why Kell had needed the phone in the first place. Kell duly conjured three more snippets of imaginary dialogue, then rang off, telling the dead phone line that he was catching his breath outside a shop halfway along the bay. He then handed back the Samsung, thanked Lacoste effusively, and watched as he strolled off in the direction of the ferry terminal.

Ten seconds later, in an act of God for which Kell sent thanks and praise to the heavens, the iPhone began to ring in his back pocket. He went into the shop to answer it.

"Tom?"

It was Elsa. Kell smiled at the coincidence.

"Funny you should ring," he said. "I've got a number I need you to check."

32

As soon as Lacoste was out of sight, Kell left the shop and limped along the promenade to a small café where he ordered a Coke and a toasted ham-and-cheese sandwich. Even ten minutes later he was still physically exhausted and made the latest in a series of private promises to join a gym and do some regular exercise. Having paid his bill he then walked back along the promenade, exaggerating his phantom limp as he passed Centonove, just in case Cecilia happened to be watching. There was no sign of her, only the bald-headed waiter attending to a rowdy table of six on the terrace.

Kell continued along the path. A group of young boys were splashing in the sea, watched over by an overweight man wearing orange Speedos and a Croatian football shirt, his topless wife asleep beside him. There was a smell of pine and engine oil, a summer sense of nothing much mattering, of people having all the time in the world.

Back in his room, Kell opened the safe. He would text Lacoste's number to Elsa. Working at her usual pace, it would probably be less than twenty-four hours before she had identified the man, traced his IP address, obtained an itemized copy of his cell phone bill, and accessed his e-mail accounts. If Lacoste was in a relationship with Cecilia—a relationship which she had run in parallel with Wallinger—it would show up on their correspondence like UV dye on a banknote.

Kell tapped in the four-digit code, swung open the door of the safe, and reached for his mobile. Sure enough, a missed call was registered on the phone icon. He tapped the screen and texted the number to Elsa. His shins and knees still throbbing from the run, Kell went to the beach for a swim before falling asleep in his room to the sound of clacking seagulls and a chambermaid vacuuming in the corridor outside.

He woke to an e-mail from Adam Haydock, filed as a CX to Amelia. To his irritation, Kell was copied on the message as "Temporary Istanbul."

EYES ONLY / ALERT C / TempISTAN/ ATH4
Case: I. Christidis / 12.6.13

1. Suicide note found by wife. (Handwriting/style confirmed). Describes financial concerns, fears of bankruptcy; regret and sense of personal responsibility for Wallinger crash; poor relationship with daughter. (Copy (Greek) in transit/VXC + TempISTAN).
2. Colleagues speak of likable, "honest" personality. Teetotal, but alcohol found in bloodstream postmortem. No history of alcoholism.
3. Greek Orthodox, lapsed.
4. Sense of surprise in community that Christidis should take his own life, but motives appear plausible to those who knew him. Coroner report seen by AH—suicide verdict obtained. Coroner's report not challenged by family.
5. Comms (PRISM) shows e-mail used infrequently. Regular cell and land calls to wife and friends (colleagues). No pornography.

No drug use. No girlfriend/boyfriend. No psychiatrist/medication.

6. Credit card debt—€17,698.23 House owned. Airport shifts cut, income down by 10% (on 2010). Wife unemployed. Christidis brother died (61) 2012. Bereavement?
7. No third-party/Cousin interest detected on Chios. Police cooperative (€500 single payment). Nothing recorded against Christidis in police files.

It was customary for officers filing CX to offer little interpretation of their own product. That was left to the wonks and analysts in London, who would direct the intelligence further upstream until a more senior colleague or minister of sufficient rank and distinction chose to act upon it. Nevertheless, the thrust of Haydock's report could not have been clearer. As far as he was concerned, there was no evidence of American interference on the island, nor any sense that Christidis had been compromised or manipulated. Haydock knew that "C" was suspicious of the circumstances surrounding Wallinger's crash and was aware that Kell had his own private doubts about CIA involvement in the case. Nevertheless, against this background, he had maintained that there was no foul play or coercion involved in the death of Iannis Christidis. It was suicide, pure and simple.

All of which left Kell with a sense that he would never know the truth about the accident. If nobody had tampered with Wallinger's plane, why had it crashed? He thought of Rachel, of the anger she felt toward her father, of the letter Paul had written to Cecilia, the intensity of his love for a woman who might not have loved him in return. A woman who, while apparently grieving Wallinger's death, had allowed another man to caress her back, stopping him only when those caresses became too intimate, too public. Had Paul taken his own life because he had discovered that Cecilia was two-timing him? Surely not.

Perhaps there was no mystery at all, no foul play, no conspiracy. Just the random accident of engine failure, bird strike, pilot error. It was one of the lessons Kell had learned many years earlier: there were always operational questions that could not be answered. Questions of motive, of circumstance, of fact. Despite all of the resources at the disposal of SIS, the tenacity and skill of her employees, human behavior was too unpredictable, the capacity to disguise and dissemble limitless. "I just don't buy the trail of breadcrumbs," Amelia had said. But perhaps she wanted to see conspiracy where none existed. God knows, it was a fault of which they had all been guilty, at some point in their careers. Amelia's desire to explain and rationalize the sudden death of a man she loved had obscured an inconvenient truth: that Paul Wallinger had most probably got into the wrong plane on the wrong afternoon, and fate had taken care of the rest.

Kell stood up, his calves aching. He took a half liter of water from the minibar and drank it down. Dinner was now an hour away and he was aware that he needed to formulate a strategy for meeting Sandor. First, though, he checked his e-mails. Rachel had been out of touch all afternoon.

He opened his private account and saw that she had replied to an earlier message, saying that she was booked onto a flight back to London in two days' time.

> Am I going to get to see you before I go? Mum's gone back to London and I've got the house to myself...x

The prospect of seeing Rachel again, of spending the night with her at the *yali,* was intoxicating. He had half a mind to catch the last boat to the mainland, charter a plane out of Dubrovnik, and leave Lacoste and Sandor to their fates. Instead, he told her that he would be back within twenty-four hours, then changed into a pair of jeans and a shirt and wrapped his ankle in a pristine white bandage obtained from the concierge. He would need to show some evidence of his injury to Lacoste should they run into each other. Heading downstairs, Kell drank a glass of wine in the bar before walking along the path toward Centonove with the stubborn, possibly foolhardy idea turning in his mind that he would introduce himself to Sandor as a friend of Paul Wallinger's, then sit back and watch the fireworks.

33

Kell became aware that there was a problem at Centonove when he saw a large group of people gathered on the pavement in front of the restaurant. The lights were out on the terrace and the tables overlooking the bay unoccupied. He stopped outside a beach shack bar and lit a cigarette, watching the crowd from a distance of about a hundred meters.

At first, it looked as though the kitchen had suffered a power shortage or gas leak, but then Kell saw two uniformed Croatian police officers emerging from the building, one of them speaking quietly into a walkie-talkie. There was no sign of Sandor. Kell assumed that she was indoors, dealing with the consequences of whatever burglary or petty crime had been committed at the restaurant.

Then he saw the paramedics. Two of them. Kell stubbed out the cigarette and walked farther along the path. He could see that perhaps as many as thirty people had gathered outside Centonove, mostly local residents in shorts and T-shirts as well as a smattering of tourists dressed more smartly for dinner. The younger of the two policemen was trying to move the crowd away from the entrance, trying to suppress an atmosphere of panic or scandal. His older colleague was still talking into the radio. Glancing toward the bay, Kell saw a police boat moored beneath the terrace and assumed that the officers had come over from Dubrovnik. Whatever was going on inside the building had required mainland assistance. Somebody was badly injured, or worse.

Kell felt a breeze against his legs as two small boys ran past him on either side, one of them clutching a football. They were talking excitedly in German, alerted by the crowds and by the scent of a story.

Movement in the first-floor window. A third paramedic in a crisp white uniform was walking around Sandor's apartment. Kell kept his eye on the window and was staggered to see Lacoste standing to one side of the room, his face clouded by shock.

Kell knew then that Cecilia Sandor was dead. He felt the same dropped-stitch shock in his gut that he recalled from Istanbul when Haydock had called with the news that Iannis Christidis had drowned. This time, however, the natural opportunist in Kell recognized that Sandor's death was the break he had been waiting for. If she had been murdered, who had killed her? The same people that had constructed the legend of a mistress mourning her dead lover? The intelligence service that had run Sandor against H/Ankara? It did not occur to Kell that she had taken her own life. One suicide on the same operation was a curiosity. Two was too much of a coincidence.

He approached a young couple standing in front of him. The man had the unmistakable late Empire self-confidence of an English ex–public schoolboy. With her careful hair and pastel skirt, his wife was straight out of Fulham.

"You're English?" Kell asked.

"We are." The woman had a single pearl earring clipped to each lobe.

"What's happened here?"

The man, who was no older than thirty, a young husband with a young wife, nodded out toward the water.

"The manager," he said. "We heard that she's been found dead."

"Found by who?"

"Cops," he replied, as though he had found himself in his own television show.

Right on cue, the older of the two Croatian police officers emerged from the restaurant and began asking the crowds to move away. The tourists went first, then the locals, gradually leaving the scene to the paramedics and a handful of restaurant staff, including the bald waiter whom Kell had seen so many times in the preceding forty-eight hours. It turned out that the young couple were also staying at the Lafodia and had booked a table at Centonove. Under instructions from the police, they walked farther into town in search of an alternative restaurant, nodding a quiet farewell.

Kell, too, was ushered from the scene and returned to the beach shack, where he lit a second cigarette and ordered a lager while continuing to watch the restaurant. News of Cecilia's death had spread to the bar. The manager was a young Croat with erratic hair who spoke good English and answered Kell's seemingly innocuous questions with a lazy nonchalance, clearly assuming that he was just another bored tourist trawling for tidbits of gossip.

"Had you known her for a long time?"

"No. She keeps private. Bought the place three, maybe four years ago."

"She wasn't from the island?"

A shake of the head.

"And it was suicide?"

"Sure. Apparently pills. Then she cuts . . ." The barman's vocabulary failed him. He was holding a glass and began to slash at his forearms, dragging the rim down to the wrist. "Opens up the skin. The artery, yes?"

"Yes." Kell had known a boy at school who killed himself by the same method. "In water?" he asked, assuming that a black ops team had rendered Sandor unconscious and then maneuvered her body into a bath.

"Yeah."

Whoever had wanted her dead had also wanted to create an impression of distress. A gunshot wound or poisoning would have left too many questions unanswered.

"What about her boyfriend?"

"Luka?" The barman's response was instant and confirmed that Sandor had been seeing Luka and Paul at the same time. The barman put the glass down. "I think he's from Dubrovnik."

Four teenagers had entered the shack, three of them smoking rolled-up cigarettes. The barman turned to serve them. Kell walked out onto the path and took another look at Centonove. The shutters on the kitchen window had now been closed and the younger policeman appeared to be standing guard outside the restaurant. Kell waited until the barman had poured out four drinks for the teenagers, then went back to his stool.

"Seems much quieter now," he said, ordering a second drink. He paid and left the change for the barman, keeping him in the conversation.

"Yeah?"

"Yeah. Just a policeman standing guard outside. Poor guy."

"Who? The police?"

"No, the boyfriend. What did you say his name was? Luka?"

"Correct." The barman opened up a dishwasher packed with glasses and ducked under a cloud of steam. "He's always in here. Maybe not so much anymore, huh?"

"No," Kell agreed, trying to sound sympathetic. "Did they run the restaurant together?"

"No. Luka works in the city. Owns a record company. Reggae and hip-hop. You like that shit?"

"Bob Marley, maybe Jimmy Cliff," Kell replied, knowing now that he could easily run Lacoste to ground. How many independent Croatian record labels were run by men named "Luka"?

"Yeah, Marley, man."

And so it went on. By nine fifteen, Kell had established that Cecilia

Sandor was an outsider, viewed with suspicion by many on the island; that she was often away from Lopud for extended periods; that she was considered to be wealthy; that Luka had left his wife and eight-year-old daughter to be with her, but had confessed one drunken night in the bar that Cecilia had turned down a proposal of marriage. Satisfied that he had garnered more than enough information, Kell shook the barman's hand just before half past nine and set out along the bay, passing Centonove in the hope of talking to the grieving Luka outside. But it was not to be. He exchanged a few words with the policeman, who spoke only rudimentary English (enough to confirm that the proprietor of the restaurant had "died sudden") and was then moved on. Kell asked him if Luka was "okay," to which he received a curt nod of the head. There was perhaps a small possibility that Sandor's boyfriend would be arrested on suspicion of murder or, more likely, would soon accompany Cecilia's body across the strait to Dubrovnik. Either way, Kell would advise Amelia to send Adam Haydock, or his equivalent from SIS Station in Zagreb, to obtain the full police and medical reports into the incident. His own work on the island was surely done.

It was only when he was in the passage outside his room, no more than ten minutes later, that he remembered the camera seen by Haydock on the CCTV in Chios. A silver digital camera, probably belonging to Cecilia, which might contain images of the bearded man at the outdoor restaurant. How could Kell have allowed himself to forget such a thing? True, given that Cecilia was a former intelligence officer, it was highly unlikely that she would have kept any compromising photographs in the camera's memory. Nevertheless, Kell had a responsibility—to Amelia, if nobody else—to get into Sandor's apartment and to try to obtain it.

He knew why he was reluctant to act. It was obvious. *Things are very quiet and dull here without you.* He wanted to be on a plane, in a cab, at the *yali*.

Kell stood in the passage outside his room. There was no realistic chance of getting into Sandor's apartment that night, or even for the next few days. Let Haydock, let Elsa, let Zagreb deal with the camera.

Kell reached into his pocket for the keycard to his room, opened the door, switched on the lights, and took two miniatures of Famous Grouse from the minibar. Within fifteen minutes he had filed a CX on Sandor's death and sent it via encrypted telegram to London. He then opened up his private e-mail account and wrote back to Rachel.

> Leaving Berlin first thing tomorrow, back midafternoon. Cancel whatever plans you've made. Have dinner with me x

34

Istanbul was just as Kell had left it: hot and crowded and traffic-stalled, the horizon a smogged screen of tower blocks and minarets. But it was now a different city, a Petri dish in which every movement and idiosyncrasy of Ryan Kleckner's behavior was being minutely examined and interpreted by a team of SIS analysts in London and Turkey. As he drove in from Sabiha Gokcen, Kell instructed his taxi driver to take him past Kleckner's apartment building, where a four-man surveillance team was already on post: a man and a woman in a branch of Starbucks a block from the entrance; two young British Asians in a van parked across the street. Kell was receiving updates on Kleckner's movements every half hour.

ABACUS had woken early, been to the gym, returned to his apartment for lunch, and was presently upstairs reading an unidentified paperback book in the kitchen. As Amelia had promised, Kleckner's residence, his routes to work, his favorite restaurants, his gym, and his car had all been decked out with enough cameras and microphones to capture the subject in almost every moment of his waking life. He was followed onto trams, trains, and ferries. A Turkish source working inside the American consulate as a computer technician was even able to provide SIS Station with regular briefings on Kleckner's work timetable, his moods and routines. If, at any point, a single element of the operation was discovered, SIS could be reassured that they were deniable: Kleckner would simply assume that MIT had put him under surveillance, and most probably report as much to his Station chief at the CIA.

En route to Dubrovnik airport Kell had spoken to Amelia, who had agreed with Kell's assessment that Zagreb/3 should handle the fallout from Sandor's death and spend a week on Lopud crossing Croatian palms with silver. "I need you in Turkey," she had told him, and Kell had readily agreed.

But he was made to wait before seeing Rachel. Kell had invited himself round for what he euphemistically described as "tea at the house," but she coolly informed him that she was "busy until dinner" and suggested that they meet instead at a fish restaurant in Bebek at nine o'clock. "You'll just have to be patient, Mr. Kell . . . ," she had told him, decorating the text message with kisses. Kell had checked into the Georges Hotel on Serdar-i Ekrem and tried to kill time by reading a novel. He had been reading the same page of the same opening chapter for well over fifteen minutes when Rachel finally put him out of his misery.

Hmmm. Just found a bottle of vodka in the freezer. Two glasses as well. Drink here first before dinner . . . ? xxx

He was at the *yali* within thirty minutes.

Rachel had left a key under the mat. Kell opened the front door and walked into the house to find the ground floor deserted. There was no sound, save for the lapping of the waves against the shoreline and the rumble of a dishwasher. Kell took off his shoes and socks and left them by the door, the air-conditioning cooling his skin as he walked upstairs and stopped at the first-floor landing.

One of the bedroom doors was open. In the reflection of a mirror, Kell could see Rachel lying naked in bed, her head propped up against a scattering of pillows, her beautiful body exposed to him. He took off his shirt and moved toward her. Rachel's dark eyes tracked him across the room.

They stayed in bed for almost three hours. Only afterward did Kell realize that they had played out a parallel version of Paul's letter to Cecilia. He remembered the words almost perfectly: *You left keys for me. I let myself in and you were waiting. I don't think I have ever seen you looking so beautiful. I wanted to take my time. I was craving you.* Yet he could not know—and did not ask—if Rachel had been conscious of this.

At dusk they took a bath together before walking north along the western shore of the Bosporus. Rachel had kept the reservation at the restaurant. They ordered *meze* and grilled sea bass at a candlelit table with views across the water to the Asian side. In the bliss of reunion something palpable had shifted between them. Kell felt entirely at peace. She was all that he wanted. It astonished him how readily, even recklessly, he was prepared to be submerged by his desire for her.

"There have been so many things I've wanted to ask you," she said, dipping a hunk of bread into a chalk white bowl of *tzatziki*. "I feel like I know nothing about you. That I did all the talking when we first met. What do you love?"

"What do I *love*?"

Kell wondered if anyone had ever cared to ask him such a thing. He obliged her, in a way that he would never ordinarily have revealed himself, and his answers took them off in myriad directions—discussions about malt whiskey, about Richard Yates, about cricket and *Breaking Bad*. Kell knew that she was making a study of him, because it was in his passions that he would be revealed to her. For years it had been in Kell's interest as a spy to conceal himself; he had remained opaque not only to agents and colleagues, but also to Claire, the woman with whom he had lived most of his adult life. Perhaps he had even been a mystery to himself. With Rachel, however, absurd as it seemed after so short an acquaintance, Kell felt *known*. At the same time, he had not felt so unstable, so exposed, so much in the grip of another person, in years. Had Paul felt the same way about Cecilia? Had she snatched his friend's heart as comprehensively as Rachel was seizing his own? Perhaps they were similar beasts—men who had taken on the IRA and the Taliban, and yet were incapable of controlling something as simple and as straightforward as their own feelings.

"Tell me about Berlin," Rachel said as she poured the last of the wine.

"I didn't go to Berlin," he said.

Her face remained impassive.

"Where did you go?"

"To Lopud."

Rachel swayed back in her chair, resting her glass so close to the corner of the table that Kell feared it would topple off and smash.

"No wonder you didn't tell me."

"I'm telling you now. I'm sorry I wasn't able to say anything before." He leaned forward, unable to read her mood. "Cecilia Sandor is dead."

"Jesus."

"We don't yet know what happened. It's possible that she was murdered. It's possible that she took her own life. We know that she had a boyfriend during the same period that she was seeing your father." Rachel's face soured and she shook her head, looking down at the table. He was giving her operational theories, classified material, secrets, but he did not stop. "There was a man on Chios, seen talking with Sandor and your father. They were eating lunch at a restaurant in the harbor the day before the crash. We've been trying to identify him. He may have been an intelligence officer, he may just have been a friend."

"Why would somebody want to kill Cecilia?"

It was the obvious question. Kell had only his instincts, his paranoia, with which to answer it.

"In a previous life she was a Hungarian intelligence officer. We need to establish whether or not she was recruited to seduce your father. We have doubts about the legitimacy of the relationship."

He realized that he was saying too much, piling theory on theory, hunch on hunch. What if Rachel reported this back to her mother? There was no evidence to suggest that Cecilia was a honey trap, other than her relationship with Luka. It was equally possible that Sandor, like Iannis Christidis, had taken her own life out of sheer despair.

"What are you trying to tell me?" she asked. "That you think Pappa was a *traitor*?"

It was the question to which Kell had always given himself a definitive answer: no. He simply could not believe in the annihilating possibility that Paul Wallinger had been another Kim Philby, another George Blake; that H/Ankara had been working in tandem with Cecilia Sandor and the SVR. As Rachel asked the question, he saw the depth of a daughter's love for her father, and the profound fear that his betrayal had extended beyond adultery into treason. Kell wanted to console her. He could not bear to see Rachel suffer with such a question. Amelia was convinced that the leak was coming from the American side, from Kleckner. For the time being, they had to believe that ABACUS was the mole.

"I'm certain he wasn't. I just don't know about the woman. I don't know if she was legitimate."

"And now she's been silenced, so you can never find out?"

"Perhaps." Kell picked up his glass and looked past Rachel, out across the water at the zigzag lights of the Bosporus Bridge. He felt that he had nothing left to say. Two tables away, a little girl in a pretty white dress was watching a film on a mini DVD player while her family ate dinner.

"Pappa talked about you," Rachel said suddenly. "I remembered it while you were away. Two years ago. There was something in the papers. Something about torture." Kell looked up. It was obvious that Rachel was talking about Gharani and Chater. "Rendition?" she said. "Were you involved in that? Were you Witness X?"

Kell remembered a similar conversation with Elsa in a house in Wiltshire. He hoped to his bones that Rachel would be similarly forgiving.

"My father said you were one of the most decent men he knew. He was stunned by what happened, by the way you were treated. Amazed that you didn't quit." Kell did not entirely trust the conviction in her voice.

"He said that?"

Rachel nodded.

"I didn't quit because I felt that I hadn't done anything wrong," he told her. "I didn't quit because I still enjoyed the job. I felt that I could do some good." Rachel looked at him as though he was being sentimental, even naïve. "Besides, what else can I do? I'm forty-four. This is all I know."

"No it's not." Her reply was quick, almost damning. "That's just something you tell yourself because the alternatives are too daunting."

"God, I hate the way the younger generation are so wise. When did that happen?"

"I'm not that young, Tom," she said.

A waiter came and offered them coffee. Simultaneously, they declined. Rachel shot Kell a look. They had both had the same thought.

"Maybe we should get the bill?" he said, holding her gaze.

"That sounds like a good idea."

35

The memory of that night, the stillness and the intensity of it, stayed with Kell for days afterward. Shuttling between Ankara and Istanbul, combing through file after file, report after report on Wallinger and ABACUS, he was fueled by visions and memories of Rachel, their separation as frustrating to him as the endless search for clues in the great mass of data about Kleckner.

She had left for London the next day. Kell, buried in meetings and paperwork, felt like a man who had become stuck on a bus in heavy traffic, the driver refusing to let him off between stops. He could just as easily have analyzed the reports, the surveillance logs, the transcripts, in an office at Vauxhall Cross. Instead, Amelia had him living out of a suitcase in Turkey, surviving on a diet of e-mails and text messages to Rachel that became less frequent the longer they were apart.

Against this background, he worked effectively. Reading the transcripts of Ryan Kleckner's private e-mails, listening to his telephone conversations, watching him on video surveillance feeds, Kell was able to build up an almost complete picture of ABACUS's day-to-day life. Kell was quickly able to deduce that there were at least five women in Istanbul with whom the handsome young American was sexually involved. He read every word of Kleckner's correspondence with Rachel, written in the run-up to his birthday at Bar Bleu, checking the language for clues, and judging the tone for any evidence of mutual attraction. To snoop on Rachel's private correspondence, albeit as part of a legitimate and pressing operation, left Kell with a feeling that he was sliding into seedy and unethical behavior that would eventually exact a heavy toll. The competitor in him was relieved that whatever attraction Kleckner had felt for her at the funeral appeared to have dissipated, but Kell was glad to set the information about Rachel to one side, and to restore her privacy.

It was while searching through Kleckner's list of friends on Facebook that Kell stumbled on a coincidence. Ebru Eldem, the twenty-nine-year-old journalist with *Cumhuriyet* who had been jailed the previous month, ostensibly for "terrorist" activities, had known Kleckner intimately. She had also been a source for Jim Chater—albeit as an unconscious asset—providing him with low-level cocktail party and conference gossip. Chater had been angry when the Turkish government had banged her up and had complained about it to Wallinger. Contacting Elsa, who was now in Milan, Kell instructed her to hack Eldem's dormant Facebook account and to search for any evidence of a relationship with Kleckner. Two hours later Elsa had sent over several pages of screen-grabbed messages between the pair, which showed quite plainly that they had been lovers.

Kell immediately called Amelia in London from the secure speech room in Istanbul. She was in her office.

"Did you know that ABACUS was involved with one of Jim Chater's assets?"

"Yes, I did."

Any elation he had felt at making the link between Eldem and Kleckner evaporated when he heard the terse disinterest of "C's" reply.

"It doesn't send up a flag for you?" he said. It was freezing cold in the sealed room and Kell had forgotten to bring a sweater.

"Should it?"

He had obviously caught her in a cool, distracted mood. At their last meeting, a lunch in Istanbul, Amelia had been relaxed and open, Kell's friend rather than his boss. She had told a story about bumping into a senior Whitehall civil servant while shopping in Waitrose. ("He looked at me in my spinster loneliness, stared at the gin and ice cream in my basket.") Today, however, she had reverted to type, her manner brusque and businesslike, wanting results from Kell, not tenuous links between ABACUS and a jailed Turkish journalist. This, he realized, was his future. If he was handed H/Ankara, their friendship would suffer as a result. Amelia would pull rank repeatedly, reminding him time and again of his place in the firmament.

"If he knew that Eldem was reporting to Chater, that she was briefing against Erdogan . . . If her agenda didn't fit with his values . . ."

Kell heard a noise on the line that he interpreted as Amelia's continued frustration with the direction that the conversation was taking. Theories. Conjectures. What-ifs. She had no interest in them. He felt that she had somehow discovered that he was involved with Rachel; that she knew the extent to which the relationship was affecting his work. Instead, Amelia said something quite extraordinary.

"We've had a break on Chios."

"Adam?"

"Yes. He's been clever. Found a camera, got the footage. Eyes on the table. We've identified the man who was sitting with Paul and Cecilia. The man with the beard."

"And?"

"Looks like an SVR officer. Minasian. Alexander Minasian."

36

It was suddenly as hot in the room as the sweltering streets outside. Kell had been listening to Amelia through a speaker system but lifted the secure telephone free of its cradle and spoke to her direct.

"Paul was at a restaurant with CCTV coverage, in plain sight, with an SVR officer?"

"Yes."

"With Cecilia Sandor? His mistress?"

"Yes."

"Jesus."

Kell reached for a cigarette, remembering in the same moment that smoking was forbidden inside the consulate. Instead, he picked up Amelia's lighter and began twisting it through his fingers, then tapping it on the table. It was impossible to know what to make of the revelation. It proved everything, yet it proved nothing.

"Are you still there?" she asked. There was a note of sarcasm in her voice, because she knew that Kell would have been poleaxed by the news.

"I'm still here." Kell scribbled "MINASIAN?" on a piece of paper, tapping the question mark with the edge of the lighter. "Was there anything from Paul or another source about running Minasian? Was he in your sights? An asset?"

"No. Of course we wish that was the case." It was the dream of every SIS officer, from Khartoum to Santiago, to recruit and run a Russian intelligence source. "All of our preliminary intel suggests that Minasian is bona fide. Directorate C, almost certainly SVR station chief in Kiev."

Ukraine was a second-rate posting. Usually that would indicate that Minasian was either a highflier in his early thirties who had been handed Kiev as a test, or had stalled midcareer with no chance of Paris, London, Washington, or Beijing.

"How old is he?"

"Thirty-nine."

What did that suggest? That Minasian was based in Kiev in order to service the mole in Turkey? Quick access in, quick access out.

"And his name didn't come up when Paul talked to you about the mole? Landau, Begg, Tremayne?"

"No." Amelia's voice cut out—a glitch on the line—and came back a second later. "He only had suspicions about Landau and Kleckner. Besides, we think Tremayne is clean."

"We do?"

"Yes. We also think he's gay."

Kell was not surprised. "I must say I had my suspicions about that."

"I think we all did," Amelia replied. "Surveillance followed him to one or two places in Ankara and Istanbul that Doug would rather not have been seen. I'm going to pull him in. Have a chat."

"There's no sense that he's being burned?" Kell asked. If the SVR knew about Tremayne's sexuality, there was an outside chance that his private shame could be exploited as a point of weakness.

"None," Amelia replied.

"So when you talked to Paul about the leaks, who raised the subject of the mole first?" Kell stretched out a tension in his lower back. "You, or him?" At last Kell could feel his brain spinning into a higher gear. "Did

Paul say that he suspected a leak, or did you go to him with your suspicions?"

"The latter."

"And you knew nothing about his relationship with Sandor? Paul didn't tell you that he was going to Chios?"

"No. As I have told you before, no."

These were not the answers Kell had been hoping for. If Wallinger had been an SVR asset, run by Minasian out of Kiev or Odessa, he could have set a crash meeting on Chios to discuss Amelia's suspicions. But why include Cecilia in the mix? Was she the cutout? Even if that were the case, why hold such a meeting in plain sight of half of the population of Chios Town? Kell said as much to Amelia, who appeared to want him to continue talking, vacuuming up Kell's analysis, digging around in his brain. He asked if there had been any developments in Croatia.

"Official verdict still suicide." Kell heard a faint gulp and swallow, then the thunk of what sounded like a glass hitting a table in Vauxhall. "Locals seem to believe that. But no note was left. Your friend Mr. Luka Zigic has been telling anyone who will listen to him that his girlfriend was murdered."

"Now why would he suspect a thing like that?"

"Zagreb 3 is still trying to find out. Luka certainly doesn't think she was suicidal. No medication in the bathroom cabinets, all fun and games as far as he was concerned. In bed and out. You remember Cecilia shut the restaurant in the first ten days of May?"

The temperature was dropping in the secure speech room. Kell said: "Yes."

"She spent most of that time with Zigic in Dubrovnik. We've also got regular telephone calls between them when Sandor was in England for the funeral. He met her at the airport when she flew home. Poor old Luka seemed to be under the impression she was attending a conference in Birmingham organized by the Croatian tourist board."

"Somebody forgot to get all their ducks in a row." Kell laid a private bet with himself that Zigic would be dead by the end of the month. If he was going around casting doubts on Sandor's legend, making people suspect foul play in her death, whoever had killed her would happily kill him too, just to ensure quiet. "Here's what I think." Kell replaced the phone in its cradle and again spoke into the room. "Sandor was being run by Minasian as a honey trap. She seduced Paul, on SVR orders. She got pillow talk out of him, maybe more. When Minasian judged that the moment was right, he confronted Paul on Chios. Tried to blackmail him into cooperation. 'We have films of the two of you together, we have letters, we have recorded conversations. Work for us or we tell the world that the married head of SIS Station in Ankara is screwing a Russian spy.'"

There was a pause in London. Kell could not know how many people were in the room with Amelia, but suspected that they were both alone. The molehunters. The circle of trust was two.

"And then Paul kills himself, crashes the plane rather than face the music?"

"Possibly. Or, more likely, it just *crashes*. Engine failure. Pilot error." Kell was struck by how coldly he was discussing the accident. It was like talking about an item he had seen on the news. "Call it unfortunate timing."

"Do you really think that, Tom? Or do you not want to face the other possibility?"

"What other possibility?" Kell began to walk around the table, pacing out his thoughts. It had always astonished him how eagerly Amelia had wanted to pursue the idea that the great love of her life had been a traitor. Why take herself down that path? It was ruinous in personal terms, it was ruinous professionally. It was as though she wanted to control Wallinger even in death. "You want me to consider that Paul was working for Moscow? That Minasian recruited him? That *Cecilia* recruited him? Amelia, if you told me that you were having dinner with Burt Lancaster at the Ivy tonight, I would believe that before I believe that Paul Wallinger was a Russian spy. These leaks, these failed ops, these system flaws all came about in the last thirty-six months, correct?"

"Correct. HITCHCOCK, EINSTEIN, etcetera."

"You have always believed that the leak was coming from the American side. From Kleckner or Landau. Correct?"

"Correct."

"Then let's go with that hunch. Forget about Paul, take eyes off Mary Begg, put everything on the Cousins."

"I'm not ready to do that."

"There's something about Mary?" Kell asked. He regretted the joke as soon as he had made it.

"Leave her to me," Amelia replied. "Begg is a London problem."

There was a brief moment of silence, humorless and tense. Kell wondered what Amelia knew about Begg: who was watching her; what they were seeing and hearing; why she was still under suspicion.

"Paul doesn't fit the profile of a traitor," he said, again instinctively defending Wallinger.

"Is there such a thing as a profile?"

"You know there's a profile." Kell retrieved the lines from Sudoplatov, lodged in his memory for years. " 'Search for men who are hurt by fate or nature. The ugly, people craving power or influence, people who have been defeated by circumstances.' Does that sound to you like Paul?" Amelia did not respond. "Look at the historical record," Kell said. "Philby: sociopathic narcissist. Blunt: ditto. Burgess, Maclean, Cairncross: ideologues. Ames and Hanssen: cash and vanity. Paul doesn't tick a single box. He never cared about money. He was vain, sure, but he was never short of women or colleagues telling him how wonderful he was. He was your golden boy."

At the end of the line, Amelia sniffed and said: "So was Philby." Kell could picture her rolling her eyes.

"Paul was cunning, yes," he said, "but his sins were there for all to see, for anyone who cared to look closely enough. As for ideological conviction, are we really expected to believe that a senior British intelligence officer, in the wake of 9/11 and Chechnya and Litvinenko, suddenly decides to work for the government of Vladimir Putin sometime in 2008 or 2009? Why? Why would he do a thing like that? For money? He's no longer paying for private education, Rachel and Andrew left home years ago." How strange to be saying her name aloud, just another building block in his defense of Wallinger. "Josephine owns a flat in Gloucester Road that's worth minimum one point four million. You saw the farmhouse in Cartmel. Add another two million to the Wallinger real estate portfolio. Plus foreign perks, plus the *yali,* plus the villa in Ankara. Paul loved the Service. He loved the job." Kell was on the point of adding: "He loved *you,* for Christ's sake," but stopped himself. In truth, he no longer knew who or what he was protecting. His dead friend? Amelia, whose reputation would lie in tatters if her former lover was exposed as a mole? The Service itself, toward which Kell felt almost wholly ambivalent in the wake of Witness X? Or was he protecting Rachel? Philby's children, the Maclean offspring, the sons and daughters of Ames and Hanssen, had all been variously ruined by association with their traitor fathers. It was better to believe in Paul's innocence, to run every other lead to the ground, before confronting the possibility that Wallinger had betrayed them all.

"I would agree with all of that," Amelia replied. "And with your analysis of what may have happened with Minasian and Sandor. But it still gives us a serious problem."

"Of course it does."

"What did Paul tell Sandor? What was the extent of her access?"

Kell scrolled through his memory of the files and e-mails, the love letters, the photographs. "Impossible to say," he replied eventually. "We need to find out if all the leaks—HITCHCOCK, EINSTEIN, everything—flowed from Paul's interactions with Cecilia, or if we still have a threat from Kleckner or Landau."

Amelia took another sip of water. Again the sound of the glass in

Vauxhall. "What are your thoughts on that? You've been looking at ABACUS. Landau looks clean to us. Doesn't strike me as the sort of person who has the *guts* to betray his country, know what I mean?"

That was vintage Amelia. Acerbic, straight to the point. *The guts to betray your country.* Kell absorbed the remark with a smile and sat down. He again took the secure phone from its cradle, aware that he had seen nothing—in any file, on any tape, in any surveillance report—to arouse the slightest suspicion in Kleckner.

"Everything checks out," he said. "But then again, that's the whole point, isn't it? We're not talking about a disgruntled bureaucrat in the State Department who can't send an e-mail to his handler without half the world reading it. We're talking about a trained CIA officer who may or may not be working in conjunction with a pedigree counterintelligence service. If Ryan Kleckner is funneling Western secrets to Moscow or Beijing, it will be in their institutional DNA to make it look as though Ryan Kleckner is *not* funneling Western secrets to Moscow or Beijing."

"Of course."

"So I'll keep looking," Kell told her.

"Yes, you will."

37

The break came within less than twenty-four hours.

Kell had installed himself in Wallinger's office in the SIS Station in Istanbul, a screen to one side of the desk showing flagged-up fragments of Kleckner surveillance footage shot during the previous six weeks. His days were mostly taken up reading reports on Kleckner—anything that London had been able to ascertain about his life and career—as well as myriad classified files relating to EINSTEIN, HITCHCOCK, Sandor, and Wallinger. Many of them Kell was reading for a second or third time, hoping to catch something that he had missed, a pattern, a flaw, an overlap that would unlock the mystery.

What made matters more complex still was not knowing whether the breaks and idiosyncrasies in ABACUS's "patterns" around the city were the results of Kleckner's own legitimate work as a CIA officer, attempting to recruit sources within Istanbul while working under diplomatic cover as a "health attaché," or whether they constituted something more suspicious. On four occasions the SIS surveillance team tasked with following Kleckner had lost him. In the first instance, a trailing vehicle had broken down. In another, the same van had become lodged in heavy traffic and ABACUS had slipped from view. But on two other occasions, Kleckner had employed active countersurveillance against a six-man team and shaken them off after just forty-five minutes. Was he meeting his handler, or an agent of his own? The leader of the surveillance team, a thirty-four-year-old British Asian named Javed Mohsin, had complained repeatedly that it was impossible to track ABACUS with anything less than ten officers. He needed eyes behind the target and ahead, anticipating where ABACUS may or may not go, based on previous behavior. That meant numbers on the ground. Most of the team—as well as two Tech-Ops specialists with responsibility for the blizzard of cameras and microphones installed across Istanbul—had already been in Turkey for six weeks and were understandably keen to return home. Amelia was reluctant to request a replacement unit, not least because it would have to be seconded from MI5. That raised the risk of too many questions being asked in London about an operation against an American ally on foreign soil. At Kell's suggestion, she agreed to look into hiring Harold Mowbray and Danny Aldrich, the freelancers who had helped in the hunt for her son, François, almost two years earlier. Elsa Cassani had also agreed to continue dedicating her time and resources to ABACUS.

Having looked at Kleckner from every angle, Kell had concluded that there was one area of his life that seemed particularly unusual: his regular visits to a small teahouse on Istiklal, no more than fifty meters from the entrance to the Russian consulate. Amelia had mentioned an attractive waitress at the café who seemed to have caught Kleckner's eye, but the girl had since ceased to work there and there was no evidence that she had ever met Kleckner socially. Two weeks after her final shift, ABACUS was still going to the café two or three times a week, usually after shopping for books and magazines on Istiklal. Nothing unusual about that, but he showed no similar loyalty to any other establishment in the city, save for the café at his gym (where Kleckner would often eat breakfast after working out in the morning) and a Lebanese restaurant close to the American consulate which was popular with many of his colleagues.

Furthermore, the teahouse itself—which was called Arada—was fairly nondescript. Kell had dropped by and been struck both by the lack of clientele and by the quality of the tea, which, even by Turkish standards, was so stewed as to be undrinkable. (It was notable on the tapes that Kleckner rarely finished, and sometimes never touched, his drinks.) Walk a few hundred meters north along Istiklal and the American would surely have discovered several places that were more atmospheric, where the girls were prettier, the drinks and snacks of a higher quality. Arada was situated down a dark passage, with no natural sunlight. It was not particularly comfortable, nor did Kleckner appear to enjoy a friendship with the manager. On one occasion, he had played backgammon, appearing to lose his temper with an elderly Turk who picked up his dice too quickly after rolling. Granted, Arada had a certain old-world charm and offered a quiet respite from the noise and bustle of Istanbul's busiest thoroughfare, but Kleckner's fondness for the place seemed eccentric.

There was also the question of the café's proximity to the Russian consulate. If Kleckner was signaling to a handler or cutout, it was an almost outrageous gambit, but perhaps that was in the nature of whatever double bluff had been orchestrated by the SVR. Who would ever assume that a CIA officer would contact his controller within spitting distance of Russian soil? Kell had ordered up the Arada surveillance reports. There was no discernible pattern to the visits. If ABACUS had a glass of tea or a Turkish coffee at the location during the day, he was either en route to or from a meeting, or shopping for clothes and books. His evening visits were usually followed by consular business (dinners, cocktails) or dates with the five local women who seemed only too happy to throw themselves into the arms of the charismatic American diplomat. On at least three occasions, Kleckner had gone to Arada with a girl.

The reports contained information about Kleckner culled by other SIS assets with whom he had come into contact in Istanbul. These included snippets of conversations at parties, minutes from meetings between the two allies, even a chat with a brokenhearted Irish au pair with whom Kleckner had enjoyed a one-night stand—anything and everything that might assist Kell in building up a picture of ABACUS's personality and attitudes. It was noted that he was "a fan" of Obama, surprisingly "ebullient" on drone attacks, that while "intoxicated" he had lambasted the whistleblower Bradley Manning—at the same time launching a "sustained and scathing attack on Julian Assange"—and that as a student at Georgetown he had supported the Bush administration's decision to invade Iraq. Other biographical details had appeared at first to be mundane—"likes Bob Dylan"; "misses his mother"—but it was one such seemingly innocuous observation that unlocked the entire operation.

At a dinner party hosted by the Dutch ambassador at his wife's private residence in Ortakoy, Kleckner had been heard to say that as a graduate he had "hoped to live the kind of life that meant he didn't have to wear a suit to the office." Kell had remembered the remark, only because it had made him smile, but as he studied the footage of ABACUS's visits to Arada, something became extraordinarily clear to him, extraordinarily quickly.

Twice Kleckner had visited the teahouse first thing in the morning while wearing a tie—on a weekend. Three times he had visited the teahouse in the evenings in a suit, twice during the week, but once on a Sunday evening. At no point had he gone there, at any other time of day or night, wearing anything other than casual clothes, even when in the company of a woman. The more Kleckner spooled back and forth through the images, the more Kleckner's clothes looked out of place. Why wear a jacket and tie on a hot spring morning en route to work, or on his day off? Why not put them on as he entered the consulate or immediately prior to a meeting? Why meet a smartly dressed girl for dinner dressed in chinos and a button-down shirt, but play an aggressive, sweat-inducing game of backgammon with a Turkish man without even removing his jacket?

Kell looked at the times and dates on the footage. He was interested in Kleckner's movements in a twenty-four-hour period either side of appearing at the café in a suit and tie. If clothing was a signal—either to a fixed camera or to somebody who had been instructed to go to Arada at a particular time of day or night to watch for the mole—then Kell had to follow it up. Were there other idiosyncrasies in his appearance? Did a tie signify one thing, a pair of shorts another? If Kleckner sat in a certain seat, did it mean that he was in a position to hand over classified information? Had the game of backgammon been interpreted as a request for a crash meeting? Kell could not know. All he was certain of was the fact that something was out of place. There was ninety-degree heat in Istanbul and Ryan Kleckner hated wearing suits. The clothes were wrong.

He rang the safe house in Sultanahmet in the hope of finding a member of the team off shift. Javed Mohsin himself picked up.

"It's Tom."

"Oh. Hello there."

A typically cool greeting. Mohsin had a habit of sounding irritated by any intrusion Kell happened to make into his day-to-day affairs. It was the insolence of the underling; a man too old to be ordered around.

"Have you got ten minutes to run something for me?"

"Suppose so."

"Don't sound too excited, Javed."

A grunt on the end of the line. Kell asked him to load up the surveillance reports for the seventy-two-hour period on either side of Kleckner's first Saturday visit to Arada, when he had worn a tie. It took Mohsin almost five minutes to get himself ready, a period in which Kell could hear a toilet being flushed and the cough of another member of the team in the background.

"Okay. Got them," he said eventually.

"Can you tell me what ABACUS was doing on Friday, fifteenth March, and Sunday, seventeenth March?"

"Don't you have these reports?" The tone of Mohsin's reply implied that Kell was either being stupid or lazy in requesting his assistance. "I sent digital files over ages ago."

"Those were edited highlights and they're right in front of me. I want a second pair of eyes on the hard copies. I want to know what you remember, what's on the originals."

The terseness of the response appeared to have no effect on Mohsin's complacency. For reasons that were unclear to Kell, he began with the report from Sunday, March 17. Kleckner had been clubbing, had gone home alone, had slept late, then spent the rest of the day reading in his apartment, talking to his mother on the telephone and "masturbating."

"Not at the same time, I hope." Kell wondered why he had bothered making the joke. "What about the Friday?"

A rustle and flick of pages as Mohsin searched through the report.

"Looks like a normal day. Goes to the gym. Train to the consulate. Long lunch with a colleague we haven't yet been able to identify. Then gets on a catamaran at Kabatas."

"Where to?"

"Princes' Islands."

Another irritating Mohsin power play. Providing only the minimum amount of information on a request. Making Kell push for more detail.

"Did somebody follow him?"

"Sure."

"Can you elaborate on that, Javed? This gnomic thing you do is starting to irritate."

There was a murmured apology, nothing more. "He got off at Heybeliada."

"What's that? One of the islands?"

"Yup."

"Sea of Marmara?"

"Yup."

Ordinarily, Kell would have lost his temper, but he needed to keep Mohsin onside, at least until the end of the conversation.

"Then what?"

Another pause. A subtle change in Mohsin's tone of voice. "Well. Then he went to Buyukada. Then we don't know. That was one of the times we lost him."

There was a map of Istanbul on the wall of Wallinger's office. Kell could see the necklace of tiny islands in the Sea of Marmara that were reached by the ferry from Kabatas: Kinaliada, Burgazada, Heybeliada, Buyukada. Motorized vehicles were banned on all four.

"You lost him on an island the size of Hyde Park with no cars, no motorbikes, no bridge to the mainland?"

"Yes, sir. Sorry, sir."

Kell at last had leverage in the conversation. "Not a problem," he said. "These things happen. Let's look at some other days." He had written down the other dates when Kleckner had visited Arada while wearing a tie. There was a Sunday a week later. "What do you have for ABACUS on Monday the twenty-fifth?"

"March?"

"Yes."

It was apparently another routine day. Kleckner had gone to the gym, gone to work, gone home.

"And the Saturday before that?"

Again the rustle and flick of pages. Mohsin moving more quickly now, trying to do a better job. "Okay. Here we are. Saturday, March twenty-third. Subject wakes earlier than normal. Six o'clock. Has slept alone at the apartment. Breakfast at the apartment, listening to music. Isis. Oh." A sudden cutout, a silence. Kell felt his heart jolt. "This is interesting. Subject took a taxi to Kartal."

"Where's that?"

"On the Asian side. I remember this gig actually. I was on it." It was like talking to a different person. Mohsin sounded engaged and anecdotal, like a man reminiscing in a pub over a pint. "Took me two hours to get there. He boarded a ferry and went to Buyukada."

"Back to the Princes' Islands?"

"Yes, sir."

Kell could feel a rush of gathering excitement. "And once he was there? What happens next?"

Mohsin overlapped him. "Let's see. Has a coffee and an ice cream with a friend near the ferry terminal."

"Who's the friend?"

Mohsin's response took several seconds. "Er, Sarah got a clear image of him. We identified him as a journalist who lives over there. Matthew Richards. Knows a lot of expats, diplomats in Istanbul. He and Ryan see a lot of each other."

Richards. A reporter for Reuters. Kell had seen transcripts of his telephone conversations with Kleckner, conducted on open lines, as well as copies of their e-mail and text exchanges. He had never paid much attention to them, because Richards was reckoned bona fide by London. Mohsin picked up the story.

"It turned out he wanted to look at one of the houses that's for sale on the beach. Right next door to where Richards lives. Maybe he recommended it. Afraid to say we couldn't get near him at times, sir. I had to make a judgment call. He would have smelled us."

"Sure."

"But I remember he took a towel down to the beach, had a swim. That's in the log. When we picked him up again at the ferry terminal he still had wet hair."

"And Richards? He didn't go swimming with him?"

"No. Don't think so. He's got two kids. Married to a French girl. Was probably putting them to bed because it was getting late. Ryan maybe went into the house before the swim. Gets on well with the whole family. Likes the son, teaches him baseball."

Kell knew that from the files and said: "Okay."

There was one more date. The midweek evening when Kleckner had played the frenzied game of backgammon in 80 percent humidity while wearing a jacket and tie. Mohsin took a couple of minutes to find the original surveillance report. This time he started with ABACUS's movements in the twenty-four-hour period prior to his appearance at Arada.

"Okay, got it," he said. Kell was staring at his packet of cigarettes on Wallinger's desk. As soon as the call was over he would walk out through the chancery and go for a smoke at the teahouse between the consulate and the Londres hotel.

"Go on," he said.

"Girl slept with him that night. The Turkish one. Elif." Kell knew her, remembered the name. Pneumatic, husband-seeking starlet from Bar Bleu. "She leaves at dawn, he goes to the gym." There was a fractional pause, then: "Jesus . . ."

Kell pitched forward in his chair, knowing in his bones exactly what Mohsin was going to tell him. The opiate rush again, pouring through him now.

"Guess where he went, sir?"

"I think I know what you're going to tell me."

"Ferry. Kabatas."

"To Buyukada?"

"You got it."

38

Kell was out of the consulate and into a cab within five minutes. The driver allowed him to smoke a cigarette—"leave window down"—and he texted Mohsin en route, who confirmed that Kleckner was in Bursa attending a Red Cross–hosted conference on the Syrian refugee crisis, polishing his cover and possibly working a recruitment. There would be no danger of bumping into him catching a ride on a horse and cart on Buyukada.

"How do you pronounce it, anyway?" Mohsin asked half an hour later, as they sat at the makeshift terminal café on the western shore of the Bosporus. Kell had arrived first and ordered two glasses of tea to kill time while waiting for the boat.

" 'Bew' to rhyme with 'chew.' 'Coulda' as in 'I coulda been a contender, instead of a bum.' "

Mohsin shot Kell a quizzical look. The phrase meant nothing to him.

"*On the Waterfront*?"

"Yeah, it's really nice here, isn't it?" he replied, looking out across the sapphire waters. Kell stared down at his glass of tea. At the side of the busy thoroughfare bringing traffic to the terminal, an old man was selling roasted chestnuts from a two-wheeled cart. The wind blew a smell of burning charcoal toward the café. Kell had missed lunch and was hungry. The café had a colored banner running above the counter, in the style of a McDonald's, advertising burgers and toasted cheese sandwiches of varying degrees of plasticity. He would have ordered something had the ferry not been announced on a crackling loudspeaker. They stood up, Kell snapping back the dregs of his tea like a shot of liquor, the heat of the liquid scorching the back of his throat and leaving a dust of melted sugar cubes on his tongue. Then they walked side by side toward the ticket gates, a screech of brakes and the blare of a horn behind them as traffic came to blows on the highway.

The ferry was not busy. Kell counted nineteen passengers making their way along the quay. Two of them were British—he could hear West Country accents—the rest seemingly a mix of Turks and tourists. He stepped onto the ship, following Mohsin to a seat on the first deck. A passenger had recently been sick—there was an odor of vomit shrouded in disinfectant. As the ferry slipped her moorings, it began to rain, clouds draining the Bosporus of color and turning the churning waters cold and gray.

"This is roughly where he sat," Mohsin muttered, settling into a seat beside Kell. "Might even be the same ferry." There was a small family nearby eating cheese and bread from a picnic. Mohsin, wearing shorts and a blend-in Galatasaray shirt, recalled the setup of the team. "Steve was on him. Agatha. Tourist cover, playing a couple. Priya up above, hijab. I was over there"—he indicated a television in the corner of the deck—"pretending to watch a local news program."

"What was ABACUS carrying?"

"Shoulder bag. Same one he usually takes to work. Carries it with him most places. Leather. Keeps books in there, newspapers and magazines, deodorant if he's going out in the evening and doesn't have time to shower at the consulate."

And product, Kell thought. Intelligence reports for a handler. Memory sticks. Hard drives. If ABACUS had made a drop, Kell needed to intercept the material, to get to it before Kleckner's handler.

"Did the bag seem any different on the way back? Lighter? Larger?"

"Lighter, definitely. He had a bottle of wine because he was going to dinner with Richards."

"At his house?"

"Yeah."

"And where is that on the island?"

"Don't worry. I'll show you everything."

The ferry stopped four times en route. On the Asian side, they moored for ten minutes while a large group of Chinese tourists boarded the ship and flocked to the interior deck, silent in hats and sunglasses, subdued by the rain. The cranes unloading container ships at the docks were shrouded in mist; Kell could make out an entire fleet of brand-new purple buses lined up on the quayside. The old railway station at Kadikoy was still standing, reminding Kell of the Bund in Shanghai, a long-ago operation to burn an African arms dealer visiting the city from Nairobi. With the rain now falling in flurries that whipped and swirled across the decks, the ferry eventually made her way to the mouth of the Bosporus and out into the open waters of the Sea of Marmara, a choppy twenty-minute crossing to Kinaliada, the first of the Princes' Islands. There the rain ceased and Kell went outside into the humid afternoon, standing alone on the starboard walkway, smoking a cigarette as a rainbow arced across his shoulder toward the distant minarets of Hagia Sophia.

Half an hour later they were pulling into Buyukada, Mohsin having joined Kell on the upper deck and continuing his running commentary on ABACUS's visit.

"Richards was waiting for him on the dock. His kids go to school every day in the city. He was waiting for the ferry from Kartal, which brings them home."

"And while that was coming in?"

Mohsin had obviously read the surveillance report en route to Kabatas. It seemed that he could remember every detail.

"A coffee in the second of the cafés over there." He pointed south, along the Buyukada jetty, past the ticket office, toward a street in the main town. "They had a beer, a game of backgammon, then went to get the kids."

"Backgammon?"

"Yeah."

Everything was now a clue, a tell, a signal—or a blind alley. All of Kell's experience told him that the island was wrong. Why would a CIA mole isolate himself on Buyukada, making dead drops in a natural choke point? Was it another SVR double bluff, like Arada's proximity to the Russian consulate? Or was Kell seeing tells and patterns where none existed?

Suddenly, with no sense of its origin or catalyst, he recalled a conversation with Rachel at the *yali,* weeks earlier. Their shared cigarette, looking out over the Bosporus while Amelia had gone for the walk with Josephine. How could he have forgotten such a thing?

Pappa had a friend who lived on Buyukada. An American journalist.

Had she meant Richards? If so, why say that he was American? Kell immediately took out his iPhone and tapped a text message to London.

HELLO YOU—AM I IMAGINING IT, OR DID YOU MENTION THAT YOUR FATHER HAD A JOURNALIST FRIEND ON BUYUKADA? IF I'M NOT GOING MAD, CAN YOU REMEMBER HIS NAME? RICHARDS? IF I AM GOING MAD, CAN YOU IGNORE THIS TEXT? SEPARATION FROM YOU HAS MADE ME DELIRIOUS—T X

Under a fierce sun that had burned away the last of the rain clouds, Kell followed Mohsin along the broad jetty. They came into a narrow covered arcade of shops selling suntan lotion and postcards, guided tours around the island, sunglasses, and imitation sailor's hats with CAPTAIN embroidered in gold across the peaks. Mohsin showed Kell into the café on the main street, pointed out where ABACUS and Richards had sat for their game of backgammon, then remembered that "the target" had gone to the toilet for "at least five minutes." That alone was enough to send Kell into the gents', where he looked around for a potential dead letter box, a place to store cached documents. Perhaps there was a storeroom or passageway in which a cutout or handler might wait for a brush contact. But the environment was all wrong—too busy, too small, too obvious. He lifted the lid on a cistern in the men's cubicle, but only because it seemed lazy not to. More likely Kleckner was using Richards as the cutout, or their friendship as a cover for his activity as a mole.

"Where next?" he said. "Show me the route."

Mohsin promptly hailed a horse-drawn carriage and took Kell on a tour of the island, following a route that ABACUS had taken on an earlier visit to Buyukada. Kell felt slightly ridiculous, sitting side by side on a narrow love seat with a humorless surveillance officer while their grinning driver encouraged his aging horses to move faster by whipping their flanks with a long wooden stick. The island was crowded at the seafront, but largely empty in its interior, a scattering of well-maintained houses on a loose grid separated by broad streets that were splattered with the dried, straw-colored dung of passing horses. After half an hour Kell grew tired of the rocking of the cart, the squeaking hinge in the love seat and the perpetual clip-clop, clip-clop of the horse's hooves. He was very hot and learning nothing useful about Kleckner. He instructed the driver to return to the main town, jumping off opposite the Splendid Palace, an Ottoman-era hotel that boasted views across the strait to Istanbul. With Mohsin beginning to flag, they went into the bar and cooled off with two glasses of lemonade under an inevitable portrait of Ataturk.

Rachel had not replied. Had she taken offense at the message about her father, or was something going on in London? Kell had not heard from her in two days and had begun to despise himself for the speed with which she had seized control of his heart; there was a dignity in his solitary life that she had completely stripped away. When he had concluded his search of the island, he would call her from the Kabatas ferry and try to encourage her to come back to Istanbul for a long weekend.

"Show me the house," he said to Mohsin when he had walked back into the bar.

"Which one?"

"The one that's for sale. The one you thought ABACUS might be looking at."

It was a ten-minute walk from the hotel. Kell settled the bill and they went outside into the late afternoon sun, returning to the quiet suburban streets to the west of the main town, disturbed only by the occasional passing bicycle or pedestrian.

"This is roughly where I had to let him go," Mohsin confessed, explaining that he had been following ABACUS in a one-on-one for twenty minutes but had become concerned that the American would "smell" him. He led Kell downhill along a narrow lane leading toward the last row of houses before the beach. There were large private gardens on either side of the road, the occasional bark of a dog punctuating the silence. "Richards lives in a house about a hundred meters that way." Mohsin gestured toward a screen of pine trees on a corner where the road split left and right in a T-junction. "We weren't able to get close because it's so isolated. Normally, one of us could play the cover. Grab a horse and cart, pretend to be a gardener or something. But once ABACUS gets ahead of us on foot—"

Kell interrupted him. He knew the reasons for what had happened and wasn't interested in hearing Mohsin's excuses. "It's okay," he said. "You don't have to explain."

They walked on in silence. Kell could hear the murmur of the sea, now only a hundred meters away to the north. The Richards family lived in a part-renovated *yali* on a road parallel to the shore. Kell could not tell if anyone was home, nor was he much interested in knocking on the front door and disturbing their peace. According to the surveillance reports, cross-referenced with e-mails and phone logs, Kleckner had visited the house three times in the previous six weeks, on one occasion staying the night and thanking Richards the next morning for giving him "a world-class dinner and a world-class hangover." Kell was more interested in the house next door, now for sale, which Kleckner had been seen to visit. Properties on the island were prohibitively expensive, particularly those close to the beach. Buyukada was a summer refuge for the city's elite; thousands of wealthy Istanbullus retreated to the island in July and August, taking up residence in second homes to escape the stifling city heat of high summer. Why would a twenty-nine-year-old spy with less than thirty thousand dollars in savings, fourteen months from his next CIA posting, be looking to buy a *yali* in the most expensive corner of the most expensive island in the Princes' archipelago?

Kell had a possible answer a few minutes later. Walking along the road toward the house, he spotted a "For Sale" sign (in English and Turkish) tacked to a tree. There was a broken wooden gate leading to the property, a tiny splinter piercing Kell's index finger as he pushed it open. The men found themselves amid very thick undergrowth, the garden grown wild. Kell could see the shadow of what had once been a large house through gaps in the foliage, but it was clear that the entire property had been allowed to fall into ruin.

"Tell me exactly what you saw," Kell said, returning to the road. Both men were soaked in sweat, Kell's shirt sticking to his back like cellophane. It had been impossible to proceed any farther through the garden. "You told me ABACUS went for a swim."

Mohsin leaned on a tree beside the "For Sale" sign, flattened by the heat.

"That's right," he said. "He went round in the horse and cart like I showed you. He left the driver in the center of town, then doubled back toward the Richards house. I started following him along the road, exactly like we've done today." Mohsin was beginning to sound defensive and impatient: either he was bored of repeating himself or was taking Kell's questions too personally. "I had to hold off when I thought I was getting too close," he said. "The rest of the team—there were only three of us that day—were back in town." He nodded east along the coast. Kell, too, was beginning to feel enervated by the heat and wished they had brought a bottle of water. "But he'd taken out his towel and I saw him later on the beach. Swimming. That's when he got dressed, climbed up the rocks, and disappeared into the house."

"This house?"

Mohsin nodded.

"Taking his shoulder bag with him?"

The surveillance man hesitated, remembered. "Yeah. It's not as overgrown on that side."

"What made you think he was interested in buying it?"

"Just this." Mohsin tapped the sign. "Why else would somebody wander round a ruined *yali* on a hot afternoon after taking a nice relaxing swim? I figured Richards must have told him about the house being for sale. Or maybe he just stumbled on it. Maybe he just likes looking around old buildings."

Maybe, Kell thought to himself, but there had been nothing in any of the files or transcripts to suggest that Kleckner had taken an interest in the property. He wondered why the hell Mohsin hadn't volunteered this information sooner.

"Let's go down to the beach," he said.

39

Through the trees and across the water, west past Kadikoy and north along the Bosporus to Kabatas, a taxi was pulling into the ferry terminal where, only a few hours earlier, Thomas Kell and Javed Mohsin had waited for the ferry, drinking their glasses of tea.

Alexander Minasian, wearing shorts, a T-shirt, and a white Adidas baseball cap, paid the driver, sprinted across the concourse, passed the terminal café, pressed a ticket into the entry barrier as a foghorn sounded on the water, then leapt onto the ferry only seconds before departure.

Delayed in traffic at the end of four hours of countersurveillance, Minasian knew that if he had missed this boat, it would have been another three hours before he could dock in Buyukada, another two before it was safe to go to the Trotsky house, therefore making it necessary either to stay the night on the island or to hire a water taxi back to Istanbul in the dead of night, a journey he had endured once before, in mercilessly rough seas.

The ferry pulled away from the jetty. Minasian made grateful nodding eye contact with a member of the ship's crew and headed for a row of molded plastic seats on the port side. He kept an eye on the jetty, looking out for any last-minute passengers racing to catch the boat. Would a surveillance team risk exposure by one of their number chasing him onto a ferry? Perhaps not. If they were well-organized, if they had people in Kadikoy or Kartal, an operative could be sent ahead to Buyukada, cutting him off at the town. It was even possible that an American or MIT team could be active on the ferry. But they were not organized. He knew that because KODAK had told him as much. In Istanbul, Alexander Minasian was always a ghost.

A second horn cried out over the water, the blast of the ship as she steered confidently toward the cut and thrust of shipping moving north and south along the Bosporus. Removing a paperback book from his jacket pocket, Minasian began to read, confident in the knowledge that his journey to clear the KODAK letter box would, as ever, remain undetected.

40

They were on the beach.

To Kell's surprise, Mohsin had removed his shirt in the heat, revealing a tattooed and belly-fattened torso of which he seemed inordinately proud. Turning back to face the island, Kell could see the façade of the Richards house, partly obscured by a high stone wall. A small concrete harbor had been constructed on the beach, offering protection to a wooden sailing boat that was tied up with no fenders beside a paint-chipped steel ladder. For fifty meters on either side of the harbor there were sharp, mussel-covered rocks and weedy inlets; in the distance, farther toward the main town, the shoreline flattened out into shingle, offering swimmers easier access to the water.

"You said ABACUS swam here?"

"Yes," Mohsin replied. "Went in off those steps, swam out into the open water, came back. I watched him from up there."

He indicated the path down which they had walked from the road. It would have been easy for Mohsin to conceal himself in the shadow of the trees and the undergrowth.

"And then he went to the ruins?"

Kell began to retrace Kleckner's steps, trying to think his way into the American's mind. Why hadn't Richards, or one of the children, of whom Ryan was apparently so fond, joined him for the swim? Why cool off, only to return to his friend's house via the property next door?

Maybe he just likes looking around old buildings.

There were steps leading up to the ruined house. Large chunks of rock had broken away so that it was difficult for Kell to find his footing. Mohsin followed him to the northern perimeter of the overgrown garden. It was now possible to see the full extent of the ruins. The roof of the house had fallen in. Trees were growing in the spaces between collapsed walls, weeds and wild flowers carpeting every abandoned room. Kell was able to navigate his way under the frame of what had once been an entrance porch and emerged into an area about the size of the secure speech room at the Ankaran embassy. On one side, a wild and impenetrable bush obscured his view of the sea; on the other, a gap in a low wall allowed him to move into a second room, where various rusted cans and glass bottles were strewn on the ground. If people came to this place, they did so irregularly: most of the litter looked archeologically old.

Kell thought of Robert Hanssen, arrested by the FBI in a secluded park in Washington, D.C., after secreting classified material beneath a small wooden footbridge. As he ducked under a splintered beam, he instructed Mohsin to begin looking for anything that might function as an effective DLB.

"It'll be something in keeping with the environment. An old rusted box. A hole in the ground. Look for stickers, marks on walls. It's possible he's using different locations and identifies them to his handler in that way."

Mohsin, still shirtless, was seemingly energized by his task.

"Sure," he said, delighted finally to have been asked to play a more dynamic role in the operation. No more stakeouts, no more foot surveillance, no more paperwork and waiting. He was playing with the big boys now. "I'll start over here."

"You do that."

At the same time, Kell began looking for a route to the Richards house, because that would surely be Kleckner's cover? A drink in the garden, a solitary stroll and a cigarette after dinner, perhaps even a wander at three A.M. while spending the night. If there was a quick, unobstructed route between the two properties, Kleckner could be there and back within a couple of minutes. Under cover of darkness, or shielded during the day by the ample foliage of the gardens, his absence would not even be noticed.

Kell was at the eastern end of the ruins when he heard a child laughing, perhaps twenty or thirty meters away. One of the Richards kids. Ahead of him there was a tangle of trees and bushes obscuring the view, trapping the heat, but as gloomy as an English forest in the depths of winter. Kell climbed over an intact wall and looked to his left. There was a clearing to the side of the house, adjacent to what had once been a doorway. Walking toward the sound of the laughing child, he was able to move through the clearing and to bend and twist with relative ease along a path that linked the two houses. This was surely ABACUS's route. So why had he approached the ruined house from the seaward side?

Now an adult's voice. A Frenchwoman, most likely Marguerite Richards. Kell froze. He could not risk being seen by one of the children, or flushed out by a barking dog. He waited, then moved slowly back toward the ruined house, where he rejoined Mohsin.

No more than half a mile away, Alexander Minasian had joined the long line of passengers exiting the ferry at Buyukada. Having stepped down onto the jetty he walked south toward the main street, past the ticket check, and into a covered arcade of shops where he had once bought his nephew an imitation sailor's cap with CAPTAIN embroidered on the peak.

KODAK favored the second café on the main street as a first point to shake off surveillance. Minasian, on the other hand, preferred a larger restaurant to the west of the ferry terminal. It was his habit to take a table outside, to order a drink and perhaps a snack, then to read for twenty minutes, building up a portrait of his fellow customers, watching for repeating faces from his countersurveillance routine on the mainland. When Minasian was satisfied that there was no threat, he would pay his bill, leave the book on the table, go inside the restaurant—ostensibly to use the bathroom—then walk out via a rear exit adjacent to the women's toilet. This took him into a small courtyard at the back of the building. From there it was possible to reach one of the quieter alleyways that ran behind the main harbor road and to set out toward the Richards house in the western corner of the island, employing whatever further countersurveillance Minasian deemed necessary.

On this beautiful summer afternoon, the Russian chose a table at the outer perimeter of the terrace, ordered a bottle of Efes lager, paid in advance, and continued to read the novel he had begun on the boat. He was enjoying the book very much—it had been a gift from his lover in Hamburg—and so it was with a measure of regret that he abandoned it on the table, in order to give the impression that he was going to the bathroom. Minasian then slipped away from the restaurant via the staff exit.

A bicycle had been left for him, as arranged with the consulate in Istanbul. Minasian unlocked it using the key he had collected earlier in the day from an SVR colleague at the Pera Palace Hotel. He then embarked on a pleasant bicycle ride around the town, passing the churches of Aya Dimitrios and San Pacifico before heading downhill in a westerly direction toward the house occupied by Matthew and Marguerite Richards and their two young children.

Kell spent more than half an hour lifting paving stones, standing up on crumbling walls, peering into the gaps between wildly overgrown trees, even pulling back a rotten hessian sack that had been wedged in one of the doorframes. He began to think that he was on a fool's errand. Mohsin had become so irritable—and plagued by insect bites—that he had returned to the beach, complaining about the "fucking heat" and saying that he needed a swim to "cool the fuck down." Again and again Kell reminded himself of the tradecraft lunacy of planting a DLB on an island. No escape route. The suicide of the choke point. And he was about to give up, about to join Mohsin in the water, when he glimpsed a rusted gas canister in the corner of what had once been a kitchen or pantry at the southeastern end of the house.

Kell crouched down. The canister was protected from the elements by a portion of wooden shelf. There were dried leaves and loose stones all around it, as well as a prehistoric cigarette packet, crumpled and faded by years of rain and heat. Cobwebs deterred Kell from picking it up; he did not want to disturb the site. Instead, he banged on the canister. A hollow retort. An insect landed on his wrist and he flicked it away, banging his head on the wooden counter as he did so.

There was a gap to the left of the canister, running under the counter into darkness. Kell took out his iPhone, leaned closer in and shone it around the corner into the empty space. No cobwebs, no obstructions here. The area surprisingly clean. Just a deflated leather football, old and worn. By stretching out his arm, Kell could pull it out.

The leather was bone dry, but the surface of the ball was not as dusty or as caked in filth as Kell had expected. He felt something slip and move inside the ball, perhaps a stone. His fingers probed at the edge of a slit in the leather. Using both hands, Kell prized it open.

He was holding a balled-up sheet of paper wrapped in cellophane and held together by two rubber bands. He knew then, in his bones, that it was product and felt an adrenalized rush of euphoria that caused his hands to shake as he removed the rubber bands and unscrewed the bundle.

The piece of paper was still crisp, the typed letters clear and easy to read.

1. JC/LVa consistently losing argument on S intervention with WH. UK will do what US will do. Trying to get more on this but veracity of chem usage a) doubted by JC and b) not a WH threshold, as stated. Intel on FSA contradictory. WH happy for LVa to arm clandestinely.
2. Assad Pharma VX to AQ intercepted GID (April)
3. New BND source inside Huda-Par/Batman—deputy chairman HA
4. New stream of reporting coming out of mayoral office. JC source. Unidentified. More to follow on this.
5. Weapons cache FSA planned for frontier crossing and interaction 5.2.13 Jarabulus. RX, license plate by SMS 4.30. Very low circulation on this.
6. Why CS termination? Explanation? PW compromised? Suggest LHR Tues 30-Fri 3 (confirm SMS)

• • •

Alexander Minasian was thirsty. There was a man selling drinks from a stall at the side of the road, no more than three hundred meters south of the Trotsky house. The Russian leaned the bicycle against a garden fence before paying for a liter of chilled water. It was still very hot on the island, even in the relative cool of the shaded suburban neighborhood, and he removed his baseball cap before swallowing almost half a liter of the water in one long, breathless gulp.

The break in his journey allowed Minasian the opportunity to check his tail for following surveillance and to make an assessment of the good sense of servicing the DLB. There were three designated approaches, each of which he had used at different times. The most straightforward access to the Trotksy house was via the Richards garden, though Minasian could only enter the property when the family were away. The second route took him down to the sea, where he would pass in front of the Richards *yali* and then approach the site from the beach. The third route required Minasian to bicycle half a mile farther west, then to double back along a narrow path that clung to the coast.

Because of the heat, he decided on the second option. He would lock the bicycle, walk down to the beach, enjoy a brief, cooling swim, then service the DLB on his way out.

Kell took out his iPhone, photographed the piece of paper four times, immediately sent a copy of the photograph to one of his e-mail accounts, then whistled to Mohsin down on the beach.

He had soon deciphered Kleckner's abbrevations. "JC" was Jim Chater, "LVa" was Langley, Virginia. "WH" was White House, "FSA" very obviously the Free Syrian Army. (The cache of weapons would be transported in a Red Cross vehicle to the border at Jarabulus.) "CS" was Sandor, "PW" was Paul. Kell assumed "HA" were the initials of a deputy chairman of Huda-Par, the Kurdish Islamist party with offices in Batman, a town about a hundred kilometers east of Diyarbakir. In item 2, Kleckner had suggested that a consignment of VX nerve agent, disguised as market pharmaceuticals by the Assad regime, and destined for al-Qaeda, had been intercepted by Jordanian intelligence.

Kell had a decision to make. Should he leave the letter in place and risk it passing into the hands of Kleckner's case officer? The product itself was not incendiary: ABACUS had not revealed the identities of any CIA or SIS agents in Turkey. The name of the new source in the mayoral office in Istanbul was not known to him. That Langley and the White House were in disagreement about the good sense of intervention in Syria was an open secret, as was Downing Street's position on arming rebels opposed to Assad. Nobody had ever believed that the use of chemical weapons would be a red line for the White House.

The obvious operational risk was to an apparent consignment of weapons designated for representatives of the Free Syrian Army. The date given for the transfer at the border crossing in Jarabulus was May second. That was in three days' time. If Kleckner was an SVR asset, it was almost certain that Moscow would pass details of the Red Cross license plate to its client state. That would lead to arrests, and certainly to the deaths of whomever the Americans hired to drive the truck. It was perhaps a price that would have to be paid. To alert Chater would be to alert him to Kleckner's treachery. It was too early to play that card.

Kell heard the sound of Mohsin coming up the shattered stone staircase from the beach. He whistled again, directing him toward the kitchen. He took a final look at the sheet of paper, then balled it in the cellophane, tied it with the rubber bands, and replaced it inside the football. Taking care not to disturb the cobwebs strung beneath the wooden shelf, he reached into the space behind the gas canister and put the football back in exactly the same place and position in which he had found it.

"You find something?"

Mohsin was standing in the doorway. He had swum in his shorts, which were wet through, his hair matted with seawater. Kell motioned at him frantically.

"Stay where you are. Fuck's sake don't come in here." He was concerned that Mohsin would drip water on the ground, contaminating the scene. "Where was ABACUS yesterday? Did he go to Arada?"

"*What?*" Something of Mohsin's default disdain had returned. He was plainly irritated by Kell's tone.

"I said was ABACUS in Arada—"

"I heard you."

Kell stood up. At last he allowed his anger full expression. "Javed, I don't have time for your attitude. Answer me. This is important. Time is a fucking factor. Was ABACUS in Arada yesterday or wasn't he?"

The surveillance man was stung by the rebuke. Looking at Kell with sullen eyes he said: "Yes" and wiped his still-wet arms clear of drying salt and water.

"Was he wearing a tie? Was he wearing a suit?"

Kell could see the cogs beginning to work in Mohsin's brain. *The boss wants to know if ABACUS signaled the DLB. The boss wants to know if somebody is coming to clear the box.*

"Yes. I think so," he said.

"And where did he go yesterday? After work?"

"I don't know," Mohsin replied.

"What do you mean you don't know?"

"We lost him, sir. Yesterday was one of the times he got away from us. I thought you knew that."

Kell walked toward him and physically turned Mohsin through one hundred and eighty degrees. If Kleckner had gone to Arada the day before, wearing a tie to signal that the box was full, his SVR handler could come to the house at any moment. If he had seen Kell in the old kitchen, had heard them talking, had watched them going into the site, the operation to identify and then arrest the mole was ruined before it had begun. Even as Kell guided Mohsin out of the house, down the ruined steps, telling him to pick up his shirt and personal effects as quickly as possible, he knew that ABACUS's handler could be sending an abort code that would put Kleckner on the next flight to Moscow, never to be seen again.

"What's going on?" Mohsin asked, as Kell guided him toward the small concrete harbor, his hand in the small of his back. They had moved so quickly that Kell had not even been able to check for signs of water in the house, droplets from Mohsin's arms and legs, drips from his shorts. He could only hope that they would dry quickly in the fading heat. There was a house about eighty meters along the coast, close to where the beach flattened out. Several bathers were swimming and splashing in the shallows.

"There's a risk that somebody is coming to the site. I found the DLB. It was loaded."

"Jesus." Mohsin was putting on his shirt. "You want me to stay? Keep an eye out?"

Kell had considered that option, but it was too much of a risk. Keep an eye out from where? The tops of the trees? A rowing boat out at sea? No. The location of the box had been well chosen. Even setting up static camera positions overlooking the site would be fraught with risk.

"Forget it," he replied, taking out a cigarette and lighting it as they reached the edge of the shingled beach. "We just need to get away from here as quickly as possible."

Alexander Minasian surfaced seventy meters from the shore, clearing seawater from his nose with a crisp, efficient snort. Treading water, he was able to study both the façade of the Richards *yali* and the outline ruins of the Trotsky house, which was largely hidden from view by a curtain of pine trees. He could hear children playing in the distance, the low moan of a motorboat engine, the lisp of water as low waves unfurled on the beach. Turning around so that he was looking out across the vast plain of the Sea of Marmara, stretching all the way to the blur of Istanbul, Minasian remembered the long arguments with Kleckner about the good sense of locating the DLB on Buyukada. The Russian had argued his case vociferously, but the American was as stubborn as he was eventually persuasive.

"Look. Matt is a friend of mine. I go to his place all the time, he has parties, he has dinners. I can get away into the Trotsky place, leave whatever I have to leave, collect whatever you need me to collect. Then I can be back before anybody notices I'm gone. Somebody finds me there, I say I'm a historian with an interest in Lev Bronstein. Either that or I have plans to buy the place and turn it into a house like Matt's. See? You send me to some park in Istanbul and I start acting suspicious around buildings, I have to drive around for five hours shaking off a tail and then leaving classified information in some toilet somewhere, I'm gonna get antsy. I'm gonna get *caught*. And I don't want to get caught, because I want to help you guys. I can't do that if I'm sitting on my ass in some prison in Virginia."

So the SVR had let Ryan Kleckner have his way. Above all, the agent must feel comfortable in his work; he must feel safe. It was a relief to Minasian that he was handling a trained CIA officer—albeit one with limited experience—whose skills in countersurveillance had significantly reduced the chances of disclosure. KODAK was a calm and thorough agent, sometimes eerily so. Nevertheless, Minasian was aware of Moscow's concerns about him and conscious that the American's attitudes did not always sit well with senior colleagues. Minasian was convinced that the order to kill Cecilia Sandor, for example, would not have been given in normal circumstances. It was a symptom of Moscow's paranoia about KODAK, a determination to protect their source at all costs. Had Minasian himself been consulted on the operation, he would have argued strongly for Sandor and Luka Zigic to be left intact.

Minasian spun around and looked back at the beach. He was far from the shore and concerned that an opportunistic islander might steal his towel or bag. Two men—a Caucasian male in the company of a dark-skinned Turk—were leaving the beach via a slip road. Three small children were also accompanying their mother back into town. It was the end of the day. Minasian looked west, toward the gradually setting sun, and knew that it was time to finish his swim and to complete his task. Turning onto his back, he began to head for shore, arms windmilling slowly in the dusk while, high above, an airplane slipped across the sky.

41

"What do you think it means?"

"Isn't that obvious?" Kell replied.

He was back in the secure speech room, still in the same sweat-soaked clothes he had worn all day, talking to Amelia in London. It was half past ten in Turkey, half past eight in Vauxhall. Amelia was looking at the final line of Kleckner's document, sent by secure telegram an hour earlier.

Why CS termination? Explanation? PW compromised?
Suggest LHR Tues 30-Fri 3 (confirm SMS)

"There's an obvious link with Cecilia Sandor," Kell said. "'PW' has got to be Paul."

"I realize that, Tom."

"Then which bit of it is confusing you?"

They had been on the line for almost an hour and Kell was at the edge of his patience. He hadn't eaten since breakfast, Rachel had failed to respond when he had called her from the ferry, and it was so cold in the secure speech room that he was wearing an undersized winter coat purloined from a lost property cupboard in the Chancery. He had wanted to go straight from the island to Sabiha Gokcen and catch the late flight back to London, but the discovery of the DLB, the proof of Kleckner's treachery—with Paul's possible involvement thrown in—was too pressing. Instead, Kell had pulled Amelia out of a meeting in Whitehall and she had raced back to Vauxhall Cross to speak to him.

"No bit of it is confusing me," she replied, reacting to Kell's insolence as he would have expected. Her voice had taken on an edge of irritated condescension, like the start of a row with Claire. "I simply wanted to know what you think. What is meant by the word 'compromised'? Was Paul an asset or was Paul a patsy? And why does Kleckner care?"

"Why does he *care*?" Kell had a sudden glimpse of his future as H/Ankara and knew that he would grow to hate these interminable conversations with London, Rachel long gone and fucking some hotshot thirtysomething barrister at a warehouse apartment in Shoreditch, while Kell deadened his soul with work, throwing himself into recruitments and agent-running as a means of forgetting her. In recent weeks he had come to think of the secure speech room as a padded cell, a freezing womb in which he felt trapped and controlled. Surely it would be better if he was back in London, dealing with "C" face-to-face, day-to-day, then heading home to a flat lined with his books and his paintings, to a midnight bed warmed by Rachel? "He cares because killing Sandor was a mistake," he said. "It draws attention to what he's up to. Somebody finds out Cecilia was seeing Paul, that makes them sit up and start asking questions."

"Of course it does."

Kell heard the tinkle of a spoon against a cup, like the prelude to an after-dinner speech. Amelia was probably drinking an espresso from the new machine in her private office.

"We are still where we were on Wallinger," Kell added. "Either he was conscious that Sandor was an SVR asset, and therefore deliberately assisting her, or he was not. What's strange, what doesn't ring true, is

Kleckner's consciousness of that SVR operation. If Minasian was running both of them—an asset in the CIA, an asset in SIS—it's feasible that he would have made them aware of each other, but it's risky. Doubles the chances of one of them getting caught, of one of them betraying the other."

"Precisely." Amelia sounded pleased to have Kell thinking along similar lines. "Though we are both agreed that the tradecraft on much of this operation has been eccentric, to say the least."

"We are both agreed on that."

Kell buttoned the coat to the neck and bit down on a stick of shortbread, the only food that had passed his lips in eight hours, save for a handful of peppermints discovered in a bowl near the consulate entrance.

"Tom?"

"Yes?"

"I have to go to the Cousins with this."

It was what Kell had expected Amelia to say. An SVR mole inside the CIA was catastrophic; that it had taken the Brits to identify him would both embarrass Langley and leave them in London's debt for years. Nevertheless, Kell recoiled at the idea.

"That is the one thing we should not do. Yet."

"Why?"

"Because they'll try to pin most of it on Paul. Say that the most damaging leaks—on HITCHCOCK, on EINSTEIN—came from our side. We need to clear him of suspicion, find out the precise nature of his relationship with Sandor and Minasian."

"There's no time for that," Amelia replied. "The Americans need to know. Jim Chater has to be told."

"All in good time. Kleckner is coming to the U.K., yes?"

"Yes."

"So get me to London. Tuesday to Friday, he'll be on our turf, we know that we can control him. Let me move the surveillance operation from Istanbul to London, get my team home, get fresh eyes and legs on him. Kleckner wants to talk about Sandor's murder. He will lead us to his handler."

"And if we lose him? If he shakes us off?"

"Then we lose him."

Kell was aware that Amelia needed him in Istanbul. The Station was going to have to try to put cameras on the DLB; to identify Kleckner's "signal in" to Minasian; to work out how to put a long-term advance surveillance team on Buyukada that would saturate ABACUS on his next visit. Kell would suggest that SIS try to gain control of the DLB and switch Kleckner's product for chicken feed, handing bogus intelligence to the SVR that would tie Moscow in knots. But London meant Rachel. Kell wanted time with her, even if it was just the few days when Ryan Kleckner would be in town. Time to track the American into the arms of his handler, yes; but also time to rekindle their relationship.

"There's no need for you to come over, Tom."

Kell heard a note of apology in Amelia's voice, as though she wanted to save him the trouble of flying back.

"Of course there is. We should talk face-to-face, line everything up for Ryan's visit. I'll get the early BA flight tomorrow, see you around lunchtime."

"What about the Red Cross convoy?"

"What about it?"

"We let the Russians inform Assad? That's your view?" Amelia sounded as though she wanted to test the direction of Kell's moral compass. "The convoy gets hit, gets discovered, Jim finds out that we knew about it, he's not going to be best pleased."

"Since when did you care so much about Jim Chater?"

It was a better reply than Kell had intended, touching as it did on Amelia's loyalty to her own.

"Fair point," she replied, with an appropriate edge of contempt for the man who had almost obliterated Kell's career. "Nevertheless, I don't like the idea of a Red Cross team getting arrested or shot by the Syrians when we could have saved them."

Kell wondered what Amelia was expecting him to say. Surely she could see the importance of delaying any conversation with Langley?

"I don't like it either," he said, "but we don't have any choice. Tell Jim and he'll ask how we found out about a top secret consignment of American weapons making their way into the arms of the Free Syrian Army. Warn the driver and the Russians will know there's blowback on Kleckner's material."

"Collateral damage?" Amelia said, as though she wanted Kell to take responsibility for it.

"Collateral damage," he replied.

42

Twelve hours later Kell was touching down in London.

He came from the ceaseless clamor and sweat of Istanbul into a city of permanent rain. It was always the same coming home. Landing at Heathrow under gray skies; the same fat-turned-to-muscle Crystal Palace supporter driving the same gargling black cab; the gradual but somehow reassuring adjustment to the smallness and the litter and the dimmed light of England. Rachel, having vanished from Kell's life for the better part of three days, suddenly surfaced again, texting him incessantly on the M4 with a customary barrage of jokes about his age and a demand that Kell meet her for dinner.

MY PLACE. I'M COOKING. DON'T FORGET YOUR PACEMAKER, OLD MAN XXX

Kell had forgotten to put out the garbage before he left for Chios. Opening the door of his flat he was hit by a nauseating smell, close to the stench of death, and had to open every window in the place before walking the bag downstairs and throwing it in a Dumpster eight doors down. Having sifted through his post, he showered and changed, then took a cab to Bayswater shortly after one o'clock.

Amelia was waiting for him in a branch of Costa Coffee at the northern end of the Whiteleys shopping mall. They walked to the empty office of a defunct mail order catalogue business on Redan Place. It was here, a year earlier, that Kell had told Amelia about the plot to kidnap her son. He remembered the conversation as one of the most difficult they had ever endured, yet as they rode the lift to the fourth floor, Amelia seemed relaxed and uninhibited, whatever memories she retained of that afternoon now happily erased. She was wearing an almost exact replica of the outfit she had worn that day: a skirt with a navy blue jacket, a white blouse, and a gold necklace. Kell noticed that it was the one she had worn to the funeral; the same necklace she had been wearing in the photograph that Wallinger had kept beside his bed in Ankara. The realization gave him an odd sense of reassurance, because such a symbolic choice surely suggested that Amelia had no doubts about Paul's innocence.

"The Office owns this place now?" he asked as Amelia tapped in the security code, switching off a silent alarm.

"Rents," she replied, dropping her handbag on the ground. She walked toward the kitchen at the far end of the room. "You want tea?"

"I'm fine, thanks."

The office had changed. Two years earlier it had been open plan, rows of plastic-wrapped dresses hanging on racks along the south wall, desks covered in coffee cups and computers. Now the room had been sectioned off into six separate areas with a corridor running down the center. Kell could see Amelia filling up the kettle at the far end of the office. There had been a red sofa outside the kitchen. That too was gone.

"This place is operational?" he called out, walking toward her.

"About to be." She turned to face him. "I thought we could watch our friend from here. Team coming in at three to arrange the layout. Agree?"

"Sounds like a done deal." Kell was impressed that Amelia had moved so quickly on Kleckner's visit to London.

"Let me get you his itinerary," she said.

As the kettle crackled and came to a boil, Amelia passed Kell a three-page document outlining ABACUS's travel arrangements. Everything was there. Flight times, hotels, meetings, lunches, dinners. All put together within the previous twenty-four hours.

"That was quick," he said. "Who did this? Elsa?"

It transpired that Kleckner had telephoned Jim Chater from Bursa, requesting some leave. The call had been picked up by Cheltenham. Chater had signed off on the trip and Kleckner had spent the rest of the evening back at his apartment in Istanbul, arranging the journey. Elsa had been watching his e-mail and credit cards, GCHQ listening to his phones.

"He's staying at the Rembrandt?" Kell was trying to recall where Kleckner had based himself on previous visits to the capital. In the beds of two or three different girls—he wasn't certain how many—but never before at a hotel. "Why isn't he using one of the embassy apartments? Did he try for that?"

"He did." Amelia was looking in a cupboard for a mug. She found one and pulled it down, muttering something about "fresh milk." Kell had a sudden flash memory of Rachel in the kitchen at the *yali*. He remembered the way she had leaned across the counter, reaching for a box of tea. "There's a delegation in town," Amelia was saying. "All the flats were full. Which makes our job that much easier."

Kell wondered if he could light a cigarette or if the temporary office would be subject to Civil Service regulations. "Could be a smoke screen. Could be he's staying somewhere else and has no intention of checking in."

Amelia turned and appeared to hesitate before answering. "Perhaps," she said. "But I've got a team going into the Rembrandt tomorrow morning, just in case. Harold heading it up. They'll rig two rooms. If little

Ryan complains about the first one, he'll be moved to the second. Either way we'll have coverage."

Kell was again impressed by the speed with which Amelia had moved on the operation.

"The Rembrandt is on Knightsbridge, yes?"

"It is, yes." Amelia was pouring water into the mug.

"Wonder if Ryan's a fan of *The Secret Pilgrim*."

She frowned and looked at him, confused. Kell came into the kitchen and poured himself a cup of water from a cooler by the window.

"Harrods," he said. "Best countersurveillance site in western Europe. A guy with Kleckner's training goes in there, he'll lose our team in less than five minutes. So many switchbacks, so many rooms within rooms. It's a labyrinth."

"A wilderness of mirrors," Amelia replied archly. He could sense that she was making a calculation about manpower. How could she organize a team big enough to saturate Harrods if and when Kleckner chose to go there? It would mean having at least twenty watchers on call for the entire five-day duration of Kleckner's visit, far more than she could justify to the risk-averse jobsworths at MI5. Kell put her out of her misery.

"Let me worry about it," he said. "He's just as likely to go to Harvey Nichols or wander around the V&A." She withdrew the tea bag from the water and threw it in a trash can. "Just tell me about women," Kell said, sipping the water.

Amelia looked perplexed. "What about them, Thomas?"

"Did Elsa look at Kleckner's Facebook? Isn't there a girl on there he likes, one he slept with last time he was in London?" He was trying to remember the woman's name. He could recall the profile photo, because the left side of her head had been almost completely shaved. Both parties had made a promise to each other that they would get together next time Kleckner was in town. "We should cover her flat, anyone else who

Ryan's been in touch with about his trip. He has a habit of setting himself up for dates, nights out, booty calls. Has there been any of that?"

"*Booty* calls?" Amelia had adopted the tone of a shocked maiden aunt. "I'll have it looked at. As far as I know, Ryan has no plans other than to see some old friends from Georgetown."

Kell left the office just after three. He shopped in Whiteleys, bought groceries at Waitrose on Porchester Road and sank a six o'clock pint at the Ladbroke Arms, where Kathy welcomed him back with the enthusiasm and excitement of a sailor's wife greeting her husband off an aircraft carrier in Portsmouth. He was aware that this would be the first time that he and Rachel had been together on home soil. Kell expected her to be different in London, more reserved, putting on a layer of armor to protect herself from deeper commitment. Perhaps they would come to see that what had passed between them in the previous few weeks was no more than a giddy infatuation; a holiday romance.

As soon as he walked into her flat, however, they were kissing, taking off their clothes, tripping toward the bedroom. Everything about Rachel was as Kell had remembered it: the opiates of her perfume and her kiss; the weight and shape of her languorous body; the sense in which he was communicating the strength of his feelings for her without words. There was a kind of frenzy to his desire that he could not and did not want to conceal. And that desire was matched by a quality of gentleness and passion in Rachel that drugged him into a state he had rarely known. Thomas Kell had witnessed violence and appalling brutality, deceit, and artful cunning. He had seen men killed, families torn apart, careers destroyed by greed and lies. He was not a sentimental man, nor did he have any illusions about people's motives or the human potential for cruelty. In his long marriage to Claire, a relationship repeatedly smashed open by her infidelites, Kell had nevertheless felt deep affection for his wife. But he had never known this narcotic agitation, the state of grace in which he found himself whenever he was in Rachel's company. Not in forty-four years.

Just as they had done in Istanbul two weeks earlier, they dressed at dusk and walked outside in search of dinner. ("I was lying about cooking," she said. "I just wanted to get into your trousers.") They talked about Rachel's new job, about a problem she was having with her neighbors, about a family holiday planned by Josephine for August. It was only toward the end of the meal that Kell decided to broach the subject of H/Ankara; in the rush of a second bottle of wine it seemed dishonest not to speak about it.

"I've been offered a permanent position in Turkey."

"That's amazing," Rachel said. "You must be thrilled."

A vain part of Kell's character wished that he had detected at least some small evidence of disappointment.

"I haven't accepted yet," he said quickly. "A lot depends on the operation I'm working on now."

Rachel's eyes dropped to the table. They both knew that Kell would not be permitted to speak candidly about his work. Though he was aware of this and sensed Rachel's reluctance to discuss the subject, he nevertheless forced the point.

"It's your father's job. Effectively." Rachel was still looking down at the table. "How would you feel about that?"

Kell was conscious that he had gone too far. The entire restaurant was filled with couples and families and groups of friends, none of whom appeared to be talking to one another. They had come to one of Rachel's favorite Thai restaurants, and the plink-plunk of piped music became as grating as nails being dragged down a chalkboard.

"Rachel?"

"*What?*"

There it was again; the sudden, flared anger of their first night in Istanbul, her face a sullen, disappointed mask. This time, however, Kell knew that she was not drunk; he had hit a nerve of impatience and grief and Rachel's mood had collapsed as a consequence.

"Sorry," he said. "That was stupid of me. Let's talk about it another time."

But she remained stubbornly silent. Kell tried to start a conversation about a book they had both read, but the ill feeling between them crackled like static and Rachel would not respond. He was irritated by how quickly the easy romantic rhythms of the evening had been dismantled. Perhaps, for all of the sex and conversations, the thousand e-mails back and forth, they would always be relative strangers to each other.

"Let's not do this," he said. "I'm sorry. I was being insensitive. I shouldn't have brought it up."

"Forget it," she said.

But the evening was over. They sat in prolonged silence to a background of harps and pipes, Rachel looking off to one side of the restaurant, her face sullen and bored. Kell, stirred by a mixture of frustration and fury at the sudden change in her behavior, proved incapable of reviving her mood. Eventually Rachel went to the bathroom and he asked for the bill. As they walked out of the restaurant five minutes later, accosted by the grayness and the litter of a damp, ill-lit east London street, Rachel turned to him and said: "It's probably better if you don't stay."

Kell felt the fury inside him simmer, but did not reply. He could still hear the plink-plonk of the music receding behind them as he turned and walked away. The romantic in him was crushed with disappointment; the man of reason and experience merely raged at Rachel's overreaction. Kell cursed himself for talking about Ankara, but cursed Rachel still more for lacking the patience and the goodwill to let his remarks pass.

He did not turn around. Nor did he respond when he felt his phone vibrating in his pocket. Instead, he lit a cigarette, walked to the Underground station, waited on a crowded platform for the last Central Line service of the night, and returned in silence to west London. Emerging from the lift at Holland Park station half an hour later, he saw that Rachel had twice tried to call him; she had also sent a text message containing a single question mark. He did not respond. Instead, he stepped out onto Holland Park Avenue and took out a packet of Winstons. A man and a woman walked past him, arm in arm. The man asked for a cigarette and Kell gave him one, lighting it wordlessly and receiving effusive thanks in return. There was a smell of dogshit in the air: Kell couldn't tell if it had been on one of the couple's shoes or was just general to the area. He began to walk east, not yet heading home, and was gripped by a determination to work. Revived by the cigarette, he hailed a taxi and was at Redan Place in less than five minutes.

There was no security guard on duty downstairs. Kell let himself into the building using a fob key. He rode the lift to the fourth floor, only to find the door to the office propped open by boxes piled three high on the ground. The lights were on in one of the larger rooms halfway down the corridor, the flickering shadow of someone moving around. Kell called out: "Hello? Anybody home?"

The movement ceased. Kell heard a grunted "What's that?" and saw Harold Mowbray's face looking out into the corridor. Harold was squinting, trying to bring Kell into focus. He looked like a man peering into an oven to see if his dinner is cooked.

"That you, boss? What you doing here this time of night?"

Mowbray had been the Tech-Ops man on the operation to find Amelia's son. Good with microphones and miniature cameras, good with one-liners to break the tension.

"I was going to ask you the same thing," Kell replied. "It's good to see you." He was surprised by how much he meant it. The kinship of old colleagues came as a relief.

They approached each other in the gloom of the corridor and shook hands.

"So what's going on this time?" Harold asked. "Amelia got a secret daughter she doesn't know about? I felt like we were in *Mamma Mia!* on the last gig."

Kell laughed, ignoring his regret at how stubborn and shortsighted he had been not to call Rachel back.

"Cousin we have concerns about. Ryan Kleckner. Based out of Istanbul. He's in London for four days, has a crash meeting at some point that he won't want anyone witnessing."

Harold nodded. Kell went back to the main door and flicked a switch, strobing the lights in his office. Harold confirmed that he was happy with the coverage in the two rooms at the Rembrandt. Kell had obtained the names and addresses of the Facebook girls and told Harold to wire their apartments for sound, not sight. The Georgetown dinner was booked for Wednesday night at Galvin, a restaurant on Baker Street. They briefly discussed the possibility of wiring a table, but concluded that it would be pointless. Instead they would have taxis in front of the restaurant timed to coincide with Kleckner's exit.

"That's more Danny's bag, yeah?" Mowbray was referring to Danny Aldrich, another veteran, who would head up the surveillance team in the absence of Javed Mohsin.

"True," Kell concurred. "At some point Kleckner is going to try to disappear." Harold was standing in Kell's office. Both men were smoking cigarettes, having pushed the windows wide open. "We'll only have seven people watching him, eight max. Ideally I'd like to get something onto him, either some dust or a microphone."

"Yeah, Amelia mentioned that."

Kell looked up. "She did?"

Harold looked as if he had spoken out of turn. Kell had the impression that he was concealing something. He remembered his conversations with Amelia in Istanbul: the sense of parallel operations taking place without his knowledge, of privileged information being withheld.

"What do you mean?" he asked, stubbing out the cigarette. Harold turned and walked back into the corridor. Kell followed him to the closed-off area in which he had been setting up the Rembrandt surveillance screens. He could not see Harold's face as he said: "You know. Usual stuff. What's the latest tech, what can we do to ensure eyes and ears on a target."

"And what *can* we do?"

Harold recovered and shot him a trademark grin. "I'm working on it, guv," he said. "I'm working on it."

43

Ryan Kleckner boarded Turkish Airlines flight TK1986 at Istanbul Ataturk Airport at 1730 hours on Tuesday, April thirtieth. Fifteen rows behind him, Javed Mohsin settled into a window seat, placed his Pakistani passport in the inside pocket of his jacket, inflated a travel pillow, and went to sleep. Five hours later, following a delay in the air, Mohsin was watching ABACUS flash a diplomatic passport at Terminal Three immigration, thereby cutting out a snaking line that would have delayed the American by at least forty-five minutes. Mohsin telephoned ahead to a second surveillance officer in the baggage area, confirming Kleckner's outfit—white Converse sneakers, blue denim jeans, white button-down shirt, black V-neck sweater—and giving a description of his carry-on bag (a molded black wheeled suitcase with a Rolling Stones lips sticker peeling on the left panel) as well as the leather satchel from which he was rarely parted. ABACUS had no checked baggage and would be mobile in the terminal building within less than three minutes.

The second officer—known to the team as "Carol"—picked up ABACUS as he walked into the baggage area and called ahead to Redan Place when she saw him buying a SIM card from an automated machine in the south corner.

"Which brand?" Kell asked. He was sitting in the smallest of the six rooms, the one he had chosen as his own office. Kleckner's move was predictable, but it was nevertheless a potential headache to Elsa and GCHQ.

"Difficult to say. Looked like a Lebara pay-as-you-go."

"Has he fitted it in the BlackBerry?"

"Not yet. Negative."

Carol followed ABACUS through the automatic doors at customs and established line of sight with a third watcher—Jez—who had joined the massed ranks of minicab drivers clustered in arrivals. Jez was dressed in a cheap black suit and holding a sign with the name "Kerin O'Connor" scrawled on the front in green marker pen. Lowering the sign, he turned and tailed ABACUS at five meters while Carol moved ahead, taking up an advanced position on the platform of the Heathrow Express in anticipation of Kleckner choosing to travel into London by train.

As it turned out, he took a cab. Jez texted the license plate to an SIS vehicle idling near the Parkway intersection at junction 3 of the M4. With Jez on a follow, the driver of the vehicle picked up the ABACUS cab as it paused at a set of traffic lights three hundred meters short of the motorway. Both cars tailed the target into central London and housed ABACUS at the Rembrandt Hotel. Carol went back to Paddington on the Heathrow Express, then made her way to a restaurant in Knightsbridge awaiting further instructions from Kell. Jez parked in a mews behind the hotel and hoped that he would be able to get some sleep; the driver of the second SIS vehicle was called onto a separate job. Javed Mohsin went home to his wife, whom he had not seen for more than six weeks.

Every detail of Kleckner's arrival was relayed live to Redan Place. As soon as ABACUS was on the road, Kell had called Danny Aldrich in his room at the Rembrandt. Harold had piped the hotel's surveillance cameras to Aldrich's laptop so that he could keep an eye on the corridor outside Kleckner's room, as well as the lobby and front and side entrances. If the American checked in and went walkabout, Aldrich would form part of the mobile surveillance team attempting to follow him. If he ordered room service and went to sleep, most of them would get an early night.

As it turned out, Amelia was right about Kleckner's desire to switch rooms. Having checked in to 316, which had taken four painstaking hours to rig with cameras and microphones, the American made a cursory assessment of the room before returning to reception and requesting an upgrade. A female officer on secondment from Australian SIS was role-playing the Rembrandt receptionist—with the connivance of the hotel manager—and reacted quickly and calmly to Kleckner's request, even throwing in the bone of a "lovely view over Knightsbridge." ABACUS was duly reassigned a room on the top floor of the hotel that had also been wired for sight and sound.

Kell wondered at Kleckner's motive. Did he simply want a more pleasant room, or did he have concerns about liaison surveillance? If the latter was the case, was the American simply being cautious, or did his decision speak of a gathering paranoia?

"We just have to hold our nerve," he told Amelia on the phone just after ten o'clock.

"We do, Tom. We do," she replied, and with that announced that she was going to bed.

It became a long night. Kleckner took a shower in his room, ordered a club sandwich, then changed into a pair of jeans and a fresh shirt before heading out into the late London evening. Jez, who had briefly fallen asleep in the mews, awoke to a telephone call from Kell instructing him to drive in loops around ABACUS while Aldrich, Carol, and two other foot surveillance officers tailed the American into Kensington.

It transpired that he had made a date to meet a Lebanese girl at

Eclipse, a bar on Walton Street. The youngest female member of the team—Lucy—entered the bar ten minutes later, where the attentions of two Dubai-based businessmen briefly interfered with her efforts to photograph Kleckner's companion.

"She's about twenty-five," she told Kell, speaking to him from the bar. It was almost impossible to hear what she was saying. "The name I heard was 'Zena.' They are intimate. They've either met before or he's on a promise."

"Why didn't we know about her?" Kell asked Elsa, texting Danny and instructing him to hold on Walton Street. It had been a long time since he had heard the phrase "on a promise." "Who's Zena?"

Elsa shrugged. "Maybe the new SIM?" she said.

Kell had asked for one of the separating walls in the office to be dismantled so that there would be a larger communal area in which the various members of the team could sit. An extra sofa had also been brought in from a shop on Westbourne Grove. Elsa was lying on it, staring up at the ceiling, tired and faintly irritable.

"It is always the case that people have e-mails, sites, new IPs that they can use to make contacts."

"True," Kell replied. "But we still need to get hold of that SIM."

Kleckner was another hour at Eclipse, leaving with Zena as the bar closed. Lucy had allowed the Dubai businessmen to pay her bill and had left in their company half an hour earlier, thereby giving Kleckner—had he noticed her—the impression that she had intended to meet the men and was not a surveillance threat. As soon as she had left the bar, however, she brushed off the men and returned home, "red" for the duration of Kleckner's visit on the basis that he would recognize her as a repeating face should she continue to follow him.

Meanwhile, Aldrich had purloined a dummy black cab from the Security Service and was able to tail Kleckner and Zena to a nightclub at the eastern end of Kensington High Street. With Lucy out of the game, Kell was aware that they were down to a team of only five. He could not risk sending another watcher into the venue. He had a hunch that Kleckner would get the girl drunk, take her out onto the dance floor, then suggest a nightcap at the Rembrandt. That was his normal Istanbul modus operandi and it seemed highly unlikely to Kell that Kleckner would break off, on the cusp of a one-night stand, to meet Minasian.

So it proved. Just after three in the morning, Kell had a text from the receptionist confirming that ABACUS was "back in his room with a woman (Arabic appearance, mid-20s). Both drunk/flirtatious." Switching on the surveillance screens, Kell and Harold were able to see Zena frantically brushing her teeth in the bathroom while a shirtless Kleckner searched the minibar for champagne. The bedspread had been disturbed, suggesting that the pair had already kissed.

"Lucky bastard," Harold muttered. "What I would give to be twenty-nine again."

"I'm sure a lot of women feel the same way," Kell replied. "Take Zena. If she had a choice tonight between you and Ryan, and you were staying in the hotel, well . . ."

"Well it's no competition, is it? She's only human."

Harold switched off the audio feed from the bathroom. The television had been turned on in the room and tuned to a music channel. There was a song playing that Kell didn't recognize.

"Shall we leave them to it?" he suggested, remembering the first night with Rachel at the Londres.

"Good idea," Harold replied, and they moved next door.

44

Zena slipped away before seven o'clock. Kleckner, who had been pretending to sleep, got out of bed as soon as she had left the room and checked the time on his watch. Having visited the bathroom, he dropped to the floor and completed fifty rapid push-ups, a series of stomach crunches, and a leg-strengthening exercise in which he assumed a sitting position against the wall. Kell had seen it all before in Istanbul, but it was Harold's first glimpse of the ABACUS beauty routine.

"I knew there was something I forgot to do when I woke up this morning," he said.

Kell, who had grabbed three hours' sleep on a mattress in his office, said: "Me too" and patted his stomach as he walked down to the kitchen.

By eight o'clock, Kleckner was eating a virtuous breakfast in the hotel restaurant—muesli, fruit, yogurt—watched by Aldrich on the first floor. Eight surveillance officers were scattered around the neighborhood—one with Aldrich, two more in the Addison Lee Renault with Jez, three on foot in Knightsbridge. Elsa had coverage of the Wi-Fi in Kleckner's room, as well as his Turkish cell phone, but still nothing on the Heathrow SIM. There had been no hint, in any of the ABACUS traffic, of

Kleckner's plans for the day, nor had he contacted Chater in Istanbul. Kell knew in his bones that the American was going to try to make a break from surveillance.

Just after nine fifteen, Kleckner was reported to have left the Rembrandt and to be heading east on foot—directly toward Harrods. He was wearing a baseball cap and three layers of clothing, including a black jacket that could be removed at any stage, effecting a change in appearance. Kell, leading the operation from the hub in Redan Place, ordered Jez to Harrods and put his two officers inside, one in the western corner, one in the Food Hall. Two others were sent ahead to Harvey Nichols.

The first sign of Kleckner's intention to shake off possible liaison came as he turned south on Beauchamp Place, less than a hundred meters from the entrance to Harrods. On Walton Street he turned right once again, effectively doubling back in the direction of the Rembrandt. Kell pulled the officers out of Harrods and put them back in the Renault with Jez. Aldrich, who had been idling in the black cab on Thurloe Place, picked ABACUS up on Draycott Avenue and managed to follow him into Pelham Street. Carol, dressed in running shorts, sneakers, and a T-shirt, was hooked up to headphones that allowed her to hear Kell's feed from the hub. She jogged west along South Terrace, staying parallel to Kleckner's position, then picked him up as he reached the Underground station at South Kensington.

"He'll go for the Tube," Kell announced, and wasn't surprised when Aldrich reported that Kleckner was making a phone call in the pedestrianized area immediately west of the station.

"Can we hear that?" he called across to Elsa.

Elsa had a constant line into Kleckner's BlackBerry, but shook her head. Either the American was talking on the new SIM, or—more likely—was garbling nonsense into a dead mouthpiece while taking the time to make a complete observation of his surroundings. Any repeating faces? Anything out of place? Ryan knew all the tricks. Javed Mohsin had lived with them for six weeks.

"Looks like a slow three sixty," Aldrich reported, confirming Kell's suspicion that Kleckner was slowly turning a complete circle in order to make an assessment of the area. "Now he's going for the trains."

Carol could not follow. Not in running gear. Instead, Aldrich and two other officers followed ABACUS into the Tube. This was the worst time on a surveillance job. Dead time. No communication from underground, save for the odd lucky text with a bar of signal, or a miracle burst on free Virgin Wi-Fi. Otherwise Kell was forced to pace and to wait, trying to communicate a sense of calm and well-being to Elsa and Harold, but inside churning with tension. He used to love this feeling in his younger days, the adrenaline surge of high stakes and risk, but Kleckner was too important—his sins too grave—for Kell to have any sense other than an intense desire to bring him to justice. He thought of Rachel, and of her dead father, and the pleasure he would gain from presenting her with Kleckner's head on a platter. If the London mission failed—and Kell was aware that there was every chance they would lose ABACUS in the next five days and fail to identify his handler—Kell would be forced back to Istanbul and to weeks, possibly months, of waiting for a second chance. His fallback plan, which he had discussed at length with Amelia, was to switch the intelligence dropped by ABACUS in the Buyukada football for chicken feed. But such a plan would mean allowing Kleckner to continue to operate, and would almost certainly require the assistance of the CIA. That would mean Chater big-footing the SIS operation, thereby spelling the end of Kell's involvement.

A signal from Elsa. A hand in the air, tapping her ear with the other. "Text from Nina. Piccadilly Line. Hyde Park Corner."

Nina was one of the two officers who had followed Kleckner into the tube. She was short and slightly cross-eyed, with capped front teeth that produced an unsettling range of colors in her mouth; Kell had met her only once and taken an instant dislike to her.

"Is he coming out?"

Elsa shrugged.

It was another twenty minutes before Kell heard anything more.

"Boss?"

Aldrich this time.

"Danny. What's the situation?"

"He's doing circuits. I got him to Green Park. He gets off, he gets on. One more stop to Piccadilly. Then he goes north to Oxford Circus."

"Have you got him now?"

"Yeah, I've got him. I'm looking at him. But I'm down to myself."

"What happened to Nina?"

"Fuck knows."

Kell swore under his breath but was glad to have Aldrich as a last pair of eyes. "Where are you?"

"Hyde Park Hotel."

A possible site for meeting a handler? Almost certainly not. It was too obvious, too quick out of the gates. An officer of Kleckner's experience would run at least two hours of countersurveillance before contemplating such a risk. The Hyde Park Hotel had to be just another stepping post on a preplanned route.

"Visual?"

"Impossible. He'd make me."

At that moment, a text came through from Jez, who, by a miracle Kell would never entirely understand, had somehow contrived to get into the hotel ahead of Kleckner and to track him as far as the men's bathroom. Acting on this information, Kell instructed the other members of the team to move back into the Knightsbridge area and to await further instructions.

"You think Harrods is coming, don't you?"

Elsa was standing beside Kell at one of the windows looking out over Whiteleys. To his surprise, she put her arm across his back, as if to try to reassure him.

"I do," he replied, turning and smiling at her. "He's less than five hundred meters away. It's always been a favorite Russian watering hole.

They would have told him to go there, if he didn't know already. NKVD. KGB. FSB. Been using the place for decades."

"Watering hole?" she said, screwing up her face. "What does this mean, please?"

"Never mind." Kell looked out across the skyline roofs and cranes of London.

ABACUS was about to go shopping.

45

Jez saw ABACUS out of the Hyde Park Hotel and passed him on to Carol, who had changed out of her running gear, tied her hair up in a bun, and put on a business suit with heels. She was close enough to touch Kleckner as the American walked west along Knightsbridge, crossing the street at a set of traffic lights and heading toward Harrods.

The entire team, barring Nina, was back in the area, but Kell had put only one officer—a sixty-two-year-old named "Amos"—inside the store. To gamble more, only to have Kleckner leave the building within three minutes and drop down into Knightsbridge Underground, was too risky. Instead, he would spread the rest of the team around all four sides of the building, covering each of the ground-floor exits. There was no point trying to follow Kleckner every step of the way around Harrods. Let him do his thing, let him adopt his tricks. ABACUS could spend five hours trying to duck and weave through eight different departments but, when all was said and done, he still had to leave the building.

"He's in," said Carol.

Kleckner had used the Hans Crescent door in the north corner, still wearing the baseball cap, still wearing the black Carhartt jacket. Jez went in behind him, continuing the live conversation with Kell while Carol stayed on the entrance.

"Moving through men's clothing. Fifteen meters." Jez's voice was a low, gravelly Cockney. "How are my exits?"

Kell and Elsa had more than half a dozen cell phones laid out in front of them, each feeding positional information from members of the team. Absorbing their messages, using them to create and maintain a mental map of the area, required Kell to focus and to concentrate in ways he had not known for years; it was exhilarating.

"All covered," he replied, as Jez moved upstairs to the first floor, allowing Amos to pick up Kleckner in the Food Hall.

"Visual," Amos said, the trace of a Somerset accent. While most of the members of the team were using earpieces and concealed microphones, Amos had been given an antediluvian Nokia of the sort favored by grandparents and lonely widowers. Kell had banked on the phone giving plausible cover. "Looking at some caviar, I think. In the delicatessen. Baseball cap still on."

Working in partnership, Jez and Amos were able to move with Kleckner as he ran countersurveillance for the next fifty minutes. Through the mists and the pretty girls in Perfumes and Cosmetics, he next went up two floors to linens, then down via the Egyptian-themed escalators past the candlelit memorial to Diana and Dodi Fayed. Whenever the American dropped out of sight, making a sudden left- or right-hand turn, Harold used a link to the Harrods closed-circuit security cameras to try to track him. This worked only twice—a sudden flickering image of a figure in a dark jacket and a baseball cap—but on both occasions Kell was able to establish Kleckner's approximate position and to feed it back to the team. At the same time, Nina had reappeared, having traveled east on the Piccadilly Line for almost half an hour under the misguided impression that Kleckner was seated in the adjacent carriage.

"I had the wrong guy," she explained sheepishly. "Fucking baseball cap. Same jacket."

"Never mind," Kell told her, and put her in Beauty and Fashion, covering doors 6 and 7 on the right angle in the southeast corner. Meanwhile, Aldrich, Carol, and three others were standing outside under natural cover, using umbrellas to shield them from a sudden shower of rain.

Just before midday, Kell was informed by Amos that ABACUS had made his way to the toy department on the third floor, via the large bookstore in the center of floor two. He had bought a copy of *Wired* magazine and was presently playing a computer game on a large-screen television in the north apex. Kell took the opportunity to switch out Jez and Amos, putting them on exterior ground-floor exits while Carol and Lucy continued visual surveillance on separate floors. Throughout the slow minutes of watching, the texts, the closed-circuit images, the bursts of talk and the long, agonizing silences, Kell nevertheless felt that he was on top of the operation, spinning the right plates, making the right decisions. Kleckner would eventually leave the building, fail to notice that Danny or Carol or Nina had picked him up, and lead SIS to his SVR handler.

In the blink of an eye, however, it was all lost.

One moment Lucy had a confirmed sighting of ABACUS in Toys, the next Carol saw him moving through Children's Clothing on the fourth floor. Then he was gone. No closed circuit. No sightings at any of the ground-floor exits. The cell phones in Redan Place stopped buzzing, the laptop screens went quiet. Eight highly experienced surveillance officers stopped talking to Thomas Kell, who felt a gathering storm of frustration as the realization hit him that he had lost Ryan Kleckner. For two hours Kell had the team watching all ten doors at street level while Aldrich and Nina swept through Harrods trying to find the American. But there was no sign of him. Shortly before three, Kell called them off and rang Amelia.

"I lost him."

"I'm not surprised."

She sounded sanguine, rather than irritated, but Kell said: "Gee, thanks," as though Amelia had doubted him all along.

"I didn't mean it like that."

"Harrods," he said. "Fucking Harrods."

"Don't worry about it." Kell had called her at the Cross. He could hear another telephone ringing in Amelia's office. "We know that ABACUS has agents outside Turkey. There's every possibility that he's meeting one of them, not his handler. He'll come back to the hotel at some point, and we can start all over again."

Kell thanked her and hung up. He took the lift down to the ground floor and went for lunch at a fish-and-chip shop on Porchester Road. He tried texting Rachel, but heard nothing back. By the time he had returned to the hub, Elsa was on her way out to a movie at Whiteleys, Harold coming back from a Thai massage on Queensway.

"Smell that, guv?" he said. "Tiger Balm." Kell squeezed out a smile. "Don't worry about it," Harold said, planting a hand on Kell's elbow. "These things happen. We have other plans up other sleeves."

"We do?" Kell replied, sounding and feeling uncertain.

Harold winked. Kell couldn't tell if he was being serious or merely trying to cheer him up.

"Anybody find the baseball cap?" Harold asked. "The jacket?"

Kell shook his head. Perhaps Kleckner had effected a complete change in his appearance—stealing a Harrods uniform, buying a new outfit in Menswear—or had simply managed to slip through one of the exits just at the point when Jez or Carol or Nina or Danny had been looking the other way. Eyes became tired. Concentration sagged. It was inevitable. Either way, ABACUS was now a ghost.

For the next several hours Kell moved his chess pieces around the board—Aldrich back to the first floor of the Rembrandt, Carol jogging through Grosvenor Square on the off chance that Kleckner would show up on a visit to the embassy—but it was a game against an opponent who would not show his face. Elsa returned from the cinema ("I see a film about Earth with Will Smith and the son of Will Smith. It was not a good film.") and began to work Kleckner's Facebook account, looking for an exchange of messages with one of his many London girlfriends. Amelia had overruled Kell's decision to wire two of the flats belonging to Kleckner's earlier one-night stands, on the basis that it would be a waste of time to do so, thereby leaving Kell with no further moves. Kleckner was somewhere in London—somewhere in *England;* it might be days before he resurfaced. All Kell could do was sit and kill time by overseeing a change of shift in the surveillance team, Carol and Jez and the rest heading home, to be replaced by eight MI5 watchers, none of whom had ever seen Ryan Kleckner in the flesh. Kell felt the frustration of a man prevented from seeing direct action in the field. He was used to playing an active part in operations, not sitting passively in an office trying to second-guess an opponent. Spying was waiting, yes, but Kell wanted to be in the Rembrandt, in the taxi on Egerton Gardens, on the streets of Knightsbridge, not stewing in Redan Place in front of banks of surveillance screens with Harold stinking of Tiger Balm and Elsa lost in her world of codes and bits and algorithms.

At ten he went out for dinner, wandering down Westbourne Grove to a Persian restaurant where he ate a lamb kebab and drank mint tea, thinking of the horses and carts on Buyukada and the moan of the ships on the Bosporus. Harold had gone home for a few hours but was due back at midnight. Elsa had fallen asleep on the mattress in Kell's office. Danny Aldrich was minding the fort, and had promised to call Kell as soon as there was any news on ABACUS.

Just after eleven, Kell's phone rang.

"Boss?"

It was Danny. Kell was smoking a cigarette outside a newsagent. Across the street, two drunk girls were climbing into a taxi. It looked as though one of them was about to be sick.

"Yes?"

"He's back."

"At the Rembrandt?"

"No. Pat picked him up walking north from South Ken tube. But looks like they're heading there."

Kell was already walking back toward Redan Place. He dropped the half-finished cigarette in a puddle, heard it fizz.

"They?" he said.

"He's got a girl with him."

"The same one as last night? Zena?"

"Negative. Someone else. Could be one of the Facebookers. We'll have visual in a couple of minutes."

Kell began to sprint down Redan Place, drawing the fob key from his pocket, jogging into the lobby and turning toward the bank of lifts. He had to wait more than a minute for the doors to open. There was a smell of curry in the cabin. Somebody had come back with takeout.

"We're in here," Danny called out, summoning Kell into the surveillance room.

Harold and Elsa were seated in front of the Rembrandt screens. Neither of them looked up, but Elsa mumbled: *"Ciao."*

"They in the hotel?" Kell asked.

"Yup. Just got out of the lift." Harold was leaning forward. "You should see the bird. Fucking unbelievable. This bloke's a machine."

The audio feed from Kleckner's room was switched on. Kell could see a long shot down the corridor of Kleckner and the woman. As the door opened, Kell heard the woman's voice first, an American accent, mimicking a line from Pink Floyd.

"Oh my God, what a fabulous room. Are all these your guitars?"

Kleckner laughed, Harold smiled, and they all watched as the woman walked inside. It was only then that Kell realized who she was.

Rachel.

46

Kell turned away and walked out of the room, stumbling toward the door, the lifts. He was aware of somebody behind him calling out *"Tom?"*—as he walked down the short passage toward the men's bathroom. He pushed through the door and as he thought of Rachel touching Kleckner, her hands on his body and her mouth on his skin, he bent double as the shock worked through him. He pitched against the wall of the bathroom, his lungs pulling at the room for air.

He reached for a cigarette. He walked over to the bank of sinks and sat against them, lighting it. He opened the window, holding the cigarette out toward the frame, somehow still dully conscious of sprinklers and smoke alarms and rules. With his first inhalation of smoke Kell experienced a surge of rage so intense in its coiled violence that he almost smashed his fist into the wall. He thought of Kleckner's broken jaw, blood on his face, and considered how and where and in what way he would exact his revenge. He would kill Kleckner. Kell was sure of it. He knew that the American had lured Rachel to the hotel to humiliate him. ABACUS had known that Wallinger's former colleagues were watching.

There was a knock on the door.

"Tom?"

It was Elsa. Kell found that he was grateful to hear her voice. He tossed the cigarette through the window, turned toward the sinks and switched on a tap.

"Yeah?"

"Are you all right?"

Kell looked at his reflection in the mirror, the collar of his shirt frayed, the cumin stench of his daylong sweat mingling with a taste of tobacco.

"I'm fine."

He thought of Rachel with her mouth on Kleckner's cock, swallowing him, then that cock inside her, her legs wrapped around his back. It was happening now, right now. Kell put his face down into the sink and covered it in water.

Elsa had come into the bathroom.

"Tom, what happened?"

"Just felt sick," Kell replied, the lie springing into his mouth. "Something I ate. Sorry for the cigarette . . ."

"Do not be sorry!" Elsa's singsong voice, the happiness in it, was a balm to him, even as he thought of the hotel room again, the noise of Rachel's orgasm slicing through him like a blade. Kell had his phone in his pocket. He could call her, right now, bring the whole thing to an end.

"I need another cigarette," he said.

"No." Elsa's arm was around his back. "You need to go home. You need to rest. Do you need to be sick?"

Kell knew that Elsa had intuited what had happened. He shook his head. If he stayed, he would be forced to watch the screens, forced to act like a man who did not know the girl, who did not care what was happening. He would have to sit and listen as Harold commented on ABACUS's prowess as a lover, made lewd jokes about Rachel's body, made fun of yet another girl who had fallen prey to the charms of Ryan Kleckner.

"Maybe it's a good idea," he said.

"To go home?"

"Yes."

47

Fifteen minutes later Elsa was sitting beside Kell in the backseat of a black cab pulling up outside his flat in Holland Park. She paid the driver. Kell walked ahead of her into the building, turning the key in the door, picturing Rachel asleep on Kleckner's chest, laughing and joking over room service in bed, showering together. He should have been more careful. He should not have let his guard down. People always betray you in the end. Kell himself had betrayed many others.

"Let me help you."

Elsa pushed open the street door and asked Kell for the number of his apartment.

"Five," he replied, and they walked upstairs. Kell was wondering why Elsa was following him. What did she want? "You really don't have to come in," he told her. "I'm fine."

"I am coming in."

As soon as he was in the kitchen, he poured himself a cognac and sank it in a shot. He offered Elsa something to drink, but she was already looking around the flat. He found her standing in the corner of the living room, staring at a shelf of Kell's books.

"Graham Greene," she said. "You like this?"

Kell nodded. He had read a Hitchens essay in January that had stripped Greene clean of his reputation. Hard to go back after that. Rachel had given Kleckner *Hitch-22* at the birthday party.

"And an Italian book! Di Lampedusa. *Il Gattopardo*. You have read this?"

Kell shook his head and said: "No, not yet." Perhaps as many as half of the books in his flat had been bought on a whim or a recommendation and he had never opened them. He was grateful for the momentary distraction of Elsa's conversation. He took out a packet of cigarettes.

"Do you mind me smoking?"

"Tom, this is your house. You can do what you want."

He lit the cigarette and fetched two glasses and a bottle of red wine from the kitchen. They were sitting side by side on the sofa facing the television. DVDs piled up on either side. Box sets. Rentals from Love Film. The collected Buster Keaton. Elsa had three earrings in her right lobe, a single stud in the left.

"Are you okay, Tom?"

"I'm fine."

"It's all right," she replied, putting her hand on his knee. Kell stared down at the wedding ring on her finger. "I know who the woman was. The woman in the hotel."

Kell looked at her and felt a shiver of anger, rooted in his own shame. Elsa held his gaze, determined that he should trust her.

"You love this woman, don't you? You love Rachel Wallinger?"

"Yes, I do."

He took a sip of the wine, a pull on the cigarette. To Kell's surprise, Elsa plucked the cigarette from his hand and took two quick drags of her own, tipping her head back and breathing smoke at the ceiling. Her jaw was tensed, her eyes steady, as though she was recalling every love affair, every heartbreak, every moment of passion she had ever known.

"She is—what?—twenty-eight? Twenty-nine?"

"Thirty-one," Kell replied.

She passed the cigarette back to him. For an absurd and illogical moment, Kell thought that Elsa was going to ask why Kell had not fallen in love with *her.* Instead, she said something that took him completely by surprise. "I have met her."

Kell stared at Elsa.

"In Istanbul. With Miss Levene. With Amelia. I understand why you feel this way. She is very special. Not just beautiful. A rare person. More than *simpatica.*"

"Yes," Kell replied, reluctant to pay Rachel any compliment or to acknowledge that he had proved incapable of securing her love. "She is very special."

"But you feel a fool for losing yourself to her."

Kell smiled and remembered how much he valued Elsa's friendship, her habit always of speaking her mind.

"Yes," he said. "You could say that."

"Don't feel that way." Her reply was emphatic. "Why else are we here? To feel love is to be alive. To let your heart go out to a person you love is the most beautiful thing in the world." Elsa must have seen something flicker across Kell's face, because she stopped short and said: "You think I am just an Italian romantic. The stereotype."

"No I don't," he told her, and touched her arm, offering her the cigarette. Elsa shook her head.

"No. No, thank you. Just to taste the tobacco was good." She stood up and walked across to the far side of the room, staring at another row of books on Kell's crowded shelves. Seamus Heaney. Pablo Neruda. T. S. Eliot. Auden.

"You keep all of your poetry together."

It was an observation rather than the start of a new line in their conversation. Kell stubbed out the cigarette. He remembered how close he had come to making a pass at Elsa on a similarly intimate night in Wiltshire when they had discussed Yassin Gharani. She had cooked for him.

She had listened to him. He wondered again why she had come to the flat. It would not have surprised him to learn that she was under instruction from Amelia.

"Tom?"

"Yes?"

"This has been a very bad night for you."

"Yes."

"I am so sorry. I cannot begin to imagine what you must be feeling. But you *are* feeling. And this is good."

He could see that she was trying to say something beyond words meant as mere comfort. Something deeper, something about himself. She took down one of the books, as though to give herself time in which to form the correct words. It was *Jane Eyre*. Kell looked at her and, for a reason he could not properly understand, tried to will himself to find Elsa attractive. But he could not do so.

"When I first met you, I felt that you were closed."

"Closed," he repeated.

Smiling, Elsa put the book down on a table in the center of the living room and crouched in front of him, touching both of Kell's knees for balance. He did not know if she was going to try to comfort him with a kiss, or if she was simply being kind and considerate toward him.

"When we began to talk in Nice, and later in Tunisia and in England, I felt there was a great sadness at the center of you. More than frustration. More than loneliness. It was as if your heart had been dead for years."

Kell looked away toward the window. He remembered Rachel saying an almost identical thing to him in Istanbul, as they walked hand in hand to the restaurant in Ortakoy. "You've been lying dormant." It had shocked him that she had intuited such a thing, but he had felt the essential truth of the remark as something close to a revelation. Rachel had brought him back to life. He knew that he had been unhappy with Claire in the same way that he knew his own capacity for vengeance.

Now Elsa sat down beside him on the sofa. She put her right arm across Kell's back, like somebody comforting the bereaved.

"This time," she said, "when I see you in Istanbul, and here in London, you are a different person. This girl has lifted you up out of your sadness. It must feel like a weight has been around you and lifted off by what you feel for her."

"It did sometimes feel like that. Yes. It no longer feels like that."

Elsa hesitated, as if her natural optimism had caught her out and caused her to be gauche. "Of course," she replied softly. "This is a hell for you. We lose lovers. We are betrayed by them. We must imagine them moving on into new hearts. But to see this with our own eyes, to be confronted by this directly, it must be unbelievable for you. Unbearable."

"I'll be fine," Kell replied and suddenly wanted her to leave.

"Of course you do not know if what you saw was the truth."

It was not in Elsa's nature to offer glib consolations with no basis in fact. Kell did not understand precisely why she had said such a thing.

"We all saw the same thing. You perhaps saw more than I did."

Elsa suddenly stood up, seized the packet of cigarettes from the table beside him. She began to move around the room, smoking, as though pacing out a private thought, a theory, coming to terms with its consequences.

"When I met Rachel, she seemed to be friendly with Amelia."

Kell looked up. "She's Paul's daughter. Amelia was very close to Paul. She probably cares about her."

"I am sure that she does. That she cares about her. Forget it. Forget what I said."

"You haven't said anything," Kell replied, aware that Elsa seemed slightly agitated.

"That's true!" she said, forcing a laugh. She was flustered, out of her depth. Elsa leaned across to the ashtray beside Kell and stubbed out the half-smoked cigarette. "I do not know what I am saying."

"I don't know either. Did Amelia ask you to do anything for her that was related to Rachel?"

"No."

Kell realized that Elsa was lying to him. It was as though she knew something that might put him out of his misery, but was prevented from saying it by official secrecy—by a promise, a commitment to Amelia.

"You have to tell me, Elsa."

"Tell you what?"

Kell looked at her. Whatever glimpse of whatever truth she had uttered had vanished. In a swift moment Elsa became no more and no less than his friend again, consoling him in a moment of loss.

"You should sleep and come back in the morning," she said. "Will you do that? I think you need to rest tonight."

"Yes, nurse," he replied, adding: "Would you like to stay here?" Kell saw a flicker of disgust flash across Elsa's face. "There's a spare room," he said quickly. "I meant in the spare room."

"No, I will leave you," she replied calmly. "Are you sure you will be okay?"

"I'll be fine. I'm a big boy. I've known worse."

"Then you must have known bad things," she said.

48

Kell slept until ten the next morning. He took a shower, walked to a branch of Carluccio's on Westbourne Grove for eggs and bacon and orange juice, then showed his face at Redan Place shortly before midday.

"Any news?"

Harold was reading the *Daily Mail* on the sofa. As Kell walked in, he looked up and produced an uncharacteristically forced smile. Danny Aldrich was in the surveillance room, looking at the feeds from the Rembrandt. There was no sign of Elsa.

"ABACUS still asleep," Aldrich announced.

Kell walked into the cubicle and forced himself to look at the monitors. En route to the office he had stopped in a pub and sunk a double shot of Smirnoff to ease his nerves. He was going to see Rachel wrapped in Kleckner's arms. He had prepared himself for this.

"Still asleep," Kell repeated and stood over Aldrich's shoulder.

To his surprise he saw that Kleckner was alone in bed. There was nobody else in the room, no movement on the bathroom monitor. No sign of Rachel anywhere.

"Where's the girl?" he said.

"Left ages ago."

Walk of shame. Hours of bliss and fucking and then she caught an early Tube home to Bethnal Green.

"What time did she go?"

"Didn't stay long actually."

Aldrich's voice was level, matter-of-fact. If he knew of the link between Kell and Rachel he was doing a masterful job of disguising it.

"Why? They had a fight?"

Aldrich spun around in his seat and looked up at Kell. Kell moved away, leaning against the wall, putting distance between them.

"I got no idea what happened. I went to bed. Harold was keeping an eye on things. How you feeling by the way? Elsa said you ate a bad kebab or something?"

"I'm fine, completely fine." Kell smiled at Elsa's cover story and looked again at the monitor. The American was waking up. He had pushed the sheets down and twisted onto his side. He was dressed in a T-shirt and a pair of underpants. It was a strange consolation to Kell that Kleckner was not naked. "Where's the team?" he asked.

"Usual positions. Carol and Nina back on today. Jez as well. Theo's got an old woman"—Aldrich looked down at a printed list of names—"Penny, who's going to role-play his wife. Geriatric couple. Always makes good cover."

"Yes," Kell muttered, hardly listening. He was watching Kleckner. Something was happening in the room. "Here we go."

Aldrich turned and looked at the monitor. Kleckner had reached for the hotel landline beside his bed. In a swift, practiced movement, Aldrich flicked three switches, grabbed two pairs of headphones, passed one of them to Kell, and placed the other over his head.

"We can listen. Probably housekeeping wondering when they can get into his room."

But it was not housekeeping. As Kell put on the headphones and crouched in front of the monitor, he heard Rachel's voice in his head, the agony of her tenderness, the same lilt and flow and mischief that he had foolishly thought she reserved solely for him.

"Morning, sleepyhead."

"Rachel?"

"Yes of course Rachel! Who were you expecting?" Laughter in her voice. "Did you only just wake up? You said you'd call me."

"What time is it?"

"Midday. Half past. I'm so hungover."

"Me too. What happened?"

Kell could see Kleckner sitting up in bed, rubbing his eyes, like a bad actor trying to convey a sense of disorientation.

"Well, you sort of fell asleep. At about two. Two thirty, maybe? I had to get home and change and come to work so I thought I'd leave you to it."

"I don't remember that. I don't remember much actually."

"Oh, thanks!" More laughter, more mischief. Kell willed himself to keep listening, to keep watching Kleckner. "You remember *nothing*?" Rachel said.

The American switched hands on the phone and reached for a bottle of water. "No, sure," he said, scrambling for tact. "Like I remember coming home. I remember how great it was being with you. I remember that stuff. I just feel like you can't have had such a great time."

Rachel paused, perhaps for effect, perhaps to tread carefully around what sounded like Kleckner's vanity and self-doubt. "Maybe that's because of the three vodka martinis, the two bottles of red, and the mojitos we drank at Boujis. We were shitfaced!"

"I pass out? That never happens to me."

"You passed out. We both passed out."

"Jesus."

There was a lengthy silence. Kell caught Aldrich's eye but there was nothing to read in his expression. He turned back to the monitor. Kleckner reached into his pants and scratched his balls.

"So what are you doing today?" Rachel asked. "What are you doing now?" It sounded as though she wanted to get together. The second act.

"Today?" Kleckner looked across the hotel room, in the direction of the television. "I gotta bunch of stuff to do. Shit, I had no idea how late it was." There was a crackle of static on the audio feed, enough to make Aldrich flinch and make an adjustment to his headphones. "I need a Tylenol. I got this dinner tonight. The college reunion thing I told you about."

"Oh, yeah, at Galvin."

"Yup. Baker Street, you said?"

"There's two of them." It was just like Rachel to know something like that. All the best restaurants. All the best places to go. "There's a Galvin in Shoreditch, one in Baker Street. You should check."

"And what are you doing after?"

Kleckner had stood up. His brain was starting to kick into gear. There was a seductive edge to the question.

"Tonight?" Rachel said. "You mean after your dinner?"

"Yeah, sure. You busy?"

Kell willed Rachel to turn him down.

"I can't, Ryan. Not tonight. Then I've got to go back to Istanbul."

He was stunned. Rachel hadn't mentioned anything about going to Turkey. The area around his neck and chest was tight and hot.

"So that trip's going ahead?" Kleckner asked.

"Yeah. Some final stuff Mum needs me to do at the house. But you'll be back by the weekend, yeah?"

"Sure. That's my plan. I'm busy tomorrow, then I could catch a late flight I guess."

"Okay. So let's have dinner in Istanbul. Saturday night. I love saying that. It sounds so romantic and international!"

"It sounds great is what it sounds. I wanna be with you, Rachel. I wanna see you."

Kell closed his eyes.

"Well that's good. Because you're *going* to be with me. You're *going* to see me. And I'm glad about last night."

"What do you mean?"

Kell wanted to tear off the headphones.

"Just that we're taking things slowly. I'm glad."

"Oh, okay." The American sounded resistant to the idea, as though he was not used to being finessed by a woman. "Me too," he added unconvincingly.

"So I'll see you in Istanbul. You can show me your favorite places. We should go back to Bar Bleu."

"Sure. You at work now?"

"I am," Rachel replied. "And I should stop talking to you and get off the phone or I'll get in trouble. Bye-bye, gorgeous."

"You too. Bye. See you in a coupla days. Take it easy."

Kell watched as Kleckner hung up the phone, walked into the bathroom, dug around in his washbag, and retrieved a strip of pills. The American ran a tap and threw back what appeared to be two painkillers, then switched on the shower. He walked back into the bedroom and began to rummage in the wastepaper basket. Returning to the bathroom, he did the same thing.

"What's this about?" Aldrich asked. "What's he doing?"

"No idea," Kell replied, and it was only as he removed the headphones and walked outside into the corridor that an answer presented itself: Kleckner had been looking for a used condom. Had he been so drunk, so disoriented, that he had forgotten whether or not he had fucked Rachel?

"Everything all right, guv?"

Harold was still sitting on the sofa reading the *Daily Mail*. Kell had been on his way to the terrace for a cigarette but sat down, realizing that Rachel had inadvertently dragged a schedule out of Kleckner. *I gotta bunch of stuff to do today. I'm busy tomorrow, then I could catch a late flight.* She was *helping* him. The team could use that information. Rachel had isolated the times when ABACUS was planning to meet his handler, and cut short his trip by twenty-four hours.

"Interesting piece?" he asked Harold, spotting a headline about a link between cancer and dieting.

Harold turned down a corner of the paper and grinned.

"Very," he said. "We're all dying unless we start eating pizza. Your man Kleckner should give up on his planks and his push-ups and just start enjoying himself."

Kell tried to smile. He had to get past what he had heard and seen. He had to move on with the job. There was still a mole to catch. It was of paramount importance to track ABACUS to his handler. Yet he could not stop himself from asking the question:

"What happened last night? After I left?"

Kell felt a check in his breathing as he waited for Harold's response. Wasn't it obvious what had happened? Two young people had found each other attractive. They had gone to bed together. Even if Rachel had left before dawn, she would soon be back in Kleckner's arms, fucking him at the *yali* on Saturday. The fact that she wanted to wait, to take things slowly, only confirmed that she was taking him seriously.

"It was weird actually," Harold replied, laying the newspaper on the sofa beside him. "For once our boy couldn't close the deal. Maybe he was knackered out by whatsername."

"Maybe," Kell replied blandly, unsure what to feel. He was about to stand up and leave when Harold frowned.

"Who was she, guv? You recognize the girl?"

"No." The lie was out of Kell's mouth before he had a chance even to acknowledge the possibility of telling Harold the truth. He wanted his private life to remain private.

"It's just weird."

"Why?"

"I got asked to wipe the tapes."

"You got asked *what*?"

"To destroy them. This morning. Throw them away."

"Why?"

"Search me."

And as Kell asked the obvious question, he realized the obvious answer.

"Who asked you to do that? Who asked you to destroy them?"

"The boss, guv. Amelia."

49

Kell went to the lifts, walked quickly out onto Redan Place and called Amelia's private number.

"Where are you?"

"Tom?"

"I need to speak to you. As soon as possible."

"You sound agitated. Is everything all right?"

Her brusque, formal manner—at the edge of condescension, even contempt—was a further irritant to him.

"I'm fine. But we need to meet."

"Why?"

"*Why?*" Kell came to a standstill and briefly separated the phone from his ear, swearing under his breath. "Why do you think?" he said. "Because of work. Because of ABACUS."

"And it's urgent?" Amelia managed to make it sound as though she had a hundred better things to do.

"Yes. It's urgent. Where are you?"

"Shouldn't you be at the office?" she asked, as if Kell was being insubordinate. "Where's ABACUS now?"

"Danny has him. Danny's in charge. This is more important."

A long silence. Finally, Amelia deigned to reply.

"It'll have to wait," she said. "I have a lunch that I can't cancel. Can you meet me at my house at half past three?"

"Done," Kell replied. "Half past three."

He was early. This time there was a security goon on the door who made Kell wait in the atrium on another afternoon of incessant rain. When Amelia texted to say that she was stuck in traffic and running late, Kell went for a brisk, umbrella-sheltered walk along Kings Road, up and down Bywater Street, then into Markham Square, past the house in the northeast corner that had once belonged to Kim Philby. He bought a packet of cigarettes in a branch of Sainsbury's and was smoking one outside Amelia's house when she finally pulled up in her official car and nodded him toward the front door.

Moments later Kell was pacing in the sitting room of the Chelsea house waiting for Amelia to reappear. She had excused herself for five minutes, wanting to change out of a business suit into "something more comfortable." Kell had always felt less fully-formed, a generation younger whenever he was in Amelia's company. He put it down to a mixture of professional awe and natural deference.

"Look at you hopping up and down," Amelia said, coming into the room while still tying the buckle on the belt of her jeans. Kell saw the flash of a tanned, gym-toned stomach beneath a sheer white blouse. "I feel like you've come to ask for my hand in marriage."

She had sprayed herself with perfume. Hermès Calèche.

"I haven't come for that," he replied.

She shot him an appraising glance, quick with the realization that her visitor was not going to be finessed with feminine charm. Kell was angry, and Amelia knew exactly why.

"Drink?" she said.

"The usual."

He regretted that response, because it sounded chummy and forgiving. The last thing Kell wanted was to generate an atmosphere of complicity.

Amelia moved toward the drinks cabinet and plucked out a bottle of single malt. "There's no ice," she said, and was turning toward the kitchen when Kell stopped her and said: "I don't need ice. Forget it. Just some water."

"You sound awfully tense, Tom."

He did not respond. Amelia continued to pour the whiskey, the glug of three fingers, then passed him the glass over a sofa. Kell remained where he was as Amelia sat down in her favorite armchair, the sofa a barrier between them, a net dividing opponents.

"So."

Two children moved past the street window ringing the bells on their bicycles. Amelia's tone of voice, allied to impatient body language, conveyed the impression of a woman who had five, perhaps a maximum of ten, minutes to spare before she would be called off to a more important assignation.

"Why did you destroy the tapes?" Kell asked.

To his surprise, she began to smile. "Isn't that how David Frost began his interview with Richard Nixon? Only I think it was the other way around. Why *didn't* you destroy the tapes?"

"Rachel," Kell said.

Amelia did not look up. "What about her?"

"Why was she in the hotel? Do you know about that? Do you know why she was with Kleckner? Did you encourage that relationship?"

"You're angry with me when perhaps you should be angry with Rachel."

Kell almost flew at her, but managed a swift return of serve. "Don't worry. I'll get to Rachel in my own good time. Right now I'm extremely angry with *you*."

Amelia looked to one side of the room, as if weighing up a number of options. She could pull rank and tell Kell to go back to Redan Place and do the job he was being paid to do. She could admonish him for the sin of becoming involved with Rachel Wallinger. She could credit Kell with enough intelligence and strength of character to be able to hear the truth of what had occurred at the Rembrandt. Or she could simply keep her counsel, shielded by silence and secrecy.

"I would be lying if I told you that I was not aware of your feelings for each other."

Those two words—"each other"—gave Kell a jolt of hope. They implied that Rachel had confided in Amelia. They implied that she cared for him. He took a sip of the whiskey.

"How did you know we were involved?" he asked.

"I guessed."

"How?"

"Is that important?"

"I'd like to know." Kell did not particularly need to hear Amelia's answer, but he was annoyed that he had been caught out, irritated that he had left clues for her to follow. Perhaps Rachel had confessed everything.

"I'll tell you another time," she replied. "Come and sit, Tom. You're making me nervous." She gestured Kell toward an armchair. He moved around the sofa, stood in front of the chair, but did not sit down. Amelia clasped her hands together and appeared to be wary of what she was about to say. "It's serious between the two of you, isn't it?"

"You tell me," Kell replied.

"I want to hear your end of it. All I know is what Rachel has told me."

"Forgive me, but I'm wondering if any of this is your business?"

"By coming here today, you have made it my business. You seem extremely upset."

"I *am* extremely upset. I want answers. I want to know what the hell is going on and I want to know what else you've concealed from me."

Amelia's normally impassive face was gradually flushed with something close to regret.

"It's important for you to know that Rachel had only one condition."

"One condition on what?"

"One condition that would guarantee her cooperation."

Kell remembered what Elsa had said to him the previous evening. *When I met Rachel, she seemed to be friendly with Amelia.* Everything was becoming clear to him. Everything was falling into place.

"She agreed to help me, she agreed to cooperate, as long as you weren't informed. She was aware that something could happen with Ryan that would undermine her relationship with you. She cares about you very deeply. She likes you. But ABACUS was more important."

Kell found himself repeating the phrase "ABACUS was more important" as he stared out of the window at the gray, rain-soaked street. His pride, his professional and personal self-esteem, were teetering on a precipice.

Amelia twisted in her seat and reached for a glass that wasn't there. Kell was drinking alone. "It would be disingenuous of me to say that the arrangement I struck with Rachel didn't suit the Office," she said, adding: "Down to the ground" after a slight pause.

"What kind of arrangement?" But Kell already knew the answer, in the same way that he had known, when Harold had informed him about the tapes, that Amelia had been the one to give the order to destroy them.

"An arrangement to track Kleckner. An arrangement to know where he was, what he was doing, who he was meeting, what he was saying."

Kell felt a skin crawl of disgust, Rachel co-opted into sleaze. He said: "You wanted Rachel as Kleckner's girlfriend."

"Something like that." To her credit, Amelia managed to look ashamed.

"You're saying you deliberately and consciously sidelined me on an operation over which I was supposed to have tactical control? And you used my girlfriend to do that? Is that what you're telling me?"

Amelia did not need to respond. They both knew the answer. Instead, she said: "I was worried that it would take months, years to get the proof on Kleckner, to have him arrested. I wasn't even sure that ABACUS was the mole. I wanted to have a backup plan just in case. For very obvious reasons, I could hardly ask your permission. And your instincts about the teahouse, the discovery of the DLB, your *triumph*, Tom, meant that I could put the plan into action."

Draining his whiskey, Kell reflected on Amelia's tireless, Blairite ability to turn disaster into triumph; to make her opponents feel that they had misjudged her; to give a watertight impersonation of blamelessness and virtue, even in the aftermath of gross, cynical negligence.

"So my triumph became my undoing?" he said. "That's what you're telling me. That's how you're spinning this?"

Amelia nodded. Kell stood up, went to the cabinet, poured himself another three fingers of whiskey, did not offer Amelia a drink of her own, sat back down and produced a resigned sigh.

"You'd better tell me the whole story then," he said, and even lit a cigarette in the living room, in flagrant breach of Amelia's house rules on smoking. She did not tell Kell to stub it out. "Start at the beginning," he said, settling back in the armchair and crossing his legs as the whiskey began to work through him. "Try not to leave anything out."

So she told him. Everything.

Over the course of the next three-quarters of an hour, Amelia Levene confirmed to Thomas Kell that she had made a private arrangement with Rachel that would help bring Kleckner to justice.

Having met Rachel in Istanbul and established that Kleckner found her attractive, Amelia told her that there was a mole inside western intelligence, a mole threatening every SIS operation in the Middle East and beyond. That evidence had shown that the mole was most likely to be Ryan Kleckner. She had told her that Kleckner may have been involved in the death of her father.

"You couldn't possibly have known that at the time," Kell interjected. "We still have no proof of that."

Amelia appeared to concede the point. It had simply been a useful weapon in the armory of her recruitment. Tell Rachel that Kleckner was instrumental in the murder of her father. That would ensure her co-operation. Kell knew the tricks, the cynicism of his own trade. He allowed Amelia to keep talking.

In the event that Kleckner's guilt was proven, she said, Rachel had agreed to get alongside him, by staging a meeting in Istanbul. As luck would have it, on the day that Kell had discovered the dead letter box, Kleckner was on his way to London. Lo and behold, who should he look up in his little black book but Rachel Wallinger—the one who got away. The beautiful daughter of the dead British spy who had made eyes at him at her father's funeral. It was a slice of great good fortune, of which Amelia was initially suspicious, but the opportunity was too good to pass up. Rachel was ready to avenge Paul; she would even risk losing Kell to do so.

Kleckner's invitation was all that they needed. He was coming to London, was Rachel free? *Love to take you to dinner. Love to see you in your hometown.* That was all it took. Everything had fallen into place after that; everything was given the green light. All that mattered was that Rachel be smart, keep calm, hold her nerve—not exactly a challenge for a woman of her caliber. After all, she was the daughter of a master spy. The DNA, the intellect, the toughness, had been passed down to the next generation.

"You do know that we tried to recruit her at Oxford, don't you?"

Kell was floored. "*What?*"

"After graduation, she applied for Fast Stream. Got all the way to the IONEC, then walked away. Her head wasn't right."

Kell stared blankly ahead. *I loathe spies,* Rachel had told him. There had been nothing about SIS Fast Stream, nothing about the IONEC. Just her contempt for her father's trade—for *Kell's* trade. He remembered Rachel's words. *A part of Pappa dried up inside. He had a piece missing from his heart. Decency. Tenderness. Honesty.*

"Honesty."

"What?" Amelia asked.

Kell gestured at her to continue.

"I gave her two objectives," she said, as if Rachel was just another officer on just another operation. "We needed to get to Kleckner's BlackBerry. If possible, to his satchel as well. Tech-Ops have replacement batteries, devices which, when switched with an existing BlackBerry battery, will continue to act as a power source, but can also provide us with audio coverage as well as precise location data."

"So that's what Rachel was doing in the hotel last night? That was her chance? That's why she went back to Kleckner's room?"

Amelia nodded.

"And did she succeed?"

The chief of the Secret Intelligence Service smiled, a lioness pleased with a cub's first kill. "Oh, yes. She did brilliantly."

"And did she have to fuck him first?" Kell spat the question.

"Tom, for God's sake."

"Did you make her do that? Is that who we are now? No better than the Russians? No better than the Mossad?"

Amelia had been seated for the best part of an hour. She stood up and walked across to the window, closing the curtains. It was some time before she deigned to respond to Kell's question, as though he had not merely offended her at a professional level, but also as a woman.

"Right from the start," she said, "Rachel was very clear about what she was and was not prepared to do. I think she finds Mr. Kleckner physically attractive. Plenty do." Kell interpreted the remark as an attempt to annoy him. "In other words, to flirt with Mr. Kleckner, to seduce him if you like, would not cause a woman of Rachel's temperament much in the way of distress. Does that make sense to you, Tom?"

"It makes sense to me, Amelia," Kell replied pointedly, and could feel his affection for her, his loyalty to his friend and to their rotten profession, disintegrating like a worn-out rag. "What doesn't make sense—"

"Let me finish." Amelia was pouring herself a glass of wine and almost barked the interruption, as if Kell was about to offend her yet again with more preposterous morality. "Rachel was prepared to kiss Ryan. She was prepared even to go to bed with him. These were all choices that she made of her own volition . . ."

"Oh, come off it."

"Of her own volition," Amelia repeated, very clearly and steadily. "I never believed that she would sleep with him, have *sex* with him, that she would allow herself to become physically intimate with him in the way that you are implying. I didn't think I had created a prostitute or a whore or that what she had shared with you meant so little to her that she would trade you in for a man she despises."

Kell was rendered silent. He felt the shame of his jealousy as something feeble and humiliating. But Amelia was not yet done.

"Find out if they fucked!" She was almost laughing, as if something as meaningless as the brief, drunk copulation of two people was of any lasting consequence to anyone. "They didn't, if that's all you care about, Tom. Fucking men and your fucking egos. Why do you think she got him so drunk at the dinner, at the nightclub? Why did she lay on the promise of a steamy night at the Rembrandt Hotel, only to see him fall asleep in his own bed just as things were heating up?"

"She drugged him."

"Bingo! Glad you could join us. Welcome to the operation."

"How did she do that?" Kell's experience told him that the use of a sedative, however mild, was catastrophically risky. He remembered Kleckner on the phone at the hotel. *I pass out? That never happens to me.* What if he suspected that Rachel had spiked his drink, spiked his food? What if he took a good look at his BlackBerry and realized that Rachel had tampered with the battery?

"A sedative," Amelia confirmed. "I believe it's called lorazepam."

"How strong?"

"Strong enough. Ours was delayed release." Kell shook his head. He could feel his anger at Amelia returning. "Enough to make a drunk, stressed, exhausted man feel even more drunk and stressed and exhausted—shortly before it knocks him out. And that's exactly what happened."

"Hence the reason Kleckner woke up at midday."

"Hence," Amelia replied, seemingly restored to a more acquiescent mood.

"And how did Rachel administer this lorazepam, this delayed release Mickey Finn? Don't tell me. A vial of white powder tipped into Ryan's mojito?"

Amelia took a sip of her wine. "Almost," she replied, weaving around any implied condescension in Kell's tone by producing an amused grin. "Rachel had it in chewing gum, as a matter of fact. Liquid as a backup if Kleckner didn't take the bait. But he was keen to freshen his breath after Boujis, accepted her offer of some spearmint, chewed it for ten minutes, kissed her, and was asleep about an hour later. The booze did the rest."

"And Rachel?"

"What about her?"

"What if Kleckner realizes that he's been duped? What if he has doubts about the new battery? What if he already knows that we are onto him and that Rachel's trip to Istanbul tomorrow is just a ruse to draw him in? He could have her killed."

"That's a little excitable, isn't it? The SVR is hardly likely to start a third world war by murdering MI6 officers."

"They killed Cecilia Sandor and she was working for *them*."

"Precisely." Amelia seemed pleased to have won the argument so easily. "In moments of disappointment, the Russians tend to kill their own. They don't kill ours." She surprised Kell by touching his shoulder as she passed him. "Besides, Rachel may not even have to see Kleckner in Istanbul."

"Why not?"

"Because she's done her job. She switched the battery." Amelia allowed herself the trace of a smile. "The phone is working. We can see Kleckner. We can hear Kleckner. If ABACUS takes the phone to the meeting, takes the battery out and leaves it even within fifty feet of their conversation, we will be able to isolate every single word."

50

It was exactly as Amelia had promised, exactly as she had planned it. ABACUS went to his Georgetown dinner, ABACUS went home to bed. ABACUS woke up on Friday morning and then ABACUS went to see Alexander Minasian.

Kell and the surveillance team stayed on him, for the simple reason that the battery might fail, that technology would render Rachel's remarkable coup entirely useless. They saw him visit the embassy on Thursday afternoon, they tracked him to a cinema in Westfield. In the evening ABACUS was housed to the eight-man dinner at Galvin, then taken home to the Rembrandt in an MI5 taxi that just happened to be passing as the Georgetown mob spilled out onto Baker Street at one o'clock in the morning. The next day, with Kleckner booked onto a British Airways flight to Istanbul at 1840, the American had set his alarm for seven in the morning and embarked on a countersurveillance routine so prolonged, so complex, and so exhaustive that Kell, by the time Kleckner had vanished into the suburbs of Clerkenwell at six minutes past twelve, never to be seen again, could only sit back and admire his immaculate tradecraft.

But it didn't matter that the team had lost ABACUS a second time. Kell was obliged to go through the motions of disappointment and regret, reassuring Jez and Theo and Carol and the useless Nina that they had been up against a pedigree CIA officer and that there was no shame in failing to cover him. It didn't matter because the BlackBerry kept beeping, the microphone kept working, all the way to a modest bed-and-breakfast in a semidetached house in Snaresbrook where Minasian was waiting in the lounge.

"Where's the owner?" Kleckner asked, exhausted by more than four hours of countersurveillance but pleased to see that Minasian had also cleaned his tail sufficiently for the meeting to go ahead.

"We *are* the owner," the Russian reassured him, and they had embraced like long-lost brothers.

Kleckner had removed his sports jacket at the door of the bed-and-breakfast. He had left the battery in the inside pocket, hung the jacket up on a hook in the hall, then carried the phone unit into the meeting.

The conversation between the two men was immediately transcribed. It was estimated that Rachel's device had picked up as much as 80 percent of the dialogue.

KLECKNER (K): Where's the owner?
MINASIAN (M): We are (emphasis) the owner.
(Muffled)
M: You look well, Ryan.
K: Ditto.
M: Having some fun in London? Seeing the girls?
K: One girl. Maybe two girls.
M: (laughter) So few!

There was always small talk at the start. Kleckner was used to that. Pretending to be friends, pretending that everything was just fine, but everybody's hearts pumping at ninety beats a minute and aware that the sooner they stopped dicking around, the sooner they could shake off the paranoia of capture and go back to their so-called lives.

M: The product is spectacular. Am I saying that word correctly?
K: I guess. Sure. You're saying it in a way that I can understand it so, yeah, "spectacular." I understand what you mean.

There was always flattery, too, the theater of reassurance. Kleckner knew the drill; Christ, he used it on his own agents. *You're the best. We couldn't be doing this without you. Have no doubt that you're helping us. One day all this will be over.*

Then it was down to business. Are you happy with the drop sites? Do you want to move from Buyukada? Is there any heat in Istanbul or a sense that Langley suspects a mole? It was always the same with Minasian.

To all his questions, Kleckner gave reassuring answers. Yes, the drop sites were fine, the signals in and out were working well. No heat in Istanbul, no worries about a mole. Minasian wanted to talk about the new stream of reporting from the mayor's office. Fair enough. Kleckner told him what little he knew. And the cache of CIA weapons heading for the border at Jarabulus? *Sure, if you think you can stop them and do Assad a favor, that's why I told you about them in the first place.*

But all Kleckner really wanted to talk about was Paul Wallinger. That was the reason he had risked Harrods and the Rembrandt. All he needed to know was why Sandor had been killed. He required answers on that. No, he *demanded* answers on that. And if he got the *wrong* replies, the *wrong* explanation, well then fuck you and fuck the SVR. Our little arrangement is terminated.

M: As you know, one of the purposes of putting Cecilia with a senior figure in the SIS was to deflect attention away from your work.

K: I'm aware of that. Of course I'm aware of that.

M: If there was any sign of difficulties, if anybody became concerned about HITCHCOCK, about EINSTEIN, the rest, SIS and CIA (sic) would look at the relationship between Mr. Wallinger and Cecilia and spend many months, many years suspecting that he was the source of the leaks.

K: Sure. So why kill her?

M: [UNCLEAR]

K: [UNCLEAR] . . . to believe that?

M: Ryan, we are investigating, using sources.

K: Bullshit.

M: [UNCLEAR]

K: Okay, so if [UNCLEAR]

M: The plane crash was also an unfortunate incident.

K: Incident or accident?

M: Excuse me? Incident? Again, we had nothing to do with this. Our investigations, your investigations, the British investigation, all concluded mechanical failure. There is a small chance that Paul Wallinger took his own life. I have to admit interest in this.

K: Okay.

M: I push it too far. I try for a burn on Wallinger.

K: You did what (emphasis)?

M: [UNCLEAR] which was what Cecilia wanted.

K: And you went along with that?

M: She wanted to bring the relationship to an end. She wanted to go back to her boyfriend, the restaurant. I felt that I had to make a choice. Either we lose all of the access to H/Ankara, or we confront him with the reality that he has been involved in a relationship with an agent of the SVR, penetrated, compromised, and then we see what follows . . . [UNCLEAR]

[DELAY—56 SECONDS]

The meeting between Minasian and Kleckner thus confirmed that Paul Wallinger had never been working for Moscow. The transcript also revealed that the SVR was lying to Kleckner. Intelligence obtained by SIS had confirmed that Cecilia Sandor had been murdered by a French assassin named Sebastien Gachon. As Kell had predicted, Sandor's boyfriend, Luka, had also disappeared a few days after Sandor's death. Moscow had been busily tidying up the loose ends around ABACUS. It was doubted that Luka's body would ever be found.

What came next on the transcript, however, pitched Kell and Amelia into an entirely new area of concern.

[DELAY—56 SECONDS]

M: [UNCLEAR] . . . this is the girl you mentioned?

K: Yup (sic)

M: Ryan, okay. Is this a good idea?

K: What do you mean?

M: You go to her or she comes to you, she approaches you?

K: What, you think I'm that stupid? I met her at Paul's funeral, we connected, I invited her to a party in Istanbul. (Pause, 3 seconds) Look, none of this shit is connected or your business in any way. I have to maintain some privacy.

M: I understand that. We understand that. So you have trust in her? Complete trust?

K: Sure I do. One hundred percent. Jesus, you think the Brits would get Paul Wallinger's grieving daughter to fuck Tom Kell just to pull me in?

M: Tom Kell?

K: SIS retread. Guy they sent out to Ankara when Paul died. They had a thing for a while. Look him up.

M: [UNCLEAR]

K: [UNCLEAR] . . . paranoid. I like this girl, man. (Laughter) She's smart, she's pretty. There's no risk.

M: Okay. So be disciplined. See her in Istanbul. Try not to get attached. This is my advice, although all advice in these situations, there is always no point? Am I correct?

K: You are absolutely fucking correct.

51

The first thing Minasian will do is run a check on you. Try to find out everything he can about your relationship with Rachel. Then he'll turn it around. Go to every e-mail she ever wrote, every text message she ever sent, and find out if she knows that you're investigating Ryan."

"I'm aware of that, Amelia."

They were walking through Notting Hill, the rain a memory, London trying its best to be warm and European. Rachel was already in Istanbul, Kleckner on the plane. Minasian had not shown his face at the Russian embassy and was assumed to have returned to Kiev.

"What do we know about him?" Kell asked.

"Very little." Amelia's frank admission took Kell by surprise. "Youngish. Younger than you, anyway. Post-Soviet, in the sense that he has no bloodstream ideological link to the old days. Still in nappies during the Gorbachev coup. Ukraine is obviously of strategic importance to the Kremlin, but I suspect Minasian was posted to Kiev solely to service Kleckner, not to work the EU angle. Married. Children. Family man. Peters thinks very highly of him." Peters was the ranking SIS officer in the Kiev Station. "Minasian is thorough, slick, ambitious. A rising star.

We think the order to kill Sandor originated in Moscow, not with him, and that Minasian may have argued against it. He might be your common or garden SVR psychopath, he might not. Either way, he's still low enough on the food chain to do what he's told when Moscow thinks it knows best."

Amelia was talking without looking at Kell, clipping along the pavement with impatient speed. Passing a policeman on the corner of Lansdowne Walk, she pressed Kell on his relationship with Rachel.

"Is there anything, in any of your correspondence, in which you discussed the molehunt?" Kell drew Amelia's eyes to his and produced a withering stare that nevertheless failed to deflect her. "Even if you didn't mention the leaks, did you discuss why you were in Turkey?"

"Of course we discussed that. Rachel knew that I was investigating her father's crash. She knew that I'd been tapped up to replace him." Amelia made a noise through her teeth; that revelation in itself constituted a breach of the Secrets Act. Kell settled on a mood of absolute candor. "She hated the fact that I couldn't tell her what was going on. We tried to avoid the subject of my job as much as possible. I now realize, of course, why she was so reluctant to talk about the Office. Because all the time she was working for you."

"Not all the time, Tom . . ."

". . . she was afraid that I'd find out your dirty little secret."

"A dirty little secret that just happened to produce the intel which will put Kleckner behind bars. But thank you for your support and understanding."

It had been plain to Kell for some time that his friendship with Amelia might easily now deteriorate to a point from which it would never be salvaged. There would be too much bad blood between them. Too many lies.

"Did you talk to Rachel about Cecilia Sandor?" he asked.

"Did *you*?" Amelia's quick, impatient glance further illustrated the extent of her frustration. Kell told her what she needed to know. "Of *course* we talked about her," he said. "She was her father's mistress. She knew all about her. So did Josephine. Rachel read their bloody love letters."

"And did you tell her that Sandor was Hungarian NSA?"

It would have been easier to lie, to react with outrage at the accusation, but Kell knew that he was cornered. He had no choice but to tell the truth.

"Yes. She knows that."

"Fantastic." Amelia was shaking her head. "Was that a conversation or did you have it on e-mail?"

"I would never commit something like that to paper." Kell's response sounded brusque, but he privately acknowledged that he could not remember precisely where or when or how he had spoken to Rachel about Sandor's intelligence background. Nor did he confess to a further sin—that Rachel knew Sandor had been assassinated. Amelia already had too much to work with.

"Have you heard from her?" she asked.

"Amelia, I haven't heard from her since we had a row in the restaurant. It's what you wanted, right? It's the *cover.* I'm the jilted lover, she's not responding to my calls."

"Good. At least that's one positive. As soon as she gets in touch, I'll let you know."

52

Alexander Minasian had left the Snaresbrook bed-and-breakfast, boarded a Central Line train into London, arranged a meeting with the SVR head of Station at a restaurant in Shepherds Market, and told him about KODAK's relationship with Rachel Wallinger.

"Kell," he said. "Tom Kell. What do you know about him?"

"The name is familiar. I can look into it. We will have files."

"He was sent out to investigate the Wallinger accident. He had a meeting with Jim Chater at the American embassy in Ankara. According to KODAK, he came with this woman to a party he was hosting at a bar in Istanbul."

"Kell knows Chater? They are friends?"

Minasian indicated that he did not know the answer to the question. He knew only that KODAK was possessed of a visceral hatred of Jim Chater. That he posed as Chater's underling and creature, an admiring junior colleague learning at his master's knee, but that KODAK despised the American's ethics and working methods. Indeed there had been times when Minasian had felt that Ryan Kleckner's work for the SVR was, in part, motivated by his animus against Chater.

"You have the date of this party?"

The head of Station was picking at a plate of chicken liver pâté. Minasian was not in the mood to eat.

"KODAK's birthday," Minasian replied. "According to the girl, that was the first night that she and Kell had met. We need to confirm that. They began a relationship that continued until Rachel returned to London. They had dinner here on Tuesday night, when she broke everything off. By then KODAK had already contacted her. She says she was more interested in seeing him."

"According to who?"

"According to KODAK. This is what she told him on the night she came back to the Rembrandt. She says Kell is too old. Maybe forty-three, forty-four. She is only just thirty, she doesn't want to be trapped in a relationship with a man she has no intention of marrying. Now she's in Istanbul, she wants to have dinner with KODAK, he thinks she likes him."

"Who do you believe?"

"It is not a question of who I believe," Minasian replied, signaling for the bill. "It is a question of what the intelligence tells us."

53

As soon as the BA flight had touched down in Istanbul, Ryan Kleckner switched on his BlackBerry. Within thirty seconds he had received a text from his mother, downloaded various work-related e-mails on three separate accounts, and sent a message to Rachel telling her how much he was looking forward to seeing her for dinner the following evening. It was after midnight, so he was not surprised when Rachel did not reply.

Kleckner was seated by a window on the starboard side of the aircraft, directly over the wing. There was the usual crammed rush for carry-on baggage as the engines powered down. Kleckner was obliged to remain in his seat for several minutes while the passengers beside him stood up, retrieved their bags, and waited in the aisle. A flight attendant made an announcement, in both English and Turkish, informing the passengers that there would be a short delay before the cabin doors were opened.

A few moments later, Kleckner was finally able to shuffle into the aisle, to find enough space in which to stand up, and to fetch his black wheeled suitcase from a locker on the opposite side of the aircraft. As he placed the suitcase on a vacant seat, he looked down the cabin at the mass of tired, impatient passengers waiting to exit the plane.

He had always hated crowds. Blank-eyed, lazy faces. Women who had allowed themselves to grow fat and sullen. Children screaming for food and toys. Kleckner wanted to push through all of them. From a young age he had been certain of his own superiority, that his intellectual and physical advantages placed him above reproach. Whatever flaws he was thought to possess—vanity, arrogance, an absence of compassion—were, to his mind, strengths. They were also easily disguised. Kleckner found it simple to win the trust of strangers; he had been able to do it long before he was trained to that purpose. To dissemble, but also to see through to the cold center of people, to intuit and understand the motivations of colleagues and friends, were gifts that he seemed to have possessed from birth. There were days when Kleckner wished that he would be found out; that somebody would have the wit and the ingenuity to see through him. But such a moment had never come.

He turned and looked back down the cabin. The stench of a three-hour flight. Too many people. Everybody crowding him up.

Kleckner looked again. A face was familiar to him. A woman in her late twenties with dark hair, standing no more than three meters away. She was traveling alone, studiously avoiding his gaze, minding her own business.

He had seen her before. He had seen those eyes. Not quite straight, not quite focused. And the teeth. They had been capped, perhaps following a childhood accident. Where had he seen her? At Bar Bleu? At a meeting in Istanbul? At a party?

It was only as he was walking down the aisle toward the exit, nodding thanks to the pilot, smiling at the flight attendants, that Kleckner remembered exactly where he had seen the woman. The realization hit him with the force of a sickness.

The perfume department. Then, an hour later, a repeating face at the exit in the southeast corner of the building. Kleckner had clocked her profile, written off the second sighting as coincidence, proceeded to a meeting with his agent.

Harrods.

54

No fewer than eighteen SVR operational assistants, in London, Kiev, and Moscow, were assigned to the case. Ten of them looked at Rachel Wallinger's digital vapor trail, eight of them at Kell's. Working all through Friday night, the SVR was able to retrieve and translate 362 e-mails and 764 text messages between the two parties.

Everything that KODAK had told Minasian was borne out by the evidence. The words "Amelia," "Levene," "crash," "Chios," "Cecilia," "Sandor," "death," "murder," "accident," "mole," "MI6," "SVR," "SIS," "Ryan," and "Kleckner" were flagged and run as cross-checks with the correspondence. Whenever these words appeared, the message was immediately forwarded to Minasian, who had caught a flight back to Kiev, via Frankfurt, on Friday evening. At no point did any of the analysts gain the impression that MI6 was investigating Kleckner. Kell's relationship with Rachel appeared to be authentic, as did her job at a publishing house in London, the e-mails she had exchanged with friends about her conflicted feelings for Kell, her growing attraction to Kleckner.

But Minasian was not satisfied. He was convinced that the analysts had missed something. At five o'clock on Saturday morning he asked that the entire file be couriered to his apartment in Kiev, where he began to read through every text, every e-mail, every message for himself, including items that were not specifically related to the sexual relationship between Kell and Wallinger. Minasian was adept at reading and absorbing large amounts of written material at speed. Though he had not slept in almost twenty-four hours, he was nevertheless alert enough to alight on the single word—"Buyukada"—which confirmed his worst suspicions about Kell's true purpose in Turkey.

According to the SVR report, the text message had been sent from Kell's O2 account to Rachel Wallinger (without reply) on April 29 at 1734 hours. The same afternoon that Minasian himself had visited Buyukada to clear the DLB.

HELLO YOU—AM I IMAGINING IT, OR DID YOU MENTION THAT YOUR FATHER HAD A JOURNALIST FRIEND ON BUYUKADA? IF I'M NOT GOING MAD, CAN YOU REMEMBER HIS NAME? RICHARDS? IF I AM GOING MAD, CAN YOU IGNORE THIS TEXT? SEPARATION FROM YOU HAS MADE ME DELIRIOUS—T X

55

At around eight o'clock on Saturday morning, a surveillance analyst watching the live feed from Ryan Kleckner's apartment in Tarabya began to report that the American was acting strangely. ABACUS had returned home from the airport at two A.M. but had not been to bed. Instead, he had spent a significant amount of time at his laptop, drunk an entire bottle of red wine, and Skyped his mother in the United States for more than an hour. The tone of their conversation was later characterized as "melancholy and affectionate," a description that made sense in light of what followed.

Just after eight, Kleckner was observed reading what was assumed to be a text message on his BlackBerry. The American "appeared to freeze, as if shocked" (according to the analyst) and "remained still for a considerable period of time." Kleckner did not reply to the message, but instead proceeded to the kitchen, where he retrieved "a passport (origin unknown), a significant amount of money (currency unknown), and a brand-new iPhone and charger" from a Tupperware box "hidden behind the pipes and materials beneath the sink." Alert to the change in Kleckner's behavior, the analyst had followed protocol and telephoned Tom Kell at his home in London. Kell had immediately doubled the four-man surveillance team on standby outside Kleckner's apartment building.

Kleckner then spent the next fifteen minutes packing a "large black wheeled suitcase." When he removed the hard drive from his laptop and placed it inside the case, the analyst—who was later to be congratulated for her quick thinking and initiative—again contacted Kell. Realizing that Kleckner was showing all the signs of a blown agent, he immediately ordered Sirkeci railway station, Ataturk and Sabiha Gokcen airports, the bus terminals at Harem and Topkapi, as well as the Black Sea ferry terminal at Karakoy to be placed under observation by two-man teams, drawing for the first time on consular staff to make up the shortfall.

Having packed the hard drive, Kleckner was seen to put two framed photographs, two bottles of contact lens solution, "a significant amount of clothing," and a second pair of shoes in his suitcase. He removed the SIM card from the BlackBerry and threw the telephone itself into a bin outside the apartment building. It was assumed that ABACUS had left his diplomatic passport and driver's license inside the safe in his bedroom, though the analyst was not able to confirm this.

A block from the front door, the American was observed making a call from a public phone box close to the branch of Starbucks in which Javed Mohsin and Priya were waiting for him. Kell assumed that the conversation, which lasted "no more than ten seconds," was an agreed signal to Minasian indicating that ABACUS was on the run.

It was not yet six o'clock in the morning in London. Looking at a map of the region in his flat, Kell deduced that Kleckner's most likely route to Moscow was across country by bus or rented car into eastern Anatolia, where he might attempt to cross the border into Georgia. An SVR exfil team might also attempt to pick him up at Samsun, or one of the other ports on the Black Sea, taking Kleckner across to Odessa or Sevastopol by ship. A route north into Bulgaria was also an option, though ABACUS would know that the border could more easily be controlled by the Americans. If he trusted his alias, he might risk a commercial airliner, but would assume that all direct flights to Moscow, Kiev, Tashkent, Baku, and Sofia—indeed any of the former Soviet satellite countries—were compromised.

Kell was completely reliant on the surveillance team. Lose ABACUS and, chances are, the next time anyone in SIS saw Kleckner's face would be on the front page of *The Guardian*. Track him to his arranged exfil point and there was a minute chance that ABACUS could be grabbed before an SVR team got to him. Kell telephoned Amelia at the house in Chelsea to update her on developments. Both were aware that Kell's relationship with Rachel had most likely triggered Kleckner's exit: Minasian had trawled through the data and concluded that ABACUS was blown. Amelia arranged to meet Kell at Vauxhall Cross, reassuring him that Rachel would immediately be pulled out of Istanbul. Kell doubted that he would have the opportunity to see her before he was obliged to leave London.

That instinct proved correct. The surveillance team successfully tracked ABACUS to the ferry terminal at Karakoy, where Kleckner was observed making enquiries about joining one of two cruise ships docked on the northern side of the Golden Horn. Javed Mohsin housed the American onto an Italian boat—*Serenissima*—obtained a copy of the timetable, and remained in the terminal building until the vessel had departed, two hours later, making sure that Kleckner did not double back onto dry land. As luck would have it, he was then photographed walking on the deck of the ship as she sailed north toward the Black Sea. An enterprising surveillance officer had rented a water taxi and followed *Serenissima* as far as the Bosporus Bridge.

"Kleckner is headed for Ukraine," Kell told Amelia as soon as he heard the news. "Unless the ship is intercepted and he manages to get off, he'll be in Odessa in forty-eight hours."

"We'd better call the Americans," she replied.

Kell was bewildered. "Why? ABACUS is our catch. Our triumph."

"You know why, Tom."

They had taken themselves into a small conference room on the first floor. Door closed, blinds down.

"You let Chater interfere with what I want to do, we will lose ABACUS. No question."

"You can't assume that."

"The Cousins will swarm all over Odessa," Kell told her. "Flood the port. Minasian will know they are coming twenty-four hours before the ship even docks. Jim doesn't do this stuff as well as we do it."

Amelia nodded in agreement, though Kell could see that she was still conceding to the political argument. Exclude Langley, and SIS would pay a heavy price. If Kell failed to grab Kleckner, there would be hell to pay.

"Just let me arrange it," Kell said. "A small team, low visibility. Minasian won't want to make a big song and dance. His prize agent is blown. He asks Moscow for backup, he's going to lose face. He's going to get big-footed by a more senior officer, a more experienced team." Kell risked a Russian accent. "*You couldn't cope, Alexander. We will take over now.*" Amelia almost smiled. "Minasian will want to do it quietly. No leaks coming out of Kiev Station, no indication to London or Langley that ABACUS is heading for Odessa. He just wants to get his man off the boat, get him into a car, drive him to the airport, put him on the six o'clock news. That way he's still the hero. That way he did everything by the book and it was Kleckner who fucked up. That's what I would do. That's what *you* would do, too, right?"

Amelia nodded but did not immediately respond. Kell could see the calculation being made behind the eyes.

Finally, she turned to him.

"You cannot fuck this up, Tom. We cannot lose Ryan Kleckner."

"I will not fuck this up," he replied, already walking out of the room. "Just give me what I need."

56

Kell put a team together inside two hours. Javed Mohsin and Nina flew direct from Istanbul to Odessa, taking rooms at a four-star hotel on Arkadia Beach, a resort area to the south of the city. To avoid a cluster of last-minute bookings appearing on the passenger manifest of a single airline, the seven other officers leaving London for Odessa took separate flights from Gatwick, Stansted, and Heathrow. Harold flew with British Airways to Kiev, Danny and Carol with Ukrainian Airlines. Kell connected through Vienna, Elsa and Jez via Warsaw. For the same reason, the team was distributed across several Odessa hotels, on standard tourist aliases. In the unlikely event that they were questioned by immigration officials, the younger members of the team were to express an interest in the city's nightlife. Harold and Danny were to declare a lifelong passion for *Battleship Potemkin* and the films of Sergei Eisenstein.

"What about you, guv?" Harold had asked Kell.

"There are some catacombs under the city," he replied. "I'll tell them I want to go caving."

Kell traveled under the Hardwick alias, rehearsing the legend as he flew east from Vienna, trying to think of every eventuality, every trick that would help his hastily assembled team snatch ABACUS from under the noses of the SVR. He pored over a street map of Odessa and learned whatever he could about procedures for passengers disembarking from ships at the port. Kell had left preliminary instructions in the drafts folder of a Gmail account to which all ten officers held the password, attaching mug shots of Kleckner and Minasian and arranging a meeting at a restaurant in the center of Odessa for eight o'clock on Sunday night. The team would otherwise have limited contact with one another, on clean U.K. cell phones, once they had passed through Ukrainian immigration.

Amelia had suggested using officers from the embassy in Kiev, both for local expertise and to bulk up the numbers, but Kell insisted on keeping the Station at arm's length. If Minasian's people were watching SIS personnel, that could lead the SVR right into the heart of the Odessa operation and blow it open.

Kell's planes were delayed out of both London and Vienna. He arrived three hours late in Odessa. SIS had reserved a hire car for Chris Hardwick, but there was a further delay of forty-five minutes in the airport while the rental firm agent tried to locate it. ("No cars," he said, in bored, spluttering English. "All gone.") It was already past midnight by the time Kell was on the road, driving with a sat-nav through a grid of time-travel nineteenth-century boulevards into the heart of the old city. He hadn't slept in almost two days, but managed several hours of rest in his room after receiving confirmation by secure e-mail that Rachel was "safe and well" in Istanbul. Amelia had pointed out the importance of Rachel maintaining cover; to fly her back to London would look like panic, merely confirming to the SVR that she had been working against ABACUS. Better that she remain in Turkey and continue to try to contact Kleckner. To that end, Rachel had sent two text messages to the American, as well as an e-mail, wondering why he was not responding to her calls. Amelia had instructed her to break off the relationship on

Sunday morning ("I can't BELIEVE you would mess me around like this"), thereby leaving Rachel free to return to London on Monday without raising greater suspicion.

Kell was woken at dawn by the rattling air-conditioning unit in his room. Mr. Hardwick had been booked into the Londonskaya, a pre-Soviet relic of Odessa's romantic past with broad, high-ceilinged corridors and a sweeping staircase that led down into an ornate fin de siècle lobby. Kell planned to spend the morning walking around the port, then to meet up with Danny to discuss the best means by which they might grab Kleckner.

It was a humid morning in Odessa, smells of engine oil and sea air as Kell left the Londonskaya and walked east along a colonnade of plane trees toward a pretty Italianate square at the top of the Potemkin Steps. He continued south on foot, familiarizing himself with the grid of streets around Deribasovskaya, the main pedestrianized thoroughfare in the center of the city. Soviet-era Ladas bumped along cobbled streets under crisp sunshine, Ukraine's famously beautiful women dressed at ten o'clock in the morning as if going to a wedding, teetering on high heels in curve-hugging dresses. Kell stopped for a coffee at a restaurant advertising sushi and shisha, then returned to the square.

A bare-chested teenage boy was standing at the top of the Potemkin Steps, a giant eagle perched on his shoulder. Tourists were taking photographs of the bird, a young German girl gasping at the size of its beak and talons. Kell handed the teenager a ten-*grivna* note and took pictures of his own, firing off several shots of the area—including the entrance to a funicular railway that ran parallel to the Steps. A group of perhaps twenty tourists were standing beneath a statue of a man Kell identified from a Cyrillic sign as the Duke of Richelieu, a nineteenth-century French aristocrat evidently integral to some aspect of Odessa's fabled past. He was dressed in the style of a Roman senator, a pigeon resting on his outstretched arm. Kell sat at the base of the memorial and looked south toward the Black Sea. There was a tall modern building in the center of the port complex, about half a mile away. Block capital letters on the roof identified the building as the Hotel Odessa. Kell was frustrated. Had the researchers at Vauxhall Cross realized that it was situated so close to the area where Kleckner's ship would dock, they would have booked Danny a room. With a decent pair of binoculars, Aldrich could have tracked *Serenissima*'s approach from several miles away while keeping a discreet eye on possible SVR movement in the port. The lobby of the hotel would also have made a convenient meeting point for the team in the event of emergency. Such were the missed opportunities and complications of a last-minute operation. Kell would try for a room as soon as he reached the port.

He began to walk down the Potemkin Steps. Vendors sitting in the dappled light of shading trees were selling Russian dolls from plinths on either side of the Steps. As the heat of the day intensified, an elderly man paused to catch his breath halfway up, exhausted by the effort of climbing but still managing to smile at the passing Kell. Kell offered him a sip from a bottle of water, but the man declined, resting his hand on Kell's arm and muttering: "*Spasiba.*"

Traffic was passing in both directions along a busy two-lane highway at the base of the Steps. Kell used an underpass to reach the pedestrian entrance to the port on the opposite side of the road. Within a few minutes he had reached a large square in front of the main terminal building, his view of the port dominated on either side by rusted cranes and distant container ships. Kell walked along the eastern side of the terminal as far as the entrance to the Hotel Odessa. To his surprise, he saw that the hotel had been boarded up: weeds had even sprouted at the base of a set of locked automatic doors. Peering inside, Kell could see time-zone clocks bolted to the wall behind an abandoned reception desk, plastic sheets laid out across the carpets. He remembered the office of Nicolas Delfas and thought briefly of Marianna Dimitriadis, wondering what had become of her. A number of people were walking in the area in front of the hotel: parents with their children; couples on a romantic stroll.

Kell carried on, walking around to the western pier until he had made a circuit of the terminal. He took photographs—of staircases, exits, walkways, and landmarks—that he would show to the team at the evening meeting. At one point, Kell passed within twenty feet of Javed Mohsin and enjoyed the fact that Mohsin was professional enough to avoid eye contact.

Kell went next inside the terminal itself, following signs directing passengers to the customs area. He was surprised by how easily he could move through the various levels of the building without being stopped or questioned by officials. It would be different in the morning, with any number of police officers and immigration officials present. For now, though, the environment was as open and as fluid as Kell could have hoped.

He spent the rest of the afternoon with Danny preparing the comms and vehicles. Earpieces and microphones had been sent by diplomatic bag to the British embassy in Chisinau, then driven across the border from Moldova by an SIS officer. Aldrich and Mohsin had rented Audis and would drive them to the terminal building in the morning, taking the slip road over the railway tracks running parallel to the highway. If the team could grab Kleckner off the ship and somehow bundle him into the backseat of one of the vehicles, so much the better, but neither Kell nor Aldrich believed that it would be that easy. At the very least, Minasian would have to be taken out of the equation. In a worst-case scenario, a phalanx of armed SVR officers would get ABACUS under control on the quayside and spirit him away within minutes. If that happened, Kell and his team would be going home empty-handed.

57

Ryan Kleckner could not come to terms with the suddenness with which his work had come to an end. Returning to his apartment in the early hours of Saturday morning, he had tried to convince himself that the woman on the aircraft was not the same woman he had seen in Harrods. It was a coincidence, a case of mistaken identity. Surely he was not being tailed? What clues had he given? What mistakes had he made? None. He was certain that if there was fault in the operation, it had to have come from the Russian side.

Then the text message from Minasian. BESIKTAS. A single word, bringing everything to an end. KODAK blown. Get out of Istanbul. Follow agreed procedure.

Kleckner had sat and stared at the screen of his BlackBerry, even as he realized that his apartment was most likely compromised and that his every move was being watched by a room full of analysts in Langley and Istinye. He felt humiliated, ashamed. It was the first time that he could remember experiencing such sudden and profound despair. He had no choice but to pack, leaving behind countless belongings—pictures, books, records, items of clothing—that he knew he would never see again. He doubted that he would make it as far as the door of his apartment. They were probably waiting for him outside.

But to Kleckner's surprise, he found that he was able to leave the building unmolested. To go to the phone booth and to call the number that Minasian had given him. When he heard the woman answering in Russian, he gave the agreed response: "BESIKTAS THREE." There was a pause, after which the woman repeated the code and hung up.

Kleckner had not known whether or not the message had been conveyed to Minasian until he had stolen the cell phone on the ship. One of the passengers had left the phone on a table in the entertainment lounge and Kleckner had scooped it. There had been no signal for several hours. He had waited in his cabin, then out on deck at night, watching the bars on the screen, like a paramedic waiting for a pulse. At last, perhaps because the ship had drawn closer to the Romanian coast, he had been able to send a message to Minasian.

SERENISSIMA. LUNEDI.

It was simple enough. The name of the ship, which the SVR could track online, and the day when Kleckner hoped to be picked up. Within minutes, the Russian had replied, confirming receipt of the message with the agreed word. Kleckner had wanted to speak to him, to find out what had gone wrong, but knew that it would be unsafe to do so. He was convinced that Minasian had been compromised. In all the scenarios that his mind rehearsed, Kleckner would not allow himself to believe that Rachel had tricked him or had been working in concert with Thomas Kell. Ryan Kleckner didn't make mistakes. The Brits didn't do honey traps. The fault lay with Moscow.

58

Kell was the last to arrive at the eight o'clock meeting. The other members of the team had already gathered at a large outdoor table on the south side of Deribasovskaya, their seats partly screened from the street by a slatted white fence entwined with fairy lights and fake vines. Kell had chosen the restaurant because of several reviews on TripAdvisor describing it as "busy" and "extremely noisy." Sure enough, there were several sources of music in the immediate area, including Russian pop tunes blaring from two speakers at the entrance to the restaurant and a folk band playing live across the street through a small, crackling amplifier.

"Nice and peaceful," Kell muttered as he took his seat at the center of the table. He shook hands with Harold and Danny, kissed Elsa and Carol on the cheek. To the rest—Nina, Jez, Javed, and Alicia, a Russian-speaking SIS analyst brought along as a translator—he nodded and smiled. "How's everybody enjoying their holiday so far?"

"I am enjoying myself very much," Elsa replied, a sentiment echoed by Jez, who said he had spent the afternoon at Arkadia Beach with Carol.

"And you?" Kell asked Harold.

"I was just educating the masses on the history of this fine city," he replied, brandishing a paperback book from which he began to read. Kell was glad for Harold's icebreaking charm. It was good for morale. "Did you know that Catherine the Great had a one-eyed secret husband?"

"A one-eyed secret husband," Kell repeated, ordering a beer from the waiter. "I did not know that."

"Odessa was once the most vibrant port in the whole of the Russian empire," Harold continued, flicking through the pages of the book. Elsa looked confused. His sense of humor had always baffled her. "Everything came through this place in the old days. Wines from France, olive oil from Italy, nuts from Turkey, dried fruits from the Levant . . ."

"The *what*?" Nina asked.

"The Levant," Harold replied, without condescension. "Otherwise known as the Middle East." Kell picked up a laminated menu on which every dish appeared with an illustrating photograph. "Then it all came to an end."

"Why?" Danny asked, from the end of the table. "Soviet Union?"

"Suez," Kell replied. "Canal."

Harold flattened the book spine-up on the table. "*Odessa: Genius and Death in a City of Dreams*." Kell looked at the sepia-tinted photograph of the Potemkin Steps on the cover and said: "What's everyone eating?"

It was a ritual he had endured many times in his career. As usual, there was very little operational conversation until the food had arrived. Kell knew from experience that it was best to allow teams to relax in one another's company before turning to business. The time also allowed him to assess each member of the team. Did anyone seem nervous or tired? Were there tensions between individuals, or particularly strong bonds of friendship? Though Carol seemed quiet and somewhat out of place, he was satisfied that there were no obvious problems and began with an overview of what was planned for the morning.

"The ship is due to dock at eleven o'clock. I'll be keeping an eye out;

Elsa has been tracking her progress across the Black Sea. There's every chance the boat could be an hour early, an hour late, so everybody needs to be ready and prepared by eight, phones live from midnight tonight. Goes without saying, keep them charged." The restaurant was now so noisy, and the activity on Deribasovskaya so unceasing, that Kell knew there was no chance of his remarks being overheard. "You've all seen photographs of ABACUS," he said. "We have a pretty good idea of the clothes he packed, what he might be wearing. I assume all of you have seen those notes on Gmail?" Kell registered a series of nods and muttered affirmatives. "Myself, Danny, Carol, Nina, and Javed will be down at the port terminal with two cars. It's vital that we identify ABACUS as quickly as possible. At the same time, we all need to be looking out for a welcoming party. If it's substantial, if for example an advance team gets onto *Serenissima* and brings the package out, that's the end of it. We walk away."

Danny looked down at his half-eaten plate of food. He had lobbied hard for a military solution that would have allowed Kleckner to leave Odessa in an SVR vehicle that would be subsequently immobilized by Special Forces. Conscious of the diplomatic fallout from such a plan, quite apart from the constraints imposed by time, Kell had snuffed it out without even running it past Amelia.

"If, on the other hand, our friends in Moscow are trying to be discreet, if there's just a car of heavies and Minasian to cope with, we've got a playable chance. Keep talking to one another, give me positions, keep everybody informed. Trust one another, use your experience."

There was a sudden break in the folk music across the street. Kell paused, draining his beer.

"Could you just tell us where everybody's going to be?" Carol asked.

Kell took out his camera and began to pass it around the table, showing each member of the team their starting positions for the morning. Harold would be waiting with Kell and Danny on the quayside, ready to touch Kleckner in a brush contact, attaching a tracker to his clothing.

Carol would be positioned inside the terminal building, waiting for Kleckner to pass through customs. Javed and Nina would be fluid in the port, an extra pair of eyes watching for Minasian, for Kleckner, for any sign of SVR personnel. Elsa and Alicia were to wait in two taxis parked close to the main exit of the terminal complex. There was only one way into the port and one way out. If Minasian came out with Kleckner, they were to follow the SVR until Kell, Aldrich, and Jez could join the pursuit. Jez himself was to park in the Italianate square at the top of the Potemkin Steps, role-playing a Ukrainian cab driver. Kell explained to the team that he was hoping to drive Kleckner away from the terminal on foot. If there were no taxis passing on the two-lane highway outside the port, the American would have no other option but to continue up the Potemkin Steps. If he failed to take the bait from Jez and made it into the center of Odessa, they would be in a game of cat and mouse with an expert in countersurveillance. Hence the need for workable comms, several vehicles, and for Harold, Elsa, and Alicia pulling information from the ether.

"And how do we get Ryan into one of the cars?" Nina asked. "What if it's just me and him and an opportunity?"

"It won't be," Kell reassured her. "The only people who are going to physically interact with Minasian and Kleckner are myself, Danny, and Jez. Nobody else is to take that risk. Understood?"

"Understood," Carol muttered.

"And how exactly are you going to do that?" Nina asked. Kell didn't much like her tone. "How are you going to physically interact with him?"

"Leave that to us," Danny told her.

59

Kell slept on and off for only a few hours, dreaming of Rachel, waking with his body drenched in sweat at two, then again at half past four. He had switched off the rattling air-conditioner in his room and it was stultifyingly hot. He climbed out of bed and opened both windows onto the tree-lined colonnade. It was still dark outside, no birdsong. He took a shower and ordered a room service breakfast. By the time Kell was ready to leave, it was not yet six o'clock. A sensationally long-legged, slim-waisted girl in a nonexistent miniskirt was coming up the broad staircase on the arm of a short, shaven-headed middle-aged man who flashed Kell a triumphant smile of lust and conquest. It was all Kell could do to prevent himself muttering: "You get what you pay for," but he continued down to the lobby in silence.

He emerged onto the broad pavement outside the Londonskaya. A couple of teenagers were sitting on a wooden bench under the plane trees, kissing. A woman wearing a dark blue pinafore was sweeping street dust with a broomstick. Kell turned east toward the Potemkin Steps. A horse and cart, newly painted in white, had parked at the edge of the square, the horse eating from a bag of grass, the driver asleep with a rug spread out across his body. A single taxi was waiting on the rank at the junction with Ekaterininskaya, a Humvee and a stretch limo parked alongside. Kell checked his phone. There were four messages. Danny, Javed, and Nina were awake. According to Elsa, *Serenissima* was delayed by an hour. Alicia had translated a message sent by the Odessa Port Authority giving the ship clearance to dock on the western quay. Neither Elsa nor Harold had picked up a syllable of local SVR chatter.

Kell continued past the Steps, encountering a pack of stray dogs asleep on the ground in front of a pale yellow building on the far side of the square. Somewhere in the distance a generator was running: perhaps the local grid was experiencing one of Odessa's frequent power cuts. Kell lit a cigarette and walked to a metal footbridge overlooking the port. Cranes as far as the eye could see, no ships docked at the terminal. Hundreds of padlocks had been attached to the railings, love tokens rusted by rain and sea air. An old man with a corrugated nose stopped close by and tucked in a loose section of his shirt, nodding at Kell as he went on his way. Then, out of nowhere, a familiar voice behind him.

"Waiting for a ship?"

Kell turned to find Harold and Danny coming toward him.

"Gentlemen," he said.

They stood on either side of him. Both were dressed in jeans and polo shirts. Harold had a gray nylon jacket looped over his arm.

"So," Harold said. "Is she on time?"

"Slight delay," Kell replied. "An hour, max."

"Maybe they hit an iceberg."

Kell stubbed out the cigarette. "Who is it in Greek mythology that waits for a ship?" he asked.

"Aegeus," Danny replied instantly. Kell had a flash image of Aldrich at home in Guildford, poring over books and encyclopedias. A pub quiz brain. "Theseus, his son, went off to slay the Minotaur. Told him that if he was successful, he'd change the sails on his ship from black to white . . ."

"But he forgot," said Kell.

"Exactly." Danny looked out at the Black Sea. "Aegeus saw the ship, saw the black sails. Reckoned he'd lost his son. So he killed himself."

"This is what people forget," said Harold. "They didn't have cell phones in those days, so Theseus couldn't call ahead."

Kell put his hand on Harold's shoulder, laughing.

"We've got time to kill," he said. "Coffee?"

60

Serenissima docked at seven minutes past twelve. Javed and Nina had binoculars trained on the decks, but reported no sign of Kleckner. It was a crystal-clear summer afternoon, the terminal far busier than the day before, with vendors doing brisk business on sales of snacks and newspapers, cab drivers queueing up to take curious cruise ship passengers into the heart of old Odessa. Danny and Harold had been at the quayside for more than an hour, looking for Alexander Minasian, watching the vehicles parked on either side of the terminal for any sign of threat or surveillance. Danny had reported "at least three men" in a Mercedes parked parallel to five empty vehicles immediately outside the customs area. If they were SVR, they would only reveal as much when passengers began to disembark from the ship.

Kell, whose face was known to Minasian and Kleckner, had remained in his rented car until a member of the crew on *Serenissima* had thrown a mooring rope from the bow. That was his cue. Kell was then mobile in the port and at risk of being spotted. Too bad. It was now just a race to get to ABACUS; if Kleckner spotted him, he might even get spooked and play into their hands. A ramp had been lowered from the ship, connecting foot passengers to the quay. Kell and Danny needed to get as close to the ramp as possible, and to grab the prize.

"Anything?" Kell asked, walking through a scrum of local teenagers who had gathered on the dock. He was talking to Danny via the commslink.

"Nothing," Danny replied.

Then, a call. Kell's phone throbbing in his back pocket. It was Javed.

"My comms are down," he said. "Possible Minasian. Alone. Fifty meters from you, eleven o'clock." Kell looked ahead. There was always bad news on an operation. To lose the commslink to Javed was a setback, but it had to be forgotten.

"Describe," he said.

"Dark hair, cropped short. I'm sure it's him. Blond woman to his right. Your left."

"I see her." Kell sighted the man with dark, cropped hair. It wasn't Minasian. "Negative," he said. "Keep looking."

Danny had approached from the seaward side and was already at the ramp. It was the only exit from the ship. No cars. Foot passengers only. A lot of elderly people starting to make their way down the ramp, two in wheelchairs. Crew members in navy blue uniforms, helping them on their way, smiling and laughing against a background of squawking gulls.

"Possible ABACUS." Nina this time. Kell felt a scratch of irritation every time he heard her voice. "To the left of the ramp. On the ship. No longer visible. I'm sure it was him."

Kell looked up at the great white mass of the ship's starboard side, twice the height of the Londonskaya. Shadows and sunlight and a mass of people bottlenecked at the exit, making it almost impossible to get clear sight of faces. He had no binoculars. His phone was ringing again. Javed.

"Boss. That car. The Mercedes. Driver just got out. Looks very serious. Black suit, muscle."

"Minasian?"

"Negative."

"Danny will take the tires if necessary," Kell told him and conveyed this message to Aldrich on the commslink. "Could be a politician. Could be business. Could be organized crime. Could be Simon fucking Cowell."

"Copy," Danny confirmed.

"Boss?"

Carol now on the comms, from her position inside the terminal building.

"Go ahead."

"Minasian confirmed. Seems alone. Blue denim jeans. White collared shirt. Black sweater. Standing left-hand side of the information desk. Black-rimmed glasses."

"*Seems* alone?"

"Affirmative."

It didn't make sense. It was too easy. There had to be others. Why would Minasian risk the chance of Kleckner being grabbed off the ramp? Why allow him to reach the customs area, to hand him over to the control of the Ukrainians?

"Do not let him out of your sight."

"Obviously," Carol replied.

Kell spotted Danny at the bottom of the ramp, within touching distance of a geriatric couple who were walking, with painstaking slowness, toward the immigration zone. Kell was still at the edge of a thick crowd, ten meters from the base of the ramp. It was like being in a press scrum waiting for a glimpse of a celebrity.

"Nina?" he said on the comms, hoping that she had made a second possible sighting.

"Nothing," she replied immediately.

Kell could now see all the way up the ramp and into the ship. Danny caught his eye. Still no sign of Kleckner. Had they missed him? Passengers had been disembarking for more than five minutes, but there were still large numbers of people queueing inside the ship.

"Carol?"

"Yup."

"Minasian?"

"Still there. I'll let you know if anything changes." It sounded as though she had moved position, possibly to get behind Minasian. The clarity on her link had dropped.

"Earpiece? Is he talking to anybody? Using a phone?"

"Negative. Nothing. Cool as a Russian cucumber."

There was a sudden long blast on the ship's horn, echoing out across the port. No reaction from the passengers, no reaction from the members of the public gathered on the quay. Kell lit a cigarette, turning through three hundred and sixty degrees, scanning the quay, the decks on the ship, the walkway above his head where Javed was clearly visible, standing beside a sculpture of a mother and child, a pair of binoculars trained on the ramp.

A second blast on the ship's horn. Laughter in the group ahead of Kell, American voices exclaiming their delight at "being on dry land again." Kell caught a smell of melted chocolate and roasted nuts from one of the carts upwind. Then, in his ear, Danny's voice so sudden and excitable that he was spun around: "Ramp!"

Kell looked up toward the ship. Ryan Kleckner was clearly visible, no more than twenty meters away, slowly walking down the ramp. He was trailing the Karrimor suitcase and looking up at the terminal building, like a boy on his first day at boarding school.

Kell immediately turned around—he did not want to risk Kleckner seeing his face—and gave the command.

"ABACUS in play," he said. "Take Minasian."

61

Traveling on a French-Canadian passport under the name "Eric Cauques," Sebastien Gachon took a scheduled flight from Paris to Istanbul in the early hours of Sunday, May 5. He had traveled overnight from Kampala, where he had been spending time with a girlfriend.

Gachon had never visited Istanbul before, nor did he speak Turkish. He waited in line for a taxi and passed the driver a piece of paper on which he had written down the address of a clothes boutique in Yenikoy. An hour later, Gachon was outside the Wallinger *yali,* wheeling his suitcase along the road, making a preliminary observation of the property. A single front door. No side entrances. Access from the sea.

The target was at home. Gachon could see her moving from floor to floor, a woman matching the description cabled from Kiev. No apparent security detail, no third parties in the building. He could have taken her there and then. Left his suitcase on the street, rung the doorbell, made the hit, walked away. But he was acting under orders.

Gachon continued along the street to the main coastal thoroughfare, where he hailed a second taxi. He retrieved the name of the hotel in Galata from his phone and showed the display to the driver. The driver stared at the screen. Gachon could not tell if the man was illiterate or merely lazy. He waited. After a delay of several seconds, the driver nodded, engaged first gear, and proceeded south toward Beyoglu.

Gachon was hot. He removed his jacket, took a bottle of water from his suitcase, and swallowed several mouthfuls. He then tapped out a message on his phone, in English, which he sent to the dedicated number.

WE HAVE ARRIVED. YOUR SISTER IS HOME.

Alexander Minasian had replied within thirty seconds.

THANK YOU. PLEASE WAIT FOR US. WE ARE STILL LOOKING AT THE ALBUMS. WE ARE GLAD YOU HAVE ARRIVED SAFELY.

62

Harold was at Kell's side within thirty seconds, at the edge of the ramp within ten. Kell turned to see Danny walking away from the crush toward an exterior staircase that would take him up into the arrivals area. Carol confirmed that Minasian was still loitering near the information desk. Kell was relying on her to have made the right call. If the man she suspected of being Alexander Minasian turned out to be just a run-of-the-mill Odessan hanging around the port, they were in trouble. If the real Alexander Minasian was currently getting out of a black Mercedes-Benz, flanked by SVR minders who would grab ABACUS from customs and take him to the airport, they were finished.

"Missed him."

It was Harold. Kleckner had passed too far away to be painted. The American had his head down and was walking along the roped-off passage toward a door in the lower ground floor. No sign of a welcoming committee. No sign of anybody trying to grab Kleckner out of the line. It was all too easy.

Kell called Javed.

"Tell me what's going on with the car."

"Driver got back in. Has Danny done the tires?"

"Not yet. He's going to Minasian. We're waiting on that."

Danny confirmed by comms that he was inside the terminal, Kleckner now out of sight in the customs area two floors below. A place where nobody on the team could get to him. Nobody but the SVR.

"Confirm on Minasian," Danny said calmly, and Kell felt a swell of relief. Carol had made the right call.

"Any company?"

"Not that I can see."

"I'll be there in fifteen seconds."

Kell sprinted up the flight of stairs, came into the arrivals area. He was out of breath. The day before, the terminal had been all but deserted; now there were at least two hundred people crowded at the top of the escalators. Noise and bustle and heat. It was impossible to move quickly.

The first American tourists had made it through immigration and were pushing their way toward the souvenir shops at the southern end of the terminal. Kell looked across the hall at the information desk and saw Danny closing in on Minasian. Carol between them, turning, watching, looking for plainclothes. And all the time Kleckner downstairs, seizable, with only Javed and Nina outside making sure that he didn't double back.

Kell's phone rang. Javed.

"Mercedes engine on," he said. "Exhaust fumes. Back doors open. Another man has got out. No suit. Just jeans and a T-shirt. Tattoos. Tires?"

"Take them," Kell replied instantly. He was convinced that Minasian was a diversion. The Russian had known that Kell was coming, positioned himself in the terminal building to give the impression that he was Kleckner's only contact, while down below a second SVR team was pulling Kleckner out of the customs line and preparing to take him to the Mercedes.

"I can do that," Javed replied. He had a knife, but no conviction in his voice.

At that moment, Kell saw Alexander Minasian begin to struggle, Danny with his arms around him, hugging him tight. As though Minasian was an old friend, encased in a welcoming bear hug, not filled with the ketamine that had just been jammed into his bicep. Kell heard Minasian shouting out in Russian, a man at the edge of losing control, trying to get a warning to somebody, trying to ask for help. But Danny was much stronger, he had the element of surprise, and the sedative was working through him. Kell saw Danny laughing, lowering Minasian to the ground, Carol still watching the terminal for cops and plainclothes, signaling to Kell with her eyes that the coast was clear.

Javed was still on the phone.

"Talk to me," Kell said, as a space formed around Minasian, crowds stepping back, as if from a drunk. Danny and Carol already long gone. "Is anybody moving near the car?"

"Negative. Engine still running. Driver looks very relaxed. I don't think it's them. I think we're watching the wrong people."

"Take the fucking tires," Kell ordered and turned toward the escalators.

At that moment, the head of Ryan Kleckner, his neck, his shoulders, his chest, came sliding up into view. There was a blond woman of about Rachel's age in front of him, two elderly cruise ship passengers behind. Before Kell had a chance to turn away, Kleckner had looked directly at him. The expression on the American's face disintegrated. Kell saw his eyes widen in alarm, then shoot away. In the next moment Kleckner had abandoned his suitcase, letting it drop as he reached the top of the escalators, seeming to understand that the commotion ahead of him, the disturbance around Minasian, was part of the plan to trap him. Kell called for Danny on the comms, because he could no longer see him.

"Outside. Doing the tires," Danny replied.

Kell shouted back: "Leave the tires. Javed has them. ABACUS is mobile."

63

Kleckner sprinted outside through a door on the opposite side of the terminal building. Nina and Javed were still on the western quay, looking at the ship, looking at the Mercedes. Danny was trying to find a way back to Kell. They were all out of action. Kell and Carol the only members of the team with line of sight to Kleckner.

"He's heading for the main square in the port. Toward the railway. Moving. Running."

Kell's voice alerted Elsa and Alicia, who confirmed that they were in separate taxis, engines running, at the gates. Harold was back in Kell's rental car, Danny sprinting for the Audi. Their voices a cacophony in Kell's earpiece as he sprinted along the eastern walkway toward the square at the northern end of the terminal. Carol was somewhere behind him. Kell could hear sirens in the distance. He had no idea what had become of Nina and Javed and only hoped that they had slashed the tires and were sprinting along the eastern side of the building. A forty-four-year-old man who smoked thirty a day, chasing a panicking, gym-fit, twenty-nine-year-old American. Kleckner would be out of sight within seconds.

"I can see him." It was Harold, parked at the edge of the slip-road linking the port to the highway. "Could have fucking run him over. Came right in front of me. Fuck."

Kell could visualize where Kleckner was. Past the rank of taxis, nowhere for him to go but out of the port, toward the highway, toward the Potemkin Steps.

"I have him."

Elsa's voice this time. In the taxi. That meant Kleckner was already at the gates.

"What's he doing?" Kell came to a halt. He was so out of breath that Elsa had to ask him to repeat what he had said.

"Looking for a taxi," she said. "He saw me, saw I was in the car. Otherwise I think he takes it. I'm sorry."

"Don't worry." Kell began to run again, moving toward her position. He was perhaps a hundred meters behind her. He thought that he had glimpsed Kleckner walking left-to-right across the entrance. Elsa confirmed this.

"He is crossing the road," she said. "He is so close to me. *Minchia*." Somebody else tried to speak on the link but Kell barked them off. "Wait, please," said Elsa. "He is going for the railway."

"What do you mean going for the railway?" There were train tracks under the slip-road, but that was *inside* the port. There was no access to them from the road. Unless Kleckner was doubling back.

"Sorry. I mean the little thing. That takes you up the Steps. I cannot remember the name in English you told me. In Italian we call it '*funicolare*.'"

"Funicular, same," Kell replied and arrived at the highway, looking across the road. He was exhausted, and just in time to see Kleckner entering the small booth at the base of the funicular railway that would take him to the top of the Steps. The American appeared to be the last passenger on board. The doors were closing.

"You want us to follow him?" Elsa asked.

"No. Stay there. I'll need you if he comes back down."

Kell had no choice. He stepped over a barrier and ran across the highway, a Lada bearing down on him from twenty feet. The driver blasted the horn as Kell spun in front of him, reaching the other side. Looking up, he made eye contact with Kleckner in the booth as the funicular began its slow journey up the hill.

"Danny!" Kell shouted into the commslink. "Harold! Get to the top of the Steps. Get to the fucking square, get to Jez on Primorskiy Boulevard."

If a reply came, Kell did not hear it. His sweat-soaked earpiece slipped free from the lobe and tapped loose against his back as he began, in the full glare of the midday sun, to run up the ten flights of the Potemkin Steps. His legs were numb with effort, his stinging lungs giving him only shallow, seizing breaths as he desperately tried to stay level with Kleckner. The progress of the funicular was obscured by a line of trees. Kell knew that he was behind the game. Kleckner would be out in the square within a minute, and then only one chance left to catch him.

Kell urged himself on, three more flights, two steps at a time, drawing stares as he sprinted forward. At the top stood the same shirtless boy with the same vast eagle perched on his shoulder. Behind the boy, the imperial outline of the Duc de Richelieu, the pigeon long gone from his outstretched hand. Kell was soaked in sweat, a searing pain in his lungs. One more flight. ABACUS was surely out of the carriage by now and loose in the square.

Kell saw Kleckner ten seconds later. Jogging away from the Steps, away from the Duc de Richelieu, toward the rank of taxis parked at the northern end of Ekaterininskaya. As he turned, Kleckner made eye contact with Kell, the hunter and the hunted. The man who had tried to take Rachel from him, the man who had almost ruined Amelia's career. Kell sprinted toward him, closing up the distance so that there was no more than twenty feet between them. Kleckner had no choice but to turn and run.

Three men, all smoking, were leaning on the same car in the taxi rank. None of them looked like they had washed in days. Kell hoped to God that the other two had been paid off.

"Taksi?" Jez asked in his best lazy Russian, taking a step toward the American.

Kleckner did not hesitate.

"Da," he said, getting into the backseat of the car. "Let's go."

64

Kleckner slammed the rear door, urged Jez—in fluent Russian—to "go as quickly as possible to the airport," then twisted around in the backseat to see a breathless Tom Kell gesticulating at one of the taxi drivers in the rank. As the Audi accelerated along Ekaterininskaya, Kleckner opened the window and tried to organize his thoughts. If Kell had come for him, he had come with a team. SIS and the Agency would have the airport, the train station, the main roads out of Odessa wrapped up. Within moments, Kell himself would be in a taxi, giving pursuit. How the hell had this been allowed to happen?

"Can you go faster, please?" he urged the driver, who had a bored, contempt-for-tourists laziness about him. "I'm being followed. I'll pay you. Just go as fast as possible, get off the main road. Take back streets."

"Da, da."

Kleckner muttered "Jesus Christ" in English. Normally his spoken Russian impressed people, broke the ice on a conversation. Not today. Not with this one. The driver missed an obvious side street at a set of lights, continuing west along a main drag in clear contravention of Kleckner's instructions.

"Hey! I thought I said get off the main roads." He wondered if the driver was from a different country. Maybe he didn't speak Russian. "You wanna let me drive?"

"Da, da."

Kleckner swore again, this time with greater ferocity. Yet his words continued to have no effect. The driver was immune to any sense of urgency or threat. Kleckner turned in his seat to see one of the cabs from the rank less than three hundred meters behind him. Kell was on his tail. At last the driver made a slow turn into a quieter side street.

"About fucking time, man," Kleckner muttered, in English, only to be thrown forward in his seat as the driver slammed on the brakes.

Jez turned around. He had pulled the Audi over to the side of the road. There were no pedestrians in sight. The taser was concealed in the hollow recess beside his left hand. He reached for it.

"You know what, mate?" he said, and saw Kleckner's eyes widen in alarm, registering the British accent. "Why don't you shut the fuck up for a little bit?"

And with that, Jez reached forward, touched the taser to Kleckner's chest, and fired.

65

Kell saw the Audi pull over to the side of the road. He instructed the driver of the cab to drop him at the corner. As he was handing over a ten-*grivna* note, Kell looked ahead and saw Kleckner's body flex and slump in the backseat of the Audi, then Jez opening the driver's door and stepping outside. It was done.

Kell took out his phone and called Danny.

"We're on Sadikovskaya," he said, reading off the Cyrillic on a street sign. "You?"

"Traffic. Harold too. What's happening? I'm sorry, we're trying to get to you. Fast as possible."

"It's all fine," Kell told him, taking over in the driver's seat of the Audi. Jez had opened the back door, got hold of Kleckner's leg and pushed a needle of ketamine into his thigh. "We've got him," Kell said. His lungs felt as though they had been washed in acid. "Meet you at the strip."

The strip was an abandoned military airfield, seventy-five kilometers northwest of Odessa, where Amelia had arranged for a chartered Gulfstream to be idling on the tarmac, waiting to spirit ABACUS out of

Ukraine. Kell couldn't risk the long drive north to Kiev, not with Minasian waking up in less than an hour and scrambling every SVR officer from Odessa to Archangel in pursuit of his lost prize. Jez had patted Kleckner down, found a SIM in the ticket pocket of his jeans, removed his wristwatch. Kell was concerned that the watch might show Kleckner's position and had thrown it out of the window.

"That thing was worth three grand," Jez exclaimed, looking back at the wheat field into which Kell had flung the watch.

"Maybe a farmer will find it," Kell replied. "He can buy himself a new tractor."

They drove on quiet country roads, avoiding the main highways, limiting the possibility of a bent Ukrainian cop pulling the Audi over as a favor to Moscow. Kleckner was out cold, slumped on the backseat after thirty seconds of hallucinogenic agitation in central Odessa when the ketamine had begun to work through him. Kell estimated that the American would be awake by the time the plane took off. Awake and ready to start answering questions.

A forest at the edge of a vast plain of fields, a metaled track leading to the airfield. Muggy in the late afternoon.

Nobody at the airstrip save for two British pilots smoking idly in the shadow of a derelict control tower, one called Bob, the other called Phil. Both of them long enough in the tooth not to ask about the cargo they were carrying. The flight plan had been filed, the right palms crossed with the right amount of silver. ABACUS would be taken out of Ukrainian airspace, the Gulfstream brushing the southern tip of Moldova, heading west into Romania, then refueling in Hungary before continuing north over Austria and Germany. Bob expected to touch down at RAF Northolt sometime around nine o'clock BST. Kell would take Kleckner to a safe house in Ruislip, an SIS team would try to ascertain the extent to which ABACUS had corrupted assets and operations in the region, then he would be handed over to the Americans.

Danny and Harold arrived five minutes after Kell. No smiles, no congratulatory handshakes as they approached the Audi and saw Kleckner's drugged body slumped in the backseat. Everybody knew that there was still work to do. Danny confirmed that the rest of the team were leaving Odessa—some by road, some by rail, some by air via Kiev—then grabbed Kleckner by the feet and dragged him out of the car. Kell stood at the back door and took the American's shoulders. He could feel the bulk of Kleckner's muscles as he carried him toward the Gulfstream, the body that Rachel had kissed. He experienced no sense of elation, no joy at Kleckner's capture. Indeed, as the American was hauled into the cabin, Jez helping to lay him across two seats at the front of the aircraft, Kell thought only of Istanbul and offered a silent prayer to the God in whom he still sometimes believed that Rachel Wallinger was safe.

66

She knew how to work the cover. She had texted Kleckner, called his cell phone, written him an irate e-mail. Even after Amelia had managed to get a message to her saying that ABACUS had fled to Odessa, she had kept up the facade, calling a friend in London and complaining that Ryan—"that American guy I told you about"—had stood her up, failed to keep to a promise of taking her out to dinner in Istanbul.

"You poor thing," the friend had said, oblivious to the masquerade, oblivious to the fact that the SVR were listening in to Rachel Wallinger's calls. "I know you really liked him. Maybe he's just had to go and work or something. Maybe he lost his phone."

"That old chestnut," Rachel replied. "Fuck him. Makes me miss Tom."

She knew that it was important to behave naturally, that Minasian's people were most likely watching her. That there was a potential SVR threat against her, but only if it could be proven that she had been working against ABACUS on behalf of SIS.

So she had tried to enjoy herself. Or, at the very least, to live her life as she would ordinarily have lived it, given a few days of leisure in Istanbul. She had been to the Topkapi, she had breezed around the Blue

Mosque, she had taken a boat along the Bosporus. And she had thought about Tom Kell, wondering if he would ever forgive her for the sin of consorting with Ryan Kleckner.

Rachel made the mistake of drinking alone on Sunday night, returning home from a restaurant in Yenikoy after dark. Too much alcohol on an empty stomach, her loneliness buttressed by grief and nerves and by Laura Marling on her iPhone. Approaching the house, she turned the music up loud, louder still when her favorite song came on, the mournful lament of "Goodbye England."

Rachel climbed the steps to the front door of the *yali*, reaching for her keys. The music and the headphones were shrouding every sound in the city. She turned the key in the lock.

She did not look back. She could not hear what was going on around her. She closed the door behind her and walked into the house.

67

The Gulfstream took off into a setting sun. Jez and Harold drove the Audis back to Odessa. As Kell looked down at the airfield, the control tower as remote and indistinct as an abandoned church, he saw a small boy standing at the edge of the woods, mournfully waving at the departing aircraft, as if it were carrying away the bodies of the dead.

Ryan Kleckner woke up over Romania. Groggy, muscle-slow, then aware of the plastic cuffs binding his wrists, the belt buckled tight around his waist. He convulsed briefly, like the start of an epileptic fit, then relaxed back into his seat, aware of the hopelessness of his position.

The first man he saw was Thomas Kell.

"Jesus fucking Christ."

"You're being flown to London," Kell told him. He was seated on a fold-down chair, facing the American. "You're in the custody of SIS."

"The custody of what the fuck? Can you untie me please? What the fuck happened here?"

It was odd to hear Kleckner's voice. Kell had listened to it so many times, on tapes and feeds and recordings of one kind or another. Only once—at the party in Bar Bleu—had he actually been in the presence of the American. He waited for Kleckner's rage and shame to subside; it would only be a matter of time before the personality and the training imposed itself. A man as immune to moral consequence as Ryan Kleckner would believe that he could talk his way out of capture. His self-confidence was bulletproof.

"You want to explain what's going on? You got people from the Agency onboard?" he asked.

"Sadly they couldn't join us," Kell replied.

"So this is how MI6 operates now? We can just grab one of your guys, drug him, tie him up? You going to be okay with that, Tom? We can *render* one another?"

Kell knew that Kleckner was being smart, trying to probe for a weakness. Jim Chater's willingness to transport Yassin Gharani to a black prison in Cairo—and Kell's failure to stop him—had effectively cost him his job and his reputation.

"Let's not get too excited, Ryan. Would you like a drink?"

"What have you got? Caipirinhas? Isn't that your favorite?"

"You have a good memory."

"Rachel told me."

A smile curled at the edge of Kleckner's lips as he registered Kell's reaction. Kell longed to tell him that he had been played by Rachel, that her affection for him had been a mirage, that every kiss she had planted on his body, every moment of lust and intimacy they had shared, had been a sham. Rachel had no more cared for Ryan Kleckner than a call girl cares for a client.

"How's that going?" he asked.

"What? My thing with your girlfriend?"

"Yeah. Got any trips to Paris planned? Taking her home to meet your mother?"

Kleckner jerked forward, as far as the belt would allow. There was a note of supercilious triumph in his voice as he stared at Kell.

"When we land, and when I get a chance to talk to the people who actually *know* what's been going on, who actually *know* why I made a relationship with the SVR, and when they find out that SIS has effectively *kidnapped* a CIA officer without permission or due process, I kind of get the feeling that *your* career, the careers of your superiors, in fact the entire relationship between my Agency and your dipshit Service, will be fucked into the next century."

Kell experienced a brief chill of foreboding before reassuring himself that Kleckner was bluffing.

"Don't worry, Ryan," he said, "you'll have every chance to explain yourself."

Kell stood up and made his way down the cabin. Danny was snoozing beside a window at the rear of the aircraft. Kell checked his watch. It was just after five Ukraine time, three in London. He was concerned about Rachel. He wondered why Amelia hadn't contacted the plane and tried to speak to him. Perhaps no news was good news: Rachel was probably already back in London.

Kell was pouring himself a glass of water in the galley half an hour later when he felt the plane begin to descend. At first, he thought nothing of it. It was only when he glanced out of the window that he saw city lights less than two thousand feet below and realized that the Gulfstream was landing. He put the drink to one side and walked down the aircraft, past Danny, past Kleckner. The cockpit door was open. He closed it behind him and spoke to the pilots.

"Where are we? Why are we so low? Refueling?"

The sun was no longer visible ahead of them. The plane had changed direction.

"New flight plan, sir," Phil replied.

"Says who?"

"They've told us to land in Kiev."

68

They've told us *what*? Who did the instruction come from?"

"I'm afraid I can't say, sir."

Kell braced himself in the narrow confines of the cockpit as the Gulfstream hit a river of turbulence. He wondered if the SVR had got to the pilots. Phil offered enough cash to land the plane in Kiev, nobody any the wiser.

"I'm going to ask you again," Kell said. "Who is telling you to do this?"

He could already see the glow of an airport, a column of landing lights shimmering in the distance. The plane would be down in less than five minutes, an SVR team swarming all over the Gulfstream within ten.

Phil pulled back a set of headphones, looped them around his neck.

"Best thing I can do is ask you to sit down, sir."

The request contained an edge of patronizing threat, the captain pulling rank on a passenger. Kell's lifelong irritation with bureaucratic arrogance kicked in like the jolt of turbulence.

"What airport is this?" he said.

"Boryspil. Kiev."

"International?"

"That's the one," Bob replied.

Phil was muttering into a mike, presumably to air traffic control. Kell looked at the banks of lights and switches above the pilots' heads, as mysterious to him as circuit boards. He had no choice but to return to his seat. They were moments away from landing. As he opened the cockpit door, Kell saw Kleckner looking directly at him.

"Trouble, Tom?" he said, with a wildcat grin.

"What makes you think that?" Kell replied, and buckled himself in for landing.

69

The Gulfstream soared down in the black night, kissed the runway, and taxied to an isolated corner of the airport. Once the plane had come to a halt, Phil emerged from the cockpit, walked halfway down the aisle, and announced that a vehicle was en route to the aircraft and that "all passengers have been asked to remain on board."

"That include me?" Kleckner asked.

There was a look of weary triumph on his face, as though he knew that his safe passage to Moscow was now assured.

"Yes," Kell told him. "That includes you."

Kell unbuckled his seat belt and approached the American. He took a knife from his back pocket and moved it in front of Kleckner's face.

"Wait a minute . . . ," said Phil.

Kell reached behind Kleckner's back, cutting the plastic cuffs around his wrists. Danny was smiling. As soon as his hands were free, Kleckner popped the catch on his seat belt and stood up. He was stiff and in pain, reaching for the area on his thigh where Jez had injected the ketamine.

"What did you guys use on me?" he asked.

Kell ignored him.

Phil returned to the cockpit as the engines on the Gulfstream powered down. Orange lights were strobing beyond the fuselage, the aircraft encased by the night. As the noise of the jets diminished, Kell looked out of the starboard window to see a second plane parked alongside. The registration mark began with the letter *N*. An American flight. Kell felt the dark echo of extraordinary rendition. Kleckner had begun to walk around the aircraft, stretching his legs, rubbing his wrists. The strength returning to him, the lean, exercised cunning. Kell watched him for a while, trying to glimpse the traitor within, trying to get some sense of the motive that had driven Kleckner to deceive. But he looked just as he had looked on that first night in Bar Bleu: tanned, worked-out, good-looking. Throw stones on a beach in California and you would hit fifty men just like him. Most likely there had been nothing more than money and a malign pleasure in deceit: no ideological conviction, merely betrayal for its own sake.

"You look tired, Tom," Kleckner said, turning toward Kell.

Again, Kell did not respond. Instead he crossed to the opposite side of the cabin. A vehicle was making its way across the concrete apron. Yellow headlights moving at speed. Bob emerged from the cockpit and opened the main door on the plane. The wind and the jet scream of Boryspil punched into the cabin. Kleckner reacted by blocking his ears. Danny winced and sat down. Kell walked toward the door and looked out over the airport.

"Who is in the car?" he shouted.

"You tell me," Bob shouted back.

There were three of them. Kell stood at the open door and watched as a black Mercedes-Benz came to a halt a few meters from the Gulfstream. A powerful wind was blowing across the apron, two passenger aircraft taxiing on the runway three hundred meters to the south. The driver snuffed out the headlights, switched off the engine, and opened the rear left door.

Amelia Levene stepped out into the night. Kell looked across to the opposite side of the vehicle, where the passenger door had opened. As a plane screamed overhead, a spotlight swept across the runway, and the short, stocky figure of Jim Chater emerged beneath the starboard wing. He was wearing a suit. He turned and looked up at the Gulfstream. With an almost imperceptible dip of the head, he acknowledged Kell. Kell did not move. Chater leaned back into the car, retrieved what appeared to be a cell phone, and slammed the door.

Kell turned to Danny and to the two pilots, who had gathered at the front of the plane.

"You'd better give us some time," he said. "Wait in the car."

"Sure," Danny replied, and followed Bob and Phil down the steps. They stopped on the tarmac and shook Amelia's hand, like visiting dignitaries. Chater ignored them. Kell turned back into the plane and called out to Kleckner.

"Ryan! Your friends have come to see you."

Kell saw the look of hope in Kleckner's eyes, his delight at the prospect of Moscow rushing to his aid. Yet his expression barely changed when he saw Jim Chater at the top of the steps. Kell had expected Kleckner to look stunned, the victory slumping out of him. If anything, he looked relieved.

Chater brushed past Kell and stared at Kleckner. Eye contact. Kleckner turned and looked out through a portside window. Kell felt the sudden, pure fear that SIS had been duped. ABACUS a triple, played against Minasian for a purpose so obscure, so brilliant, that Langley had been prepared to give up HITCHCOCK and EINSTEIN just to sustain the deceit.

Amelia was at the top of the steps. She walked into the cabin, nodded at Kell, playing a hand of cards to which he was not yet privy. Chater raised the steps on the Gulfstream and sealed the door. It was suddenly very quiet.

"So we're all here," Amelia said.

Kell could feel his heart quickening. He knew that if Kleckner spoke next, if he stood up and went to Chater, the game was up. A handshake between trusted colleagues, an operation blown, and two high-ranking Brits to shoulder the blame. Kell could tell nothing from Amelia's expression. Chater simply looked angry and tired. Kell had to keep reminding himself that the notion of Kleckner's innocence was absurd.

"Ryan," said Amelia, narrowing her eyes as though she was having difficulty bringing Kleckner into focus. It seemed enormously significant to Kell that Amelia, rather than Chater, had opted to speak first. "Jim has kindly agreed that Tom and I should be allowed a few moments with you before you are taken into American custody."

Kell felt a surge of relief, even as he absorbed what Amelia was saying. SIS was to be given no opportunity to interview Kleckner, to measure the extent of his treachery. ABACUS was Kell's catch, the Service's triumph, but Langley was taking him home.

"Ryan?" Amelia said again. "Can you hear me?"

"I can hear you," Kleckner muttered.

He was going to play a long game. Acting cool, trying to stay calm. Kleckner had been cornered but would not allow his captors the satisfaction of seeing him fold.

"My Service has some questions regarding an asset in—"

"I'm sure you do . . ."

"Don't interrupt, Ryan."

They were the first words Chater had spoken. Kell found something touching in the use of Kleckner's Christian name. How many times would Chater have sat with Kleckner in meetings, secure speech rooms, in restaurants and bars, assessing him, teaching him, trusting him?

"Thank you, Jim," Amelia replied, with regal precision.

Kleckner stood up. He began to move toward them, only for Chater to erupt in sudden fury.

"Sit the fuck down."

The sudden outburst caught all of them by surprise. Kell saw the hate coiled in Chater's face. He thought of Kabul, the cramped room, the sweat and the fear of the Gharani interrogation. Chater feral and raging, spewing venom in the heat. His mood had turned in an instant.

Kleckner sat down. He seemed aware of the wretchedness of his situation, but there was a look of forced pride on his face, as though he was determined to go down fighting. Kell heard the smothered roar of a jet landing on the far side of the airport.

"So," said Amelia, arranging her handbag on the floor as she took a seat opposite Kleckner. "As I was saying. We have a question about an asset in Iraqi Kurdistan. Somebody that Paul Wallinger was looking at."

Time was a factor, but Kell instinctively felt that Amelia was moving too quickly into interrogation. It did not surprise him when Kleckner ducked the question.

"You know Tom well, right?"

Amelia turned and smiled at Kell. "For many years, yes."

"So you know about these two?" Kleckner indicated Chater. "You know their story?" Amelia produced a weary sigh. She had no interest in being drawn into second-rate mind games. "Must be just like old times, huh?" Kleckner said.

"Just like it."

"Yeah? Wanna throw a punch, Tom? Wanna put a sack over my head? These fingernails sure must look attractive to you." Kleckner had raised his hands, palms facing toward his face. "I'm sure Jim can find some pliers. Why don't you guys make yourselves comfortable, start pulling them out? It's what you're best at."

Kell felt nothing. His conscience was clear. Amelia also remained impassive. Both of them were too experienced to react to Kleckner's simple tactic.

"That what this was about for you?" Chater asked. Kell was disappointed that he was taking the bait. "You had some trouble with our methods, Ryan?" Chater took a step toward him. Kell saw then that

Kleckner was physically afraid of him. There was a moment of cowardice in his eyes. "You feel like getting it off your chest?"

"I would certainly like to make a statement," Kleckner told him.

"Let him talk," Amelia replied.

Kleckner leaned back in his seat. After a long pause, he said: "I know what you guys did, Jim," his voice seemingly rich with the moral disappointment of a young man whose innocence had been stripped away by men and women in whom he had once fervently believed.

"Yeah? And what did we do to you?" Chater replied.

"I know that you walked prisoners around on leads. I know that you sanctioned waterboarding. I know that you had OMS check Yassin Gharani to make sure he was healthy enough for you two guys to continue torturing him."

The OMS was a medical unit within the CIA. Amelia folded her arms and let out another quiet sigh. Kell was waiting, biding his time. He did not want to waste words on Kleckner.

"How do you feel about working for an Agency that kills innocent women and children every day?" It wasn't immediately clear to whom Kleckner had directed the question.

"We're gonna do the drone conversation?" Chater replied wearily. "Is that what you want? Really?"

Kleckner turned toward Kell. "What about you, Tom?"

Kell knew that the exchange was pure theater. "We are at war, Ryan," he replied, and tried to convey, both by his manner and by his tone of voice, that Kleckner's moral and philosophical musings were as inconsequential to him as they were naïve.

"Really? War? That's what you call it? Thousands of innocent people living in targeted communities, frightened to come out of their homes, living in fear not just of the *violence* of a drone strike, but the *noise* of a drone strike? Psychological torture. You think that's part of a *war*?" Kleckner was fueling himself on rhetoric. Amelia stood up and wandered down the aircraft, like someone in a bar waiting for a drunk to sober up. "These communities are now ravaged by psychiatric disorders, kids too afraid to go to school and get the education they need to keep them *away* from extreme Islam"—Chater snorted derisively—"and all the time we're creating and sowing the idea around the world that my country, the United States of America, thinks it's okay to participate in extrajudicial killings, targeted assassinations. We are *creating* terrorism. We are *generating* threats."

"And you thought the way to stop that was to get into bed with the SVR?" Amelia asked the question from the back of the Gulfstream. Nobody did merciless condescension quite like Amelia Levene.

Chater weighed in. "You thought the way to stop that was to give the names of SIS and CIA assets inside the Iranian nuclear program? You thought the way to stop that was to have a truckful of Red Cross volunteers murdered by Bashar Assad? Tell me, Ryan. How does the blowing up of a high-ranking Iranian general, a man who fully intended to cooperate with the West in his determination to *resolve* the conflict between the United States and Iran—"

Kleckner interrupted him. "I had no idea that Shakhouri would be killed," he said, looking at Kell as though he alone had misconstrued his involvement in the HITCHCOCK debacle. Kell was mesmerized by the intensity of Kleckner's self-delusion. A sociopath dressing up betrayal as a moral position.

"You didn't consider that Moscow would pass on that information to Tehran?" Amelia asked, walking back down the plane. "By the way, did you know that Alexander Minasian was lying to you in the safe house? Cecilia Sandor was murdered on the orders of the SVR. Luka Zigic has gone missing. Were you aware of that?"

Kleckner did not reply. Chater muttered something under his breath and stared at the man who had betrayed him. There was a fold-down seat behind him. He lowered himself into it, tetchily adjusting his ill-fitting suit, as though he had borrowed it for the meeting. Amelia looked out of a starboard porthole. Kell remained standing. Kleckner's motives for betrayal were as prosaic as they were predictable. Sophomoric arguments from a first-class mind. Almost everybody in the intelligence community with whom Kell had discussed droning had expressed doubts about the long-term consequences in the battle for hearts and minds. But nobody—from Amelia Levene to Jim Chater to Thomas Kell—was in any doubt about its political expedience and military efficacy. Kleckner was talking like an activist but it was no more than a pose. Treachery was treachery. Kleckner could dress it up all he liked, but he no more cared about a villager in Waziristan than he cared about Rachel Wallinger. He had been motivated solely by self-aggrandizement. For such men it was not enough to affect events collectively; the narcissist had to put himself center stage. The moral and philosophical arguments for Kleckner's behavior could be all too easily made; it was just a question of self-persuasion.

"How much did they pay you?" Chater asked, but before Kleckner had a chance to react, Kell's phone began to ring. He glanced at the screen, saw that it was a Ukraine number. Harold, perhaps, or one of the team back in Odessa. He ignored the call, but whoever was trying to reach him immediately rang again.

"Give me a couple of minutes," he said, going into the cockpit. Amelia and Chater nodded. Kell closed the door, sat in the starboard pilot's seat, and answered the phone.

"Hello?"

"Mr. Thomas Kell?"

"Speaking."

"This is Alexander Minasian."

70

There were no pleasantries. Minasian said that he was speaking from the Russian consulate in Odessa. He knew that Ryan Kleckner was "now in the hands of the United States government." He said that he wanted to offer a trade.

"A trade," said Kell.

"We have a woman. In Istanbul. Rachel Wallinger. I believe that you know her."

Kell felt an inversion inside himself, a fear of loss so great that he struggled to respond.

"I know her," he replied.

Minasian waited. Perhaps he had expected Kell to sound more shocked. "She is being held at an address in Istanbul. If Mr. Kleckner is taken to my embassy in Kiev within the next six hours and handed to the Russian diplomatic staff, we will convey Rachel to your embassy in Istanbul. I can be reached on this number if you wish to inform me of your decision. You have six hours."

The line went dead.

Kell placed the phone on the seat beside him and stared out at the black night. Fewer lights on the apron now, the runway quiet. He picked up the phone and dialed Rachel's number. The line failed to connect. Not even a voice mail. Not even a chance to hear her voice.

"Tom?"

It was Amelia. She had come into the cockpit, closing the door behind her. She saw the look on Kell's face as he turned around.

"What's wrong?"

"I told you Rachel needed protecting. I told you she wasn't safe."

"What's happened?"

Kell indicated the phone. "That was Minasian. They've got her. They want to trade her for Kleckner."

The confidence seemed to go out of Amelia, all of her experience and strength gusted away by what Kell had said.

"Oh, God. I am so sorry."

Kell could not tell whether or not she would countenance the idea of trading Kleckner. He pictured the scene in which Rachel was being held. Her terror, her isolation. He felt the same rage against Minasian that he had felt toward Kleckner, moments after seeing Rachel in the hotel room.

"Where did they get her?"

"I don't know," Kell replied.

"Have Station been in touch?"

"You tell me."

Amelia took out a phone, began to scroll for a number.

"When was the last time you heard from Rachel?" Kell asked her.

Amelia appeared not to have heard the question. "What?"

"When did you last have confirmation that Rachel was safe?"

"Sunday," she replied uncertainly. "Sunday, I think."

More than thirty-six hours had passed since then. Amelia Levene had been more worried about pacifying Jim Chater than she had been concerned about protecting Paul's daughter.

"I'm calling Istanbul," she said. "I'll find out what's gone wrong."

Kell looked out of the plane. He could see the driver of the Mercedes smoking beneath the Gulfstream. Not a care in the world. He knew that it would be only a matter of time before Amelia told the Americans. After that, Rachel's life would be in Chater's hands.

"Let me deal with this," Amelia said, flicking her eyes in the direction of the cabin. "Keep talking to Kleckner. Find out whatever you can about other operations." It irked Kell that Amelia was not solely focused on Rachel's safety, even as he acknowledged that the Service's opportunity to interview Kleckner had now been even more severely curtailed. "Give me five minutes," she said.

Kell pocketed his phone, opened the cockpit door, and went out into the cabin. Chater was coming out of the bathroom at the far end of the plane, adjusting the collar of his shirt. Kleckner looked up and popped his eyebrows.

"Problem?" he said.

Kell felt the impotent fury of a man without choices. Rachel's fate was now out of his hands. Every effort he had made—to recover from her betrayal, to track and capture Kleckner—had been rendered meaningless by the counterplay from Minasian.

"Tell me about Ebru Eldem," he said.

He wanted to silence Kleckner, to wipe the sneering, unapologetic look from his face, to skewer him on his own hypocrisy. Chater caught his eye, coming back to the front of the aircraft.

"What about her?" Kleckner replied.

Kell took a step toward him. "I just want to hear about her. What she meant to you."

"What she *meant* to me?"

"Isn't it the case that she shared some of your political views, as you've expressed them? On droning? On Abu Ghraib and Iraq as well? Isn't it the case that you two had a lot in common?"

Chater sat down and hunched forward, staring at Kell, wondering where he was going. Kell could sense that Kleckner was wary of a trap. The American seemed determined not to reply.

"My understanding of Miss Eldem's personality, having read her newspaper articles, her blog, her journal, suggests that she was outraged by the hounding of Bradley Manning, the targeted killing of bin Laden, the invasion of Iraq." Kell was looking at Kleckner but thinking of Rachel. He took a beat, trying to control his anxiety, and said: "Where do you stand on those issues?"

"We didn't talk about stuff like that," Kleckner replied.

It was a lie. Chater saw it too. Kleckner was folding up inside his own hypocrisy.

"Well that's not true, is it, Ryan?" Kell paced to the side of the aircraft, his mind spinning with ideas on how to deal with Chater when the moment came. Would Langley agree to the swap? Would Chater try to buy time? Kell wanted to be in a separate aircraft taking off for Istanbul, helping in the search for Rachel. Kleckner and his false idealism was now just an object in his path, something to distract him while Amelia made her calls. "You exchanged e-mails about bin Laden on the anniversary of his death." Kell could feel how easily Kleckner was going to fold. "You agreed with her that he should have been captured and brought to trial. Did you believe that or was it just your cover?"

"Yes, I believed that."

Chater shook his head and muttered: "Jesus Christ" as Amelia came out of the cockpit. Kell turned quickly, trying to disguise his desperation for news. She passed him a note on which she had written: "Uncertain where or when R was taken. London investigating. Istanbul going to the yali." Chater seemed irritated to have been denied eyes on the message. He frowned and looked at Amelia. Kell, certain that Rachel had been seized in Istanbul, remained impassive. He did not want Kleckner to know that he had a shot at safety. Instead, he turned to him and said: "Ebru didn't know that you worked for the American government."

"Is that a statement or a question?" Kleckner replied.

"It's a fact."

Kleckner seemed shocked by Kell's response. It was as though he knew that he was cornered. He began to reply but swallowed his words.

"I'm sorry?" Kell said, urging him to speak up. "I missed that."

"I said that she thought I worked in pharma. They all did."

" 'They' meaning the women you slept with? Your girlfriends? Did Rachel think that?"

"Yes, she did," Kleckner replied, and looked pleased that Kell had mentioned her name.

"And yet you betrayed Ebru," Kell said. He hoped to his soul that Rachel was not frightened. That she had not been physically harmed. That London was already in negotiation with Moscow to secure her safe release. He wanted Kleckner out of the plane and in the car. "You gave Ebru up. You allowed the Turkish government to know that she was an asset. Why did you do that, Ryan? Why would somebody like you, who believes what you profess to believe, send someone who shares your political outlook, someone whose views you respect and admire, to certain imprisonment?"

"I didn't give her up. That's a lie."

"We have the evidence," said Amelia quietly. "We've spoken to the Turkish authorities."

Kell was grateful for the interruption but not surprised that Amelia had so quickly picked up on what he was trying to do. Her response cleared away the last of Kleckner's hypocrisy.

"I was *bored* of her, okay?" he said, and the ruthlessness at the center of Kleckner's personality was finally visible, like an open wound. "She was needy. She kept telling me she was in love. She was always taking offense at the smallest things, pissing me off. And she was working for you." A glance at Chater. Kleckner sounded like a spoiled child. "That was the position I was in. I had a relationship with Moscow. The larger responsibility was toward maintaining the balance of power."

"Total bullshit," said Chater and stood up, shaking his head. Amelia knew what Kell knew: that an extraordinarily bright young man had been corrupted not by a system, not by events, but by himself. Sensing their mood, Kleckner tried to press his point, as though he still held out some slim chance of winning the argument.

"I believed that I was doing important work that could still—"

Kell had heard enough. He wanted to start talking about Rachel face-to-face with Chater. The debrief could surely wait. "Let it go, Ryan," he said. "You're talking to people who see through you. This was about pleasure. The pleasure of manipulation. The joy of thumbing your nose at the state. The sadism of control over those whom you consider to be lesser mortals. You degrade the suffering and the complexity of the issues about which you profess to care by using them to validate your treachery. You slept with Ebru Eldem and you sent Ebru Eldem to prison. That is all that anyone will ever need to know about Ryan Kleckner."

"Let's put him back in the car," Amelia said, indicating to both men that SIS had no further interest in continuing with the interview. Chater looked stunned. Kell felt a burst of gratitude toward her. He opened the door of the aircraft, walked halfway down the steps and signaled to Danny. Then he returned to the cabin.

"Danny can take him," he said to Chater.

The American, who had been in the process of putting on his suit jacket, had sensed that something was wrong. He quietly nodded his consent. Kleckner's hollowed-out expression barely changed. The wind was funneling into the cabin, but the airport was now almost entirely silent. Danny came to the top of the steps holding a pair of plastic cuffs.

"I'll do it," Chater told him.

He took the cuffs and turned to Kleckner. "On your feet."

Kleckner stood up, held his hands together in front of his stomach. Chater looped the cuffs over his wrists and pulled them tight, with a fast upright jerk of the arm. As Kleckner winced in pain, Kell felt the nausea of losing Rachel. He wondered how long it would take Station in Istanbul to get over to the *yali*. Ten minutes? Fifteen?

"Hold him in the car," said Chater.

As he spoke, Amelia's phone began to ring. She nodded at Kell, handing him the responsibility of the primary negotiation with Chater. Moments later, Danny had taken Kleckner outside and Kell had sealed the door. He could hear Amelia in the cockpit, but could not make out what she was saying.

"So what's going on?" Chater asked. "Talk to me."

He sat in Kleckner's seat and folded his arms, smiling in a way that reminded Kell of the meeting in Ankara. It was the first glimpse of Chater's smooth, natural arrogance. In Kleckner's presence, Chater had seemed angry, even humbled.

"Minasian's people have kidnapped one of our officers in Istanbul. He wants to trade Kleckner."

Chater tipped his head back in disbelief.

"How the fuck did that happen?" he said to the ceiling. "Which officer?"

"Does it matter?" Kell replied.

"Who is it, Tom?"

He was reluctant to give up Rachel's name. He did not yet trust Chater to keep her alive. "Paul Wallinger's daughter. Rachel."

The American's reaction surprised him. Chater looked at Kell and smiled admiringly.

"Jesus. You got her working for you? Rachel is on your books?" It was as though he was more impressed by the sleight of hand than he was troubled by Rachel's capture. "How'd that happen?"

"Long story," Kell replied, beginning to feel the edges of a long-suppressed rage. It was as though Minasian's call had put him in shock. He lit a cigarette and, without offering one to Chater, put the packet back in his pocket. Kell could still hear Amelia talking in the cockpit. He did not like it that Chater seemed so relaxed.

"Do you know where she was taken?" the American asked. Kell shook his head. "How do you know Minasian isn't bluffing?"

"We don't," Kell replied.

"So a few hours ago, he's lying on his ass in Odessa. Now he's somehow orchestrated the kidnapping of an SIS asset five hundred miles away?"

"Apparently." Kell could not afford to take the chance that Minasian was lying. The clock was ticking. He said: "Presumably Rachel was taken in the last thirty-six hours. As an insurance policy. In case Ryan didn't make it."

"Presumably," Chater replied, as though Kell was being willfully naïve. "Got a proof of life?"

The question had a ghastly simplicity. Chater's tone of voice suggested that he did not care, one way or the other, what Kell's answer might be.

"Amelia is trying to find out more."

Proof of life. Did Chater know more than he was letting on? Kell drew on the cigarette, taking the smoke deep into his lungs. He felt no loyalty to the Service, no concern that Langley might lose ABACUS to the SVR. All he cared about was Rachel's safety. The rest was just a game between spies.

"We have less than six hours," he said. "If we do the swap, we take Kleckner to the Russian embassy in Kiev, they take Rachel to the British—"

Chater did not let him finish.

"*If* we do the swap," he said pointedly.

Kell now experienced an intense anger. He knew that it was of paramount importance not to corner Chater, not to make him feel that the decision was being taken away from him; but nor did he want to give the CIA any sense that there was a choice to be made about Rachel's future.

"Once we have confirmation that Rachel is alive," Kell said, "I suggest that you prepare a press release about Ryan, counter whatever claims Moscow will make about the nature of his work for the SVR, try to get ahead of the PR battle before—"

Chater interrupted again, shaking his head and muttering: "Tom, Tom, Tom . . ." as though Kell was being naïve. "Let's not get ahead of ourselves. I don't like the idea of doing anything until we have all of the facts about your girl."

It had been a mistake to tell him that Minasian had created a six-hour window. Chater was going to try to run down the clock. He didn't care about Rachel. He didn't care about the life of a British agent. All he cared about was making sure that Kleckner was debriefed and then thrown into prison for the rest of his days. Chater knew that Langley would most likely not survive another spy scandal. Moscow had been scoring too many points for too long.

"All of the facts," Kell said, loading the remark with as much contempt as he could risk. "Here are the facts, Jim. Rachel works for us. Her life is in danger. If we don't give Kleckner to Minasian, she will be murdered. It's that simple."

To his absolute astonishment, Chater said: "I understand." At first, Kell was not sure that he had heard him correctly, but the American looked up and nodded his head, conveying in a simple gesture of reconciliation that he would not countenance the idea of risking Rachel's life.

Kell was briefly speechless. For so long he had thought of Jim Chater as little more than a thug, the living embodiment of a certain brand of American recklessness, swinging from country to country on missions of vengeance and control. But beneath the anger and the bravado there was a keen mind, a man of learning, even of reason. Unable to shake off the memory of Kabul, and convinced that Chater would put Rachel's life at risk, Kell had allowed himself to forget that.

"What are you saying?" he asked.

"I'm saying that obviously we have no choice. We've got to get your girl back, right? But I don't want to be rushed. I don't want us to make a move without knowing exactly what Minasian is doing. He says we have six hours. Fuck him. He knows anything happens to Rachel, I take Ryan back to Virginia and Minasian loses his career."

Kell felt an enormous sense of relief, even as he became aware that he could no longer hear Amelia's voice in the cockpit. It would be necessary to involve her in the conversation as soon as possible, to put together an agreed strategy, then to contact Minasian, whether he was still in Odessa or en route to Kiev.

As if reading his thoughts, Chater said: "We need to get 'C' in on this," and Kell nodded, dropping the cigarette into an empty bottle of water.

At that moment, the door of the cockpit opened. Amelia's head was lowered as she emerged into the cabin, but when she looked up Kell could see that something was terribly wrong. There were tears in her eyes.

"What is it?" he said.

Kell knew the answer. He dreaded it. Amelia was looking at him with utter dismay.

"Tom." He wanted to stop her saying what she was going to say. Kell would have given his life not to hear her words. "I am so sorry." She was imploring his forgiveness with her eyes. She walked toward Kell and held his wrists, squeezing hard at the bones, just as she had held them at Paul's funeral. "It was a bluff. Minasian was bluffing. They didn't have her. Station rang the house. The police were there. There was never going to be any exchange. Rachel has been killed."

71

A small boy swimming in the shallows of the Bosporus had seen blood sprayed on the ground-floor windows of the *yali*. The body of Rachel Wallinger was found in the kitchen, a single bullet wound to the head. Minasian, stranded in Odessa knowing that Kleckner would be out of the country in less than six hours, had played a final, desperate card, not knowing that his superiors in Moscow had ordered Rachel to be killed.

Kell and Danny immediately flew to Istanbul. Amelia returned to London on the Gulfstream, breaking the news to Josephine at the flat in Gloucester Road. In his anger and despair at what had happened, Kell became numb to the sinister ease with which SIS conspired with the Turkish authorities to make the murder look like a random act of violence. Press reports described Rachel as "the daughter of a former British diplomat killed in a plane crash earlier this year." Though Kell blamed himself as much for Rachel's death as he blamed Amelia, he avoided speaking to her and refused to meet when she asked if they could discuss the case over lunch.

"What's left to discuss?" he wrote back. "Rachel is dead."

Kell also made it clear that he no longer had any interest in taking over as H/Ankara.

The day of Rachel's funeral, Kell was woken at five in the morning by a call from Elsa Cassani. She told him that the wires were reporting the death of a twenty-nine-year-old American diplomat in Kiev. The story, subsequently carried in the international sections of all four British broadsheets, described Ryan Kleckner as a "health attaché" at the U.S. consulate in Istanbul.

> Eyewitnesses reported that Kleckner, who was on holiday in Kiev, became involved in a heated argument outside a nightclub in the small hours of Tuesday morning. His body was discovered in a suburb east of the city.

"SVR?" Elsa asked.

"No," Kell replied. "The Russians have always prided themselves on getting their people home."

"The Americans, then?"

"Yes."

Chater would have given the order. Made it look like a violent crime. Ukrainian tough guys taking exception to an uppity Yank and putting a bullet through his brain. Further "eyewitnesses" would emerge in the coming days claiming to have seen Kleckner in a brothel or lap-dancing club, behaving in a drunken or sleazy fashion. Something to put a slight stain on his reputation so that he did not return to Missouri as a hero. Something for his family and friends to be ashamed of as they stared at the coffin.

"He was too much trouble to Langley," said Kell. "They couldn't have survived the scandal."

"What about you?" Elsa asked.

"What about me?"

"How are you, Tom?"

Kell looked across the room at the black suit hanging near the window. The light was coming up outside. He had to drive to Cartmel in a few hours' time, to sit in a church surrounded by Rachel's friends and family, nobody knowing what had happened between them, what Rachel Wallinger had meant to him. He could be no comfort to Josephine, to Andrew. Kell felt that he had betrayed them all.

"I'll be fine," he said. "Will you be there today?"

"Yes."

He was wide awake now. He reached for a packet of Winstons, sitting on the edge of the bed and lit a cigarette. He was determined to avenge Rachel, to make Minasian pay.

"So I will see you later?" Elsa asked.

She had rung on the landline. Kell knew that the SVR would be listening to the call, picking up every word of the conversation. He spoke very clearly and steadily into the receiver.

"You will see me later."

Acknowledgments

To Keith Kahla, Hannah Braaten, Steve K., Sally Richardson, Bethany Reis, Rafal Gibek, Paul Hochman, Dori Weintraub, Justin Velella, and everybody at St. Martin's Press in New York (and beyond) for their patience, professionalism, and support.

To my agents, Will Francis and Luke Janklow, and to everyone at Janklow & Nesbit, on both sides of the Atlantic: Kirsty Gordon, Rebecca Folland, Jessie Botterill, Claire Dippel, Dmitri Chitov, and Stefanie Lieberman.

My thanks to Marika and Malachi Smythos for guidance on Chios. To Owen Matthews, for his generosity and kindness, not least in introducing me to the wonderful Ebru Taskin in Ankara. Owen has written two great books—*Stalin's Children* and *Glorious Misadventures*—both of which I strongly recommend. Jonny Dymond, Cansu Çamlibel, Nick Lockley, Banu Buyurgan, Alex Varlick at Istanbul's Georges Hotel, Omar, GG, and Frank R. were all great sources of information in Turkey. Thanks to A. D. Miller and Simon Sebag Montefiore for Odessa tips. Narges Bajoghli and Christopher de Bellaigue, author of *Patriot of Persia* and *In the Rose Garden of the Martyrs,* gave me very useful insights into life in Tehran.

I am also grateful to: Harry de Quetteville, Mr. and Mrs. Adam le Bor, Boglárka Várkonyi, Ben Macintyre, Ian Cumming, Mark Pilkington, Siobhan Vernon, Mark Meynell, Rowland White, Robin Durie, Alice Kahrmann, Rory Paget, Catherine Heaney, Bard Wilkinson, Anna Bilton, Hasmukh and Minesh Kakad, Boris Starling, Pat Ford, Saveria Callagy, Meredith Hindley, Kate Mallinson, Ros O'Shaughnessy, my mother, Caroline Pilkington, and all the staff at *The Week* in London.

I owe unrepayable debts to Elizabeth Best and Sarah Gabriel (www.sarahgabriel.eu). I would not have started *A Colder War* without one, nor finished it without the other. Thank you.

C.C., London, 2013

Don't miss any of Charles Cumming's novels

Also available:

The Spanish Game

Typhoon

The Trinity Six

A Foreign Country

A Colder War

The Hidden Man (AVAILABLE NOVEMBER 2015)